BAD BOYS BRING HEAVEN

Bad Boys Bring Heaven

Masquerade series
Book 1

Leah K. Plamm

Leah K Plamm

Bad Boys Bring Heaven
Copyright © 2023 Leah K. Plamm
All Rights Reserved.
Paperback ISBN 978-619-7592-02-3
eBook ISBN 978-619-7592-04-7

Without limiting the rights under copyright reserved above, no part of this publication may be reproduced, stored in or introduced into a retrieval system, or transmitted, in any form, or by any means (electronic, mechanical, photocopying, recording or otherwise) without the prior written permission of the copyright owner, except in the case of brief quotations embodied in critical reviews and certain other noncommercial uses permitted by copyright law.

This is a work of fiction. Names, characters, places, brands, media, and incidents are either the product of the author's imagination or are used fictitiously. Any resemblance to actual persons, living or dead, events, or locales is entirely coincidental. The author acknowledges the trademarked status and trademark owners of various products referenced in this work of fiction, which have been used without permission. The publication/use of these trademarks is not authorized, associated with, or sponsored by the trademark owners.

Published by: Leah K. Plamm 2023
leahkplamm@gmail.com

This book has been previously published under the title Masquerade in 2020

"Ironically, when we own the shadow aspects of our self and put down our masks—this is when we become truly lovable."
—Jane Monica-Jones, The Billionaire Buddha

To my grandparents, thank you for raising me and supporting me every step of the way. I love you.

Playlist

"Masquerade"—Elina
"Tell Me"—Diddy ft. Christina Aguilera
"Devil Devil"—MILCK
"Love in This Club, Pt. II"—Usher, Beyoncé, Lil Wayne
"God Is A Dancer"—Tiësto, Mabel
"Secret"—Maroon 5
"Dance for You"—Beyoncé
"Secret Love Song, Pt. II"—Little Mix
"Lose My Mind"—Dean Lewis
"Back to Black"—Amy Winehouse
"Rewrite the Stars"—James Arthur, Anne-Marie
"New Year's Day"—Taylor Swift
"Fire on Fire"—Sam Smith
"All or Nothing"—Theory of a Deadman

Music is a big part of my writing process and I'd like to let you into my world.
You can listen to an extended playlist, each song placed in an exact order to take you through every stage of Ivy and Damien's relationship:

Spotify link

YouTube link

Synopsis

She's the inconvenience he never saw coming . . .
and the one he would kill for

Damien Black. American royalty. Gorgeous asshole. Shameless rake.
Also . . . my new boss.
One night of mistakes and he's running to my rescue like the prince on a white horse.
But a liar is no damsel.
There's no escaping Rosehill's bad boy when fate keeps pushing you together.
But if the souls of the foul are doomed, why does every night feel like heaven?

What do you do when a pretty little thing walks through the doors of your exclusive nightclub?
You take a front-row seat to the show.
Ivy Thanos. Brilliant dancer. Dangerous vixen. Dark enigma.
Breaking all my rules, she's my personal hell. I would rather burn than let her go.
How do you fight for love when the whole world is against you and everything you know turns out to be a lie?

Bad Boys Bring Heaven is a full-length steamy contemporary romance with a twist of suspense. It's the first book in the Masquerade series and can be read as a standalone.

Chapter One

IVY

"I fucking hate men."

Stella giggles on the other side of the phone. "What is it this time?"

I slam the back door of the bar closed, my black apron discarded somewhere on the floor. Good riddance. I'm not going to miss wiping down the sticky tables, nor will I shed any tears for the refined clientele of this oh-so-fine establishment. There is one thing I'll miss though, I've grown fond of Ricky the rat that lives in the bathroom, ironically one of our least scummy patrons. And honestly, if someone's stupid enough to bring their child to a trashy bar, where the servers are dressed in lingerie and some sorry excuse for a skirt, then they deserve to get their ass bitten by a feral rodent.

"I got fired."

Lightning split the sky open. A couple of raindrops slide down the sleeve of my black raincoat.

It is official ladies and gentlemen, God is a man.

Fuck you too.

"Again?" Stella sounds more amused than concerned.

"Technically, the first two times I quit."

In the year I've spent in Rosehill, a lively town on the coast of the Mexican gulf, a Miami wanna-be as I like to characterize it. Since being here, I'd gone through a few jobs, none of which lasted very long. The first one was in a bar that turned into a brothel at night. I still can't believe it took me two nights to figure out the sordid scheme and run the hell out of there. The second one was at an ice cream parlor, but I didn't make enough to meet ends so I had to search for something better.

In comes Johnny's bar. Johnny the namesake and owner, didn't ask questions, paid on time, and didn't try to sleep with his employees, all three of which are necessary requirements for someone like me. A ghost.

"I never liked that place anyway," Stella does her best to console me but we both know neither of us can afford to lose their job right now. The bills are stacking and the rent was due two weeks ago.

"Wait, it gets better." My heart ups its rhythm with every step that I take toward the bus station. "I got fired because that guy put his hands on me again."

This is the third time the same guy has tried (and succeeded, in spite of my best efforts) to grope me. The first time I smiled as I took his order and spat on his food later. The second time I told Johnny, who said he'd do something about it as I watched him proceed to scribble in his crossword as he dismissed me. It wasn't like I was expecting him to ban the guy from the bar, he was one of our regulars after all, but I at least hoped he'd throw him a thinly veiled remark. Nothing. He did nothing.

"How is that a valid reason?" Stella's sewing machine rumbles to life in the background.

"I kind of, sort of, broke his fingers." I pull the hood over my head as the rain intensifies. "I have you to thank for that.

If you hadn't dragged me to Krav-Maga I would've still had a job."

"Good riddance," Stella huffs. And this is why I love my roommate. She would never tell me to sit quietly and take it, even though we might not have dinner on the table tomorrow. Or hot water. Or a roof over our heads. She would sleep on the street with me if it meant I was happy.

"What are we going to do?" Pain shoots through my finger. I look down to realize I'd been chewing my nails to the point where I bit on flesh. Good Lord, my heart is going a mile a minute. I didn't think of the people I'd be letting down when I made that stupid decision. I can't let my sweet Stella live on the street. She might feel indebted to me because I helped her a year ago, but she's too soft for all of it. She wouldn't last a night without the comfort of her bed. Or a sewing machine for that matter.

Booming thunder interrupts my worries. I become aware of the fact I completely zoned out for the options Stella has been rattling in my ear. I manage to focus enough to catch the last of her words.

"…and I'll probably sell enough after the fashion show to keep us afloat for the next month or so."

"Wait, wait. I'm not living off of your sweat and tears. You deserve to use that money to get a vacation or something, you've been killing yourself night and day."

The line is silent for a second. "There might be one more option left. I'd have to call in a favor."

"What is it?" I couldn't take her money, but I'm not above having her help as long as it means I won't have to mooch off of her hard work.

"You used to be a dancer, right?" One of the few things Stella knows of my old life is my passion for dancing. I'd slipped up one night after a few too many glasses and then she'd come to the bar a month ago when I was doing my Friday night dance routine on the pole left by the previous owner of the bar that Johnny never bothered to remove. I wasn't proud but at least I wasn't taking my clothes off for tips. I got them in bulk when I started swinging my ass to the beat of the music or wore my long. dark hair in pigtails.

"Contemporary but yeah, I've done a couple of years of aerial dancing."

Something inside my chest squeezes. It does so every time I'm reminded of the life I fled. Of all the things I lost I miss dancing the most. I should've been at camp this month. It would've been my first time as a teacher rather than a student.

You wouldn't have been free.

The voice inside of my head reminds me. As if I am now, I want to scream back. But, I don't. Instead, I keep on walking, my cowboy boots soaked, and my confidence slowly washing away with every drop of rain that slips into the gutter.

"Yes!" Stella exclaims.

"What?"

"He's free. Go to the address I just sent you and call me. I'll tell him to go out and meet you in front."

"Who is he? What is going on, Stella? I'm soaking wet." And I look like an escort. Not that I have anything against sex workers, God knows I'm in no position to judge, but I'm in no fit state to meet with a potential employer. I'm still in a skirt that could pass as an eye patch and my top that is nothing short of a bra underneath the raincoat.

The sound of our doorbell chirped through the phone.

"Raquel's here, gotta go."

And just like that, I'm left alone with my thoughts once

again. I check the address on my phone, not too far, about a twenty-minute walk from where I was headed.

Twenty minutes alone with my mind. I might as well jump in front of the next car.

The voice of my mother keeps repeating in my head. Failure, failure, failure.

My father's disapproving ts-ts.

With every step that I take, the weight on my chest bends me down a little more.

I'm twenty-four with no income, no family, and no name. I have my roommate who doesn't know half of what I've done. I have this beautiful town, even if it hasn't exactly been the most welcoming over the past year. Or maybe I'm the problem. I can't keep a job, I can't go back to where I came from, I can't even make a freaking meal for myself.

Breathe in. Breathe out.

The closest I've come to affording therapy is YouTube and not even premium. At least I had managed to teach myself the five senses grounding technique and a few breathing exercises to calm my mind in times of crisis.

In. Out.

I can do this.

As I'm concentrating on remembering how to breathe, I almost bump into something. A red telephone booth. Who the hell uses these anyway?

The rain escalated while I was spaced out and the constant beating of the drops on my raincoat feels like a thousand whip cracks to my bare skin underneath.

I look around. An old movie theater sign hangs on the red-brick building the telephone booth is attached to. No cafes, no restaurants. Nowhere to hide until the rain calms down.

"You've arrived at your destination," the GPS scares the hell out of me.

"Where?" My question hangs in the air. I go inside the telephone box to unlock my phone. It's wet from the rain even though I held it underneath the raincoat. God, I hope I didn't screw this up too. I can't afford a new phone. I can't even afford an old one from the pawn shop.

Sure enough, the location on the map points to this building. I open the door and stick my head out in the rain. The place looks like it hasn't worked in decades. I try to call Stella but it goes straight to voicemail. I try again, and again. Nothing.

My heartbeat picks up again. I'm supposed to meet this mystery guy who can supposedly solve my unemployment issue. The sun has set, and the roads are empty and dark, the street lights casting a mysterious glow on the wet pavement.

"Come on, come on, come on," I chant, biting my nails as I lean against the inner wall of the telephone box.

"You going in?"

I jump with an embarrassing little squeal. A woman dressed to the nines in a sparkling mini-dress, and her two friends, another woman and a man sporting an amused smile, are standing at the entrance of the booth.

"Huh?" I look around confused. Going where?

"The club." The girl rolls her eyes. "You going in or not?"

Club? What are they talking about? I…

A conversation with Stella about her friend's club dawns on me. She mentioned it some months ago, but nonetheless it left a mark in my mind thanks to the elaborate dancing shows she talked about. Could this be it? No. It couldn't. A place like that would never take me. Unless…

"So?" The guy drums his fingers on the door. "We're getting wet over here, darling."

"Yes, yes." I hurry out of the box. "After you."

I expect them to lead me to a side door or something but the life-sized Ken goes inside the booth and dials a number.

"Umm, I don't think it's working," I start to say but my mouth hangs slack at the last word. The wall opens in front of us.

What the hell! Stella mentioned the club was exclusive and the waiting list for membership was a year long but she said nothing about hidden entrances.

The girls trail after him and I follow suit. My jaw is on the floor as I look around the vintage movie theater.

It's like stepping into a time machine. Popcorn makers on wheels and wooden benches are sitting under sparse lighting, not a single speck of dust on any of the surfaces despite the years.

I notice I've been left behind by my little group, while climbing the red carpet stairs. I hurry after them, touching the golden handrails as if they might disappear in a dream.

In the back of my mind, I calculate how quickly this could become a scene in a thriller movie.

There's muffled music on the second floor behind the black wall. Ken walks over to a polished black grand piano sitting on the empty balcony, opens the lid, and presses a combination of three keys, the echo of their sound circling the large building.

Something behind me clicks. I turn around to see a large man dressed in a black suit and a masquerade mask. He's holding open the door to an entrance that wasn't there before.

"Welcome to Masquerade," he says, gesturing for us to follow him. He leads us through a dark hallway. The group stops in front of a table with various masquerade masks on it. So many colors to choose from, each one more exquisite than the next. They each take one so I do the same. A black one with a gold feather and details.

A petite lady with a red glowing band around her wrist escorts us through another hallway to the club. I, being me, get distracted by the detailing on the mask and stop to put it on, losing the group.

"Hey!" I call out but no one answers. The hallway is long and dark, I can barely see my own legs. "Hey, guys!" I continue walking in the darkness, calling for them but nothing. It's a long, long hallway and I can hear the music coming from the other side of the wall but there's no door.

I end up back at the mask table but the woman is no longer there. I'm alone in a dark hallway in an abandoned building.

My fingers tingle to get my phone. I dial Stella's number again. No reception.

Wonderful. I'm about to end up in the morning news.

I turn on the flashlight cursing myself for not thinking of it sooner. I continue down the same hallway, touching the walls for another hidden door.

"Ouch," I bump into something. Someone. A wall of a human in a suit.

"Watch where you're going," he snarls at me. His scowl is sitting harshly against his granite jaw. Why is he so rude? It's not like I spilled my drink on him or something.

"I'm sorry," I draw back, not wanting to get myself kicked out for bothering the guests before I even have the opportunity to see this club.

"You're staring," the scowl deepens. His voice is dark and velvety like chocolate.

He looks down at my hand and I realize I'm shining my flashlight in his face.

Darkness envelopes us like a thick cloud and with my

vision blurred his cologne drifts to my senses. Woodsy with lingering traces of vanilla.

My thighs tremble. It's been over a year since I felt the touch of a man. Voluntarily anyway. I lean forward, the warmness of his body beckoning me.

"Are you…" he startles me out of my trance, "sniffing me?"

Oh my God!

Ivy, get your shit together.

"I'm sorry." I feel like he can see my flushed face even through the darkness.

"So I've heard." His smirk is devastating. "See you around," he leaves the end open probably for me to fill in my name.

"Yeah, see you." I hurry down the hallway and out of his sight. A minute later I finally find the door and push it open.

Mind-blowing.

A red neon sign Masquerade with a carnival mask above it glows on the brick wall of the spacious building. The club is packed with guests mingling between black leather booths, drinking at high tables, and grinding against each other in their masks.

The stage catches my eye. The curtain is drawn and butterflies erupt in my stomach. Just thinking about being on it makes me giddy.

I sneak to the only empty seat at one of the bars and order the least expensive drink on the menu. My voice is muffled by a loud bang. The music stops, the lights go out, and the only sounds come from the whispering people. Two girls next to me jump in their seats and whisper, "That's it! It's starting."

The curtains draw back and with the start of the piano intro of Annie Lennox's "I put a spell on you," a spotlight illuminates a beautiful dark-skinned dancer lying on an air hoop above the stage. She's dressed in a white glittering bodysuit and a white mask. With the first line of the song spotlights illuminate four more dancers. The dancers grasp the hoops with both hands and stand on one foot while rotating gracefully until they reach the ground.

The crowd explodes with applause, whistling, and shouting in ecstasy.

They bow to the audience and sit on their hoops again as they ascend for a few more spins.

In the end, they roll over and grip the top of the hoops with their feet as their bodies hang down over the gazes of a hundred enchanted people.

The lights go out and when they start again the dancers are gone but the security is in front of me.

"Would you follow me, miss?" He gestures to the exit. A hostess is standing next to him, giving me a once-over. At some point during the performance, I took off my raincoat and am now standing in my work attire. She probably thinks I'm a prostitute who sneaked in. Only one of these is true but the shame of getting kicked out before I even finished the drink that I bought with my last money is greater than my will to find this imaginary employer.

I stand up, throwing the raincoat over my half-naked body, and follow them.

I expect to be escorted to the hallway and into the street but instead, we end up backstage. Dressing tables are neatly stacked next to each other, and a white bodysuit hangs from a folding chair.

"What is going on?" I ask the gorilla guy. Both he and the hostess shrug.

"Rob, I can explain." A woman shrieks somewhere behind the wall.

My throat dries. What is he doing to her? Why the hell am I here?

"I don't want to hear it. You're going to rehab." He says back in a British accent, exiting through the door. He stops in his tracks when he sees us as if he didn't expect us here.

"Boss," the gorilla nods.

"I'll take it from here." My heart threatens to puncture my chest. What is he going to do to me?

He gestures to another room. "After you."

I walk inside what seems like an office, the British guy on my feet.

"Who are you?" He closes the door behind him and leans against it. "This is a private club. I know everyone inside this building, yet I've never seen you. How'd you get inside?"

"No one," I shake my head frantically, "I'm no one."

"Well, no one," he crosses his arms, "we can do this the easy way or the hard way. It's your choice."

Easy way? Hard way? What the hell?

God, I knew I was begging for you to take me but I didn't mean it literally. I'm not ready to die tonight.

"What are you going to do to me?" I go over the moves I still remember from the Krav Maga classes. This man is at least six foot three, muscled but not as big as the gorilla. If I'm strategic maybe I could take him down. But how would I get out of this maze of hidden doors?

"You can either tell me who you are and what are you doing here or I can call the police and let them take care of you and whoever your pimp is." He delivers his statement with no emotion like a robot.

My heart stops for a second. I can feel my head getting dizzy.

"Are you alright?" He asks but I can barely hear him from

the pounding in my ears. No police. No. I can't go to the police.

"No," I say, sitting down on the chair as my knees buckle. I gather myself. "Yes. Yes, I'm okay. My friend Stella sent me here to talk to someone about a job offer."

Realization dawns on Rob's sharp face and he untangles his arms. He brings me a glass of water and sits in the opposite chair.

"Why are you dressed like that?" His brows furrow. His tone isn't condescending, more like... worried.

"It's a long story," I gulp down the water. "No police, please. I'll go. I'll never come back. I promise."

The door flies open. A woman dressed in the bodysuits the dancers wore steps in, wobbling on her high heels and barely keeping her balance.

"You can't fire me, Robert. I've got a solo tonight." She screams. It's the same woman I heard before. She looks high as a kite.

"I damn well can," Robert mutters under his breath, pressing a button. "You're going to rehab, end of discussion. I've found a replacement."

The woman zeroes in on me. "This?" She spits out like poison. "You replace me with this?"

While it's true I've lost the perfect shape I kept on for years from the dancing, I am in no position to be judged so harshly. I might've put on a little weight but my body was still a machine. I still kept dancing in our living room when Stella was out of the house.

The gorilla guy shows up and wraps his arms around her, lifting her off the ground as she keeps screaming profanities.

When I look back at Robert his shoulders are hunched over and his head is between his arms. I don't dare move or say anything.

In a few silent moments, he raises his head again. "So you've already seen more than you should've." I gulp. "This has never happened before but I want you to know whatever happens that we value hard-working, transparent, and discreet people. What you've seen now is a one-off. Naomi will get the help she needs but in the meantime, we need a dancer for a solo. What can you do?"

I spill out the type of dancing I'm best at. Contemporary, burlesque, aerial, and ballroom. I've trained almost every style there is since I was a child, plus gymnastics. I was training to be a dance teacher before I had to disappear.

His phone lights up with a message and his frown deepens as he reads it.

"It's your lucky day," Robert says, his tone enthusiastic, the look on his face anything but. "The boss is here. Show what you got to the other dancers and if they approve you've got one chance to impress him."

"But I thought you're the boss?" I ask confused because of how the gorilla guy addressed him.

"I'm the manager," Robert says. "You'll meet him if you get the job. Now hurry," he rushed me off the chair and into the hallway, "there's not much time."

He spewed off instructions to me and the other dancers and let us do our thing. They filled me in on what was expected of me. Naomi's dance was an aerial routine on silks but since I haven't trained them in over a year I opted to do my favorite burlesque performance. Robert allowed it as a one-off even though it was aerial night.

As I look at myself in a mask in the mirror I can't help but feel a pang of guilt.

Life is not about waiting for the storm to pass, but learning how to dance in the rain. My nonna's voice echoes in my mind as I fasten my costume. That's what she told me after my very first dance class when I wouldn't step out because I was afraid of the storm. She made me show her all the steps I learned, and we both danced our way to her car. I miss her as much as I miss dancing.

Before going on stage, I look at myself one last time and close my eyes. Breathe in. Breathe out.

Only tonight.

I can forget who I am, where I come from, and what I'm running from. I can be myself, the real, raw version, behind this mask and let the lights guide me home.

Let the curtains fall.

Chapter Two

DAMIEN

Robert, the club manager and my best friend, fucking finally shows up at the bar.

"Damien, I didn't expect you tonight."

"I didn't know I needed an invitation to my own club."

He shakes his head, grinning. "Already in a good mood, I see."

"Thought I'd do a check-up."

On the liquor.

"Lucky me," he grunts.

"Whiskey, neat." John, my bartender, takes the order.

Robert takes a glance at the second floor where the VIPs are. "Your booth is ready."

"Pass. I'd rather stay closer to the booze."

He stares at me with suspicion while I tip back the first glass and slide it to John for a refill.

"Is there something else I can help you with?" He's not asking about the booth or the drink, but I don't feel like bitching to my friends. I've got whiskey to forget my first-world problems and Masquerade to escape in my little anonymous universe.

My phone lights up every five seconds with messages from my mother. Jesus, this woman is impossible. I switch it off just as the lights go out.

This is my favorite part of club nights. The shows. I sit back and tip the glass. John takes care of the problem, but another arises.

A shadow enveloped in fog and illuminated by a single spotlight on the stage. The club is freakishly quiet and everyone is staring at the smoking-hot body pressed onto a wooden chair.

"Wicked Games" by The Weeknd starts and the girl, dressed in a black bodysuit, opens her legs slowly, revealing tanned and tight hips wrapped in knee-high black boots.

The singer's voice comes through the speakers as she flings her head back, long dark hair spraying in the air. She flips the chair and smashes the boots' thin heel in the wood. My dick jumps, urging me to take notice, but that's my employee. I shouldn't be thinking about her sexually. It must be the frustration and the whiskey. It shouldn't be hard to find someone willing to help me take it out later.

Still, I can't stop thinking about the other places I'd like this heel to press right now.

With the gait of a predatory cat, she demands attention.

The light goes out and the music stops. My breath catches in my lungs like someone punched the air out of them.

A second later, a beam of purple light illuminates her silhouette. Her body glides across the chair. Slowly and gently she traces her fingers from her toes to her juicy, red lips.

I look around the room. Starving eyes like zombies in an apocalypse, she's mesmerized every single person in the room, turning them into her willing slaves.

I can't lie. I'm picturing her grinding on top of me while I'm buried balls deep inside her.

And it's so wrong.

I know all my dancers pretty well, I've watched them perform a million times, but there's nothing about this body and the way it moves that's familiar.

I'm lost in her curves when she crawls on all fours.

A hint of something green and ugly creeps up when I realize not a single man in here can take their eyes off her, not even the women. In my fantasies I make her crawl to me so that everybody knows this pretty little kitten is mine.

Red lights illuminate her, like a devil hidden underneath the body of an angel.

I'm reminded she's not mine to take as the crowd pushes around me to get closer to her. I didn't realize I moved but I'm in front of the stage now.

Bending over a chair, she traces every edge and every curve of the wood with the tips of her fingers.

For the finale, she does a handstand split and lands with finesse in the fog creeping on the stage. I'm a goner—but no, not yet. Her eyes lock on mine.

The lights go out.

I blink, shaking off the trance and she's gone like a figment of my imagination. If it weren't for the confused people around me I would've thought I made her up.

I don't know who she is, but I know one thing—I want her, and I'll have her.

Rob sneaks up from behind me and slaps me on the shoulder with a wolfish smile. "She's good, isn't she?"

"Who is she?"

He sighs, muttering something under his breath.

"Come again?"

"Fuck, man, I didn't ask her name."

"Explain." I touch the bridge of my nose. It's like I don't have enough trouble with my mother and the board at the company, I don't need more here, in my safe haven.

"Stella recommended her."

Double shit. Stella and I have an agreement, her friends are off-limits. And if she's working for us now that means I can't even look at her without getting slapped with a sexual-harassment case.

"I wasn't aware we were looking for dancers." My sour mood just turned murderous. I'm horny and frustrated, never a good combination.

"Naomi's going to rehab." Rob doesn't need to explain more. We'd been keeping a close eye on Naomi for months now. I had a feeling something was off when I talked to her a few days ago. I should've known.

"And I thought this day couldn't get any worse." I tip the third glass. The club is our little family. I insist on keeping good relationships between the employees and the management. Masquerade is a well-oiled machine that delivers only the best quality to our refined clientele. This is the place celebrities and millionaires salivate over. We offer the most expensive of all luxuries. Anonymity. If someone from the staff isn't well enough to handle our strict policy it creates a bad name for the brand.

Still, one question swerves around my brain above all else.

"How do I find this mystery girl?"

"She should be backstage." Robert takes the hint and we take the bottle to the back only to find an empty dressing room.

Tasha, one of the other dancers, exits the bathroom.

"Where's the new girl?" Rob is one step ahead of me.

"She was in a hurry and left."

"Left?" I growl, taking both Robert and Tasha aback. I clear my throat. "I apologize."

"Did you happen to catch her name?" Robert shakes his head barely visible with a hint of a smirk. The bastard. He's onto me.

"I gave her your card and told her to come back tomorrow."

Without wasting any more fucking time, I run to the back entrance. She couldn't be far. There's a familiar silhouette at the corner of the street. "Hey! You!"

She whips around, catching sight of me, and jumps into a waiting cab before I can reach her.

Dammit!

I didn't even see her face.

Chapter Three

IVY

I open the flaky white-painted gate carefully and slowly, but the rusty hinges always give me away.

"Who is it?" Stella's voice rings out across the empty yard.

"It's me, Ivy," I call out. I cross the sunburned grass of the backyard and find the door of our one-story tiny house wide open. "Stells, why is the door open?" I walk into our sea-blue living room, but as soon as I see her lying facedown on the ground, I know the answer.

"Huh?" My best friend and roommate replies in a weary manner, biting a worn-out pencil not even looking up from her sketchbook. Her normally expressive Italian tone absent.

I sit on the wooden floor beside her and caress her blond hair. My eyes flick over all the clothing sketches surrounding her. Some are finished, others are halfway done, but their total number is probably somewhere in the twenties.

"Stella! Did you get up from this floor at all today?"

"Huh?" she repeats.

That's the second time this week she forgot to lock the door. Stella wouldn't notice if thieves had robbed the house around her. I love her for her dedication, but she needs to take better care of herself.

"Did you eat at all today? Drink water?"

By the size of her eye bags, I can tell she didn't sleep despite her repeated promises to me. She takes notice of me for the first time since I walked in.

"No, Mom." She pouts.

Her innocent big blue eyes remind me of a child even though she's just a year younger than me. We've played this game a thousand times before. I scold her, she doesn't listen, repeat. Since the very first day when I learned she was bulimic. I've made it my mission in life to keep her from relapsing and so far it's going well.

"Dio Mio!" I imitate her signature overdramatic Italian exclamation and accent. Her ringing laughter fills the house. "Let's feed you."

"I should be prepping for the fashion show. I came up with this great design last night." Her eyes sparkle with joy. "Just wait 'til I sew it! You're going to love it."

I pull out a half-drank bottle of rosé and pour it into our cheap glasses. Stella microwaves yesterday's spaghetti and the divine aroma of basil and tomato sauce spreads across the kitchen.

One thing you need to know about Stella: she's the best pasta cook in the world. Ever.

Before we met, I didn't even like pasta very much. Now I can't imagine not tasting hers again. My heart skips a beat at this possibility, but I quickly push all emotions to the side.

Tonight's about celebrating my first exciting experience since the day I met Stella. If I have to thank God for one thing, it's that He sent the sun into my life, on my darkest day.

I was sitting on a park bench, feeling confused and frustrated, just hours after arriving in Rosehill, my new home. I had just opened a bag of cookies when I raised my gaze and saw a petite blonde running toward me in a freaking wedding dress. Mind you, I almost choked. She threw herself on the bench beside me, with all the dramatics of a soap opera actress, crying her eyes out. Romantic comedy movie material right there. Until she raised her head, and I saw the purple swelling around her aqua eyes and the dried blood on her split lip.

I couldn't bring myself to leave, even though I knew I was in no position to help anyone, so I offered her a cookie and stayed by her side until she stopped crying and told me her story. The groom had hit her right before the ceremony when he realized she wouldn't inherit the fortune of her godparents. She didn't have anywhere to go.

She seemed to have no one, like me. I couldn't just leave her all alone at night in the park. So, I invited her to stay with me and the rest is history.

Stella's personality is rare and untainted by this vicious world we live in. Love and positive energy radiate from her. You can see her thoughts written on her face, and I've never once heard her say a bad word about anyone.

It was one of those immediate connections you feel in your bones. A soul mate, if you will.

So we ended up renting this house and living together even though Stella made up with her godmother. We've been working non-stop to achieve this wonderful illusion of being independent. I, on my way to avoiding jail, Stella on her way to Milan's fashion week.

We head to the backyard, with a plate in one hand and a glass in the other, and sit on the swinging bench.

We took the house for the low rent knowing we'd be dealing with a junkyard. We've refreshed it a bit since but neither of us expected to stay in this place long enough to make it a home. It seems like we've become home to each other.

The storm has long passed, leaving the smell of rain in the crisp air. We dig into the plates, eating in silence. The adrenaline from the dancing is starting to wear off and I feel my lids get heavier.

"Dio Mio!" Stella jumps up from the bench at about halfway through the plate. "I absolutely zoned out of our conversation earlier."

I've been waiting for that.

I shrug. "I'm not saying I'm not going to hold it over your head, but I mean everything turned out… fine?"

"Fine?" She repeats.

"I met Robert."

"You did? How'd you get in Masquerade?"

"I snuck in." I grin. I tell her the whole story from me getting fired from my job to landing a new one. Or rather the part where I ran out of the club scared of how good it felt to be back on stage. Scared of how much my heart would break if I had to turn down a good offer, assuming they had one for me.

"Why'd you do that? Are you insane?" Stella throws her hands in the air.

"You know why," I push the spaghetti from one side to the other. I can't sign a contract and a place like that doesn't work on the gray side. Even asking to work without one would raise eyebrows.

"I can help," she offers. "I know the owner, he's like a brother to me."

I stop her before any more craziness comes out of her mouth. "I can't." My voice is trembling, water pooling in my eyes.

"Look, I know you're hiding from something…"

I swallow the lump in my throat and look up to the sky to blink the tears away.

"I would never put you in any danger. I could just ask. I don't have to give details, and I don't know them to begin with."

Stella and I have this unspoken agreement. We're both hiding. Me, from the world. Stella, I suspect, from herself. We both have pasts we don't talk about. We don't ask questions. We just support each other.

This would be going one step too far. Asking her to dig into her past to hide me from mine would be breaking an invisible boundary.

"I'll think about it," I lie. There's nothing to think about. I wouldn't put her in a position to ask for favors on my account.

That calms her down a bit. She stays silent throughout the night, listening to my tails of how beautiful the choreography of the aerial dance was.

When we go to bed, there's a knock on my door.

"I was thinking," she starts. "Would you at least go tomorrow again? As a favor to me." She pleads. "Just dance one more time. I promise not to say anything. I just want to see you glow the way you did tonight."

I nod. One more time wouldn't kill me, right?

Chapter Four

IVY

I leave Masquerade's building but my heart remains inside.

Who can I really blame for my stupidity? When the clock struck four in the afternoon I put my sports bra and a pair of shorts in a duffel and headed toward the club, skipping on the sidewalk like a kid going to an amusement park.

I can now see I am my biggest problem. I should stay out of trouble, out of sight, yet I put myself under the spotlight once again just to feel the rush. My body knows with its whole being that dancing is my calling. That moment when my feet feel the rhythm of the music, the waves reverberating off the ground, is like an addict injecting the first dose in their veins.

At first, it was just the girls and me, then Rob came over. He insisted I stay for the next party and dance on stage again. I had my speech prepared. Stella is having a fashion show and I've promised to help her. He didn't budge. Any excuse I found, he had a counteroffer.

This is, I learned today, one of the twenty top nightclubs

in the country, even though it just opened six months ago. The other dancers showed me one of the most amazing dancing and aerial shows I've ever seen during rehearsal. Any performer would fight and claw their way up for the chance to dance in Masquerade.

Everyone but me.

God, what am I going to do?

I tend to ask this question a lot but I never get any answers from the Big Guy. I think He's mad at me.

As I wrestle with these thoughts, I arrive home, but the living room window isn't lit up. Stella never goes to bed so early and it's rare for either of us to stay in our bedrooms. Unlike the huge living room, our bedrooms are the size of a matchbox, and the only option for being inside without becoming claustrophobic is to fall asleep.

I rummage through the duffel for my keys with one hand and knock on the door with the other, but there's no answer. I empty the contents of it onto the grass. Wallet, training clothes, chewing gum, two scrunchies, one fake passport, and gloss. No keys. I search the whole thing again, tap all the pockets and shake it three more times, but nothing except for a toothpick falls out.

Panic slowly creeps inside me, as I resort to banging my fists on the door while trying to reach Stella on the phone. No answer on both fronts, even after I kick the shit out of the door. She finally answers on the second call.

"Where are you?"

"Ivy, I can't hear you very well. Is everything okay?" Her voice is ripped through the hiss of the phone.

"I forgot my keys and I can't get inside," I yell because why not, maybe it'll help the breaking connection.

"Oh no! Raquel found the perfect fabric for the design I showed you last night, and we went to Savannah to pick it up. I won't be home until at least four or five in the morning." It's eight o'clock in the evening. Shit. "What are you going to do? I can call Rob. Maybe you forgot them at Masquerade."

I sigh, resting my head against the door. "I don't remember taking them at all. I guess I'll be waiting for you on the swinging bench."

"The room at the Black Rose Hotel is jam-packed with clothes we need to iron but you can go there. I'll call the front desk. Just be careful with the clothes, the show is in two days."

It's too cold outside for my summer dress, I don't have much of a choice. Agreeing with a sigh, I decide to walk there. It's only a mile and I've got a lot of energy to kill.

Despite my troubles for the evening, only one question bothers me along the way.

What will I do about the job?

Chills sneak up my spine at the thought of declining it. If that was an option, I would give up everything in the world to stay at the club. There's nothing worse than knowing your dream is at your fingertips but you can't quite reach it. I feel empty with no purpose in life and that's as close to being dead as it gets.

At least when you're dead you don't suffer, but my parents didn't give me that opportunity. No. They left me alone, escaping their responsibility and depriving me of the right to live the life I dream of. But isn't that what they've been doing my whole life?

It's rare that I give in to emotions but I can't help myself.

I hate them. I hate them for not giving me an explanation or at least the right to choose. Once again, they left me at the mercy of fate without even thinking about how their actions might affect me. One could say that after twenty-four years I should've known better. But of all the selfish things they did, this one is by far the worst.

I'd been forgotten at school and dance lessons countless times. They missed most of my birthdays. I graduated from the fancy boarding school they shoved me in without either of them in attendance. Then, after living two decades in New York they decided to return to Bulgaria, and still, they forced me to go to MIT, not Juilliard, where I'd been accepted. And they missed that graduation too.

When I was eleven and broke my fibula, I couldn't walk for a month. And what did my mother do? She left me with two crutches and a computer and told me I was a big girl. I lost five pounds in three days because I couldn't get out of bed to eat.

The only thing that kept me going was the banana she left me in the morning when she was pouring water into the kettle. I was lucky that Nonna Ivanka came to visit, found me half-starved, and took care of me until I healed.

The only thing that touched my mother's stone-cold heart was the discovery that I was a genius when she saw the algorithms I was writing while bedridden that month. From there on, my parents' mission was to make me their copy.

But they failed. I will never become a heartless, self-absorbed robot like them and that is my punishment.

Life is tough when you're cursed to feel so strongly. There are three ways to drown out all the voices in my head, all the emotions I've been suppressing for the purpose of surviving. The three Ds. Dancing, drinking, dick.

Screw everything—I'll do at least one of these tonight.

Lord knows it's been too long since I last did either.

DAMIEN

"Gentlemen, as you can tell for yourselves, everything is impeccable at my hotel. Are you satisfied?" I grit my teeth and smile at the grouchy faces in front of me.

The two morons' bellies bounce over their tight belts as they nervously tap their feet and look around, trying to think of anything else they haven't checked for violations. But there will never be a violation because I'll never give Richard the pleasure.

"Of course. We never thought otherwise, Mr. Black," Tweedledee says with an equal amount of hypocrisy and bile.

I just deprived them of their early Christmas bonus.

Tweedledum gives me the meanest look he can manage, considering he has to bend his neck to look at me. "We'll be back, Damien."

I step forward, shadowing over them, my smile in place. "I'll be waiting."

Tweedledee visibly shivers. Coward.

Once they're gone, my hotel manager scoots closer and puts her hand on my shoulder. "That was close. Their checks are becoming more frequent."

This is their third visit since the beginning of the year, and we're barely past halfway. There's only one person to blame. Fucking Richard. The bastard is trying to get dirt on me in any way he can. He'll have to send in an army before I give him a chance to fight.

I pull away from her touch and give her a pointed look. She straightens her spine, tweaking her black skirt.

"They've never been close and never will be. I pay you to keep an eye on this shit."

She lowers her eyes to the ground like a guilty puppy.

Maybe I was a bit harsh, but I cannot afford employees who don't follow the highest standards. If I wasn't paying the Health department chief of staff to warn me about these visitations, I wouldn't have been able to fix the problem we had before they stormed in here.

A problem that the manager was supposed to check for regularly.

"I expect close attention to detail to be a priority and your performance to show vast improvement from now on. Don't make me regret giving you another chance."

Her shoulders slump. "It won't happen again, Mr. Black," she says, avoiding eye contact before turning and striding to her office.

I slam onto one of the sofas in the lobby bar.

Fucking shit.

The old motherfucker is starting to lose patience. Richard has been trying to embarrass me in front of the board of the company for years. He almost succeeded a few years back but I managed to rectify the situation. Honestly, I should be a little insulted. Does he still think I'm just a stupid boy? He showed his cards way too early.

The question is, how far is he willing to go?

When it comes to Richard, I wouldn't doubt his greed.

He's been trying to throw my family out of our own company for as long as I can remember, though he started actively targeting me after I made the mistake of sleeping with his daughter. It wasn't enough that her little obsession cost me my freedom.

I'm no Hollywood star like my sister but I've been known to make a headline or two. One wrong decision and a picture of your naked ass on someone's yacht ends up on the front page of tomorrow's newspaper, magazines, and all over the internet. One of the many benefits of being the heir to a multi-billion-dollar hotel chain.

One of the other benefits is that I can get shitfaced at my own hotel bar, with no cameras around, until I pass out, forgetting about this fucking day.

I rub my temples, feeling a headache coming on. Something tells me this evening won't be easy.

Chapter Five

IVY

When I walk into the hotel bar and all heads turn to me, I realize this might be a mistake. My baby-blue polka dot summer dress definitely doesn't fit the scenery. I make my way to the bar in the quickest way possible and take a seat. All eyes break away from me like a spell and I take a deep breath.

"Vodka, straight," I slap a bill on the bar. When one wants to forget vodka is the safest choice. Soon I won't remember my own name.

Neither the false nor the real one.

The bar is, to put it simply, magnificent. Brown leather armchairs, the smell of sandalwood, and polished wooden tables, most of them occupied by middle-aged men in suits and ladies dressed in the latest fashion pieces. Beautiful and elegant, all of them perfect. From the sophisticated hairstyles down to the beautiful neutral-colored dresses and stilettos.

Cheers to always feeling out of place, especially now.

Every once in a while someone glances at the length of my minidress. I can only imagine what my mother would say.

Cheers to you mother and the island you're probably sunbathing on while I struggle daily.

The alcohol's familiar burn soothes the bitterness inside of me.

Mirrored columns reflect the lights of the city and separate the booths. Floor-to-ceiling windows reveal the most breathtaking full-angle view of Rosehill.

I've heard that the three bars and four restaurants at the Black Rose Hotel are among the most elite in the country. I got lost twice while looking for this bar. I can only imagine what the penthouse suites would look like.

The bartender slides over a fresh glass of vodka as he removes the empty one from the black marble bar. With it in my hand, I move cautiously between booths and to the front of the window.

The lights from the buildings are reflecting in the dark water of the Gulf of Mexico. The waves break them apart into twinkling stars. Traffic isn't slowing down at this hour and people walking on the coastal street look like ants from up here. In the distance, you can see the flashing lights from the Ferris wheel.

I take a sip, frowning at the burning sensation in my throat. Just as I head back to the bar a reflection in the mirror column stops me in my tracks.

A pair of green eyes are staring at me with a burning glare.

Eyes so familiar, but I don't know why.

The vodka must've caught up with me.

I return to the bar and lean back in the high leather chair. Another sip. I can't help it. I glance at the mirror.

I wasn't imagining things.

Where only half a face was reflected a few seconds ago, now a whole image of a man is visible. One hell of a man.

The same eyes that ate me up in front of the stage my first night in Masquerade look at me in the mirror. I thought I was imagining him because of the euphoria that enveloped me on stage, but is it possible?

Turning my gaze away to down the second glass, I decide it's unlikely I'd see the same person again. Though I can't help but admire the man in the mirror.

My sensitive parts awaken from the deep hibernation they've slipped into this year and take notice of Mr. Smoldering. Wild brown hair, emerald green eyes, and stubble lining his sharp features. Perfectly shaped muscles stretching his white shirt. Black ink adorns his chest behind the three undone buttons on top, disappearing under his shirt and continuing down his forearms where his sleeves are rolled up.

Without looking away, he raises his glass and takes a swig of the golden-brown liquid. I grip the third glass the bartender slides over to me, close my eyes, and swallow down my poison.

When I open them again, he's still there, and all doubts that I imagined him evaporate. He drapes an arm over the back of the booth, never once taking his eyes off me. The warm feeling south of my stomach, no doubt awakened by the vodka and this stranger, reminds me I am still a woman, a woman who hasn't had sex in far too long.

It couldn't hurt to play a little with this stranger, right?

DAMIEN

The woman in the mirror looks away for only a few seconds before her gaze finds mine again. She looks familiar but I can't put my finger on it.

Have I slept with her before? Is that why she can't take her eyes off me, or am I just interesting to her?

In the usual settings, my reputation precedes me. I doubt there's a woman in here who doesn't know my last name.

When the fuck did that start to matter?

My dick wants what it wants. I've become more selective with the company I keep in recent years after a few too many mistakes. Is this strangely familiar woman another mistake? Sure. But how much could it hurt? I'd make sure to check she's being a good girl and her phone is not recording like the last one. And if she starts running her mouth, well...

If there's one thing I know, it's how to get a woman on her knees. And no, I'm not talking about praying.

She'd be too occupied.

Life has been too easy lately, I need some danger and the flames in the dark eyes of the stranger are promising to burn me.

She gets up and heads for the end of the bar where the restrooms are. Her graceful gait reminds me of a wild cat, her hips swaying from side to side in the most seductive way. Her tiny dress accentuates the tan on her long legs.

When she disappears behind the door, I look around and notice all the men are staring at the door she just went through.

This woman has a charisma that attracts everyone like a magnet. When she entered the bar, we all felt her presence. Against the backdrop of all the gray and beige, she came forward as a fresh vibrant color.

She might be trying hard for that innocent appearance, but those scorching eyes give her away.

Multiple glares from the other women in the bar follow her as she leaves the restroom and returns to the bar. None of them radiate this kind of sex appeal.

I grit my teeth as a man reaches out to grab her arm when she walks by his table, but she evades his touch with such grace, without so much as giving him a look.

Interesting.

Every woman here comes to this bar with the same goal. To bed the richest man in the room. That would be me, and my attention is on the most clueless one.

Is she that good of an actress? Playing the long game? I don't understand what her plan is.

As soon as she sits, her eyes go to the mirror again. Does she see me as I see her? From the angle I'm sitting, she should. In the back of the mirror, I see movement. My gaze breaks away from her and lands on one of the Forbes 30 Under 30, who made his millions designing computer games at nineteen. He's slowly gathering courage with every step toward her.

I look back at the mirror and her eyes are on me again.

I get up and with a few strides, I'm behind her just before the kid reaches her. From my periphery, I can see the crushing look of disappointment as he stares at my back shielding her body from his eyes.

Sorry, pal. This woman is mine.

"Whiskey for me and whatever the lady is drinking," I tell the bartender before he can open his mouth. He nods and gets to work.

The woman in front of me stiffens for a moment but quickly recovers. She slowly turns, and her dark-chocolate eyes find my face. "So I wasn't imagining you after all," she says so softly I almost don't hear her.

"I'm as real as they come, baby." The smirk tugs at the corner of my lips.

"Baby," she rolls her eyes and tips back the last sip from her glass. "Thank you for the drink."

"What kind of man would I be if I leave a beautiful woman to drink alone?"

Her cheeks flush and my cock takes it as a wake-up call.

IVY

The bartender leaves the drinks in front of us and scurries to the other side of the bar to take care of the newcomers. I take a sip and chance a look at the man next to me. In the mirror, I could tell he was tall, but standing next to me he's huge. The effect of him towering over me with his broad shoulders is almost unbearable.

To add insult to injury the breeze from the door opening carries the scent of his cologne to my nostrils. He smells like an aphrodisiac. The fresh woodsy fragrance, with hints of vanilla and mint, is making my already unsteady legs twitch.

Armani shirt and a gold Rolex. I know his type. Arrogant, smug, and king-of-the-fucking-universe type. I've been dealing with the likes of him my whole life.

Vodka will definitely help. Whether it be with my confidence or with enduring him talking about his days in private school which will no doubt be something he mentions. They all do. That's their way of making you feel smaller so they could manipulate you into bed easier.

Luckily for him, I want him for his looks, not his money. Preferably on top, behind, and under me. This shouldn't require much talking.

His deep voice interrupts my staring. "What are you drinking to?" His eyes bounce to my glass.

"To forget."

He grants me a smug smile, which I'd usually knock right

off of his face with a snide remark if I didn't have other plans for that face.

"I can help you with that." He raises his glass. I grab mine just to have something to do with my hands that doesn't involve tearing his clothes off.

His amused gaze travels to my summer dress.

"Do I look that out of place?" I bat my lashes innocently.

Here we go.

His roaring laugh booms through the bar and a few heads turn to us. Masculine, deep laughter, so sexy I want to grab him by the shirt and climb him like a tree.

"Don't give me those innocent eyes," he says, then bends down and whispers in my ear, "You look"—he takes a step back and his eyes rake over me, leaving a small fire behind—"fucking perfect."

I'm mesmerized by the green in his eyes slowly beginning to darken.

"I'm D—"

I press my finger to his lips. The four glasses of vodka have removed most of my inhibitions, and if I want to try sex with a stranger for the first time in my life, then he must remain a stranger.

"I don't want to know your name...and you don't need to know mine."

My finger lingers on his lower lip and traces it. His smirk twists into a predatory smile, flashing his perfect white teeth. "Then how are you gonna know what to scream when I fuck that mood out of you?"

My jaw falls on the floor. Sweet Jesus. "A little self-absorbed, don't you think?"

"Nah," he tips his glass. "I can tell you want me by the way your thighs are rubbing against each other. It's just a matter of time."

I look down. Dammit. I am grinding a little on the chair. Can you blame me? The man is sex in clothes. And that is exactly what he'll be for me tonight. Sans clothes.

"Well, beautiful stranger, what brought you here?"

"This hotel…unlucky fate." I put my hand on the burning hot skin under his unbuttoned shirt. "But I think my luck has changed."

"Give me a bottle of both." He gestures to the bartender. He grabs my hand and pulls me up. "You don't mind moving the party to a more private place, do you?"

I nod, incapable of saying actual words, as he grabs the two bottles under his arm and leads me to the exit.

"My room or yours?" My squeaky voice betrays me. Oh, the hell no. I won't give up now.

"Your decision."

I fill the awkward silence as we wait for the elevator in the hotel lobby with calculations. Stella's suite is full of clothes. We're both drunk. There's a good chance he fucks dirty.

"Your room," I say as the door opens.

As we enter a little awkward, a little wobbly, he turns to me completely. "Are you sure? We're both drunk, I don't want to take advantage of you. If you want to leave, now is the time to tell me 'cause once you're in my hands, I won't let you go." There's not a hint of amusement in his eyes.

I swallow loudly and nod.

Chapter Six

IVY

Wrapping one hand around his neck, I bury the other in his soft hair. He tilts his head and his lips come at mine hungrily, kissing, biting, ravaging me. His mouth tastes like whiskey.

He pulls away and rests his forehead against mine. I can feel his hot breath inches away from my skin.

"I want you to tell me. Let me hear the words." His voice is husky and full of lust, producing a new wave of heat in me.

Fuck it. Today I'll give in to the madness, and I'll think about the consequences tomorrow.

I pull my face from his and look him in the eyes. "I want you. Now."

His lips are on mine in a millisecond, his hot tongue invading my mouth. I hear the muffled thud of the bottles hitting the carpet. He pushes me against the elevator wall, grabs me by my thighs, lifts me, and places himself between them. One of his hands drops my thigh, reaching somewhere behind him and suddenly the elevator stops. A strangled moan comes out of my mouth as his hand slides up the inside of my thigh and touches the wet lace of my underwear.

The way he captivates me is everything I've ever imagined and better.

His fingers slide under the lace and he spreads the moisture from my pussy to my clit. He growls softly, his teeth biting into my lower lip.

"You're so wet and I've barely even touched you."

I pull his hair harder because I'm ready to go just from his touch and his words.

"Do you want to come, my greedy girl? Do you want me to finger fuck you right here, right now?" The words have me burning from the inside out as I push my body into his.

"Yes," I gasp out.

I unbuckle his belt and press my hand along the length of his hard cock.

Fuck me. This is going to hurt.

Contrary to my worries, my inner muscles tighten, eager for him.

As if reading my thoughts, he slides one finger inside and starts moving it faster as his thumb circles my clit. I can't stop my moans and the sound bounces off the elevator walls and echoes around us.

I'm riding the wave of orgasm as he inserts a second finger into me. When he puts a little more pressure against my center, sensations flicker up my spine, and I dig my nails into his crisp white shirt, releasing the built-up tension.

He silences my cry with a kiss, and my whole body relaxes in his strong arms.

The beautiful man I'm wrapped around drops my feet carefully to the ground. He runs his hand through his sexy bedroom hair and looks at me with an even more intoxicated expression.

"I hope you're ready for what I'm going to do to you."

I swallow hard, the moisture gathering in the same spot

where his fingers made me crazy a few seconds ago. I take off my panties because they're a lost cause and curl them into a ball in my fist.

He pushes a button and the elevator shoots up, opening into an enormous room.

The floor is dark wood, and curtains of the same color decorate huge windows, like the ones in the bar that reveal views of the bay. Big crystal chandeliers hang from the high ceiling, and the low light creates an intimate atmosphere.

"Where are we?"

He grabs the two bottles from the elevator floor and gestures for me to follow him.

"This is my room." He opens a mirrored cabinet and takes out two glasses.

I saunter to the gray couch in front of the large fireplace and try to look around the suite more, but my eyes always seem to drift back to the man.

His white shirt is already wrinkled and almost completely unbuttoned, and I desperately want to touch the abs showing underneath it. Some script is tattooed on his chest, with tribal designs around it and across his abdomen, ending just above the mouthwatering V disappearing under his black suit pants.

My mouth waters and I lick my lips, imagining what it would be like to trace the perfect lines of his body with my tongue.

"The presidential suite." He hands me a glass of vodka, raises his whiskey, and we both drink them down in one go.

Any words in my head are lost as I take a few steps toward him. Our arms wrap around each other like we've rehearsed it a thousand times before. My fingers find the remaining three buttons on his shirt, unbutton them, and send the shirt flying to the other end of the room. His hands grip the hem of my dress and pull it over my head before throwing it over his shoulder, mimicking me. I'm not wearing a bra underneath it, and with my panties abandoned somewhere on the sofa, I'm completely naked in front of him.

He pulls back and his eyes rake over me. They stop at my breasts and my nipples harden even more in anticipation.

"So perfect." His words cause another wave of moisture between my legs. Both hands grip my breasts as his fingers play with my diamond-hard nipples.

Usually, I'd feel uncomfortable being naked in front of a stranger, but he looks at me with so much desire, all thoughts leave my head.

If I have anything to say about tonight, it's mission accomplished.

Alcohol mixed with the heated passion between us not only dissolves every thought in my head but also makes me feel lighter than I've ever felt before.

DAMIEN

The mind-blowing woman before me makes me lose my breath. With a body made for sin, tanned and toned in all the right places, and the face of an angel, she makes my every thought evaporate. She smells like vanilla, making my head even dizzier. I want to eat her, figuratively and literally.

She made me lose all patience when she looked at me with those big doe eyes in the elevator. And when my fingers slipped into her wet pussy, I couldn't hold back from making her orgasm just to see her expression. It was worth every second.

The fact that she wants me with the same hunger is driving me completely mad. Her lips are eagerly swallowing everything I'm giving her.

Her fingers unbutton my pants, and with a single move she pushes them down along with my briefs. A low growl leaves my throat as her soft hand wraps around my throbbing cock.

Hell, she has me doing math in my head like a fucking teenager just so I don't come too soon and embarrass myself. What sort of sorcery is this?

She moves her hand fiercely along my length and my fingers imitate her moves, spreading her wetness all over her pussy.

Wrapping my arm around her waist, I lift her in the air and her legs lock around me.

When her ass touches the cold surface of the glass table, she gasps. Pressing both her shoulders, I push her down until she's lying naked and spread out before me on the table, her ass on the edge at the perfect height.

I kneel before her and spread her lips in front of my face.

"I want that pussy coming in my mouth."

She whimpers and without any other permission, my tongue steals its first taste.

Sweet heaven.

That's what the girl in my hands tastes like.

I want to tease her, push her to the edge and back, but her moans provoke me to devour her.

Her walls clench on my tongue, her body on the edge of orgasm. I pull away.

"Hey! Come back. You can't leave me like that," she screams after me when I go to the other room to get a condom.

"I can do whatever I want, baby, and what I want is to feel this wet pussy pulsating on my dick while I'm buried balls deep in you," I call back while I'm rolling the condom on my painful erection on my way to her. Yeah, that's how impatient I am.

Her mouth opens in a big O, but I'm not wasting another second, sliding her to the edge of the table I coat my cock with her juices. I thrust without warning, her scream of surprise circling the ceiling of my big suite. With a few slower moves, she takes all of me.

"Harder." The word slips out between her cries and awakens the beast in me. She rises, digging her nails into my biceps. I squeeze her hips and fuck her as she likes, our hands tearing at each other like wild animals.

I glide my thumb along her clit, and it quickly shoots her straight to the edge, her arousal coating our inner thighs. Her pussy clenches, trying to choke my cock. "So fucking tight. You're making me crazy, baby."

I keep banging into her relentlessly, her nails digging into my biceps as a second orgasm makes its way through her body. Her cries are muffled as she bites my shoulder, and her whole body trembles in my hands.

With two more thrusts, my orgasm follows hers and my release fills the condom.

For a few minutes, the only sounds in the room are our rapid breaths. Our bodies remain in a semi-hug on the glass table. I pull out to go to the bathroom and get rid of the condom. While I wash, I look in the mirror at the stinging bite on my shoulder. There are small traces of blood on it.

This might leave a mark.

I grin to myself like a fucking idiot, though I'm not even drunk anymore because this girl knocked it right out of me, and I hope it stays that way so that I'll remember every second of what happens tonight. The mere thought of her makes me hard again. I grab another condom, but then I change my mind and take the whole box.

When I go back out, she isn't where I left her, so I figure she's found her way to the other bathroom. I pour myself a fresh drink and when I turn around, I notice her dress and panties aren't where they landed earlier.

Fuck, she wouldn't leave, would she?

"Hey!" I call out while I search every single room because I didn't even learn her fucking name.

But there's no trace of her.

The only clue my stranger left behind is the scent of vanilla mixed with hot sex.

Chapter Seven

IVY

"You," Raquel calls out to me with her squeaky annoying voice, "come here."

I leave the girl I'd been helping to get dressed and stride to the start of the long runway where Raquel's watching the models rehearse for Stella's fashion show tomorrow and giving them instructions. Raquel is Stella's everything in her business. Her agent, her critique, and her sort-of assistant. She does everything Stella can't or doesn't have the time to do and that's why I respect her despite her antics. Her appearance on the other hand... let's just say she never left the 80s.

The loud music buzzing in my ears is making my hangover ten times worse, even though I drank three cups of coffee and took two Advil. I haven't gotten that drunk since my freshman year at MIT.

This morning I woke up naked in my bed after Stella found me passed out on the swinging bench in the yard when she came home. No memories of how I got there, nor of me stripping my clothes off and throwing them on the floor on my way to the bedroom. Stella, the bitch, left them there so she could enjoy me doing the walk of shame this morning when I collected them while she watched me.

Raquel sizes me up, turns to her assistant, who nods approvingly, and puts a hand on my shoulder. "You'll replace one of the models."

My eyes must've fallen out of my head because that's definitely how it feels. "No way. I'm five-seven on a good day and I'm not that thin."

"Dear, the trends are changing. The figure's no longer determining the model and more curvy models are well-received by the crowd." And to highlight the more curvy models she pats my hips.

I squint at her. I may not be a model, but my hips are perfect. Well, I did gain a few pounds when I stopped training this year, but not too much. If anything my thighs and butt are juicier. I've always been curvy though, that's why I didn't continue with ballet and did every other type of dancing instead. It's impossible not to have a tight and well-shaped body after putting so many hours into a killer daily training schedule.

"That's so very nice of you," I mutter under my breath.

"I'm not here to be nice but to make sure everything's flawless," she squeaks out like a rubber duck, having apparently heard me. "Now, follow my assistant. He'll show you where the clothes are."

"But I won't..." Before I complete my sentence, Raquel's already power-walking away and shouting at one of the models at the other end of the room.

"I can't be in the show." I turn to the assistant, who doesn't even look at me, just grabs my arm and pulls me behind the curtains.

Nobody listens to my protests, and after a while, I just stop talking. I have to find Stella and explain. I don't know what I'll explain, but I can't afford to be photographed and seen by so many people.

Backstage, two makeup artists and two hairdressers make the models look even more fantastic. One of the makeup artists grabs me and positions me in front of the mirror.

After fifteen minutes of hard work, my face looks better than it's ever looked. The dark circles under my eyes are gone, and in their place is a perfectly contoured face and spotless skin. Smoky eye makeup and sharp eyeliner make my eyes look catlike.

While I'm still looking in the mirror, a woman pulls me out of the chair and positions me in front of the next one. After another fifteen minutes, my hair is lifted into a high, messy bun with two curls coming down in front of my face.

Before I can even thank her, the assistant shoves me behind a black curtain and two people start undressing me without even asking.

What's wrong with these people? Some good manners would be appreciated.

Five minutes later, one of Stella's dresses I saw her sewing this morning is on me. Must be the new design. I look in the mirror and my lips silently mouth Wow. I've never doubted Stella's capabilities, but this dress is next level. And the fabric! The fabric is soft as silk and slides on my body like a second skin. It's also the reason I'm walking funny with a massive hangover but nevertheless. The floor-length dress is fiery red with a slit so long it reaches my hip. Tightened at the waist to emphasize the female figure, with a large V-shaped neck that reaches down revealing my cleavage. My stilettos are silver, shining from the many crystal stones on them, with a red sole.

I look like a fairy tale princess.

With each passing second, my confidence grows. I don't

have to be a model to walk this runway. I just need to look like the girl in the mirror.

But in the next moment, the ugly truth slaps me in the face. I can't get on that stage tomorrow, no matter what.

The assistant returns and without saying anything signals his two helpers to follow him. Just when I think they'll finally leave me alone to find Stella and fix this misunderstanding, they take the bottom of the dress—so it doesn't drag on the floor—and start leading me to the stage. No one listens to my protests. The music has already started and the models are lined up behind the curtains.

Raquel's assistant grabs me by the shoulders and stares blankly into my eyes. "This is Stella's day. I know you love her, so go out on that stage and don't disappoint her."

His words are like a razor slicing through my chest. A pang of guilt engulfs me. He used the perfect persuasion method.

Every time my parents asked me for something, they did it by planting guilt in me for everything and nothing in particular.

But I know one thing. I'd never disappoint Stella. Not because of guilt, but because of love.

I straighten my shoulders and prepare for the runway. I'll get out there and do my best. It's only a rehearsal, after all, I'll figure out what I'm going to do later.

When my turn comes, I walk out with my head held high and the most seductive gait I'm capable of. I briefly look at the organizers and their assistants in the chairs scattered around the runway. Some sit and write something in little notebooks, others just stand around the stage and look around.

My eyes fix on a couple of people in the distance. Stella wraps her arms around an all-too-familiar figure of a man, and as she lifts on her toes to kiss him on the cheek, his eyes lock on me. I can feel his gaze burning a hole through my body.

Not able to take my eyes off him, I miss a step, stumble over the hem of the long dress, and land facedown on the runway in the clumsiest way possible. Awesome move, Ivy.

I look up and see Stella, eyes wide, staring at me.

The man beside her is gone.

Oh Gosh, I hope I imagined him.

The next model has already reached my spot and as if this couldn't get any more humiliating, she jumps over me without so much as looking at me.

The shame I feel cannot be described in words. I'm sure the color of my face is the same as the dress.

I stand up, of course stumbling twice more as I do, and step off the runway.

"What happened? Are you okay? Why were you on stage in the first place?" Stella shoots the questions at me at the same speed she's walking toward me.

A glance behind her gives me all the proof that life isn't fair.

A few steps behind her is the sexiest man I've ever seen, in a black suit. Unlike last night, his brown hair is neat, casually slicked back, his white shirt buttoned, and the lighting makes his jawline appear even more cut. Memories of that stubble scratching my inner thighs flood me as I'm standing there staring at him.

What's he doing here? Is he following me?

Stella stops in front of me and looks at me expectantly. I remember she's waiting for answers.

"I tripped. I'm fine. I don't know why I was on stage." I answer all of them without taking a breath, trying not to look at the tall man a few feet from me.

"How do you not know that? You're wearing one of my dresses."

Apparently, she doesn't know about Raquel's little change to the lineup.

"Raquel made me fill in for one of the missing models. Stella you know I'd do anything for you, but I can't. I just can't show myself in front of so many people."

The man, who's now standing next to her raises an eyebrow, but Stella's expression changes to a soft grimace.

"I understand. You don't need to explain. I would've never asked you if I'd known. I'll go talk to her right now." She hugs me and when she pulls back, she takes my hand and spins me around. "But I have to say you look stunning in my dress. Maybe I should save it for you. And these boobs"—she squeezes my breasts—"look phe-no-menal."

The gorgeous stranger coughs.

Stella blushes as if she forgot he was there.

"Not that I want to ruin this little show, but I think I can help you with a model. I know a few that I can call for you, I'm sure one of them will be available to step in," he says as he unsuccessfully tries to cover up his amused face.

Well, of course, he has a few models' numbers on his phone. I'm sure they'd gladly give him a private show. I roll my eyes at my pettiness and grunt internally.

"You've already done enough. I'll...I'll just think of something," she stammers.

"Nonsense. I insist. I'll call them right away." He turns and heads out of the hall.

It's not fair that even his walk is sexy. Confident, like he owns the fucking world.

The eyes of every model in the room follow him as he walks out the door.

Stella and I go backstage to the changing rooms so I can

take off the dress before I damage it. I change into my short denim skirt and black crop top and let my hair out of the high bun. It falls in gentle waves and it looks amazing. I wish I can keep it like this forever, but I know that soon there'll be no trace of it.

I pull open the curtain of my changing room and surprise, surprise.

The man from last night is standing on the other side, patiently waiting. His eyes travel over my face, hair, then fall on my chest and linger there a little longer than necessary before continuing down to my bare belly and finally slide down my legs.

I fold my arms across my chest and raise an eyebrow. "See something of interest?"

Before he can say anything, Stella comes out behind me and gives us a questioning look.

"Stella, you haven't introduced me to your friend," he deadpans.

The sweet ache between my thighs wakes up.

Does he even remember what happened last night?

"Damien, this is Ivy Thanos. Ivy, this is Damien Black." She points between the two of us, tension heavy in the air.

Damien...a sexy name for an even sexier man.

Like a true gentleman, he takes my hand, bends down, and kisses it. His lips linger on my skin for a few seconds, eliciting a shiver down my spine.

"It's a pleasure to meet you, Mr. Black," I say in a syrupy voice.

"Please, call me Damien." My skin prickles from his deep voice and his devilish gaze. "The pleasure is all mine."

Oh, he definitely remembers.

Chapter Eight

IVY

The rehearsal takes longer than expected, and because of all the yelling and noise backstage, my headache is now the size of Alaska.

The model Damien found is gorgeous. She throws her arms around his neck and gives him a peck on the mouth. The same way several other models do when they greet him as if they're old friends. Every single girl here is eyeing him like a juicy steak, and I'd bet my duffel bag full of stolen money that at least half of them have warmed his bed.

As much as I hate to admit it, I nearly break a tooth clenching my jaw. For God's sake, I didn't even know who he was until a few hours ago. And I didn't care. He was a fantasy. The gorgeous stranger you have hot sex with and never see again.

Well, the second part didn't work out.

Now that I have a name to put to the gorgeous face I can't stop thinking about it.

Oh, who am I fooling? I haven't stopped thinking about Damien since I left him in that hotel room.

Stella caught me looking in his direction several times and is now casting ambiguous glances my way.

When his green eyes catch mine, a heated tremor runs through my body. I look away for a second, but I can feel his eyes burning through me. He stays halfway through the rehearsal, but never approaches me.

I can't understand why I feel disappointed. What did I expect? For him to find out who I am, sweep me into his strong arms, and carry me to his suite so we could continue where we left off yesterday?

Yeah, no. That only happens in fairy tales.

"Are you ready to go?"

I jump at Stella's voice behind me. "Sweet Jesus, don't scare me like that!" I slap a hand over my heart, which could pop out at any moment. "I'm ready."

I throw away the cloth I used to clean the makeup stations and mirrors and we head through the hotel hallways to our suite.

"Why are you so distracted?" There's something strange in her tone.

"No reason. I'm just really tired," I lie. I'm still trying to find a way to tell her the man she introduced me to, her good friend, is the man who ignited every nerve in my body last night. It was the most intense experience I've ever had in my life. And the best. I mean...the man was perfection in every way. The last thing on my mind right now is sleep.

"Me too. I'll faint as soon as my head hits the pillow. Not to be ungrateful, but I can't wait for tomorrow to be done and over. I haven't had a decent night's sleep for centuries." Stella yawns.

I don't know much about Stella's life before we met except that she's Sicilian and her godmother adopted her into the family after she moved to Rosehill. I've gathered bits and parts. She's still fighting insomnia after a traumatic experience she won't talk about. I tried to convince her to see a doctor, but she swears she's over it.

"It's him, isn't it?" Stella chirps while changing into her pajamas.

I freeze midway to the bathroom. This morning, while she was enjoying her coffee and my humiliation, I told her about my mystery man from last night. How did she figure it out?

"Who?" I yell back, hoping she'll drop it.

"Damien. The man who put you in this wonderful mood today."

"Sarcasm isn't your forte."

She rolls her eyes. "Oh, please! I saw it in your eyes. You knew each other. And the way he said 'The pleasure is all mine.'" A chuckle escapes me at her imitation of Damien's husky voice.

I hate how observant she is, with that button nose and cute face she could fool anyone, the little minx. I'm secretly jealous of the way she's able to read people and still see the best in everyone. It must be refreshing to see the world through her innocence.

As for me, I'm the girl who always second-guesses, who sees the world through all its negativity and still takes on the weight. It's in my nature to take care of everyone. I'll never admit it out loud, but I long for someone to take care of me for once.

"So I'm right," she insists when I don't answer. "I knew it!" She jumps onto her tummy on the bed beside me, leaning her head on her elbows, and stares at me expectantly. "So? Spill it."

"There's nothing to spill. We saw each other, had sex, end of the story."

"Oh, come on! You know my sex life is even worse than

yours. Give me something. As my best friend, you are obligated to give me details so I can live vicariously through you. Even I can't deny the man is mind-blowingly gorgeous. I mean...that effortlessly messy hair, those eyes, the sharp cheekbones, and those muscled arms..." she says dreamily.

"Okay, okay, I get it." I laugh and slap her on the shoulder.

"The whole time I lived with him I wondered if"—she fake coughs—"is as big as his feet. You know what they say, men with big feet, big...thing." She giggles, blushing.

My jaw hits the floor.

"You...you...with him..." I can't get the question out.

"Ewww, I haven't touched him if that's what you're asking." She makes a face letting me know she finds the idea repulsive. "He's like a brother to me. I'll tell you something but you can't tell anyone." I nod. "We introduce ourselves as cousins but we aren't. His family took care of me when..." She stops and looks at the carpet for a second. "Whatever, I don't want to talk about it. You get it. But, sis, come on, I'm not blind. Even I am not immune to his charm."

"All I'm saying is that if the women knew about little Damien, it would be more than his charms they'd need an immunization for." We both burst out laughing, but a few seconds later the realization hits me.

"Wait a minute. You said you lived with Melanie, your godmother." Melanie is the person who owns this hotel and the one who organized the whole fashion show to help Stella draw in the more elite buyers. It's her apology gift for not supporting Stella a year ago when she almost got married. She also threw in this cool suite for three days.

"Melanie Black. As in Damien Black...her son?" She explains.

"So that means this hotel..." The words get stuck in my throat.

"Is his," Stella finishes. "The Blacks are American royalty. So that makes Damien…"

"The king," I mutter. I knew my instincts were right. You don't exude that kind of poise and confidence with nothing to back it up.

Stella yawns. "As much fun as it is seeing your stunned expression, I need to get some sleep if I want to survive the next twenty-four hours. Good night, babe."

I roll in bed for the next twenty minutes, trying to sleep, but every time I close my eyes, I see Damien's face. I get up, nervously pacing the room, but every step makes me even tenser. I jump back onto the bed and turn the TV on. News, music, children's channel, everything annoys me.

A cold breeze blows through the open door of the balcony. I get up to close it, but the gentle movement of the water in the infinity pool is mesmerizing.

Our suite is on the VIP floor, which houses a private bar and pool. I think for a second and decide the best thing I can do right now is cool down the heat of my torrid thoughts in the water and distract myself with the beautiful view.

I put on one of Stella's creations—a sexy red two-piece bikini with a triangle top, giving the girls a little lift, and cute bottoms with two strings on the sides—and I step outside.

It's after midnight and the moon is giving the clear water a silver glow. There's no one around, which gives me the perfect opportunity to clear my head once and for all and still get some sleep before tomorrow.

The water is cool, and with each step I take down the steps inside the pool, my shoulders relax. With each stroke, my head and body loosen up. I allow myself a second to indulge.

I don't know how much time passes while I'm swimming, but when I stop at the edge of the pool, I feel a mild burning in the muscles of my arms. I put my forearms on the tiles and stare into the distance.

The downtown and the lights of the buildings glow like millions of stars on Earth. I watch some of them go out and others light up, thinking about how big the world is and how small our problems are. Behind these windows, there are thousands of people, each of them having their concerns and problems, joys, and misfortunes. Every one of us looking for our place under the sun.

The thought is sobering and for a minute, I choose to forget about the weight of the problems heavy on my shoulders. I'm just another one of these people fighting to survive.

With a smile on my face, I rest my head on my arm at the edge of the infinity pool, close my eyes, and shut off my brain.

A splash disrupts the surface of the water and startles me. Amid my mental harmony, I didn't realize I almost fell asleep. I see movement at the end of the pool, but I can't register anything with my blurry vision. Little by little my eyes clear, revealing a jaw-dropping sight standing on the second step of the pool.

Damien's hair looks darker, wet, and slicked back out of his face. Beads of water reflect the lights on his abs, and his relentless gaze is burning me from within. My eyes slide down his body, only to notice his wet shorts clinging to his cock.

With each step he's slowly approaching, I'm gripping the edge of the pool as if my life depends on it. The water has hidden most of his body and my thoughts begin returning one by one.

"What're you doing here?" My voice comes out squeaky and quieter than I wanted.

A predatory smile appears on his face, reminding me of the wild animals on the National Geographic Channel.

He stops two feet in front of me and leans in, just inches from my face. I swallow audibly, my legs twitching.

"This is my hotel. I can be wherever I want."

Smug asshole.

I slip between him and the edge and swim to the other side of the pool. I need distance between us to think straight. I'm sure his midnight swim is no accident.

I glance over my shoulder and see he's following me with his eyes. He swivels around and starts swimming in the opposite direction. The long strokes make every muscle in his arms and back stand out. I allow myself to ogle him while his back is to me. He stops at the end and turns to me. Hypnotized by the gleaming of his golden wet skin, my gaze lingers following a drop that makes its way past his six-pack abs, slides down the V line, and disappears into the waistband of his swim trunks. I lick my lips, imagining what it would be like to follow its path with my tongue.

"Enjoying the view?" His arrogant tone snaps me out of the trance, and I realize I'm very obviously staring at him.

I quickly turn my back on him. A moment later I feel the water behind me stir, two hands grip the tiles on either side of me and cage me in. Goose bumps erupt on my body, a blend of the cold air and the hot body pressed against my back.

"Why don't you come with me and put an end to our misery?" His warm breath caresses my ear, and I feel the gentle swipe of his tongue as his mouth slides down my neck. The butterflies fluttering in my stomach move south.

I close my eyes for a moment.

Why not give in to him?

But the cool breeze and the late hour remind me.

What happened was only supposed to be once. Despite what I did I'm not the one-night-stand type. And then there's his smugness, which was dulled by the vodka I consumed, but I've no desire to relive it sober. My experiences in the past have taught me that men like him never bring anything good except their bedroom skills.

I cling to the wall to put as much distance as possible between us. "I don't have time to deal with you. Now if you'll excuse me, I have to go catch up on some much-needed sleep."

I try to get out of his arms, but they're as solid as rocks, pinning me in place.

He grabs my chin with two fingers and twists my face so that my eyes fall on his. "Is that why you escaped me when it just started to get interesting?"

"I don't owe you an explanation." My bittersweet retort ignites a flame in his eyes, and he leans over me.

"Yeah, but you owe me an encore."

His lips lock on mine and his body presses me against the tile wall. There's no escape route, and the worst part is I don't want to escape. His tongue plunges into my mouth, wiping all my thoughts as he did the night before in the elevator. His lips separate from mine for a brief moment as he grasps my legs with two hands, wrapping them around his middle. His erection presses into my bikini bottoms and the electricity of his touch sends sparks straight to my clit. I bury my hands in his wet hair, and he slides his tongue down my jaw and throat. He sucks and nibbles the skin on the curve of my shoulder. He grunts, pulling down one of the triangles of my swimsuit, and licks my nipple.

I can feel the tension gathering at that point below my belly, and a tormented moan is ripped from my throat. He swallows it with his mouth and bites my lower lip. My nails trace the muscles on his back, and his movements become faster and more aggressive. His hand slides across my chest, down my belly, and just as he pauses at the tie of my bikini bottoms, hysterical female laughter comes from the other end of the terrace, and we both freeze.

We turn our heads at the same time to see a group of girls in bikinis laughing, surrounding another girl who fell on the ground on her butt. A few of them reach out to help her stand up. Behind them, a man in a Speedo comes out, puts his hands around two of the girls, and heads toward us.

Damien sets me down abruptly and backs away. I look at him, confused, but his gaze is on the group approaching.

"Damien!" screams one of the girls, who runs to the pool.

She splashes into the water and hooks herself onto his neck. He releases himself from her grip and turns my way, but I've already adjusted my swimsuit and am on my way out.

As I walk past them, the other girls enter the pool and I recognize some of them. These are the models for the fashion show. All twenty of them look at Damien like he's a chocolate cake for their starved bodies. A few more surround him, squealing and giggling.

The man with them greets him and settles around the pool with a blonde and a redhead on his lap. I start climbing the stairs but a hand grabs my wrist and pulls me back.

"Don't sneak out on me, baby. I'm keeping score," he says quietly.

Thank goodness for the girls around him splashing and spraying him, helping me to come to my senses with the force of a plane crashing to the ground.

A few more minutes alone with him and I would've let

myself be his toy. How he manages to scramble all the thoughts in my head, I don't know.

With the eager hands of the models all over his body, even as he grips my wrist and doesn't look at them, I can gather that this is nothing new to him.

Damien Black is just that—a cocky, rich playboy, and nothing more.

I've been there, a couple of times in my college years, and I know how much it hurts when he's tired of playing with you. Especially if you're the sensitive type, which only makes them want you more, so they can crush you harder later.

No, thank you.

With a sugarcoated tone, I say louder than necessary, "I'm sure there are plenty of women here who would gladly take my place," and wink at the giggling girls around us.

Several "yes," "sure," and cheerful cheers follow.

I smile my sweetest smile at Damien and pull my hand away from his, waving goodbye. The group of women surrounds him like a hungry pride. I get out of there before he can make his way through them and catch up with me.

Later, after hours of tossing and turning, I finally manage to fall asleep when the sun has almost risen, only to be awakened by dreams of two green eyes.

Chapter Nine

DAMIEN

Soft full lips bite and suck on my neck. My hands find the ties to her red bikini top and free her tits. Incapable of resisting, I start playing with her pink nipples. She moans with pleasure and settles on my pelvis. Without wasting any more time, I find the right angle and push my cock into her to the hilt.

She screams my name.

I thrust into her slowly and with every bump of our bodies, there's a knock.

"Damien," she repeats, but her voice is distant and different.

I grab a hold of her and squeeze her shoulders so hard I'm afraid it'll leave bruises. But she's getting farther away and becoming blurry.

"Damien Black, open this door!" My mother's voice echoes in the hallway of the suite and I jump out of bed.

What the hell?

Jesus Christ, did I just dream of fucking Ivy while my mother called my name?

I shudder in disgust and shake my head, hoping it'll erase

that thought from my mind. I rub my face with my palms and sigh heavily. Blinking a few times, I pray I'm still dreaming, but Melanie's yelling is growing stronger and depriving me of my last hope.

I drag myself to the door and open it wide but before I can react, my mother pushes past me.

"It's like a cave in here." Her voice reaches a higher octave than usual and tugs at one of my last remaining nerves. I have no strength to deal with her after the evening I had.

The tight purple skirt of her suit forces her to walk in short steps, making her look like a penguin. Her black bob hairstyle jumps with every step, but no hair dares to escape the perfect coiffure. Her small hands wrapped in white silk gloves grab the thick curtains hiding reality from fantasy and pull them open.

The light burns my eyes, and I raise my hands in front of my face. "Jesus fucking Christ, you'll blind me!"

She looks at me with a haughty, incredulous expression, and with a slight stumble reaches the couch, settles in, and crosses her legs.

"Mind your manners, Damien. May I ask why you're sleeping at this hour and not working?"

"You may not. Did you come to scold me, mother?"

Her face tries to form a grimace, but the Botox injections don't allow it. "I'd sacrifice myself if I could convince you to take your job more seriously."

"What are you talking about?"

"Are you aware Richard had an emergency meeting with the board this morning while you were rolling in the sheets with God knows what skank?" She looks at my bed and my messy sheets, and her nose wrinkles in disgust.

I don't bother to explain to her that there's only one girl I want to roll with, and I'm in this state because of the dirty trick she played on me last night, refusing to get under my sheets.

"I'm not sleeping with anyone…" I start, but then the first part of her sentence penetrates my sleepy head. "Wait, he can't have a meeting without me. I'm the CEO of the company."

"Not for much longer. I can't believe you were so irresponsible! Why would you give him a reason to humiliate you in front of the board?" Her angry tone betrays the expressionless façade she's attempting.

"I don't understand what you're talking about. I haven't done anything. His minions didn't find anything at the hotel."

She fishes her phone from her clutch bag and starts typing on it. Then she turns the screen to me and plays a video of last night's pool party. It shows the moment when the models came at me like hungry hyenas after Ivy unleashed them. The video looks very different than how it felt when it was happening.

At that moment, watching her swing that ass while walking toward her suite, I was stunned and couldn't take my eyes off her. When she disappeared around a corner, I turned around and looked at all the woman who had their hands on me. Under normal circumstances, I wouldn't deny any of them. Hell, I'd take them all at once. But that night none of them could get my dick hard. Just seconds before they appeared, I'd been ready to rip the swimsuit off the girl in my arms with my bare teeth and bury myself in her until I recreated every feeling I experienced the previous night.

But when she left, so did my desire. I angrily returned to my suite and jacked off trying to get her out of my head. Unfortunately, the only thing I accomplished was a temporary release before she filled my dreams and I tossed and turned all night. Which explains my fucking mood, and why I decided to sleep in on the worst possible day.

I replay the video, confirming my fears. The only thing you can see are the girls around me, my eyes on them, and the camera turning to the dude who organized the little gathering. His smile is triumphant as if he just won the casino's jackpot, and it ends with the two women in his lap licking whiskey from his abs. It's uploaded on Instagram and had over a million views in less than twenty-four hours. The caption reads, *VIP party with my man, Damien Black*.

I run my fingers through my hair, grunting.

What the fuck was he thinking? I don't even know him. I've only seen him a few times at the bar and every time he greeted me, I only answered him as a courtesy.

"And it's not just that." My mother's voice, cold and distant again, makes me turn toward her. "It all started when one of the hotel's guests complained about the loud noise disrupting their stay." Her voice turns colder than usual. "Then security went up to investigate and he found one of these"—she points at the phone and spits the word out—"*ladies*, with her head between the legs of this young man. The others were swimming naked in the pool. Apparently, it was some kind of a challenge or whatever you call it on social media. There's a video of them swimming and kissing each other." Her expressionless face doesn't change for a second. "It seems you have a weak link in the hotel because the information was passed to Richard and the videos confirmed it. Thank God, most of the board still respects me and felt obliged to tell me about the meeting. According to them, Richard tried to make you look unreliable and incompetent to manage the company, accusing you of having orgies at your own hotel and not even hiding it." You can't help but feel the malice behind her words. "The apple doesn't fall far from the tree," she mutters to herself.

Even if I explain what happened and tell her I'm not guilty of anything, she'll never believe me. Years of my father cheating on her resulted in her negative opinion of men that'll never be changed. It's not like I haven't given her reasons to think that way about me, especially in my younger years when the quantity of alcohol, drugs, and women exceeded my age tenfold. But at least I didn't cheat on anyone because I've never had a monogamous relationship in my thirty years.

I sigh and sit on the couch next to her. I know exactly what she's thinking. "Mother, this isn't a repeat of history. I've been guilty in many cases, but this isn't one of them. Someone's framing me. You know I wouldn't risk our family legacy for such nonsense."

"Do I?! Your father had no problem doing so. And now his son follows in his steps." The venom in her voice feels as lethal as a weapon in her hand.

My jaw tics, I grit my teeth and stand up. Of all the things she could say about me, being compared to that pitiful excuse for a father and a husband is what I hate the most.

"I. Am. Not. Hyland." I pace the carpet, arms crossed behind my back.

There's distrust in her eyes, but I can live with that. Before everything, I'm her son, and I know deep down under this façade of an iron woman, Melanie loves me and wants to believe I won't become like Hyland Black. The man who made my sister and I can be called many things, but not a father. Thankfully, he leaves us alone as long as I wire him enough money to feed his vices.

But my hatred of him won't help my situation, so I concentrate my thoughts in the right direction. "I'm sure there's a way to remedy this. What did the board say? They can't make a decision without me."

"Most consider the act of Richard going behind your back unfair, but that doesn't change the facts. They're waiting to see what your next move will be." Her lips press into a straight line and she sighs.

One of the few times you can see weakness in my mother's eyes is when the family business is affected. It's her third child, and although Hyland inherited the business from his father, Melanie is the reason we're currently one of the highest rated luxury hotels.

"Damien, I hope you have a card up your sleeve because otherwise, the chance of losing everything is..." Her words are lost and I think for a moment her eyes will grow wet, but she quickly recovers. She gets up, wipes an imaginary speck from her skirt, picks up her purse and takes a few short steps toward me.

"I trust you'll fix the problem and clear our name. Again." She taps me with her white glove on the stubble of my cheek, spins around, and leaves.

For long moments I remain fixed in place, watching after her as she does her penguin walk to the elevator, the only sound her heels clacking across the wooden floor.

How could I be so stupid?

The dark-haired beauty playing with my head is to blame. If I wasn't so captivated by her, I wouldn't have even been in the pool. The only reason I went downstairs was because I saw her from the balcony of my suite. The moonlight shining on her wet ass as she was lying on the edge of the pool.

The way she left me the night before, hungry, wanting more... I couldn't stop thinking about her.

That day, when I'd gone to check on Stella and saw Ivy on the runway, I thought I was hallucinating. Her hair up, catlike eyes and sinful red lips...a true vision of every man's wet dreams. The red dress made her body look juicier, accentuating the curve of her waist and hips. Her long leg, protruding through the slit, and the swell of her tits could've tempted a monk.

She's made for sin.

And if it wasn't for the shock on her face and her stumbling when she saw me, I would've still thought she was just a vision.

Just the thought of those moments makes me horny again, and my curses echo in the empty room.

What the fuck is wrong with you, Damien? Your hotel is in jeopardy, that clown is playing with your future, and you're lying in bed with a boner like a fucking teenager.

I need to come to my senses and prioritize.

Thank goodness I have cameras in every corner of the hotel, they've been a lifesaver with all the sabotage that shithead has been attempting. I could acquit myself somewhat, but it won't have the full effect because the video has already been seen by too many people. At least it'll prove I'm not irresponsible and if I play my cards right, I could even turn the situation in my favor.

Richard will never see it coming.

I leave the *Black Rose Group* building with a triumphant smile on my face and, closing the door, I turn to see Richard's furious glare on me. I let the door hit him in the face and climb into my black Aston Martin. I press the keyless ignition and my beast growls before taking me far away from that whole circus. At the next traffic light, I close my eyes for a second and enjoy the small victory. Not only did I refute

Richard's accusations, but I suggested he might be behind the whole thing.

There's no way to blame him, and honestly, I'm sure it's not true, but that doesn't mean I won't play dirty and plant suspicion with the board. Worse than him attempting to expose me for some trumped up violation, is sabotaging the company on purpose. Something Richard has been trying to do for the last five years, but I've never had the chance to prove it to the board.

Now that priority number one is over, it's time for number two. Find Ivy and fuck her out of my system so I can think straight again and avoid making mistakes like this.

After a quick change at the hotel, I find my mother in the first row five minutes before the fashion show starts.

"It's all fixed," I whisper in her ear and the same triumphant smile I had a moment ago rises on her face. One of the many things I inherited from her.

The lights go out and with them, the talking turns into whispering. The music starts and everyone is enraptured by the clothes on the runway. At the end of the show, I almost break my hands applauding Stella. I always knew she was gifted, but this collection is an undeniable hit. With my mother's connections and the talent of the little blonde, in a few years, her name will be on every major fashion event, store and magazine.

I look around but there's no sign of Ivy anywhere. My mother graciously invites the VIP guests and attendees to join her for the after-party in the banquet hall where they'll be able to meet the designer. I make my way backstage and find Stella smiling ear to ear and bouncing with happiness as she helps a model out of her dress. The dark-haired model rolls her eyes and sighs as Stella bounces from foot to foot and tugs on her.

"Let me help you." I step in and help the model out of the dress, she mouths a *thank you* and disappears. I turn around and Stella is standing there with both hands on her hips and a shit-eating grin on her face. "What?"

"You're good at taking model's clothes off, Damien. Actually, you're good at taking clothes off, period."

I take two glasses of champagne from a passing tray and hand her one. "I don't know what you mean." I shrug innocently and clink our glasses together. "Come here." I pull her into my arms and squeeze her the way I did when she was little. "You did great! I'm proud of you!"

A tear rolls down her cheek, and I instinctively reach out to catch it with my thumb. She puts her hand over her mouth, smiles, and wipes her eyelids. "Thank you! It means a lot to me. I really wanted Rosalie to attend, but I know she's busy with work." My sister couldn't come because she has a concert gig for the promo of her new single.

"Don't worry, I'm sure mother will send her the video. The woman hired a thousand photographers."

Our laughter echoes in the half-empty hall.

"I can't thank you enough for everything your family's done for me." Her eyes tear up again.

"There's nothing to thank me for, you are my family. But you know Melanie always loves a little ass-kissing." I wink at her. "Don't make her wait too long. She'll get bored and start telling family stories."

"God forbid," she says with a hand to her chest and sits in front of one of the mirrors to fix her makeup.

I look around again but there's almost no one left here, and Ivy is nowhere in sight. Strange, she seemed very close to Stella yesterday, and I was under the impression she'd be taking care of things backstage. The wrong side of the stage, if you ask me. Maybe she's at the party already.

"She's not here." Stella watches me from the mirror and smiles as if she can read my thoughts.

If she's already noticed, then there's no point in denying it. Or maybe she knows about the evening we spent at the hotel. "So I better get to the party, then." I button my jacket and fix an escaped strand of hair in the mirror.

Stella chuckles, shakes her head and turns my way. "You obviously don't know Ivy. You won't find her at the party either. She wanted to stay in the room, but I sent her for a well-deserved treat at the spa so what happened last night would not be repeated. Or the one before that." She narrows her eyes and pokes her little finger into my chest. "Damien, Ivy isn't just another one of your pawns. I see how you look at her. I love you as a brother, but she's my best friend and if you hurt her, I'll have to cut your balls off. I know how much you like them."

Over the years, I've let Stella think she's a badass so I wouldn't hurt her feelings, but her angry face is adorable and the self-confidence that makes her think her threats could stop me is just too entertaining. With a grin, I remove her finger from my chest, where she's barely left a crease in my shirt. "Stella, what has happened or will happen is between Ivy and me. We are grown-ups and we don't need parental guidance." I try to maintain a serious tone, but I fail because she looks just like those cartoon characters with steam coming out of their ears. If it was anyone else, I'd be worried, but Stella changes moods every five seconds.

She folds her arms. "I'm serious, Black. This affects me too 'cause we live together, and I won't stand back and watch you play with her. Find yourself another toy!"

Dammit, why do they have to be roommates?

"Okay, okay," I say, raising my hands, and she narrows her eyes. I can't say she doesn't have a right to question me.

Even I don't believe me. "Are you ready?" I offer her my arm and we walk into the banquet hall side by side, camera lights blinding us.

I'm not the biggest fan of the press, so I back away the moment the vultures surround Stella, and I head straight for the bar. I endure exactly thirty minutes at the party, enough to drink two whiskeys and tell myself *fuck it* before I sneak out unnoticed. Without even having a plan in my head, my feet lead me to the spa. A glance at the guest sign-in sheet gives me all the information I need.

What was it that Ivy said in the pool? No time to deal with me?

Well, an hour just opened for me to deal with her.

Chapter Ten

IVY

The masseur's hands slide down my shoulders with just the right pressure and I feel my stiff muscles relax. I almost groan in pleasure, but somehow I keep it to myself. My eyes are growing heavier and heavier thanks to no sleep and the warming coconut oil he's rubbing into my skin. With each rub on my back, I drift away more until all I hear is relaxing music somewhere in the distance.

"Miss, I'm sorry, but I have to step out for a second." The masseur's quiet voice barely registers in my head and *"Mmm"* is all I can say before it all goes dark and quiet.

I'm startled by the clicking sound of the door, and a displeased sound falls from my lips. I open my eyes and immediately close them because the white tiles under my face are too bright. The darkness swallows me up again and I relax under the warm towels.

Lost somewhere in between the clouds and Earth.

I'm on the glass table in the presidential suite, and in the place of the short masseur guy is the man who made me fall apart that night.

His thick fingers massage my feet, toe by toe, until he

reaches the arch and presses on the right spot. He spreads the warm oil on my leg and rubs my calf. With each caress, his hands move higher. His palms glide on my thighs and knead my sensitive skin. He runs his fingers along the inside of my thigh, almost to my center, and the sensation mixed with the scent of the oil is not as relaxing as it is arousing.

He repeats this motion twice more, each time reaching higher, and when his fingers press against my panties, I tremble. Two big hands press down on my legs, so I don't move, and that brings me back to reality. But I'm not ready to leave my dream yet so I let myself fade again.

The hands of the divine man in my fantasy are rubbing and squeezing my ass. One finger slowly slides down to the ball of nerves between my legs. It swirls around my clit and I lift my hips seeking more contact. Another finger touches me and moves slowly along my labia.

The soft touches aren't enough and I can't hold back a quiet moan of protest. A deep growl nearby startles me and I freeze in place.

I open my eyes and gasp when I realize I'm still in the massage room and there's an erection pressing against my thigh.

Oh my god, I didn't just let the masseur touch me while I imagined Damien, did I?

My blood runs cold just thinking he might've abused me while I was asleep. I raise my head from the face port in the massage table and almost turn when a hand gently grabs my neck and pushes me back down.

Just when I become fully aware of what's going on and I'm ready to scream, an all-too-familiar palm slaps my butt. "Be a good girl, Ivy, or I'll have to punish you," Damien's hoarse voice is so close his breath tickles my ear, then he bites it and I squeak softly.

My brain is sluggish, still in sleepy mode, and before I can say anything, a harder slap lands on the bottom of my ass. His fingers caress the burning spot and the pleasure-pain makes me wet. My ass instinctively lifts higher and he slides a finger under my thong.

I hear the squeeze of a bottle and a few cold drops slide down my pussy lips. He spreads the oil with his fingers, the warming sensation shooting me straight to the edge.

I want to bitch-slap myself for allowing his touch. All night I kept repeating like a mantra that I wouldn't allow this man to come near me again, and here I am like putty in his hands. The stubbornness in me struggles with the desire, but the truth is that after that first night, I couldn't stop thinking about the things he made me feel. I've had sex before, of course, but there's something different about this man and the way he put my needs first. No one has ever paid so much attention to my pleasure, nor has anyone ever looked at me with such intense hunger. Like he'd tear me apart, feast on every single inch of skin, and make me love every second of it.

"You tried to escape me, but I found you. There's nowhere to hide, Ivy. I'll make you want me, need me, crave me." He slips a finger into me and starts moving it slowly, while another one strokes my clit. My arousal dampens the sheet beneath me, and my walls flutter around his finger.

Nobody has ever talked to me like that. And I've never wanted anyone as much as I want this man. From the moment our eyes met in the mirror at the bar to the stolen glances as I peeked at him from behind the curtains of the runway. Oh, how I love a man in a suit. Is he still wearing it?

I turn my head to the side to see him standing right next to me in his three-piece black designer suit. I sigh and his eyes dart to mine. There's that look I was dreaming about. There's something special, so raw and yet delicate...like a gemstone. His deep green eyes with little black lines in them remind me of a Trapiche Emerald—one of the rarest and most majestic gemstones in the world.

He slaps me on the ass once more and at the same time inserts a second finger into me. A whimper, needier than I'd like to admit, slips out of me and his fingers curve in search of my G-spot. Another moan follows when he finds it and presses that magic button. I arch my back in search of deeper penetration, and he answers my unasked question. His fingers fuck into me faster and deeper, and his thumb carries the moisture across to my swollen clit before he goes back to swirling around and over it. My thighs tremble and he rubs his erection against my hand. I twist my arm backward to reach out and caress his hard cock straining against his suit pants.

Ready to explode, I wrap my hand around him through the fabric of his suit pants and squeeze. My moans fall silent and I hold my breath, expecting complete destruction.

Suddenly his fingers freeze inside me and I look up to meet his darkened gaze.

"What are you doing? I was almost there." There's no way he could miss my angry tone.

"You'll come when I say you can." His devilish eyes look at me defiantly.

"What the..." My words die mid-sentence because his fingers start moving in me faster than before and I'm on the crest of the wave again.

My hips move in sync with his hand, and my moaning gets louder. I'm right on the edge and all I need is a little push to detonate. But his fingers only stroke me for a split second, just enough to drive me crazy.

"Touch me." I'm panting.

"Only if you ask me. Nicely." His sugary tone mimics mine from the night before when I left him with a boner in a pool full of hungry women.

"Asshole."

He bares his perfect teeth in a predatory smile. "I never said I wasn't. You deserve it."

His hand goes up and another slap lands on my butt cheek. A loud whimper follows and my thighs become sticky with my arousal.

This game excites me even more.

His gaze grows darker and more intense. "This will teach you not to play with me. Ask me like a good girl." He looks down at the middle of the table, where my ass is in the air, and his fingers continue thrusting lazily in and out of my dripping hole. He bites his lip, and the memory of his tongue being in that same place makes my inner muscles contract. "I know you want it. Be an obedient little girl and you'll be rewarded. Pretty, pretty..." he whispers in my ear, his tongue sliding down my neck.

Shit. That's all I can handle.

"Please," I whisper and feel his smile on my skin.

The next second, his fingers pump in and out of me hard and fast, making me see stars and explode like an atomic bomb.

He covers my mouth with his hand to silence my cry and my whole body shakes. I close my eyes, my nails digging into Damien's legs through the fabric of his pants as the orgasm consumes me.

When the swirling stars behind my lids disappear and I return to the living, all my limbs feel like Jell-O, my body melted into the table.

I open my eyes, but he's no longer beside me. I sit up on the bed and see him walking toward the door.

"What game are you playing?" My words are weak with fatigue, but Damien hears me.

He turns to me, a smug smirk on his face, one hand fastening his gold cufflink on the crisp white shirt without so much as a spot on it.

"Oh, Ivy. We both know my fingers won't be enough for you. That game takes two players and it's only getting started. You know where to find me." He winks at me, opens the door and disappears.

Only now do I begin to realize what just happened.

Damien Black just played me the same way I played him yesterday. He left me wet, confused and turned on.

But he didn't realize his mistake. He gave me a piece of what I wanted.

Chapter Eleven

DAMIEN

I enter Masquerade late for my meeting with Rob. The security clears the path in front of me until I reach my table in the VIP area.

The theme of the night is *Angels and Demons* and the club is bursting at the seams with men and women dressed in white or black, wearing masks and wings. We do thematic shows three or four times a week. Everybody' is begging for access. They all want a piece of the exclusive paradise I've created.

From the second floor I can see the staff, hidden in the darkness on stage, installing poles.

I look at my Rolex—a quarter to three. Just in time for the last show.

I love watching our shows but my favorite part is when it's over and I get a chance to look at the shocked, joyful, or naughty faces of everyone in the audience. It pleases me to see my own business, not something I inherited, thriving. Hell, we made our two-year plan in six months. If Masquerade continues at this pace, I'll be opening more clubs around the country.

With a smile, I settle into the booth and open the bottle of whiskey as Rob emerges from the stairs in his signature style—black Tom Ford suit, burgundy tie, and matching handkerchief.

"My man, what's good?" We shake hands, and he sits next to me.

"Whiskey?" I hand him a glass.

"Just a little." He pinches his fingers. "I don't drink on the job."

I snort out a laugh. Some of the craziest nights in my life have been with Robert, but when work is involved, he's unprecedented. One of the many reasons I give him so much authority in the club. Also, because he's my best friend and I trust him with my life.

"Are you ready for what's coming?" he asks with a sly smile.

"Bring it on." I grin. "I'm ready to see something good."

Rob points to the stage where the boys are finishing their preparations. I'm eager and even excited, which I haven't experienced in a long time. Actually, now that I think about it, maybe I lied a little. I felt excitement last night when I left Ivy's wet pussy in the spa and went back to my apartment, alone, convinced she'd show up at my door for more.

Spoiler alert: She left me hard and furious. When the sun started to rise, I realized she wasn't coming, and I cursed myself for not bringing her to her knees and fucking her right there on the massage table.

Fucking ego.

"What's bothering you? The wrinkle on your forehead might become permanent and damage your beautiful face." He pouts mockingly and pats my cheek.

"Long story short: I got stood up," I admit reluctantly.

He bursts out laughing. *Great*, not only was being stood

up by Ivy a blow to my confidence, now I'm Rob's entertainment as well.

I roll my eyes, wanting to punch myself for acting like a moody bitch.

So what if a woman ditched me? A woman who gave me the hottest sex of my life.

But still, just a woman.

Another one.

And she's the only one who's ever left me alone and hard. *Twice.*

"You"—Rob points at me when he's able to catch his breath—"Damien"—he tries to maintain a serious expression, unsuccessfully—"Motherfucking Black. You were shot down by a woman? *You*?! I won't believe it even if I see it with my own eyes." His laughter subsides, but his eyes are still tearing.

"Believe it. Twice."

I'm worried this time his eyes will pop out of his head. "Come on. You're fucking with me, right?"

I shake my head.

"In all these years we've been friends, I've never once seen a woman even take her eyes off you, let alone get out of your bed and leave you dry. I have to meet this one." He pats my shoulder.

No woman has ever refused me before. Not one. They are always the best version of themselves around me. It's faker than a Playboy cover girl's tits. And I should know, I've seen a lot of them. Who doesn't want to be with one of the richest and most sought after bachelors in the country?

"She thinks she's gotten away from me, but I'll find her sooner or later and the game will end faster than it started." The determination is clear in my tone. No one plays me and goes unpunished. You never know, I might end up liking this little game of ours.

"I'm sure she won't get off easy." Rob nods and stands up next to the railing. "Are you ready for the show? It's something new. This is also the official debut of the new dancer. I told her we'd offer her a contract if she performed well tonight, but I'm more than sure she'll crush it. She even helped with the choreography." A glimmer of pride flashes in his eyes. He loves to find new talents, and after the Naomi fiasco he needed something to lift his spirits.

"Let's see her." I stand beside him on the railing and raise a toast.

The lights go out. Memories of the dance I watched pass through my mind, and a lot of dirty ideas dance beside her in my thoughts. But as interesting as she is, I have one rule at work.

Don't fuck the staff.

As many temptations as I've had over the years, and there've been a lot, I've never broken my rule and I definitely won't start now.

The music starts and a red light illuminates the four poles and the girls curled up on the ground around them. With the first words of MILCK's song "Devil, Devil" the girls lie on their chests on the floor and raise their asses up in the air. They roll on their backs and their breasts rise upward, as if they're possessed, in time with the lyrics of the song.

This is exactly what I love about my dancers. The way they connect with the music and convey every word with their bodies. It took us a while to find the best of the best, but it was worth it.

They crawl on stage and when the bass hits, they climb the poles in sync. No one would even think that one of the dancers has only been here for five days. They're in sync as if they've been a team all this time.

The red light doesn't illuminate much of the dark stage, apart from the silhouette of their bodies, and I can't tell which one is the new girl.

They're spinning on the metal poles, hanging by their hands and simulating walking on air as if they're walking on clouds. Descending to the ground, they bend over, stand up, and make a full spin around the pole. Then they climb it with each beat of the song, cross their legs around it in a sitting position, and stretch their upper body and arms backward.

The white light comes on and my eyes fall right on the temptation.

I spit the sip of whiskey in my mouth all over Rob's shoes.

"What the hell, man?" He jumps up cursing, but I can't give two shits about him. My eyes are blazing with what I saw on stage.

No, it can't be true.

The words of the song ring in my ears. There's no better way to say it. Well, I'm no saint, but she's most definitely torturing me with a glance.

My heart races a hundred miles an hour as I watch her body, way too familiar than it should be, perform complex acrobatic stunts in the air.

I'm not one to believe in coincidences. But then she sits up while gripping the pole, straightens her legs up in the air, her upper body hanging downward, and her eyes fall on mine. I would know her face even hidden behind a mask.

Fuck. I knew she seemed familiar in the bar.

Fate is a bitch and she's toying with me.

I take a sip, and the burning liquid slides like honey through my already hot body. Ivy places her hands on the ground, still hanging from the pole, and flips over, landing in the splits on the ground. She crawls forward, her spine curved, and flings her long hair, that gorgeous mane I've thought of burying my fingers in all day.

I swear I haven't seen anything more erotic.

The two devils surround the angels and in a beautiful mix of dance moves, possess them, along with the whole audience and myself.

The lights go out and the next moment, a dim white light shines on their bodies hanging crucified on a metal stick.

With that, the song ends and the stage lights turn off again.

Thundering applause follows as the stage lights up again, and the curtains, as always, close.

This is the moment I've been waiting for but right now I can't look anyone in the face because I'm too busy adjusting my erection.

In her previous performance, the pleasure was sweet because I didn't know who she was, and I was just a part of the crowd she enchanted, but now that I have a face and memories invading my mind, I can't stop imagining her climbing me instead of that pole and twisting her body around mine that way. Remembering how she opened her long legs in front of my face and I buried myself between them to drink up the sweetest juices I've ever tasted.

Did she know I was her new boss? What are the chances she did it because of that? She wouldn't be the first to try.

Hoping I was able to adjust myself so it's not obvious, I take a deep breath and turn to Rob, who's smiling like the devil himself.

"I told you!" His tone is as enthusiastic as a five-year-old in a candy shop.

"Congratulations. What's the name of the new girl?"

"Ivy. She didn't tell me her last name, though. But it doesn't matter, we're signing her tonight."

If she googled me, there's a big chance she knew who I was. But what would be the point of running away from me if that was the case?

Interesting.

Well, there's only one way to find out. "Send her to my office. She'll sign with me."

Chapter Twelve

IVY

When I get off stage, my heart is beating so fast I'm worried it'll pop out of my chest. Applause and whistles bring back memories of all my other performances. There have been hundreds, and yet none of them have ever stirred so many mixed emotions.

It's not just the adrenaline of dancing that's making me bounce toward the changing rooms. Really, I had no plans to return to Masquerade at all. What's the point when I know there's no way I can sign a contract? An elite club like this would never hire me illegally, even if Stella asks. The only thing I'm going to get out of this is a bunch of questions I can't answer.

I don't know what possessed me to come back. When the clock struck two in the afternoon, my feet just started moving toward Masquerade, and before I knew it I was on the pole, rehearsing for tonight's performance. I kept telling myself I was doing the right thing and I shouldn't leave without saying goodbye.

Subconsciously, or maybe on some conscious level, I knew if I didn't dance this last time, I'd regret it. A bit overdramatic, I know. But such are the true passions. Primal, and thrilling, they swallow you whole, and all you're left with is praying they never spit you back out because it will hurt like hell.

Throughout my life, I've known two things: dancing and programming. The first came from the soul, the second from family obligation.

I know. An extremely strange combination. But we'll get there.

The question now is how quickly I can get out of here, hopefully unnoticed and before someone tries to shove a contract and a pen into my hand.

I enter the backstage area and, thank goodness, there's no one there, because I have to pee. I'm washing my hands in the bathroom when I hear some of the other dancers giggling behind the door. As soon as I exit, Tasha pushes her phone in front of my face.

"Ivy, sweetie, you have to see this." She plays a video of us on the stage. "My boyfriend recorded it. Look how hot we are! We make *the best* team!" She raises her hand in a high five and all of us smack it.

During these last few days, the girls were very nice and fun, and I really liked them. Tears well up in my eyes at the thought of leaving them, but I refuse to cry in front of anyone. I'll have plenty of time for that when I go home alone and unemployed.

I blink the tears back and smile. "I didn't know you had a boyfriend."

"Yes, the most wonderful man on the planet. And I don't say that just to brag." Her eyes light up with love.

"It's true, he's so supportive. Unlike the shitty men I always find." Christy, one of the other dancers, laughs. "You can't dress in these short skirts, you can't dance in these skimpy costumes," she says in a mockingly deep voice and proudly swings two manicured middle fingers in the air. "Fuck you, controlling men! I can dress any way I want because I'm free." She sticks her tongue out and laughs triumphantly.

All of us burst out laughing and enter the dressing room. I barely get my heels off before Rob knocks on the door and calls my name.

I freeze on the spot. *Shit*. What do I do now? How am I going to explain my situation to him?

Think, Ivy, think. There has to be something to get me out of this.

I get up and drag my feet to the door, buying time to think up an excuse before it's too late. I open it and step forward, but before I can say anything, Rob grabs my shoulders and starts pushing me down the corridor.

"What's going on?" I protest.

"Boss is here and wants to sign you personally. Don't worry, he's very impressed," Rob says with a gentle squeeze on my shoulders, which perhaps is meant to be comforting, but the only thing I feel is the hum in my head.

Crap. It wasn't supposed to happen this way.

"But I..." Again, before I can finish, Rob pushes me into the room and closes the door.

What's wrong with this man? It's rude to interrupt people. And to push them around like they're a sack of potatoes.

Still facing the door, I hear movement behind me and realize my not-future boss is supposed to be here. As I turn slowly, still contemplating an escape plan, I feel all the blood drain from my face.

What the hell?

There must be some mistake. Yes, for example, this must be the wrong room.

Or I'm having hallucinations.

That would explain why the main character in my latest wet dream is sitting in front of me on a leather chair, legs crossed on the desk, looking at me curiously.

For a few too long seconds, we both stare at each other in complete silence without moving. I'm sure he can't miss my shocked expression, but he doesn't seem the least bit surprised. He knew I was dancing on that stage. Did he know who I was that first night at the hotel? Or the next two?

His gaze slides down my body but instead of feeling dirty, the ice in my veins thaws, making way for the heat.

Bravo, Ivy, a great start to your job interview. Turned on by the boss. Is there a bigger cliché?

It's just that when you know what your boss can do with his fingers, and that crooked mouth, you can't help but get a little fired up.

But then I remember what I have to do and that there'll actually be no job, and no sexy boss. It helps to reign in my dirty thoughts while Damien continues to look at me with an inscrutable expression.

He gestures for me to sit down and I scurry to the chair across from his desk.

When Robert pushed me into the room, he failed to notice I was still wearing only a red bodysuit and knee-high socks. The mask and my shoes are missing. Thanks to him, the majority of my body is on display.

Damien's eyes track my every move, and when I finally sit on the edge of the leather chair, he stands up and starts pacing.

I take the time to appreciate his appearance. He's wearing a white T-shirt, black leather motorcycle pants and a black leather jacket with white and neon green elements. I've never seen anyone wear motorcycle gear better. Seriously. Those

Hollywood macho men could only dream of looking this hot in that outfit.

His brown hair is styled casually but still somehow neat. His piercing green eyes steal my breath for a second. The stubble is gone and his face looks so smooth I want to run my fingers over it.

He leans over me and puts his hands on the arms of my chair. Our faces are close, but far enough away for me to put my last surviving brain cell into action.

"What am I going to do with you, Ivy?" He speaks breathlessly.

I swallow hard and try to get around the inevitable collision. "I don't know what you're talking about."

After my words come out, I realize how stupid they sound, but it's too late.

"Oh, you know..." One side of his mouth curves up. "I want you, and you want me...even if you don't want to admit it. But your skills are too good for me to pass up the opportunity to hire you. Rob swears by your talent, and he's never wrong."

My heart struggles to be free from the cage of my chest, and I shift in my chair, leaning back to put even more distance between us. "You won't have a problem with either—"

"I don't shit where I eat," he interrupts.

I scold him. "What's wrong with the men in this club? Why do you love interrupting people so much?" My questions come out in a tone that I shouldn't use when talking to my boss, but that's a moot point, anyway, so fuck it. "If you'd let me speak, you would understand that's not going to happen. I can't sign a contract with you."

He raises an eyebrow and pushes away from my chair. Only now do I manage to catch my breath. "What do you mean you can't? Our benefits are the best. You won't find a better employer anywhere." He starts pacing again.

"It's not about that. It's just..." My words get lost. There's no way to explain it.

He stops abruptly. "What is it about, then? If it's because of us, I already told you, I won't interfere with your work. I have a strict policy regarding personal relations with the staff."

I don't know why his words make me more disappointed than happy. "No, no. Nothing like that. I just... I can't sign. That's it."

Understanding flashes in his eyes, and I wonder if he'll guess that...

"Are you running from something, Ivy?"

And bingo.

I don't know why I even thought I could have this conversation.

I get out of the chair and before he can catch me, I run out the door, straight to the back exit. But of course, with my luck, the door is stuck and when I finally manage to open it, it's too late. Damien's standing before me and nails me to the wall, his arms caging me in.

"What are you running from? Or whom?"

His eyes burn holes through me, and it feels like he can see into my soul.

I look away and purse my lips. His arm shoots up and my first reflex is to lift mine to protect myself. His eyes widen and anger settles in them.

"Jesus, Ivy, did you think I was going to hit you?" The shock of that insult is written all over his face, but I still don't dare look him in the eyes.

Only one person has ever hit me, and that was my ex-boyfriend Vladimir. The first time I closed my eyes, the second time I was stupid and forgave him, and the third time I kicked his ass out of my apartment after I threw all his junk from the balcony. It wasn't that big of a deal, but I've always had quick reflexes, even before that bastard came into my life.

"Did someone abuse you? Is that why you're running?" His angry questions are blasted one after the other. He raises his hand again but I don't move this time. He caresses my cheek and tilts my chin up so I'm forced to look at him. "Listen, Ivy. I've never in my life and will never raise a hand to a woman, unless she's in the bedroom and bent over my knee. Do you understand me?"

I hate myself for letting him assume such things, especially when it's not true and there are women all over the world who suffer from domestic abuse daily. But there's just no way I can tell him the real reason. I prefer to let him assume whatever he wants, as long as it's far from the truth.

His fingers caress my lips, and his gaze lingers on them a little longer. He sighs and his eyes return to mine. "I'll let you work without a contract. If you're running from something this is the safest place for you. I don't want you hesitating for a second before calling me or Rob if you feel threatened in any way."

My eyes widen. I can't believe he's willing to take such risk when he doesn't even know me. He knows my body, but that's not enough to risk your business.

"Did Stella put you up to this?"

"Stella?" His brows scrunch. It wasn't her.

"You don't have to do me any favors just because we had sex, Damien. I'm doing fine by myself."

His angry look turns furious. "I don't want to hear another word. If I wanted you in my bed, the last thing I'd do is hire you. Don't get me wrong..." His hand slips down to my waist and the cold touch makes me shiver. He looks down at my goose-pimpled skin and whispers in my ear. "I want you as much as you want me."

Then he pulls back, his face serious as a heart attack. "But I made a promise to my godfather, Stella's father, that I'd protect her. Not only do you live with her, but you're also her best friend. I can't let any harm come to her, and if you're in danger, she's in danger. But even if you weren't connected to Stella, I wouldn't leave you unprotected, no matter what you think of me. I have no tolerance for violence against women." His teeth snap when he utters the word *violence*.

This is the second time I've heard of Stella's family and none of it was from her mouth. Just as she doesn't ask about my family, I don't ask about hers. It's an unwritten rule between us. I guessed she didn't have any or they weren't in the picture anymore, but Damien's words make me think maybe the story is more complicated than I thought.

His piercing gaze brings me back from the world of probabilities, and I wrap my arms around my body. "I can't accept. My situation could cause you a lot of trouble."

His lips press into a thin line, and that wrinkle of anxiety appears on his forehead. He didn't think about that. "Doesn't matter. It's against my nature to leave you unprotected. I could never forgive myself if something happened to you. Besides, where have you worked so far?" I list the bars I've worked at in the recent months and his wrinkle deepens. "Ridiculous. There's no way a beautiful woman like you should be working in shitholes like that. I forbid it."

My jaw drops before anger overtakes me. "Forbid? Who are you to forbid me?" I pull my hand from his. "Nobody can forbid me to do anything. I. Am. Free." I pronounce the lie of the year. I'm anything but free. But even so, who does he think he is?

I bend under his arm to get out of his way and start down the street, but in two steps he's in front of me again.

"I'm sorry. I'm just angry." He puts two fingers on the tip of his nose, takes a deep breath, and goes on. "You're obviously overqualified and you dance from your heart. Stay with us."

Wow.

No. Fucking. Words.

Twenty minutes ago, I was ready to collect my things and give up my dream, and here he is now serving it on a silver platter.

I know it's unfair on my part to even think about it, considering I can get him into a lot of trouble. But what can I do when I'm currently unemployed, broke, and I haven't come up with a single prospect? And this man is offering me the opportunity of a lifetime which will solve all these problems.

I've heard people say this but I never understood it.

Don't negotiate with the devil;

You're human, you'll be tempted.

At that distant moment I had everything in my life.

Today I understand it more than I understand myself.

How can I refuse this proposition from the devil himself, in black leather gear and burning green eyes?

And here he is before me, leaning against the wall, innocently kicking pebbles on the sidewalk, after throwing this once-in-a-lifetime proposal straight into my unprepared hands. He doesn't even know how much it will cost me. I'm good at lying, but I hate it. And accepting means lying to everyone around me. But if I refuse, I know I won't forgive myself.

The answer is simple. I'd give him my soul if he promises to bring back the greatest happiness in my life, dancing.

"Okay."

"Okay what?" He pushes off the wall.

"I'll dance at the club if it won't cause problems for you."

His jaw tightens. "Don't worry, I'll be fine. But not a word about this to anyone. The only ones who will know are you, me, and Rob."

"No problem." What's another lie to the already forming list. "And Stella. Stella will ask and I can't lie to her."

"That's okay, Stella's family."

It's on the tip of my tongue to ask how Stella is family when he's American and she's Italian, but I don't.

He sizes me up and sighs. "Go get dressed before I drive you home. *Or before I throw myself at you*," he mumbles and it makes me chuckle.

Only now do I realize I'm still half-naked on the street in the middle of the night.

"You don't have to drive me. I can get home myself."

He frowns. "I won't leave a lady to walk the dark streets alone." His tone leaves no room for argument.

His eyes rake over my whole body again, and it feels like hot lava running through my veins and settling in my stomach.

Calm down, Ivy. This is your future boss.

Equal shares of excitement and horror pass through me like tidal waves, and I try to stuff them in my little box.

Control your overly-emotional self, Ivy.

I make my way inside, change clothes, and say bye to everyone.

I go out the back door, and the first thing that catches my eye is the divine man leaning on the coolest motorcycle I've ever seen.

I don't know how I didn't notice it before; it's freaking huge. Black with neon green elements, like his jacket, and polished on all sides without so much as a scratch. The metal plate reads *Ducati*. It looks really expensive.

The man and the bike seem to complement each other, and it's a great contrast to the business Damien I saw at Stella's fashion show. This Damien looks more like the bad boy your mother warns you about.

"Is Batman going to come after us when he doesn't find his vehicle?" I raise an eyebrow.

"I'm saving your ass, baby. You can call me whatever you want." His laughter is so deep and raw it melts my *ass*.

I take a few precarious steps toward him and raise my hand to feel the surface of the black beast. The one with the engine, not the one with the taunting smirk.

"Do you even know how to drive this thing? I mean...it's huge." I can't hide the admiration in my voice.

I don't know shit about bikes, but this one deserves some adoration and respect.

Damien doesn't even grace me with a response, just rolls his eyes, hands me a black helmet, and helps me fasten it. Then he puts his own helmet on, helps me onto the leather seat, and climbs in front of me. "Hold on to me." He grabs my hands and places them on his sides under the jacket.

Oh, dear god.

Where did these side abs come from? It's just not fair to feel his hot skin, his strong muscles pressed against me, and not be able to throw myself at him.

I already feel enough tension from last night's *massage*. I barely gathered enough strength to keep myself from running to his suite in the middle of the night. Good thing he made the mistake of getting me off earlier. The resolve to withstand his arrogant ass and taunting smirk was far stronger after I got mine. Even if it was just a tiny bit.

The beast's engine growls with a deafening roar and pulls me out of my thoughts.

I realize I've dug my nails in his abs and pull my hands down, but only until he starts the beast and fear takes over.

I've never ridden a bike. All I know about them is they're dangerous but sexy.

Kind of like Damien.

Oh, how I'd love to ride him.

I squeeze him tightly, close my eyes, and rest my head on his back.

Chapter Thirteen

DAMIEN

I take a few wrong turns to extend our ride down the coastal street so I can enjoy her touch for a little longer. I don't know what's happening to me; I don't usually crave intimacy. But it's different with her.

I roll the throttle and release the clutch and my bike flies forward. Her nails dig into me through the thin fabric of the T-shirt and bring back memories of the night they were scratching my back.

Damn it. How could I hire her when I can't stop thinking about fucking her? *Bravo, Damien, really smart.* Now my own club will be the den of temptation.

I had my plan of fucking her until I got bored and stopped thinking about her. But I won't break my only rule, even if I have to suffer blue balls every time I see her on stage.

But what else could I have done? Leave her unprotected and at the mercy of some asshole? Not my style. I'd rather use her as bait to find him and kill him.

One thing that brings out the worst in me is someone abusing women. I nearly broke my jaw, clenching it with fury when she raised her hand to protect herself from me.

No woman should have to go through that.

My hands are gripping the handles, trying to break them. A memory, as clear as day, replays in my head. My mother's screams when the pitiful excuse for of a husband came home drunk and stoned most nights and decided the best way to shut her up was to slap her around.

The first time I woke up from the noise of one of their arguments, I went to check on her, and just before I opened the door, I heard a loud clatter and then the voices quieted. I peeked through the open door and saw my mother on the floor, her cheeks red, blood pouring from her nose. I was seven or eight, and I was afraid. I ran to her crying, but Hyland stopped me, gripped my arm and dragged me to my room.

Back then I didn't realize what had happened, and I stayed up all night to keep her safe from the monsters.

Who knew the monster was right under my nose?

Over the years, history repeated itself many times, and I only found out the truth when I was eleven and the jerk hit her right in front of me. By then, I was ready to protect her and jumped between them, and that was when I received my first slap. It was also the day I started hating my father.

The memory of the helplessness I felt every time I couldn't help her burns a hole in my chest to this day.

But today I'm not helpless. Today I can do everything in my power to protect Ivy so she can avoid that fate. This is the reason I took such a risk and hired her without a contract. It might be disastrous for me if Richard finds out, but I'll think of something.

The pressing of a warm body against my back drives away the thoughts spinning in my head. I stop at a red light and turn to look at her face. She didn't put the face shield down on her helmet and now her cheeks are rosy from the cold, and her lips are swollen. She smiles at me with the most innocent smile, and I forget everything around me. She nudges me and points at the green light with a vibrant laugh.

I roll the throttle, but I turn right to the beach instead of left for the city. If this is the last night I can be with her as something other than an employee, I'm not ready for it to end.

I reach the pier and stop the bike. I get off it and reach over to help her.

"Why did you turn here? I live in the opposite direction." Her words are muffled by the helmet.

I unbuckle it and lift it to see the questioning expression on the most beautiful face. She rushes to smooth her hair, but the wind blows it in all directions making her look like one of the women in the shampoo commercials on TV.

"Why aren't you answering me? And why are you staring at me?"

Her sweet frown when the wind blows her newly arranged strands mesmerizes me. I want to bite her puffy lips and kiss her until she forgets what she looks like.

But I don't.

Instead, I smile and tell her, "Because you're cute when you're pouting."

Her lips open but no sound comes out of them. *Well, well, who's speechless now?*

She takes a step back, reclining on my bike. I shorten the distance between us and press myself against her body. For a long moment, we stand still and silent, incapable of taking our eyes off each other.

"Look up." I point a finger at the sky and we raise our heads. There's not a cloud in sight, and all the stars are clearly visible. As if someone dropped a bag of diamonds on a dark canvas.

"Wow."

My gaze returns to her. "This pier is the least lit and is one of the few places where the stars can be seen so clearly."

A baby smile rises on her face, and my conflicting emotions from earlier evaporate just like that. Her eyes sparkle with the reflection of the stars. We remain silent, the only sound coming from the crashing waves on the shore.

She looks back at me and whispers, "It's beautiful."

My thoughts slip out of my mouth. "Not half as beautiful as you."

I can't restrain myself any longer.

I wrap my arms around her waist and press my mouth to hers. At first, our lips touch in a gentle, slow kiss, but with each twist of our tongues, it deepens. I grab her thighs and set her on the seat of the bike. Her legs twist around my waist and I bite her lip. She whimpers, the sound making me crazy.

The kiss gets rougher when she answers me with a nibble, and we both jump on each other like we can't get enough. Her body is bent under mine, and with each rub, the erection in my pants grows. Her hands are tangled in my hair, and I push her hard against the bike so she won't have anywhere to run this time.

I kiss her jaw, her ear, her neck. My tongue slides down to her collarbone and she bites my neck. A deep growl rumbles from my chest, and my cock presses between her legs. I swear I could fuck her right here on the beach, on the pier, on my bike, and I'm sure it would be perfect. The idea is turning me on even more. Her breathing quickens and...light blinds us both.

Ivy covers her face with her hands. I grunt and twist my head but I can't see anything behind the light. A man in a guard uniform lowers his flashlight to the ground and puts his hands on his waist.

"What's happening here?" He comes up a few steps closer and almost drops the flashlight when he sees us. "Excuse me, Mr. Black. I didn't know it was you. I didn't mean to bother you. I'll be on my way. Continue with what you were...doing," he babbles, his face and tone changing between shocked and embarrassed several times.

Frankly, I don't know whether to be angry or amused. The poor guard knows who I am very well, as does everyone in this city, and he knows he could easily lose his job with a single phone call. I had dinner with the mayor just before I came to the club. He values his friendship with my family as much as his 1966 Shelby Cobra 427 and a little more than his wife.

I nod and he turns to leave but stops with his back to us and says, "Sir, just so you know, I'm not alone and it's possible some of my coworkers may bother you."

"Thank you."

Hell. I forgot about the guards.

I'm not sure if the guy just did me a favor or not. It'll be easier to forget about Ivy and how sweet it was to fuck her if she stays in the past. But dammit, how I want her.

My gaze returns to her as she adjusts her blouse. The flames in her eyes are barely there anymore.

"Um, I'm not sure this is the best way to start my job." Her tone is uncertain but enough to put some common sense back into my head.

Jesus, Damien, what's wrong with you?

It seems like every time I'm around her, she pulls me in like a magnet. And when my lips touch hers, I forget everything but the two of us.

This must stop. I'll force myself to forget her.

How hard can it be?

IVY

Disappointment hits me, and I want to slap myself for feeling it.

What's wrong with me?

This man...this charming, hell-of-a-man will be my boss. I wouldn't feel comfortable knowing I'm breaking the rules by sleeping with him. And the opportunity he's giving me is a once in a lifetime kind of thing. What if he decides we broke his rule and takes his offer back? I can't screw this up just to screw him. Even if it's the best sex of my life.

He pulls away from me, and I instantly miss his body heat. I stand on my unstable legs and smooth out my jeans.

"It's time to go home. The sun will rise soon." His voice is soft; there's no trace of that heat he just gave me.

"Yes, I should get some sleep before rehearsal tomorrow." Mine, unfortunately, sounds more desperate than friendly.

We ride in awkward silence. He parks in front of the white gate with the peeling paint and looks at the house reproachfully.

"You live here with Stella?" His tone is more than offensive.

Our house might not be on *MTV cribs*, but it's ours and it's not as bad from the inside as it looks from the outside.

"Don't judge the book by its cover," I scold him. "Stella didn't invite you over? I thought you were like family." He doesn't miss my sardonic remark and throws me an irritated glance.

"We are, but she never even let me go near it. Now I see why. If I knew she lived here, I would've made her come back..."

Before he finishes insulting our home, I swing my middle finger in the air and head for the gate.

"Bye, Damien. And don't forget—you're my boss starting *tomorrow.*"

His laughter sounds like a clap of thunder behind me, mixed with the revving of the engine. I hear the hiss of the tires behind me as I open the gate.

I turn to steal one last look at him, but I'm blinded by bright lights.

The next moment everything passes in front of me in slow motion like a movie.

Chapter Fourteen

IVY

The lights divert to the side and a big car comes into sight. Its headlights illuminate the black motorcycle and I realize it's flying toward it too fast. The motorcycle deviates, but then I hear a loud crash and glass flies everywhere.

The car slides sideways and hides the bike from my sight.

The hissing of the tires rings through the night, and thick smoke rises from the rear. The car rushes up the hill, fleeing the scene of the accident.

The smoke behind it floats up into the sky, revealing the bike laying on its side on the curb.

But there's no one behind the bike.

For a second I stay on the sidewalk, paralyzed and startled. My feet react before my brain and without realizing it, I start running toward the bike.

The pungent smell of gasoline fills my nostrils and panic envelops me.

"Damien!"

He doesn't answer my cry.

The glass under my feet crunches and grinds into my

shoe. I pass the squashed bike and rush to the grass behind it. It's still dark outside, and the little light from the rising sun isn't enough for me to see very well.

"Damien," I scream at the top of my lungs.

The silence is deafening. The experience is so unreal it feels like I'm dreaming.

God, I hope I'm dreaming.

After a few more steps, I see a piece of leather and white fabric. Looking around more closely, I see an arm sticking out from behind a bush.

Once again, my legs move faster than my brain, and I reach him in a second. Damien's lifeless body lies in the bush.

I kneel next to him and call his name, but he doesn't answer. I check him for a pulse, but I can't feel it with my trembling hands and the pounding of my own heart in my ears.

His head is turned to one side and blood is pouring from his lip and forehead. His clothes are torn and thorns from the bush dig into his flesh and clothing.

Tears are running down my cheeks and my body is shaking even more. I force my hand to still and check his pulse. With a barely noticeable movement, his chest rises and my lungs fill with oxygen as if I've never breathed before.

I grab the phone from my back pocket and call 911. The operator tells me that he's sending an ambulance and I should calm down. *Yeah, right. Like that's an option.* My breathing quickens more and more. My lungs are closing in on me.

I sit on the ground next to Damien, take his hand and start doing my calming exercises. In a minute or two, I stabilize as much as I can. I lean over him, my tears never stopping. The blood is drying on his face, and I gently caress his cheek in an attempt to wake him up without having to move his head in case there's a fracture.

"Please, Damien, please. Wake up. Damien. Come on. Wake up. Please." I keep repeating my prayers but they're in vain.

I inspect his body for more wounds, but I can't see anything under the dark leather except his torn skin on one knee. A thin stream of blood trickles from it, and I start praying out loud asking that the ambulance hurries.

Among the prayers, I curse myself for not paying attention at the first-aid course I attended and now I can't do anything without risking further damage.

The fingers I hold in my hand tremble and I stop. Damien's eyes open slightly and he blinks. "Ivy." He whispers my name softly, and his eyes close again.

"No, no, no. Don't leave me, Black. You son of a bitch. Wake up, Damien." My voice is weak and squeaky.

I slap him very lightly in an attempt to bring him around, but to no avail.

I hear the sirens of the ambulance a few blocks away. The seconds feel like hours until the sound is finally clear and distinctive. I rise from the ground and start waving in the air in their direction. Once the paramedics start running in our direction, I fall to the ground next to Damien.

"Can you hear me? Help is coming." My voice is broken, but I refuse to cry in front of the people coming and swallow my tears.

They load Damien into the ambulance, and I insist on coming with them. On the way to the hospital, they put an oxygen mask on him and give him first aid. The terms they use when they speak to each other are unfamiliar to me, and I can feel myself spacing out. The voices around me are replaced by a loud humming.

The scene of the collision plays out in front of my eyes again and again as if I'm stuck in that period of time. My breathing quickens and I look down at my bloody hands. The red spots start blurring.

I feel someone touching my shoulder and hear a voice in the distance. I'm trying to concentrate on it. "Miss? Miss, are you okay? You look pale. Are you sure you weren't injured?"

The voice comes from the woman in the blue uniform next to Damien. Her eyes wander over my body and return to my face. I look at my shoulder and see a man's hand pinching me. My eyes focus on the paramedic it belongs to, and my vision starts clearing.

"Y-yes." My whispering is too quiet for anyone to hear so I clear my throat. "Yes. I'm all right, I'm just...in shock."

"It's normal to be in shock after what you saw. You were able to react immediately and although your boyfriend is still in danger, he's a fighter."

"He's not my..." I start denying, but my voice is lost again when I realize what he said. *He's still in danger.* My chest tightens again, but I dig my nails into my palm, and the pain helps me stay in the present. I clear my throat, but before I can finish, the man opens the ambulance door and I see the ER sign.

Three hours later, I'm still pacing the halls of the hospital under the *Black Rose Group* sign.

The man has his own private wing named after his business, damn it. And he could be anywhere behind those doors, suffering or worse. The doctor told me they're taking care of Damien, but they couldn't tell me anything more because I'm not a family member. I have to wait for one of them to come.

The nurse at the front desk called his mother as soon as we arrived.

Three hours for God's sake. Three hours have passed since her son was taken behind those doors. Rosehill isn't small, but it's impossible for it to take three hours to get anywhere within the city limits. I can't believe she's still not here.

I dig my nails into my scalp in frustration. I'm sure at this point I'm balding. The typical hospital scent is palpable, but it's as if the smell of gasoline and burning tires has been absorbed into my nostrils.

It would've been much easier if they had told me at least something. *Is he conscious? Is he breathing?* I know I'm probably overreacting but I've seen a lot of motorcycle crashes on the news and most of them don't end well. I realize I've known the man for less than a week but I can't make myself leave until I know he's okay. The words of the paramedics keep repeating in my head like an echo.

In danger, in danger, in danger.

"Miss, I have to ask you to sit down because you're making the other people nervous," one of the nurses tells me in a soft voice but fails to hide the annoyance behind it.

I look around and for the first time since I arrived, I realize there are a lot of people here. And they are all staring at me.

Great. A good way to be conspicuous.

I sit on a plastic chair and grip the edge of it, but I shoot to my feet when I hear the voice of the nurse.

"Hello, Mrs. Black. Would you like to wait for your son here or should I prepare a private room for you?"

"Private room will be better." The emotion in the slim woman's voice is barely noticeable, but I can detect it.

She's dressed in a vanilla-colored business suit and looks

like she just got off the runway of some Haute Couture fashion show. I've only seen her twice around Stella, and I've never come too close because, honestly, her icy green eyes and porcelain skin, in combination with the raven-black bob, scare the shit out of me.

"What happened? I was told on the phone Damien had an accident. How is he?" The calmness with which she says all this is a mix between frightening and laudable. In her place, I'd be a hysterical mother in need of a straitjacket.

"Your son was in a motorcycle accident. He was hit by a car. You'll have to talk to the doctors for further information on his injuries."

Her eyes widen for only a second, and fear runs through them before they harden into the most chilling look I've ever seen. "Why didn't anyone tell me it's so serious?! What car hit him? How?"

I try to justify the three-hour delay by telling myself no one told her exactly what happened, but I fail. I don't think I'd ever put anything before my child if the hospital called me.

"His girlfriend witnessed the accident. You can talk to her, she might be able to answer your questions." The nurse points in my direction, and I freeze on the spot when Melanie's gaze connects with mine. "The police will be here soon to take your statement," the nurse says to me.

Shit! The police. I hadn't thought of that.

Every click of Melanie's thin heels on the tiles feels as if they're being hammered into my head, and I can tell by her eyes this is what she's imagining. With small and quick steps, she approaches and stands before me with her arms crossed. She gives me the once-over and I feel her coldness creep into my veins.

"Girlfriend? Damien doesn't do *girlfriends*." Her tone is

the embodiment of calm and businesslike, and if I didn't see the scorn in her eyes, I wouldn't have guessed that's what she felt.

"I'm not his girlfriend. I tried to explain to the doctors, but..."

Her hand rises in front of my face. "Save it. I know exactly what you are."

I can barely keep my jaw from dropping. How does she know what I am? When did Damien find the time to tell her, given he's been with me ever since I agreed to work for him?

"What happened? Who hit my son?" she demands from me.

"A car hit him and the driver fled the scene. I found him in the grass, after he'd been thrown off the bike. He wasn't conscious, but he was breathing."

"What car? Color, brand? How could he escape like a coward? I'll find him and kill him myself."

This time, my jaw drops with shock when I hear the undisguised emotion in her voice. "I can't tell you. Everything happened so fast, I was in shock and didn't see."

"Could you be any more useless?" She mutters but I decide to pretend I didn't hear her. Her son was just in an accident, after all. Three hours ago... "At least tell me what kind it was. A hatchback, a van, an SUV?"

"SUV. It was definitely an SUV." I keep replaying the memory in my head. "It was very strange; the car was flying straight at him and at the last moment, it tried to swerve to avoid him but couldn't. The driver didn't stop for even a second, it just kept going until it disappeared."

Her eyes widen and I'm worried they'll pop out. Quickly, her expression returns to its normal cold grimace, she smooths out her perfectly straight skirt, and looks at me with indifference.

"Thank you. You may give your statement and go."

"Go? What do you mean go? I need to know what's happening with Damien." My voice breaks despite my effort to sound strong. I hate that I'm showing weakness in front of this icy woman.

"Your place isn't here. Damien has a family, and you're...nobody."

The harsh truth hits me like a punch to the face. I nod, turn around, and disappear through the doors as quickly as possible. Melanie Black is right. I don't belong here. Damien has a family to look after him. He's not alone.

And, I...I'm just nobody.

Chapter Fifteen

IVONNE MOLEROV

One year ago in Bulgaria

"What do you mean they ran off?" I ask my aunt Maria. My head is getting dizzy, my knees buckle, and I drop into the fancy suede armchair in my parents' house in Bulgaria, where they'd moved back to a few years ago.

My soon-to-be-convicted-criminals parents.

"You're not listening!" She screams back at me in her Balkan accent, because she's lived her whole life in Bulgaria, but at least she speaks English well. She knows Bulgarian isn't my forte because even though I was born here and my parents are Bulgarian, we moved to the US when I was only a few months old. I speak the language with Nonna, even though she understands English. She wants the language to stay in the family.

Aunt grabs me by the arm and yanks me off the chair. "We've got to be moving! Come on, take only the necessities, you'll get the rest when you land in New York. You should decide if you want to leave after that or stay there, but I advise you to run far away. Keep me posted on your location."

I pull back from her grip and look at her like she's lost her goddamn mind. "I'm not running away. I didn't do anything!"

She storms through the door of my bedroom and starts rummaging through my closet. T-shirts and dresses are flying through the air. "I bought you a wig. Put it on for the flight and make sure to get rid of your awful blonde hair as soon as you land. Your natural brown is much better."

"Aunt stop!" I stop her before she continues this madness. "I promised Nonna I'd stay the rest of the summer in Bulgaria. I'm not leaving."

"According to the police, you're an accessory in this, so yes, you are. I'll be taking care of her and unless you want to make your visit to Bulgaria permanent, so she can visit you in jail for the rest of her life, I suggest you move your ass." She points a finger at me and looks me dead serious in the eyes. "I didn't risk my job and possibly a criminal record for you, so you could fuck it all up. Get moving!" She dials someone on the phone and runs out in the hallway.

My head is getting dizzier and my heart's racing faster with every second that passes. My back presses against the wall and the realization slowly starts sinking in as I'm lowering to the ground.

How do you tell your kid you've committed the biggest crypto currency fraud in the world and embezzled billions? One point three billion to be exact.

You don't.

You leave the aunt to announce the news while you're running away to Lord knows where and leaving your own flesh and blood to face the consequences of your actions.

Yep. That's my folks.

Running away before the criminal investigation is even

announced without at least calling or leaving a note. Yeah, I guess a note would've worked.

We screwed up your life. Run, before you're arrested and sentenced for life. Love, Mom and Dad.

I guess they didn't have time to write it, just like they never had time for me in the last twenty-four years unless they needed to guilt me into doing something. Something like helping them support the online banks they apparently stole from for years.

Anger bubbles through me and the adrenaline rush is filling my veins at realization I wasted my whole time and energy on them instead of chasing my dream. Why did I even agree to work with them in the first place? I should've known better. All they ever did was think about themselves.

The rage inside helps me get my shit together so I don't have a panic attack on the floor in the bedroom, like the pathetic person I am, and screw Aunt Maria even more than my parents screwed me. Not that I can prove it, but at least I didn't do anything. She risked her corporate hacker for the government job so she could warn me and get me out of the country as soon as possible before the warrant for my arrest was issued.

I run to my room and storm through it. The few clothes I have here, designer clothes I once loved, now disgust me. I bought them with money from the work I did for them. Living my dream, or rather dancing at a few gigs in New York doesn't pay enough for these Louboutins. My parents would never let me off my leash and allow me to search for a real job as a dancer. And I'm too much of a pushover to ever disobey them.

If only I'd known.

I bypass all of it and grab the few sweat suits I keep here. I open my Nike duffel bag, and what I see stops me dead in my tracks. Beneath the dirty clothes I brought back from practice yesterday, there is cash. Lots of it. Stacked up nice and pretty like I just robbed a bank.

What the fuck?

I guess they did think about me after all. Just not enough to break the news to me themselves. I doubt my indifferent father would care enough to leave me a bag of cash, so that leaves mother dearest. But that's not what gave her away. It's the sight of my oldest laptop tucked away under the stacks of bills because God forbid mama's little genius stop programming.

Of course, they wouldn't think of taking me with them, but they'll leave me a computer. This sums up my relationship with my parents perfectly.

"Ivonne, get your ass down here. You've got a plane to catch." I jump at the sound of Maria's voice coming from downstairs, and I quickly hide the money away under some clothes and a pair of tennis shoes.

I take one last look at the room in a house that never felt like home and a strange feeling settles in me. One I can't put a label on.

"Ivonne!" my aunt screams again, and I quickly put my brown wig on and make my way to her.

At the private airport, a jet that belongs to one of our family friends is waiting for me.

"Aunt, please take good care of Nonna. Tell her I'm sorry and I love her, and I'll miss her every day." A tear slips down my cheek when it occurs to me I may never be able to see her again. It breaks my heart into pieces, and it hurts much more than the betrayal of my parents.

Unlike them, Nonna is the best person I know and the only one who supported me through this bullshit I call life. I don't know what I'm going to do without her.

"Don't worry about her. You have nothing to be sorry about." She hugs me and the tears I'm trying to hold in, start to fall.

"Hey, hey, hey. Don't cry." Maria tries to calm me down, but she has about the same amount of motherly instincts as her sister, my mother. I have no idea how these two came out of the wonderful person that is Nonna, but at least my aunt was decent enough to take care of me in this situation.

I wipe away my tears and try to push down the fear that's growing in me.

"Here's your new passport and license. Here are the details on your new identity, memorize it and then destroy it. I'll put it in the system when I get back, but it won't be enough because I didn't have time. You have to keep a low profile. My advice is: study your documents and embrace the person you have to become once you're out of here. We don't know how long it'll last."

She hands me the folder with my fake identity and a satellite phone and we say our goodbyes.

Once I'm in the private jet, I settle down and look at the documents.

Name: Ivy Thanos

Ivy is the nickname my friends at MIT used to call me.

Nationality: Greek

I guess she picked Greece because it's close enough to Bulgaria, and I have some very distinctive Balkan traits in my appearance.

Sure, there's my photo, but instead of my dyed blonde hair, there's my natural dark brown color I haven't had since I was sixteen. I read the rest of the documents in the folder, my fear of the unknown, my sadness and anger only growing with each word.

I don't know what I'm going to do.

There's no way I can hide in New York. I may be Bulgarian by origin, but I grew up in the Big Apple. There are too many people I know that I could run into.

One place comes to mind when I think about where I could go. Rosehill.

I open the brochure I've been carrying around in my wallet for five months.

It's a nice city I was planning to visit later this year. I've always wanted to go to Florida and swim in the Gulf of Mexico. Rosehill is said to have the cleanest beaches in the state and the travel brochure describes it like a smaller Miami. A lot of celebrities have residences there too, as it's not as commercial and they can enjoy the experiences it offers privately.

Aunt is right that I don't know how much time I'll have to be this new Ivy person. If I have to start a new life, I might as well make it somewhere warm with a beach.

That feeling from earlier—the one I couldn't put my finger on—is back and it's strong.

The more I feel it, the more I think it's hope.

Hope that I could maybe, just maybe, live my own life there. Be my own person.

Who knows?

Maybe my fake name will give me a real start.

Chapter Sixteen

IVY

The tension of waiting for the food delivery is killing me. I can't stop pacing on the newly-worn path on the carpet. I pull at my hair and bite my fingers because I already bit my nails off.

Oh, who am I fooling? It's not the late delivery guy that's brought me to this state.

Today marks one week since Damien's accident. Because of me. I don't know if bad luck is following me or if it's the other way around, but if he hadn't brought me home that night, he wouldn't be in this condition now. I try to forget, to forgive myself, to be glad he's alive at all, but that guilt is embedded so deep into my brain and it gets worse every day.

Nobody in the club is talking about it. I only know what Stella told me—he got off easy, with only a few sprains, because he jumped off the motorcycle before the car hit him and he landed on that bush. But he still forbade her from going to his house, which makes me think he's worse than he's admitting, and it's killing me that I can't hear or see him myself. But his mother was right; he needs his family now.

Speaking of family, I have to thank my aunt for making

such a perfect copy of my real license that the police didn't suspect anything when they questioned me. They also didn't find any cameras or witnesses at the crime scene.

I considered using my hacking skills to find Damien's address. But what would I do if I had it? I can't just show up at his door and endure more humiliation from his mother or any of his other relatives. Also, when I got on that plane a year ago, I swore I'd never use my computer again for anything other than watching movies.

My parents started teaching me computer skills as soon as they found out I had an aptitude for it and over the years, I learned a lot from them. I had no choice because it was the only way I could keep dancing. They didn't understand my love for the arts and wanted me to quit, but Nonna intervened, and we came to an agreement that I could continue to take lessons if I spent the rest of my day learning all about programming. They hoped I'd grow up to take over the family business since I am an only child. But maintaining online banks never excited me as much as breaking impenetrable defenses. That's what really got me into my love for programming.

Unfortunately for them, I turned out like my aunt. She's an exceptional hacker who works for the government and other institutions whose names she's not allowed to disclose. Much like her, I concentrated on hacking and soon became one of the best. By the time I was eighteen, I was breaking into her system just to mess with her.

When I got accepted into MIT, my interest switched to programming languages. I still helped my parents with their work and any spare time I had I spent in the rehearsal studio dancing. All my life pretty much revolved around these activities.

Three years ago, I had enough resources to start my own project but unfortunately it never saw the light of day.

The sound of the bell startles me and pulls me out of my thoughts. I get the pizza and try to stuff a piece down my tight throat. I'm not hungry at all, but my stomach is growling like a bear. The combination of barely sleeping and not eating will surely make me pass out at rehearsal later. I swallow with much effort and keep chewing, repeating the process. The house is quiet, the only sound coming from the ticking of the grandfather clock. I feel like the hands are slowing down more and more and time isn't moving forward.

I force myself to eat another piece of pizza.

I go to the bedroom and put on my workout clothes.

I return and look at the clock again. *Damn it.* Only four minutes have passed.

I have too much free time to pace around, trying to remember anything from that night that could help the investigation. I've been wracking my brain all week and it's not doing me any favors. Rehearsals in the daytime and performances at night keep me sane, but tomorrow is my day off and frankly, I'm worried about myself.

Maybe I should put on my big girl panties and go to Damien's. Melanie made it clear I'm not welcomed there, but what if I remember something I need to tell him? Yes, I should definitely have his address or number, just in case, right?

I open the laptop before I can talk myself out of it, for the millionth time, and in ten minutes, I have all of his personal data. I write it down and close the window, but my fingers have a mind of their own and somehow the cursor is hovering over the program I created, showing me that I have new messages I'm trying to avoid.

Yes, I technically violated my own rule to hack into the

community server and find Damien's data, but it's for completely different reasons. It doesn't count, right?

I leave the computer next to me and take a drink of my water, but I can't shake the bad feeling in my stomach.

What if it's something important?

The program is designed to track certain key words on the internet regarding my identity, location, and a few other things. At the beginning of last year, it was bursting with tons of messages, but for a while now I've had hardly any. It may be another check by the Bulgarian police, but my sixth sense is telling me to look.

I pick up the laptop and sit on the edge of the couch. The program's interface appears, looking like a video game with dragons. I type in the code and messages start popping up one after another on the screen.

The police, the police, Europol, the police. All with my parents' names and only one with mine. As usual, they found nothing. Aunt and I erased every trace that I even existed with the exception of my birth certificate and my photo as a baby that they already had. Nothing else.

My eyes stop on one word on the next window. *Hack.* My eyes widen and I freeze, staring at my computer.

Not possible. Not after I wiped all traces. But the proof is right in my face, mocking me.

Someone managed to pass the second defense of my firewall.

Of course, I have a third, even a fourth, but no one has ever made it past the first. I hired some of the best in the world to try to break it. Every single one failed. But here's someone who succeeded. And that means only one thing. They'll try again and again until they get through the rest.

I know you can't physically feel the color draining from your face, but I'm sure I'm white as a sheet right now.

None of the institutions would devote so many resources to attempt breaking in. There's only one likely reason why someone did.

My project.

Very few people know about it, mostly family and a few people from my father's company. I exclude my family because they knew about the project for a long time, and none of them wanted to get involved. Everyone thought it would be a failure. There's no reason to look for it now, given it's not even finished.

But several people in the company were interested in working with me. Yet, none of them have enough skills to work alone. Which leaves only two possibilities. They either hired someone or sold the information.

Bad. Very, very bad.

No one should know about this project. I made everyone involved sign a NDA, but I guess now that I'm a fugitive they decided they could break it.

If my work falls into the wrong hands it could be used as a weapon of destruction and chaos in cyberspace. It will take time to reinforce my firewall, but I don't have it right now.

I leave the window on standby and open another one. What I find stuns me even more.

Someone is actively searching for me.

Shit.

What if they know the laptop is with me? Nobody, not a soul, knows I took it with me. No one even knows on which of my eight laptops my project is. I have only two of them with me, but they all have different defenses. Why would someone pick this one specifically?

As much as I'd like to believe it is, this doesn't seem coincidental.

My anxiety multiplies tenfold when I see the big picture.

Someone is onto me and they're looking for a way to locate me and my project. If they succeed, it'll result in one of two possible outcomes: a prison cell or death.

My chest is tightening and my breathing is becoming labored.

The worst case scenarios run through my mind. I'm just a dancer/programmer, dammit. I can't go to jail for something I didn't do. And worse, I didn't even listen much in Krav Maga to defend myself if someone finds me before the police do and decides to kidnap me or get rid of me. I'm not in a fucking action movie. Or a thriller. I don't even like watching them. How am I supposed to save myself if it comes to that?

With so many thoughts racing around in my head, my breathing speeds up and my heart starts pounding in my ears. I feel like my head is going to explode.

How did I get here? I'm just an ordinary girl.

I thought I could handle it all and just hide out, but I can't.

My hands start trembling and I feel sick. My vision is blurring too. My legs are starting to feel numb. What is happening to me?

I put my computer on the table and get up to move a bit, but the room starts moving and rotating. The pain in my head is excruciating. I look around, but it feels like the walls are closing in on me, trying to trap me.

I want to escape, but I don't know where to go. There's nowhere I can go. I've already escaped. And now someone is going to find me.

Tears are flowing down my cheeks and I can hardly breathe. I kneel on the floor and try to catch my breath, but I can't get any air.

Lord, am I dying? Am I having a heart attack?

The pain in my chest intensifies, and I can barely keep

myself from vomiting when everything around me starts spinning faster. My legs are still tingling, and little by little, my body becomes numb from my toes to my shoulders. My wheezing sounds like the cry of a dying animal because I can barely breathe. Fear overwhelms me and my whole body is shaking.

I hear a jingle in the distance, and I make an effort to focus on the opening door.

They're coming for me.

They found out where I am and they're coming to get me.

I hear screaming and realize it's coming from me.

The next moment everything turns dark.

Something cold hits me in the face and I open my eyes. A hand waves in front of my face, and ice water splashes into my eyes. I try to move and realize someone is holding my body down. The only thing I see is brightness because my vision is still blurry.

"If you kill me, you'll never get the project." The threat is out of my mouth before my brain switches on. The hand that is holding mine squeezes harder but it's still gentle. Like a woman's hand.

"Ivy! Ivy, are you okay? What happened?" Stella's voice is coming from the blurry figure above me and my chest tightens again.

They got her too! How could I let that happen?

"Stella, I'm so sorry. Run. I'll be okay, I promise. I won't let you get hurt." My cry is pathetic, but it's the best I can do right now.

Her hand caresses my cheek. "Ivy, how hard did you hit your head? What are you talking about? Who's going to hurt me?" There's fear in her voice. My vision is clearing. I blink a few times as I focus on her blue eyes looking down at me.

"Where are we?" I turn my head from side to side to see what's around us and the sharp pain makes me cringe. I blink twice. An old TV, white walls with peeling paint and an old cabinet.

"We're at home. What happened, Ivy? Did someone attack you?" Her hands holding mine tremble with each word.

I put my palms on the floor and force myself to sit up. Stella's hands are instantly around my shoulders, keeping me from falling back. My head hurts worse than any hangover I've ever had.

"No, I don't think so. Unless...when did you get here?"

"Like, two minutes ago. When I came in, you were lying on the floor, shaking and screaming. The next thing I know, you'd closed your eyes and"—her voice breaks—"I was very scared, Ivy. I didn't know what to do. You didn't answer so I threw water on your face to wake you up."

My brain starts registering the symptoms little by little. "I think I had a panic attack." I've had a few over the years, but there was always someone around me to snap me out of it. This time it was stronger than it's ever felt before.

"Who were you talking about? Is there really danger? Should I call Damien?"

Damien. I have to see him. I don't know why, but I just need to see him.

I get up slowly and sit on the edge of the couch. I look around and see my laptop on the table. The program is still open. *Shoot.* I hope Stella didn't see it.

"No, no, everything's fine. Just..." How can I explain I had a panic attack because I'm a fugitive and someone came close to finding me?

Stella starts pacing and talking fast about how worried she was, and then she switches to Italian, so I stop listening. I use the time she's distracted to grab the laptop and close it.

She turns to me with the most serious expression I've ever seen on her. "If you're in danger, you need to tell me, Ivy. You're like family and I already lost that. I'd never forgive myself if I lose you too."

My heart breaks because I know she's the same for me, and our whole relationship is based on lies. Also, I didn't know she lost her family. Or she's referring to the Blacks? "No danger, Stells." I force myself to smile. "I think all the crazy stuff I was saying was a mixture of the blow to my head and the movie I watched last night."

"Then why did you have a panic attack?" Her tone is soaked with doubt, her eyes studying me with concern.

I need to incorporate my best delusional skills. I shake my head and sigh. "Because I've been worrying too much about Damien." At least it isn't a lie.

Stella sits down on the couch and wraps her arms around my shoulders. "He's getting well. It's not your fault. I've told you a million times. It's not you who hit him." Her hands caress me reassuringly.

"But it was because—"

"Yes, yes, I know. Because of you he was here, because he drove you, blah, blah." She grabs me by the shoulders and gently shakes me. "Ivy! Come to your senses. It was his decision, and you didn't know what was going to happen. It's no one's fault except for the coward who hit him and ran away. Promise me you'll stop blaming yourself."

"Okay, Mom. I'll try."

We both chuckle and I start to relax. Usually, I'm the mother who scolds Stella for not eating or sleeping or resting enough, and she's the kid who pouts but listens to me.

"Honestly I don't know how we would've survived without each other if we hadn't met at the park that day."

She snorts out a laugh. "You mean if you hadn't saved me at the park."

I thought Stella wouldn't recover from the failed wedding, but only a month later we were both laughing about it and thanking God for bringing us together.

"Well, we're even." I wink at her.

My head already feels better. Suddenly, I freeze and look at my watch. "I'm late. I'm late." I jump to my feet and start running around the house, while Stella laughs at me and tries to get me to stay home and rest today, but after all the stress, dancing is my only medicine.

Chapter Seventeen

IVY

During rehearsal at the club, I manage to work out the tension and realize the situation isn't nearly as dramatic as I made it out to be. Not that I'm surprised I overreacted. I tend to be a bit overdramatic. Sue me.

All my life, there's been someone trying to bring me down, starting with my parents, my teachers, my boyfriends, all the way to the authorities. But no one has succeeded and I plan to keep it that way. I'm stronger than them. Or at least I have to repeat it until I believe it.

With my new attitude, I plaster on my smile in the rehearsal studio mirror, close my eyes and take a deep breath.

You can do it. You'll handle everything life throws at you. And no one will ever find or hurt you.

I exhale everything negative, open my eyes and scream in horror.

I'm not alone.

Rob's reflection in the mirror laughs.

A great start to Ivy 2.0, absolutely fearless. I roll my eyes. "How do you move so quietly?"

He's dressed in a white T-shirt and jeans and looks younger than before. I'd only ever seen him in a suit before and the change looks good on him.

He puts a finger to his mouth and whispers, "Don't tell anyone. I'm a ninja."

"Shouldn't ninjas be short and slim? The way you look, I'd say more like a soldier or a mercenary," I joke, but he straightens his perfect posture and gets serious.

"Do you have any plans right now?" His tone sounds rather cold than pleasant. His eyes don't tell me a thing.

"Umm, I don't think so."

He passes me a big brown envelope. "I need you to bring this to Damien. Something came up and I can't go myself." I think this should've been a request, but it sounds more like an order.

"Can't his mother take it? I don't think she'll be too happy to see me at the door after she kicked me out of the hospital."

"Melanie's out of town. It's urgent, otherwise I wouldn't ask you." He taps his foot nervously. "Besides, I think he'll be glad to see you." His lips twist in a mysterious smile, and I can't tell if it's sinister or kind. Or mocking.

He puts the envelope in my hand and takes a few steps to the door, but then he stops and turns back to me.

"Oh, and please bring him some food and alcohol. Whiskey. Whiskey will do the job." He smiles even wider. "And get the fucker to eat before he starts drinking. He doesn't want to listen to me, but I have a feeling you'll be more persuasive." He shoves two hundred dollars into my hand and disappears through the door. I'm sure I hear him laughing in the hallway.

I was planning to go see Damien tomorrow, but to be

honest, I don't know if I would've had the courage. But now that I have no choice, it feels easier.

Or is it because I know I won't have to go through the Ice Queen at the door?

I don't know how such a small woman can scare the living shit out of people, but I have no desire to understand.

I look in the mirror again, glad I don't look like death after the day I had.

Okay, I'm not at my best, but it'll have to do.

I leave the studio and with each step my confidence and mood improve. By the time I reach the back door of Masquerade, I'm already giddy with happiness. For a week I've been dying to find out how Damien is doing, but now I realize I just want to see him.

The taxi drives down the coastal street until we're in the middle of nowhere, and just when I'm starting to worry I have the wrong address, a large metal gate with the words *Crystal Bay* on it comes into view. Damn Robert, he didn't tell me I'll be going into the richest gated community of Rosehill dressed in a forty-dollar sports outfit from the thrift shop. Freaking rock stars own houses here!

A security guard approaches the taxi. "Name?" His voice is thick and suggests *Don't fuck with me*.

I swallow audibly. "Ivy Thanos."

He goes into the security booth. There's a long minute while my heart is beating the shit out of my rib cage.

"Robert called for you." This time his voice is more welcoming and a little of the tension eases.

He opens the gate and lets us in. As we drive through the streets lined with palm trees, I gawk at the huge houses we pass by mostly hidden by bushes. We take a right turn, and at the end of the street the driver takes a left to the driveway of one of the biggest houses.

Damien's two-story house, in a modern design, with white balconies and reflective windows sprawls across the property. There's a big garage for at least five cars and another small building. The Gulf of Mexico stretches out like an endless pool behind the house.

The whole landscape looks like a postcard, and it feels like a dream until the cab driver coughs roughly and turns to me. "Miss, are you getting out? I don't have all day."

Only now do I realize I'm staring forward with my mouth hanging open, drooling. I wipe the corners with my hand like the classy lady I am and hand him a twenty. Taking the envelope and the bags of food and booze, I get out. He drives off before I even close the door.

I ring the bell at the front door and stand there for five minutes. When no one answers I round the house, looking for another way in but end up looking around like a kid in an amusement park. There is a tennis court, and a large swimming pool with a freaking lounge sofa with a fireplace in the center. There's even what looks like a mini river-pool surrounding a big water slide.

I don't know where I thought Damien Black would live, but I sure as hell wasn't expecting paradise.

When I get to an open glass door, I stop and contemplate what to do. There's no bell. There's no one around.

"Damien," I call out and peep through the door.

I hear a clicking noise and it's getting closer. Suddenly, a huge black Doberman appears in front of me and stands in a defensive position. He's got a silver chain collar with little rhinestones. *Oh wait*, I take that back. Seeing where Mr.

Billionaire lives, it must be platinum with diamonds or some shit.

The dog growls in my direction, squinting. *Oh my!* It looks like a little horse.

"Hey, buddy!" I reach out with the back of my hand toward him so he can smell it. The Doberman looks at me distrustfully and takes a cautious step toward me. He thrusts his wet nose into my hand, sniffs three times, and licks me. I hope this was the trust test and I passed it. I step forward through the threshold and the dog growls. "Easy, buddy. Easy." I take a step back. "Where's your daddy? Come here, let me pet you." I beckon him and he approaches slowly. I extend my hand toward him to sniff it again, and he buries his head in it. I scratch him behind the ear and the neck, and he waggles his foot and tail.

"Where's Damien, buddy?" The dog pulls away and steps back. I make another attempt to get in, and this time he lets me.

He turns and heads across the room so I follow him. We walk through a great room, then down a long hallway, and the dog stops at the last door. It's half open and from where I'm standing I can only see the light coming from the huge windows and a few clothes thrown on the floor. A man's clothes. Sounds are coming from the other side, and it sounds like moaning. I wait a few more seconds until I'm convinced that what I'm hearing is exactly what I think it is.

Damien's having sex with some woman who's moaning like a fucking porn star. The moans intensify and I feel stupid for worrying about him for the past week while he's been fucking around. I can't explain why this makes me uncomfortable. He's obviously healed.

Just as I'm about to turn around, the dog pushes the door open and I see the bed. But I'm not prepared for *that*.

On the bed is Damien. Naked. One of his wrists and one of his legs are bandaged and his other hand is wrapped around his cock. He doesn't notice me and keeps fisting it up and down faster. The woman's moans grow louder with the movements of his hand.

I stand there with my eyes bugged wide, unable to look away. All I can think about is that I want to ride him like a stallion, and break whatever is left of his body that's not already broken. I squeeze my thighs together to ease the ache this scene is causing me.

The dog is lying in his doggy bed on the floor and playing with a stuffed toy, minding his own business.

My eyes go back to Damien just as his eyes close, his head tilts back and his lips part. It's the sexiest expression I've ever seen. His quiet growl signals his release and his cum spills all over his hand.

I bite my lip with the unfamiliar desire to lick it clean.

His body shakes as his cum continues to spurt, and he squeals like a pitiful puppy dog.

The Doberman lifts his head from the toy to look at Damien, tilts it to the side and yips.

Uncontrollable laughter escapes my mouth and announces my presence. Damien freezes in place, the porn is still moaning in the background. It makes me laugh even more, and he turns his head in my direction. I lean into the doorway when I realize he can't see me and his eyes widen. I drop my bags and the bottles clank together when they hit the floor.

"Did you enjoy the show, baby?" Damien throws a pillow at me, and hits the dog that's between the bed and the door, looking at us in confusion. I'm already rolling on the floor but that sets me off even more. Damien cracks up with me, his laughter mixed with groaning and swearing, but when he cries out, I realize something's wrong.

I get up from the floor, still amused, and approach him. He's lying on his bed, naked, covered in cum, staring right into my eyes without an ounce of shame.

My eyes widen when I notice the huge bruises around his ribs and the many cuts and scratches all over his body. He lies there without moving and keeps his gaze on my face. My eyes bounce to his cock, and the urge to jump on it is still there, but I ignore it.

"What are you doing here, baby? Did you decide to pay your debt?"

All the pity I felt for him evaporates with the appearance of his smug expression. I turn and stalk to the door, stop in front of it, and point at the grocery bags and bottles of booze on the floor. "I brought food and drinks, but since you're feeling so cocky you can get them yourself."

His smile only widens and he makes a puppy dog face. *Shit.*

"You'd leave your poor helpless boss lying naked, hungry, and thirsty, in bed?" His gravelly voice is so sexy, instead of feeling sorry for him, I'm turned on even more.

I bend down the slowest way possible, with my ass facing him and my low-rise sports shorts showing more than they should, and take a bottle of whiskey and a chocolate bar from the bags. Slowly walking toward him, I open them one by one and sit on the edge of the bed near his plastered hand. I pull out a piece of the chocolate from the cellophane and suck on it. Damien bites his lower lip. I slip the piece into my mouth, lick my finger, and moan with pleasure. His eyes are dark with lust as he licks his lips. I lift the bottle of amber liquid and pour some in my open mouth. Swallowing, I look him straight in his predatory eyes. "Yeah."

I get off the bed and he growls. "Yeah what?"

I leave the bottle next to him, but at a distance he can't

reach. "Yeah, I'll leave you naked, hungry, and thirsty if you want to act like an asshole." I start walking away.

"I'm sorry, baby. Will you be a good girl and come back?" His question sends me back to the massage room when he'd made me beg for an orgasm. My inner muscles clench.

I turn around, welcomed by his smoldering gaze, even hungrier than before. I need to kill this sexual tension before I ravage him and give him some more injuries.

I pick up the bags from the floor. "Rob told me to give you this envelope." I pick it up from the ground and hand it to him. "And to feed you before you start drinking. So what do you want to eat?"

"So Rob sent you." The surprise in his voice tells me he wasn't expecting me. That and the masturbation I inadvertently witnessed.

"He said he had something urgent to take care of and left me some money to shop. Too much money. You'll have food and alcohol for the whole week ahead."

"Whatever you can cook, it doesn't matter." I turn to the hallway, but his voice stops me. "And Ivy...can you help me get up?" The plea in his question makes me grin but immediately after my smile disappears. He has to ask because he was hit by a car. Because of me.

"Of course."

I go over to him and hold out a hand, but he shakes his head and points behind me. "I'll need a ride."

I turn in the direction he's pointing and see a wheelchair in the corner. Shit, how did I miss that? "Exactly how injured are you?"

"Don't ask... I'm fucked up everywhere." He points to his left side, where almost every inch of skin is bandaged and his leg is in a brace. "When I jumped I fell to one side and by some miracle I didn't break anything. I ended up with some cuts, a lot of bruising, and a torn muscle in my leg. I also sprained my knee, ankle, and wrist, and dislocated my shoulder and elbow. Because of all that, I can't use crutches for another couple of weeks so I have to use this..." He glares at the wheelchair and instantly my amusement disappears.

"I'm sorry. I'm so sorry, Damien. If it weren't for me, you wouldn't be going through this..."

He tucks a fallen strand of hair behind my ear, grabs my chin and looks at me seriously. "Not a word! You're not guilty of anything. I don't want you blaming yourself!"

"But I..." I start, but he puts a finger to my mouth.

"The last thing I remember about the crash is your face. When I woke up, you were gone, but the doctors told me you saved me." The irony of the situation. He got hit because of me and I saved him. "Now let me hold on to my last bit of dignity and help me get out of this bed."

I put on his boxers but he refuses to wear any other clothes. I help him into the wheelchair and pile the grocery bags on his lap. I push it down the long hallway, through the great room, and straight to the kitchen.

The gray kitchen looks untouched and sterile from the silverware to the alphabetically arranged spices. I bet Stella would fall in love with the island bar. But now that I think about it, she must've already seen it. This girl deserves a medal for choosing to live in our little house that seems like a shack compared to this modern residence. But if I were in her shoes, I'd choose independence, too.

I open the four-door fridge that has a touch screen with a grocery list displayed on it and there's nothing inside. Not a single thing. As if it was brand new from the appliance store. "Damien, where's your food? Did I miss another fridge?"

He shrugs and throws a peanut, from one of the bags I brought, into his mouth. "Alexa, play "Secret" by Maroon 5."

I raise an eyebrow when the song starts playing from the fridge. "Oh, so it sings. Does it 3D print food, too?"

He tilts his chin down, amusement sparkling in his eyes. "My housekeeper usually takes care of the supplies, but I told her to cancel them while she's gone. It's not like I can get up and raid the refrigerator or do some cooking."

"Don't you have a chef or something?" I look around the big freaking house that's nothing short of a mansion while I'm preparing him a ham and cheese sandwich. He shrugs again. "Then how do you eat?" Stupid question. Of course, whoever cares for him feeds him too.

"I order delivery and my security brings it to me. Usually I don't stick around much and I rarely eat at home."

"Doesn't your mom cook for you?"

He laughs, but then gasps and leans forward. "Stop making me laugh or I'll need more painkillers."

I look at him puzzled.

"Melanie and kitchen, two words that aren't compatible in the same sentence. She could hardly bear to take care of her son when he almost died before leaving for the Bahamas." He says it so casually as if it's the most normal thing.

"I get it. My mother did the same, only she left me alone without someone to help me when..." I stop when I realize what I'm saying.

What the hell is wrong with me? Why am I sharing my childhood with him? I'm hiding. I can't afford for him to know too much about me.

"When what?" Damien's staring at me now.

"When I broke my fibula at eleven. Your sandwich is ready, come on. Straight to the whiskey or do you want something else to drink before?" I drop the subject and hand him the plate. He takes a bite and groans. "Are you hurt?" I crouch to the level of his eyes.

He shakes his head with his mouth full and swallows. "Mmm, amazing. I want ten more. I'll leave the whiskey for later."

I laugh and turn around to make him some more sandwiches.

"How could your mother leave you alone at eleven? Mine's an ice queen, but at least when I was little she cared for me."

His question surprises me and I stutter. "She...she had a lot of work to do and wasn't big on caring for sick children or any children."

"Well, I'm not one to judge. Mine left me to go on vacation. At least yours had some justification."

I wouldn't call negligence and self-absorption a justifiable excuse, but he doesn't know that and I can't tell him too much.

"At least you have someone to take care of you. I was alone in the beginning." Until Nonna came.

"What makes you think there's anyone to take care of me?" His tone is curious rather than annoyed.

"Don't you have family and friends for that?"

His expression is indecipherable. I take a bite from my apple and put my hands on the countertop.

"No," he answers simply.

I don't understand. "That's impossible."

He bites his sandwich and pauses until he swallows. "In case you didn't get the memo, my family isn't the most caring. My only real friends are Stella and Rob, but they're both working so much they don't have time to deal with my problems. No one else shows up unless I pay them." The calmness with which he says this is disturbing.

"Don't you have a nurse or something?"

He laughs and sets his plate on the countertop. "You can be my nurse if you want, and as soon as I get better I promise to play doctor and give you an examination."

I roll my eyes. "As tempting as that offer is, I'm going to call you on your bullshit. Stop distracting me." I fold my arms across my chest, and his eyes fall to my breasts before returning to my face.

"No, I don't." The simple answers he gives me are extremely unsatisfactory for a curious person like me.

"How do you handle everything else then?"

"Alone."

"Come on, you can't handle everything alone. You can barely get out of bed."

However, his serious face tells me he's not joking at all. The rage rising in me is directed at his mother and the words she spewed at me at the hospital. If Damien had a family to look after him, he wouldn't be alone right now. Damn that woman. Now I feel guilty for not coming sooner. He needs someone to help him. "What about your housekeeper? When is she coming back?"

"She and the rest of the staff are taking one month off, with three weeks left. I wasn't planning on staying in town this month, but as you can see my plans went south."

"Why don't you hire someone to help you?"

"I don't trust easily." I swear he inherited the stoic face of his mother.

"But I'm here, so...you trust me?"

He raises an eyebrow as he looks up from his sandwich. "I suppose...yes. I trust you."

"Why?"

He shrugs and finishes the third sandwich. "Call it a sixth sense."

Contrary to all logic, his words make sense because I feel the same way about him.

"Then meet your new nurse." I decide there's no point in asking him. Even if he said no, the guilt would eat at me and I'd stay here until I force him to accept anyway.

At first, he looks bewildered, but then a small smile lifts the corners of his mouth. "Why?"

"Because you helped me when I needed work. You gave me my dream job. Now it's my turn to help you. Let's say we're even."

"You don't have anything better to do than watch your invalid-but-oh-so-sexy boss?" He gestures to his body from head to toe, his smile widening even further.

God, his smile almost melts my panties off. And his sculpted body... I know it's wrong to think it, but the bruises give him an edge, making him look even sexier. Combined with his scratched face, his freshly-fucked hairstyle, and his tattoos, he looks like every good girl's dream of a bad boy.

"Not particularly..." I remember that I need to fix my program's firewall and find my stalker before they find me, but I'll make time for him. I'll sleep less and work on it tomorrow night.

Damien's blinking sleepily, fighting to keep his eyes open.

"Do you want me to take you back to your bedroom?" If he wasn't bruised and bandaged and sitting in a wheelchair that question would've had my thoughts going in a completely different direction. *Okay*, maybe they did go there. But I'm sure there isn't a part of his body that doesn't hurt.

"Yes, I won't argue. Those pills are killing me," he says through another yawn.

"What painkillers are you on?" I ask as I push the wheelchair down the hallway. I can't see the rest of the rooms, but so far everything seems to follow the same beige-gray color scheme. The hallway is light beige and various paintings are arranged on the walls.

"Hey, I had one of these"—I bend down to see if I correctly guessed the artist and the signature below confirms it—"in New York."

The moment I say the city I realize what I've done.

What the hell's wrong with me? Why don't I have a filter with this man?

"Mmm." He mumbles and I sigh quietly in relief. Apparently, the pills are working.

I help him back into bed and as soon as his head hits the pillow he's out. I leave him some water, a few bags of munchies, and his pills on the nightstand. That should do it until I come back tomorrow.

Before I leave I turn around and lean against the doorframe. Damien is sleeping peacefully on his back. Although he looks like he's been beaten black and blue, I've never seen such magnificence. His hair and stubble are a little longer, giving him a more casual appearance. Lying serene, without his expensive clothes, minus the perfect hairstyle, he looks like an ordinary man, not a playboy billionaire. It makes him even harder to resist.

The dog moves and startles me. I look at Damien once more and smile. I leave the house and decide to take a long walk home. The whole way home my smile doesn't leave my face.

Oh God, what did I get myself into?

Chapter Eighteen

DAMIEN

I've spent most of the week knocked out by painkillers. When I'm awake, my activities consist of two things: watching TV and eating. Honestly, make that three things since half the time I don't even look at the screen because I'm busy staring at Ivy. It's impossible to concentrate on anything when she's around me.

I lean back on the couch and look out the window where she's playing with Six in the yard. She tosses the ball and he runs after it to catch it. This scene has been playing out for half an hour, and I don't get tired of watching it. Hell, I watch it daily. And every single day I can't take my eyes and smile off her. It's like I'm constantly high when she's around me.

Her ringing laughter carries all the way to the empty house when the big dog almost knocks her down and I can't help the giggle that escapes.

Giggling, Damien. Really?

But Six doesn't leave her alone and jumps up once more, pushing her into the pool. My giggle transforms into laughter mixed with swearing because of the pain from my bruised ribs.

Ivy climbs out the pool, putting one bare calf in front of the other and my jaw drops to the floor. Her hardened nipples are peeking through the white fabric of her tank top that's clinging to her tits and her long hair is shining in the sun, dripping water. The whole scene plays out in front of me like a wet dream in slow motion.

My dick also takes notice.

She runs to the dog, catches him, and knocks him down to smother him...with hugs and kisses. It would've been a very sweet moment if her tits weren't bouncing around, and I wasn't thinking about how nice it would be to bury my face between them.

Six has earned an extra doggy treat for the show he started. *Good boy.*

It's a good thing I'm bandaged up like a mummy; otherwise, there'd be nothing to stop me from throwing her in the pool myself and playing out my fantasies live.

These last few days have been pure torture. I'm sure God is punishing me for something I've done in the past. Most likely more than a couple somethings.

I've never violated my anti-fraternization policy before, but the temptation to touch her is too strong. I try to think of her as just an employee. I really do, all the time, but I'm failing spectacularly. Even during the week I didn't see her after the accident, the harder I tried not to think about her, the harder my erection became. And my erection hurts more than a blow to the gut. Finally, by the end of the first week, the pain subsided somewhat and I decided to release some tension. Never in a million years did I imagine she would walk into my house at that exact moment and catch me watching porn and jacking off to fantasies of her dancing. The possibility of her offering to stay and take care of me was even more unbelievable.

If it had been anyone else, I would've sent them away. I'm used to being by myself. At first, I told myself it would be a healthy change for me. I rarely spend time with women unless sex is involved. They tend to bore me quickly.

But now my plan is sinking like the Titanic, and when she enters the room, soaked to the bone wearing a wide smile and a twinkle in her eyes, I know I'm going down with the ship.

"Your dog ambushed me." She laughs, pointing to Six, who's looking all innocent, sitting quietly and wagging his tail.

"You get a double dinner, boy," I say to him, and he happily jumps up and comes over for me to pet him.

Ivy rolls her eyes, crosses the room, and squeezes her wet hair over me. The water is ice-cold, but the only thing I feel is my erection growing with her nipples this close to my face.

She must've noticed because she pulls away, her cheeks turning rosy. "Can I borrow something to wear? I doubt you want me dripping all over your floor."

Ahh, Ivy...naïve Ivy. She shouldn't say things like that when I can't do anything about it. *Right now, more than anything, I want you to drip everywhere, not just on my floor.*

The moment of silence and my heated stare may have betrayed my thoughts because she blushes, fidgeting and bouncing in place. Or, maybe she's thinking the same thing.

"Of course. Take whatever you need, my dresser and closet are at your disposal."

I watch her run upstairs, her denim shorts clinging to her perfect ass.

"Wow," comes from the second floor, followed by "this thing is huge" and I laugh. She apparently found my master bedroom.

A few minutes later she appears wearing a T-shirt that hangs almost to her knees. A primitive and unfamiliar sense of ownership overtakes me when I see her wearing my clothes. I've never been the jealous or possessive type. I like no-strings-attached hookups, I don't do relationships. Now I'm even more confused by my feelings.

"I didn't know you're into football. You don't look like the sports type."

"What do you mean?" I frown.

"Well...you just look more like the business type. You know...the one that's working twenty-four seven and doesn't have time to watch TV."

"I'm sitting and watching the game right now." It's a complete lie. I'm not even keeping up with the score because I'm too busy watching her.

"That's different. You don't have a choice while you're recovering. And even now you're still talking on the phone and trying to work from home."

"It's because work waits for nothing and no one. But there are many sides of me you don't know yet."

She leans on her elbows on the back of the couch and our faces come so close I can feel her breath on my cheek. "Show me."

For a few moments we just keep our eyes fixed on each other until Six stands up on the couch beside her and shoves between us. Sometimes I feel like this dog knows exactly what to do at any given moment. I can't afford any more slipups as much as I want her. I'll have to keep my dick in my pants and act like a grown-up, make better decisions. No, not better. Smarter.

"Well, I wasn't always like this. After a certain age the parties get boring, I'm way more excited to see my businesses thriving now."

"What about the club?"

"The club's...something I do on my own. My family built

the hotel business that I run, but I wanted to have something I created. Something different that has my character in it." I lean toward her and whisper, "Can I tell you a secret? But you have to promise not to tell anyone." She nods, a smile spreading on her face. "I'm a sucker for chocolate soya milk."

She gasps, raising her hand to her chest. "I'm scandalized." She can't help but snicker and she whispers back, her lips only inches from mine. "I wouldn't dare tell anyone."

Six yawns beside us, then jumps off the couch and rolls over onto his back, sticking out his tongue, waiting for someone to rub his belly.

I roll my eyes as Ivy immediately sits down on the floor to pet him. "You spoil him too much."

"There's no such thing." She laughs, and the big dog stirs at her feet, happy to receive attention. "I was surprised you have a dog with all the traveling that you do. Don't you miss him?"

"He came as a guest to one of my parties. Some asshole brought him to brag about his new pure-bred acquisition, but the dog bit him and he kicked it. I threw his fucking ass out and kept the dog. No one will hurt animals under my roof. Besides, if you think Six is cute now, you should've seen him when he was just a little ball of fur." I chuckle at the memory and a huge sweet smile appears on Ivy's face. "I miss him and whenever I can, I take him with me, but I know he's in good hands here."

She stares at the dog with huge hearts in her eyes, as if she sees him as a puppy dog. For a moment I feel envious because she isn't looking at me that way.

Seriously, Damien? Hearts?

I'll settle for the lust in her eyes when she gets too close to me.

"Wanna eat?" She changes the subject abruptly and heads for the kitchen.

"You know you don't have to cook. We can order something."

"I don't mind cooking. We've been eating takeout and sandwiches the last few days," she shouts from the kitchen.

Half an hour later, the divine aroma of rosemary spreads through the air and my stomach rumbles. I can't wait to see what she'll tempt me with this time.

In the distance, I hear the crash of breaking glass and a few curses. "Oh, ouch. Shit."

"Ivy, is everything all right?" I yell and see Six taking off through the open door, followed shortly by the barefoot brunette wearing my T-shirt. The dog's running in the yard, he keeps evading her, sneaking right under her nose every time she almost catches him. Ivy's shouting angrily, holding something in her hand.

The fuck? Is that a shoe?

She throws it at him. Six lets go of whatever he had in his mouth and rushes off in the direction of the shoe.

"*No*. Let go of it, Six!" she calls out as the dog bites it and carries it all over the yard. In her other hand, she's holding something resembling a chewed package.

A burnt smell invades the air, and I look toward the kitchen, only to see a billowing cloud of smoke above the stove. *Shit*, something is burning.

"*Ivy!*" She doesn't hear my shouting. I fucking hate how helpless I am right now. "*Ivy!*"

She turns in my direction. Her eyes widen when she sees the smoke coming out the window and she rushes back over.

"Shit. Shit. Damn it." Her words echo and mix with the sound of the fire alarm.

My hands and feet are itching to get up and help, but it's

impossible. I can barely go to the bathroom at night, and it takes me at least fifteen minutes. "Ivy, should I call security?"

"No, no. Everything's under control." After a few more minutes and many words that sound like cursing in a foreign language, the smoke clears and the alarm stops. Ivy walks into the room and flings herself on the couch. She looks devastated. Her frowning face is so cute I can't help but snicker.

"What? Do I have something on me? Why are you smiling like that?" She looks down at herself. My laughter is apparently contagious and before long she's cracking up too.

I've been laughing more this week than I did all last year. It's so easy to be around Ivy without having to keep a mask in place all the time. Just being my goofy self.

"What happened?"

"Your dog stole the meat I was planning to cook and broke a glass on the way out the door."

"And you decided to chase him with your shoe?"

"Don't judge me. That's all I had." She shoots me a glare. "We have no food now and you have one less pan."

"Did you manage to start a fire? I heard a lot of yelling."

"It was close but I caught it in time." She sighs and leans her head back.

"What language was that?"

I can see her posture stiffening and her breathing stop. "Greek."

"Are you Greek? I thought you were from New York." I take a closer look at her. Greeks are really beautiful women, but her features look more Slavic. I don't know how I didn't notice it until now.

She still hasn't moved and I feel like she's holding her breath. "Yes, I have relatives in the Balkans, but I've always lived in the States."

I want to know everything about this woman, and now that I think about it, I know next to nothing. "Interesting. Why did you move?"

"Because my parents got a job offer. What's with the questions? I'm here to help you, not tell you my story." The way she says it and moves to the edge of the couch I can tell I'm making her uncomfortable.

"I want to know more about you. You already know a lot about me."

"Not true. I know the same things you know about me. What food you eat, what movies you watch, and how you like to have sex. I have no desire to relive my past. To me, that's exactly what it is. In the past." Behind the coldness in her tone, and though she tries to hide it, I see the pain. Whatever her life was before, it clearly hurts her to think or talk about it. I don't want to bring back those memories no matter how curious I am.

I change the subject. "What do you want me to order?"

"Whatever you feel like eating. I lost my appetite." Her voice is cold and distant.

I order pizza and ice cream because that's what they do in romantic comedies when the girl is miserable. It's not like I have a lot of experience to help me in this area. And apparently, they know what they're talking about because it works. We eat in silence, leaning against both ends of the couch, pretending to be watching TV when we are both actually lost in our thoughts. Then we move to the guest room I sleep in and for the first time ever, Six doesn't come to me on the bed but instead lies at Ivy's feet. She indulges him and snuggles into him.

At the beginning of the week, she kept her distance and didn't cross the invisible line separating us, but in the last two days Ivy has started approaching me little by little. Since she's sacrificing all her free time caring for me and receives nothing in return, it's selfish of me to dig where it hurts. So far, I've never seen her so down and the fact that I made her feel that way is killing me. All I want to do is pull her into my arms and hug the shit out of her until she's happy again.

"Ivy, come here." I pat the mattress. She looks at me questioningly and keeps petting the dog without moving. "I don't like that frown. You know I can't get up and drag you over here." No, I'm definitely not above using my injuries if it will put a smile back on her face.

Jesus, I'm even more pathetic than I thought.

At first, she looks shocked, and rightly so. She knows I want to fuck her. It's obvious since I'm rock hard all fucking day when she's around. But I've never done anything to show her that I like her.

Or do I?

Another thing I've never done is cuddling. I'm not the type to cuddle even after sex. But these days that's the first thing on my mind when I see her. *Okay*, maybe the second.

I see her contemplating for a moment, but eventually she jumps up, steps over Six and comes to me. She gently moves into my embrace without pressing any of my injured places. Unlike the half-hugs we shared a couple of times, I pull her into me and squeeze her despite my pain. She melts into my arms and I feel her smiling against my neck.

Shit. I'm so fucked.

Holding her, I finally feel like I'm home and I fall asleep, only to wake up later that night and find she's no longer beside me, again.

Chapter Nineteen

DAMIEN

Over the last few days the pain has been more tolerable so I'm not taking as many painkillers, resulting in much less sleep. Ivy is still taking care of me and despite my newly acquired addiction to having her wrapped in my arms, neither of us has taken it any further.

She's still distant, but during the late evenings that we spend by the beach or in my bedroom, she's opening up to me. With every word that leaves her mouth, I suspect she's much smarter than she lets on. There's probably even more I don't know about her past than I thought, but given how quickly she shut down after our last conversation, I decide not to dig any deeper.

I'm sitting up and watching her across the room as she gets ready for a rehearsal at the club. Every time I see her reflection in the mirror it takes me back to that first night at the hotel bar.

She's without any makeup, in white yoga pants that outline her perfect ass and make my cock stand at attention yet again. The matching sports bra is slightly lower than usual and her tits are on display, not helping my situation at all. She's putting her hair up in a ponytail, and the only thoughts going through my head are how I want to pull on it as I take her from behind. *Shit*. If I keep going like this, I'll go crazy or explode. Someone needs to give me a medal for keeping myself under control in spite of all the agony I endure.

I know it would be easier on me if I just let her go and continue living by myself. It would be more painful physically without anyone to help me get around, but at least I wouldn't have a painful erection twenty-four seven and have to take matters into my own hands every night. Last night, after she left I almost broke a finger clutching the tiles of the shower as I was jacking off to fantasies of her. Even more embarrassing, it only took me three minutes to blow my load all over the bathroom floor like a teenager. My ribs hurt like a bitch when I move too much but relieving the pressure is not only nice but necessary.

I don't know if I should be glad or upset that Ivy is so good at deflecting my hints for her to stay and sleep in my bed. Though I must admit that if she's in my arms when I wake up from yet another wet dream, I can't promise I'll be able to stop myself from ravaging her. And though my mind is all for that, it would hurt a lot.

She places her hands on her hips and turns to me. "Do I look okay?"

I look at her from top to bottom and say the obvious. "Better than okay."

Her cheeks flush and her eyes narrow. "Come on, don't tease me. I'm asking for real." She takes a half-bounce step and sits next to me on the couch.

"I'm serious." I look into her chocolate eyes and catch her chin with my fingers. "You're beautiful." The compliment makes her blush even more. She jumps up like the couch is on fire and runs to the kitchen to make our afternoon meal. I'm so used to our daily routines by now that it'll be hard to get back to reality. Which is getting closer and closer.

Three weeks have passed since the accident and my injuries are almost healed. I'm using the crutches every now and then, but I still need the wheelchair for longer distances. A few more days and I'll be able to start working toward resuming my normal activities.

Normal activities that don't include Ivy.

This thought makes me frown every time I think of it.

I can't say I'm a workaholic, but I love my job and I spend a lot of time doing it. When I'm not at work, I'm constantly on the move. I don't think I've ever been in one place as much as I have been lately. And I never thought I'd enjoy a simple laid-back lifestyle without all the partying I'm used to. Or maybe what I really like about this situation is experiencing it with the beauty making me another sandwich in the kitchen right now.

As much as I try to imagine going back to my normal daily life without her, I can't. Knowing that as soon as I start walking or when my housekeeper returns she may decide to leave me makes me crazy. I can't keep her here against her will, so all I can do is just hope she feels the same way and decides to stay a little longer.

I don't even know when I became so pathetic. *Damien Black relies on hope.* No one would believe me if I told them.

I've never had to pursue a woman, they've always come after me, but when it comes to Ivy, I feel like I'm in uncharted territory. Even if she decides to leave, I'll find a way to bring her back to my house. Without her, it would be empty.

"There you go." She hands me the sandwich. "I don't

have time to eat with you 'cause I'll be late," she says as she puts hers in a paper bag.

"Put mine in there too. We'll eat on the way."

"You're coming with me?"

"Yes, Rob wants me to see the new show you've been rehearsing so much." Also when he stopped by to drop off some papers, he mentioned there was something important he wanted me to see at the club.

Her face brightens at the mention of the word *show*. I don't know if I've ever seen anyone as happy to go to work as Ivy. Every day I'm more convinced I made the right choice when I took the risk of hiring her.

"But you want me to ride with you?" Her surprise is strange. Despite her protests, three days ago I finally managed to persuade her to use my driver when she needs to go somewhere. I don't want her to spend hours walking around the city alone no matter how much she says she likes it. What if something happened to her when I could've protected her?

"Yes? What did you think, that we'd go separately?"

"No, it's just...won't it be strange for the new girl to show up with her boss? People might get the wrong idea."

Well, I didn't think about that. But Robert knows, anyway, he's the one who sent her, the British bastard. "If someone gives you shit you tell me, I'll take care of it."

She giggles. "*I'll take care of it*," she repeats in a mocking deep voice trying to imitate mine. "You sound like a mobster. What are you going to do, make them swim with the sharks?" She continues laughing while putting her shoes on. I remain silent and she looks up at me with one eyebrow raised.

"I don't think it'll get that far, but if I need to, I know the right people."

She laughs, probably thinking I'm kidding. I'm not.

"Come on, Al Capone. Jump in the wheelchair and let's go 'cause I'm late."

The fucking wheelchair.

After these weeks of helplessness, I feel like an ant. It'll take me a while to get my man card back in this woman's eyes if I decide to break my rule. Oh, who am I kidding? I've already broken it in my mind a couple thousand times. When the time comes, I'll have to start in the bedroom. There's no mistaking who's the boss there.

Once again I'm sitting in the club mesmerized by their show. Not that my other dancers aren't good; on the contrary, they're brilliant, but my personal dancer shines above them. Whenever there's a routine hole or mismatch, she immediately fixes the problem.

I noticed another quality in her. Besides being a unique dancer, she's also a good leader. She manages to coordinate the girls with ease and they instinctively listen to her.

"Okay, let's take ten and then move on to the next part," Tasha shouts.

When we're at Masquerade Ivy acts as if she doesn't know me and barely speaks to me. Most of the time, she's with the other girls or at the bar where she talks with one of the bartenders, fucking John, too much. I don't like the way he looks at her while she's dancing. And the fucker doesn't stop there, when she leaves the stage and goes to the bar, his eyes follow her, glued to her tits. Every time she turns her back to him, his eyes land on her ass. I swear I can hear what he's thinking. And if I wasn't so fucking helpless in this fucking wheelchair, I would've already knocked his fucking teeth out.

I turn to the table and pretend to read the documents while eavesdropping on their conversation.

"Hey, Ivy. You were amazing on stage."

His pathetic compliment won't work.

"Thank you."

From the corner of my eye, I see Ivy blush. *Shit.*

"I'm glad you listened to my advice and chose to be happy."

What advice is this fucker talking about? I can make her happy, she doesn't need this little punk.

Damien, listen to your pathetic ass. You sound like a jealous boyfriend. You're neither jealous nor her boyfriend, my inner voice speaks, but I quickly muffle it.

I'm not her boyfriend, but Ivy is mine. I don't care how selfish it sounds. I know the sounds she makes when she comes, and I know how she likes to eat her pizza, while wearing my T-shirt.

Mine.

"Actually...you're right, I'm happy." She smiles at him. I'm openly gaping at them right now, and I don't feel any shame about it. "I really am happy."

"You sure look like it. You're glowing."

Oh, please.

Ivy blushes even more, the way she does when I compliment her, and for the first time ever, I think she might like someone else. I don't know why the hell I ever thought she liked me, now that I think about it. Maybe because I occupy so much of her time and there's none left for anyone else.

John pushes a shot glass to her and she picks it up.

"To happiness."

Ivy clinks her glass with his and looks at me before drinking it.

How big of an asshole would I be if I go there and tell them there's a no drinking on the job policy starting right now?

Yeah, I guess I'd hit the top of the jerk-o-meter.

"I'll expect your gratitude in a drinkable form." Rob startles me when he appears and sits down in the chair across from me. "And something more expensive than the bottle you gave me for sending Ivy over to you."

I couldn't hear what they were saying, but now Ivy is laughing and showing John a new bruise on her body. Squeezing the glass so hard I wouldn't be surprised if it breaks, I drink the whiskey in one gulp and slam the glass on the table. "I don't know what you're talking about."

"What? Don't tell me the interaction between the two of them doesn't bother you." I want to punch the smug smile off his face. "I told you there was something important you should see and now you have." He points with his glass toward the bar where Tasha has joined the party.

There's no point in denying it, Rob can see it in my scowl. "How long has this been going on?"

"From the first moment Ivy walked into the club."

"Motherfucker," I hiss.

Robert snickers while pouring some whiskey into my empty glass. "I figured you'd want to know since you two are playing house. You don't strike me as the sharing type."

"I'm not playing anything. I'm her boss and her friend. Ivy's free to do whatever she wants." I growl. The fucking truth hurts.

"Whatever you say, don't kill the messenger." He raises his hands in the air with a shit-eating grin. "I'm just saying, if I wanted a woman like her...I'd stop at nothing."

"And what makes you think she's not just another one of them?"

"Please. I think you forget who you're talking to. I connected the dots a long time ago. She's the mythical woman who turned you down...several times, to be precise. Why do you think I sent her your way to keep you from dying hungry, thirsty, and pissed in that bed? I was sure if anyone could deal with Damien Black's stubbornness, it'd be her. And I was right. Again."

I know the fucker's right.

The laughter of the girl we're talking about reaches us across the bar and Rob and I turn to see John lifting her by the waist and carrying her around the room.

I'm so fucking glad I can't get up right now; otherwise, the fucker would be in a hospital. Or a cemetery.

Ivy's laughter stops abruptly when her eyes lock with mine and John follows her gaze. His happy smile turns upside down and he drops her to the floor. But he clearly didn't get what my glare was about because his eyes are still on Ivy's ass as she walks to the stage.

"Don't kill the bartender, we need him. Besides, you can't blame him. If you weren't like a brother to me and I wasn't engaged, I would've tried to tap that. You'd be a fool to let a woman like her slip through your fingertips."

Rob's comment makes me squeeze my glass even harder. "You're right. I'll make it clear to you, *and* fucking John, and to any other miserable fucker who decides to give it a try. Ivy is mine!"

Rob's Cheshire cat grin tells me he got exactly what he wanted. "This is the Damien Black I know." He raises his glass and we both sip. "About fucking time. I was worried that fucking accident messed up your brain."

I knew the fucker had a plan.

The problem is, Ivy is as stubborn as a mule. I have to be careful with this one. Then again, I've never had any problems charming a woman before. I'll need a surefire approach and a foolproof plan to convince her she's mine. Unfortunately for me, the *I want you so I'll keep you* argument won't work with her. If there's one thing I've learned about her in our time together, it's that she's built up an emotional wall to protect herself, but secretly she wants to give in to someone.

Ivy knows what passion is...hell, she's passion personified, but she hides from it because she's afraid of getting burned. If only she knew she's the flare that could set everything ablaze. All she needs is a little spark. And luckily for both of us, a striving Damien Black is a whole damn fire.

Nothing and no one can stop me when I want something. I'll charm my way into her head, her body, and ultimately her heart so that when I'm done with this fucking wheelchair there'll be no question who she belongs to.

Chapter Twenty

IVY

Damien is quiet on the way home. Usually, I can't shut him up. He always has something to say and it's rarely empty words. Every day I learn something new from him. And with each lesson, I'm convinced there's much more behind the gorgeous façade.

A question came to me earlier and has been bothering me ever since.

"Why Masquerade?" My voice breaks the silence.

Damien raises an eyebrow. "Isn't it obvious?"

"Yeah, I can guess where the name comes from, but what made you decide everyone should wear masks? Was it spontaneous or was there intention behind it? And why in an old movie theater?"

His smile is halfhearted but his tense face softens. "The building is old, but beautiful, it deserves a better fate than to be deserted. I wanted to create a place where people like me, people who always have to wear a mask in society, can let go. It's ironic when you think about it. You put on a mask so you can be your real self."

I purse my lips, thinking how true his words are. The only reason I can be myself on that stage is the mask.

"Anyway...that is why the club's exclusive. I want my clients to feel safe without worrying that someone will recognize them or sell their photo to a gossip rag or post it on social media. It's not unheard of to see celebrities or even the most prudish people shaking it on the dance floor and flirting. It's the ambiance, the never-before-seen shows, the themes, the whole experience we provide. We don't advertise. It's strictly word on the street. Everyone's heard rumors about the club, but they can't see who goes in and out because we have a lot of different entrances and exits around the building, according to the client's status and needs. The waiting list is at least a year ahead, and we only opened seven months ago."

I can hear the pride in his voice but he doesn't sound arrogant. On the contrary, it makes me feel proud to be part of his success, even if it's only a small part.

"That's actually really smart. I've only seen two entrances. I had no idea there were others."

"That's why they're secret, baby." He winks at me.

When we get to his house, I go take a shower and put on one of his T-shirts. I wonder how long it'll take him to figure out I "forget" to take spare clothes every day because I like to wear his. Damien's woodsy scent on them is an addiction I can't get enough of.

I lean against the bathroom door and look at the bed where Damien fell asleep in my absence. Even when I'm here, he refuses to wear any clothes except boxers. I don't know if he's doing it on purpose, but it drives me crazy. I feed him carbs all the time, and yet the difference in his abs is barely noticeable.

The bruises and cuts from the accident are healed, and my pity has been replaced with desire. Every time I see the tattoos on his muscles, that million-dollar smile or his burning emerald eyes, I want to devour him like a triple-chocolate cake.

I don't know what the hell is going on with me. I've never reacted this way to any man. But with Damien, I've been losing control of my body and my thoughts since day one. With each passing day, it gets worse, and at this point, I'm sure that if he says jump, that's exactly what I'll do.

What's making me even crazier is that every time I'm near him, I can feel his erection, but he never makes a move. I know about his rule, and yet I'm dying for him to break it, even though a potential relationship with my boss could get too complicated.

This bubble we're living in makes me forget all my other problems but that doesn't mean they're gone. I'm still a wanted criminal in Europe and as of three days ago, I'm wanted by Interpol as well. And I still haven't found out who tried to hack my laptop. After that first try, there have been more but I've upgraded the firewall, and they can't get past level one now.

I sit quietly on the ground next to Six and open my laptop. I've been filling my time with improving my project over the past two weeks I've spent here. In Bulgaria they say hope is the last to die and mine isn't dead yet. I hope one day all of this will be behind me, and I'll be able to sell my project. Then I'll have enough to live on for a lifetime, and I'll be free to pursue my dream of becoming a professional dancer or even open my own dance studio.

The next moment I look at the clock—it's been three hours. I didn't even realize when it got dark outside. I stretch and look over the top of the laptop where I find two green eyes staring at me.

"Hey." Damien's raspy voice sends a new wave of excitement through me, and I try to push it down but fail.

"Hey." I leave my laptop and stand up to stretch. "When did you wake up? Why didn't you say anything?"

"You were so focused. I didn't want to bother you. What were you doing?"

"Just a little programming." The words are out of my mouth before I can stop them. *Why do I keep doing that?* I've already slipped up more than I can afford, but this is my biggest overshare so far.

Damien's forehead creases and his brows draw together. "Programming?"

"Uhh...yeah."

"Care to elaborate? I thought you were a dancer?" His tone is serious, and he seems almost offended.

"Can't a girl be smart as well as athletic?"

"Don't get me wrong. I know you're smart but..."

"Actually, my IQ is one hundred forty-five, but judging by the stupid decisions I make in life, you can't tell." I shrug and toss myself onto the bed beside him. And, of course, the bed sinks from my weight, jostles his body, and he grimaces with pain. "Sorry. You see what I'm talking about?"

Damien looks like he doesn't give two shits about the bed shaking and raises his hands in the air. "How do you have a hundred and forty-five IQ? You're a genius!" His statement doesn't sound rude, critical, or skeptical unlike everyone else I've ever told. On the contrary, he sounds proud.

I feed him what little crumbs I can. "I don't like people calling me that. They usually expect me to come up with the cure for cancer or a new space station, when what I love to do is dance. My parents made me take an IQ test as a kid and after they discovered my aptitude for it they forced me to learn programming, and dancing became my hobby instead."

"Wow. I've never met a person with such opposite interests."

"It depends on how you look at it. I'm an artistic person. When you think about it, programming can be art if you do it with passion. It's just art with numbers. Isn't dancing full of numbers too? Steps, rhythm, beats, timing. In the end, everything comes down to math."

Damien is looking at me in a new way I've never seen before, and I can't decide whether it's good or bad. Did I say too much? Some men don't like women to be smart. I even had boyfriends that felt threatened by the results of a test if I scored higher than they did, and I had to play dumb.

"What?" I ask as his smile widens.

"I just... You're just so smart..."

And, here we go...

"It's sexy."

I stare at him. "Well, that's the first time I've heard that."

He frowns. "What do you mean?"

"Most men feel threatened when a woman has a brain and it functions properly. At least the ones I've been with."

His face relaxes. "Because most men are weak. You can reach the top of the pyramid only with the help of a smart woman. And if the man is smart enough he won't hide the woman in the shadows." He looks into my eyes and brushes a strand of hair from my face. "He'll make her his queen."

I shudder when his fingertip brushes my cheek. I don't want to delve further; it's taking my feelings to the danger zone.

"You sound like you're talking from experience. But you're already on top, so who is the woman?"

"My mother. Everything I've learned about business came from her. If you're a bystander, you won't see under her façade of a royal-class bitch, but in reality she's one of the most brilliant businesswomen I know. When she married Hyland, she was poor, and the bastard never let her forget it. That's why she hides beneath all the layers money can buy. To the world, she's his little wife and he's the great businessman. But the truth is that throughout his rule, my mother was the woman behind the man, in the shadows. When he refused to listen to her, we almost went bankrupt, and we only got back on our feet because of her strategic planning. Thank God, I was old enough to take control of the company, but unfortunately not mature enough to rule. I was the face, and she was the brain. Without Hyland, Melanie flourished, and we became one of the strongest competitors in the hotel and resort industry." The way he talks about his mother with such adoration and respect makes me teary. That is not the first impression the woman left me with, but now I'm sort of understanding why she was so cold. Anyone would become hardened if they were treated as if they were worthless for so many years.

I think about my own mother. Melanie might seem like a cold bitch, but at least she's standing behind her child. Mine left me.

"I didn't mean to make you sad." Damien kisses my forehead and wipes away the single tear I was unable to hold back.

"No, you didn't. What your mother did was inspiring. Better yet, she raised a son like you. She must be very proud. My mother didn't waste a second of her time nurturing. Unless you count punishing me when I did something she didn't like. Which included every time I danced. She hates art. She's only interested in herself and her work. But I guess I have to thank her for that too, she made me strong. If it wasn't for her, I wouldn't have been able to handle everything on my own."

"What about your father?"

"He's the most indifferent person I know. I'm not even sure he knows he has a daughter. I rarely saw him. He spent most of his time in his office and every once in a while he took my mother on trips. All in all, those were his only two activities. My nonna raised me. She's everything to me."

"Remind me to thank her, because without you, I would be dead. Remember, my mother may be a good businesswoman, but she's also selfish. I guess with the way her life went, she can't help it. But what kind of mother abandons her son when he's bedridden to go on vacation?"

I raise my hand. "Mine did it several times."

Contrary to all logic, we both burst out laughing. We have more in common than I thought.

I lean on his shoulder, and he pulls me to him. We put on some rom-com '90s TV show and watch it, each of us lost in our own thoughts. The silence between us isn't awkward or deafening. It's calming.

When the show is over, I look at my watch and jump out of the bed. "I have to go. Tomorrow we'll be rehearsing the routine again, and I have to go to the club earlier. Then I'll stay longer to practice my solo, so I'll be here by late afternoon."

A line appears between his brows. "You spend a lot of time at the club lately."

"The other girls have been there for months, I have to catch up to them. I haven't danced in the last year and I'm out of shape."

"Baby, you're in better shape than every single one of them."

I narrow my eyes at him. "No, I'm not. I have to train more and I can't put it off anymore."

"Will John be there?"

Hmm? Where is this conversation heading? "I suppose. Why?"

"Aren't you a little too friendly with him?" I don't like his tone at all.

"Sorry, what?" This is absurd. John is just a friend to me. I wouldn't even call him that because we only see each other at the club.

"I've noticed his interest in you," Damien says through gritted teeth.

"Is that why he stayed away from me after you talked to him today?"

What is he thinking?

He looks at me dead serious. "Let's just say he won't bother you anymore."

"Damien, he isn't bothering me..."

"Ivy," he interrupts me and puts a finger on my lips, "I've gotten used to having you around me. I can't let you go for too long." His words touch the feelings I've buried deep and nourish them. "The small building next to the pool is a rehearsal studio. You can use it instead of the one at the club. That way you'll be closer to me."

I try not to let his last sentence touch my feelings and instead focus on the first one. "Why on earth do you have a rehearsal studio on your property?"

"For my sister."

I look at him, puzzled. Apparently, I missed something.

"Haven't you googled me yet?" This time he's surprised.

"No? Do I need to?" Frankly, with everything that's been going on, I hadn't even thought of it.

"God, you are..." He bites his fist and smiles.

Maybe I really should've checked him out before I practically moved into his house.

"Uh, sorry...I guess." Warmth is creeping up my cheeks.

He laughs and squeezes them between his palms. "My sister's a singer. She moved to LA, trying to break into the business on her own. But when she was growing up, mother didn't approve of her career path and my father...let's just say it was better not to be in the house around him. That's why I had the studio built, so she could rehearse here. There's a stage and everything."

"Really? And you've been hiding it from me for two weeks?" I shriek and punch him on the shoulder, which only hurts my knuckles.

"What can I tell you...I wanted you all to myself." He winks at me with a playful smile.

And *bang*...a direct blow to my heart.

Chapter Twenty-One

IVY

I arrange the bouquet of colorful tulips the housekeeper brought me in a crystal vase on the table, and smile. A home should always have fresh flowers. It gives it cheerfulness and a refreshing aroma.

When I started taking care of Damien I noticed he had dozens of green plants, but the flower vases in every room were empty. It didn't bother me at first, but the more time I spent here, the more I noticed it wasn't just the fresh flowers missing. The whole house lacked the little things, you know —like the aroma of food and spices, a fireplace that actually has firewood, photographs, the sound of laughter from the people who live there. Such little things, small and basic, that make a house a home.

I look around and I'm pleased to see some positive changes. The sterile kitchen isn't so neat anymore, the empty refrigerator is full to the brim. All over the house, there are Polaroid photos of me, Six and Damien. In the great room, on the previously pristine couch, there are two messy blankets and many fluffy pillows he ordered after I complained one afternoon about how uncomfortable his decorative leather pillows were.

Seriously, who buys pillows as hard as stone?

I suppose a person who doesn't eat a single meal at home or stick around for more than a few days.

But with every day that passes, this house is becoming more of a real home. I think it's even growing on Damien. Maybe when he gets better and back to his hectic daily routine, he'll stay here more often.

My inner voice adds a silent *with me*. But fortunately, I still have some common sense telling me that a man like him would hardly throw away his fun lifestyle to watch movies on the couch with me.

Who am I kidding? I knew he was a playboy from Stella and the girls at the club, but I didn't even know what we were talking about until I googled him after he reminded me.

Countless pictures of him, each with a different woman on his arm. Each article described his lavish lifestyle, overflowing with details about the most elite parties, the most expensive vacations, and the most beautiful actresses, models, and socialites who shine more than the diamonds around their necks. Some of them gifted by the billionaire himself. After the tenth article, I stopped reading.

I admit, when we met I was quick to judge Damien because he seemed like the best fit for the arrogant player type. Or maybe it was because I was hurt too many times before and I didn't want to look behind the mask. But here in our little bubble, he's the other side of his public image. He's kind and caring. We fool around like children during the day and cuddle in front of the fireplace in the evening as he rubs my legs while I scratch his back.

If it wasn't for our stoic restraint one might mistake us for a couple.

Earth to Ivy. What do you expect, for Damien to barricade himself at home with you and avoid the cameras?

I can't give him anything more than what we have right now. I couldn't accompany him to an event or walk around the streets on his arm. I'm the girl who lives in the shadows. The match is impossible.

As much as I try to push down my emotions, I can't and my heart cracks in places. I have to pull myself together before it's too late. But I don't know if I'm fooling myself and it's too late already.

Damien is in with the doctor to see about his progress and to hopefully get the go-ahead to remove the brace. It's been a whole month since the accident. As the day approaches when he'll no longer need me, my heart sinks a little bit more. However, I try to enjoy every moment while I still have him.

I rise from the couch to stretch a little and turn up the music so I can no longer hear my thoughts. Six hides out in the bedroom because the music's too loud for him, and I'm completely alone. I stretch from side to side, do a handstand against the wall for a few minutes and keep stretching.

With the hit of each beat, my thoughts leave one by one and ideas for new steps and new combinations fill their place. When I have a whole new routine in my head, I get up and start dancing.

Step, two, turn, leg high, step, six, seven, eight. I submerge myself into the dance.

Something touches my shoulder and I jump with a scream. Behind me stands an unfamiliar platinum-blonde woman, staring at me with a hand on her hip and an indignant expression on her face. She bends over to turn off the music and folds her arms under her generous breasts.

"And you are?" She beats me to the question I should've asked her.

"I'm Ivy. Who are you and what are you doing here?"

"Where's Damien?"

I don't like her bitchy attitude or the fact that she's ignoring my questions. "Damien's at the doctor. You need to introduce yourself before I give you any more answers." If she wants to be a bitch, two can play that game.

Concern appears in her eyes and only now do I notice they're the same color as Damien's. Her features aren't as sharp as his, but they remind me a little of his mother.

"Oh Gosh! He never goes to the doctor. Is he all right?" She looks genuinely worried, and I'm convinced I've figured out who she is.

"You're Rosalie, aren't you? Damien's sister?"

"Yes, and who are you?"

"I'm Ivy, his...friend."

"Yeah, I bet." She snorts out. "Friend? Damien doesn't have any female *friends*."

"So I've heard..." I roll my eyes at the reminder. I guess the apple doesn't fall far from the tree. "I'm taking care of him until he's back on his feet." Obviously, he didn't share that little detail with her. *Way to feel special.*

"Why?"

"Because of the accident."

Her eyes widen. "Accident? What accident?"

I ask her if she would like to sit down while I explain, and I join her on the couch and tell her the whole story.

In the end, she tears up. "How could no one have told me? I spoke to him and my mother several times on the phone, and they didn't mention anything."

It takes her a few minutes to calm down and during that time, I'm able to get a better look at her. I don't know how I didn't see it first, but she's stunning. Even with her tears and her makeup running, she still looks like she just stepped off a movie set. Her body is thin, almost too thin, but given that she lives in LA she's probably on some gluten-free, meat-free, sugar-free, carbs-free diet consisting of ice, water, and air.

"Excuse my attitude earlier. I thought you were one of his bimbos, and what can I say...old habits die hard. You'll understand if you've met my mother."

I nod. "Oh, I've met her and I do understand."

"I'm not usually like that. It was very rude of me."

"Don't worry. I'm starting to get used to this behavior around your family." I laugh nervously. I hope I didn't offend her, but she laughs with me and leans back.

"I guess so, if you've endured Damien for an entire month."

"Three weeks, but yes...it was difficult at first." I think of the first week when Damien thought he could be an asshole and boss me around. I had to set him straight and threatened to leave him alone to enjoy his own company. Not that that worried him very much, since that's all he knows, but he saw I was serious and he didn't want me to leave so he made an effort.

"Tell me about it. You didn't have to grow up with him. Although, he's the most normal person in our whole family. I owe him a debt I can never repay for making sure I didn't end up like mother. Or worse, like father." She laughs but it doesn't come from her heart, and she brushes her blonde hair away from her eyes. I'm just about to ask her how he helped her when she screams, "Damie!" She leaps off the couch and runs on her six-inch gold heels past the pool and straight to the yard where Damien's slowly approaching on his crutches. I giggle at the shock on his face when he sees who is running toward him, but my giggles turn into hysterical laughter when I see him blush with embarrassment. Finally, something to shame the shameless Mr. Black. Apparently, the recipe's one lie to his baby sister. Who would've guessed?

She throws herself into his arms, and his eyes meet mine through the glass window. I'm genuinely happy for him now that he's getting back to his old self. It doesn't suit a man like him to be tied to a wheelchair. He's cut out to lead and instill respect.

Goose bumps pop up all over me when I think about the way he took control of me when we were hot and naked together. That is most definitely his role.

But the chills quickly leave me when I hear the slap of Rosalie's hand across Damien's cheek. I fist pump the air and yell *"Yes!"* They both turn in my direction. Damien squints but an amused smile tugs at the corners of his lips.

Rosalie is watching him, then me, and back to him, with an unreadable face. She points her finger at him. "That is what you get for not telling me you got hit by a car."

They spend hours talking and catching up, so I decide to give them space and move to the bedroom. I haven't slept much the last few days and decide there's no harm in closing my eyes just for a second.

DAMIEN

In spite of my efforts, I can't resist hugging Ivy when I see her on the bed in that sweet pose she fell asleep in. I join her and pull her to me, but of course, she feels me and wakes up. *Shit*. I was hoping she was too tired, and I could have her all to myself for a few more hours.

I'm glad my sister came home, but the only person I wanted to be with, to share the joy of being able to walk again, was Ivy. And she didn't stay around us even for a minute.

"What's happening? Where am I?" She sits up, blinks a few times, and looks out the window. "It's dark outside. How long have I been sleeping?" She rummages through the covers.

"What are you looking for?"

"My phone. What time is it?" She finds it and texts someone. When they respond she growls and slams her head against the headboard.

"What's wrong?"

"Nothing, nothing." She slides under the covers, lies back and stares at the ceiling.

I'm no specialist in women, but *even I* know when a woman answers *nothing* to this question, there's always *something*.

"Just a few more minutes and I'll get up and go," she says before I can ask again.

The disappointment strikes again, right in my heart. But then I remind myself I'm a man and it's time I start acting like it.

"You don't have to go. You're exhausted. Why don't you stay here?"

She seems visibly surprised by my suggestion, which is very strange considering the million times I've hinted for her to stay. Apparently, she didn't understand or I'm not that good at hints. "No, no, I can't. Anyway, I got some sleep so I'll be good to go to get through the night."

"You're not working today. Why won't you sleep? Don't tell me you're rehearsing again." The girl doesn't know how to rest. Every moment she's away from me, she's either glued to her laptop or in the rehearsal studio.

"No, Stella and Max are in that love phase where they

can't get enough of each other, and if I'm not working, I have to stay in the backyard and work on the laptop until they're finally done with the fucking and I can fall asleep without hearing them. Thin walls—you know how it is."

When I hear that I can't help but be frustrated, about two things. First, I'm angry at Stella for depriving Ivy of her sleep. Second, I'm angry at myself because I didn't know things between Stella and that guy she started dating a few weeks ago, Max, had reached that point already. I don't even have a background check on him yet.

But what I didn't expect to feel is jealousy. I'm jealous because I want to be in that phase with the girl beside me and never leave it.

Fuck. What's wrong with me? I don't recognize myself. Damien Black never asks for anything; he just takes it. And now I'm acting like a coward. It's time to get back to business and grab what I want with both hands, starting with the beautiful woman lying next to me.

She gets out of bed and I jump up and walk (*okay, more like hop on one foot*) to the other side to catch up with her. My leg still hurts, and the doctor told me to walk with the crutches for a few more days to keep it immobilized a little longer, but, God, how nice it feels to be on my own two feet. I'll never take it for granted again.

I grab her wrists in my hands and look into her warm eyes. "Ivy, why would you think I'd let you stay in the fucking yard in the middle of the night when you could be under my warm covers getting some much-needed sleep?"

The girl is too proud to ask or even accept. I have to make her understand that when it comes to her well-being, I won't ask her. I'll just do whatever it takes to keep her safe. Like she did for me.

She turns her head and pulls her hands away from mine.

"I don't want to take advantage of you, Damien. You must be sick of me already. I'm here all the time."

"Not nearly enough time if you ask me," I murmur. "I'm not asking, Ivy. You need quality sleep if you want to keep working as hard as you do and still be able to take care of me." I confess, this is a cheap trick to see if she'll tell me I'm capable of handling myself from now on, but she doesn't fall for it. She just sits on the edge of the bed and sighs. "What are you doing?" I ask as she removes her blouse. She stands and takes her jeans off, leaving only a red lace bra and matching panties. I have to remind myself (*several times*) I should be a gentleman and refrain from throwing myself at her like a hungry lion. Not until I'm at my full strength at least. I want to be able to take her the way she deserves.

"I'm changing for bed. What does it look like? You don't think I should sleep in these uncomfortable clothes, do you?" she says with a yawn while putting on one of my T-shirts. "Which side do you prefer?"

"Not here. We'll sleep in my bedroom, not in this guest room."

"What's wrong with this room? You've been here for a month now."

Oh, my sweet naïve Ivy. I want the first time she falls asleep in my arms to be in my own bed.

"Yes, a very long recovery period that's ending now. From now on I'm free to sleep where I want, and I want to sleep in my bed. Come on, you'll enjoy it more."

I grab the crutches that are propped up against the wall because so much tension from day one can't be good. She picks up her bag and walks barefoot, wearing just my T-shirt. I'll admit, climbing the stairs is more challenging than I expected, but with a little more time and effort, I manage it.

We finally enter my dark gray bedroom and before I can even close the door, Ivy jumps on the bed.

"Oh my! It's like I'm lying on a cloud," she says drowsily and runs her hand over the cream silk sheets.

"I told you you'd like it." I leave the crutches next to the armchair.

"I don't like it. I'm in love." She slips under the duvet. "So which side?" she asks through a yawn.

"I don't care."

"Come on! Everyone has a side."

I scratch behind my ear. "Okay. The right I guess."

"But that's my side." She pouts and shifts to the left.

I push her back to the edge of the right side and lay beside her, leaving the left space empty. I wrap my arms around her body. "Then I guess we'll both take it."

She puts her palms on my chest, and thrusts her nose into my neck. I feel her breathing and find it soothing. "I won't protest." Her words are heavy and when I look at her, she's already closed her eyes and drifted away.

"Good night, baby." I kiss her forehead and she whispers one last *good night*.

In the morning, when I wake up before her, holding her warm sleeping body in my arms and listening to her steady breathing, I realize two things.

1. I have never slept before this night. At least not fully.

2. I don't know if I'll ever be able to sleep without her again.

Ivy doesn't even know what she did last night. Now I'm addicted.

Chapter Twenty-Two

DAMIEN

For the past few days, I've been the happiest and most tortured person.

Max and Stella haven't left her bed in forever, which helped me convince Ivy to stay at my house all these nights. That's the good part.

The bad is every time I wake up, she's already up and practicing. During the day she has rehearsals at the club, works on her computer, or she's helping my sister with the choreography for her next music video. I'm spending my days in the office, now that I'm finally good for something, and it turns out, there's a lot more work than I expected. We're both spending so much time working that we only see each other at night when we go to sleep, drained.

I realized something the other day when I managed to get out of the office before the show at Masquerade ended. The second I stepped foot in my club, the usual one night stands surrounded my table. They each expressed their regret over my accident, but none of them were beside me when I was at my worst.

No, the girl that was beside me didn't feel sorry for me.

She told me to get my shit together and stayed without asking for anything in return. How many times have I fallen asleep in her arms, sedated by painkillers? How many times have I been just inches from her face and longed to kiss her? But I didn't. I followed my stupid rule.

I'll break every fucking rule for this woman if it means I'll get to lie beside her at night, fuck her, hug her, and call her mine. Hell, I want Ivy to know I'm hers. I want to hear it from her juicy lips and bury myself between them.

I open the front door and the aroma of freshly baked bread invades my nostrils. Six runs to me and I bend down to pet him. "Hey, buddy, are you happy to see me?" I scratch him behind the ear and he licks my face. The moment I let him go, he runs in the opposite direction, his large clumsy paws sliding on the floor, toward the kitchen where I find the cook I hired shortly after Ivy nearly lit up the kitchen. Again. "Hi, Eduardo. Where are the girls?"

He turns to me with teary eyes and shrugs. "I haven't seen them all afternoon, sir." Then he continues chopping onions on the wooden cutting board.

I check both the bedroom and the great room and find no one. I go to the rehearsal studio and I hear music from inside before I even open the door. I should've known. Where else would the two most stubborn and hardworking women I know be?

"And one, two, three, four...five, six, seven, eight," Ivy repeats, she and Rosalie in perfect sync with their steps in front of the large mirrors.

I grin and sit in one of the chairs by the empty stage. I was sure they'd like each other. All I had to do was throw the dance and music theme on the table, and they instantly hit it off. Since then, they've been inseparable in their spare time, which only proves I'm once again right.

Ivy notices me, misses her step, and stumbles. I instinctively jump out of the chair to rush to her, ignoring the pain in my leg, but she manages to recover before falling.

Rose points at me and grabs Ivy's hand to draw her away from me. "Don't even think about it! Ivy has to show me a few more steps before you kidnap her from me."

"Okay, okay." I raise my hands, back off and go sit on the chair again. "But you have limited time, Eduardo's almost got dinner ready. And I'm staying." I lean back and fold my arms across my chest.

Rose props her hands on her hips and rolls her eyes. "Great. Now you'll distract her."

Ivy waves in the air. "Hey, you forget I'm here?" *As if I could forget.* She turns her back to me. "Nothing can distract me when I dance."

It's good to know you're special...

"I'll show you, and then we'll do it together." She nods to Rose and starts, "Five, six, seven, eight..."

From here on, the only things I see are the curves of her perfect body, underneath the tight blue leggings and the small sports bra. My eyes follow every movement of her ass, my dick standing at attention. As if the one-month sentence I've already endured wasn't enough.

The pain of having a constant boner when your whole body is black and blue and your ribs are bruised is equal to someone jabbing your lungs with a thousand knives while kicking you in the balls. I couldn't even think about sex without hurting.

The more I look at Ivy, the crazier she drives me. A woman straight off the *Sports Illustrated* swimsuit calendar. Dark brown waist-length hair, playful chocolate eyes, perfect heart-shaped face, lush breasts, sculpted body, round ass, and legs for days. She's training like an Olympian and she's naturally beautiful. Most women would need at least three plastic surgeons to get anywhere near her level of perfection.

Her instantly falling asleep as soon as her head hits the pillow is the only thing that has kept me from fucking her these last few nights. I want her awake and aware the next time I'm with her.

At dinner, my sister starts the conversation pointing her fork at Ivy. "How is it that my brother hasn't made you a choreographer yet?"

Ivy clears her throat, sipping water, and stares at her plate without saying anything.

"Not that it's any of your business, but she already choreographs a lot of the performances," I deadpan.

Ivy raises her head from her plate and looks at me.

"Ah, so she's working both jobs and getting paid for one. Is that right, Damien?" Rosalie's doing this on purpose to fuck with me, but she doesn't realize she's making Ivy uncomfortable. "I've never pegged you for a cheapskate, brother." She laughs and stuffs a bite in her mouth.

Ivy lets out a chuckle and quickly swallows it with her next bite. I roll my eyes and sigh heavily. Rosalie loves to embarrass me in front of other people.

"Ivy knows it isn't like that. I'd make her a choreographer in a second, if that's what she wants." I look at her, but I can't read anything in her expressionless gaze.

"Thanks to both of you for the compliment, but I don't want to change my position. I'm not a choreographer—end of discussion. Let's talk about something else." She leaves her napkin on the table and takes a few sips of wine, trying to avoid eye contact the whole time.

"Brother, I can't believe you've been walking again for days and you're not out celebrating at a party yet." Rose taunts me again. What's with her? She isn't usually such a bitch. I managed to control that behavior as soon as she stopped living with my mother and moved in with me before leaving to pursue her dream.

"I don't feel like partying. Life-threatening experiences tend to do that to you. Makes you appreciate the more meaningful things..." I steal a glance at Ivy.

Even before the accident, I was starting to get fed up with that lifestyle. At thirty I've had enough pussy and parties for five lives. I knew I needed a change, I just didn't realize what I was looking for before I met her. I never knew any other life.

"Forgive me for having a hard time believing that the man known for his attendance at Playboy mansion parties when he was barely legal and his appearance on the red carpet with the whole damn calendar of cover girls on his arm has suddenly become a homebody."

Both Ivy and I freeze. None of us has ever discussed my previous scandalous behavior.

"I think I forgot my phone in the bedroom." She jumps out of her chair and quickly disappears. I know her well enough to know that was a lie. Ivy's rarely on her phone.

"What's up your ass? Why are you being such a bitch?" I growl at Rose and she narrows her eyes.

"Me? What's wrong with you?" She hisses and drops her fork on the plate.

"What are you talking about?"

She whisper-yells, "Who, you genius! Ivy. Can't you see the poor girl's head over heels for you? Don't you have a little bit of compassion, dammit. Stop toying with her."

"I'm not playing with her Rosalie. I like her too." Even more than I want to admit.

"Then what're you doing, Damie? The girl gave you one month of her life, running after your invalid ass and you're playing house with her, without actually being with her. I'm telling you this as a woman, brother. I see how much you're confusing her, and if you don't pull your shit together, you'll sink and she won't be here to save you again."

Before I can answer, Ivy comes around the corner. My sister and I wipe our frowns and put on a smile.

"Excuse me, where were we?" Ivy sits and sips her wine. She's visibly brighter and it makes me wonder if Rose is right.

"I was just telling my brother I need to go shopping with his black Amex tomorrow. Ain't that right, Damie?" She kicks me under the table.

Sisters, what can I say...you can't strangle them; you just have to love them.

IVY

My mood's been a little off all night and after dinner I excuse myself to the bedroom. I can't shake the feeling I friend-zoned myself in this situation with Damien. I thought we had something more. *Damn it*, I like him so much it's freaking me out. It's not just lust anymore... I want his mind, his touch, every single part of him.

I go straight to the closet which is bigger than my bedroom at home. I remove my blouse and my shorts and take out one of his T-shirts. I bury my nose in it and smell the divine aroma of vanilla, mint, and cedarwood, something that's become like a little ritual to me. I just can't get enough of his scent, and now more than ever, I feel like I have to take every opportunity while I'm still here. Who knows when he'll decide he's had enough of the simple life and leave me for something more fun?

I'm unfastening my bra when Damien comes in, startling me. The bra falls to the floor, leaving me on display, my back to the large mirrored doors of the closet. I grab the T-shirt to cover myself, but before I can, he reaches me and pulls it out of my hands.

He lowers his head and his lips touch mine, desperately searching for contact. His tongue slides into my mouth, as if he can't wait a minute more. His arms wrap around my naked body, tracing every curve. He pushes me back a few steps until my back presses against the cold mirror. He lifts his head for just a second, long enough for some sense to return to my head.

"Damien, are you sure—" My sense is gone again, replaced by shock when he grips my lace panties and tears them right off my body with a single pull.

"I've been waiting for this moment for a month." He grabs me by the waist and spins me around, pressing my cheek to the mirror. His fingers trace the curve of my spine starting from the bottom, sliding up my neck, and wrapping around my throat.

"Do you see that, Ivy? Me and you, the vibrations of our bodies..." He pulls me back and rests his chin on my head, one of his hands squeezing my wrists behind my back, the other gripping my throat. "Answer me. Do you see how hot we are, body to body, excited and ready for each other?" Eyes dark as a rainforest, he watches my every breath, every lift of my naked breasts in the mirror.

"Yes," I mewl, the tension in my stomach growing with his every word. The view in the mirror is so sexy I want to freeze it and keep it as a picture so I can look at it every day, every minute.

His hand releases my wrists and traces the shape of my breasts. He encircles my nipple and pinches it lightly, sending vibrations to my clit. I moan, my ass lifting, seeking more contact with his body and rubbing against his hard cock.

"Do you feel how you're making me crazy? Do you have any idea what you're doing to every man when you look at them with those big eyes? You don't even notice how they look at you"—he moves to the other nipple and strokes it—"how they want you"—his hand slides agonizingly slow down my stomach—"but, my sweet Ivy, they can't have you. Only me. You're mine." His finger slides over my clit and my body trembles at the long-awaited touch. With two strokes I'm ready to blow.

My hands are still behind my back so I find his belt and unbuckle it. I take his dick out of his briefs and stroke it with the same speed he's moving his fingers through my arousal. He slaps my pussy and slides his middle finger into me while his thumb works my clit. My whole body stiffens, my orgasm on the edge. He squeezes my throat a little more, causing the flow of oxygen to my brain to decrease and my sensations to increase. Tingles creep up my spine, and all the energy from the accumulated tension is released with my cry. My muscles tighten and my clit pulses under his fingers.

"Open your eyes. I want you to see how perfect we are together," he orders in my ear, and I comply.

His hand releases my throat and slides down to catch my nipple and send the last waves of my release through my body. Lips glued to my neck, he bites, causing my body to sink into his.

"Come here." He pulls me into the room and pushes me onto the bed. Pulling down his jeans and briefs, he climbs on top of me like a hungry lion ready to devour its prey. He tears the condom package with his teeth, and I roll it over his erection. Without any warning, he grabs my hips in his hands, pushes them up and buries himself inside me.

"Oh God," I call out, my spine curving back.

"My name is Damien Black, baby, but you can call me God if you want."

He starts moving in me with steady thrusts, increasing with each passing second. We're wrapped around each other like vines, my nails digging into his back, his teeth into my neck, and we fuck like two wild animals. The feeling is too strong...the friction of our bodies, the tension in the air, the sparks every time we kiss...

His fingers slide down my ass, carrying my moisture, and one of them presses on the sacred place where no man has ever been. Shocked, I bounce back, but he kisses me until I go dumb.

"If you don't like it, just tell me," he whispers in my ear.

His finger moves, pushing more and more. The feeling is unfamiliar and strange but it excites me until I forget it's there at all. A second orgasm floods through me, and a loud cry tears out of my lips. Damien fucks into me faster and rougher until finally he stiffens at the deepest point. An animal roar comes out of his mouth, one hand clutching the pillow next to me and the other my thigh, so strong it'll be bruised. But I don't care. His rough touch, biting, and squeezing just make the sex even hotter. I'm fine with being all black and blue if it means feeling this strong man falling apart in my arms every time.

He relaxes and he rolls over next to me. Wrapping around me with both hands and both legs, he pulls me so close I can feel every beat of his fast-paced heart.

He kisses my cheek and whispers in my ear with that low, hoarse voice. "I told you, baby. Together we're explosive."

Chapter Twenty-Three

IVY

The next afternoon Damien reluctantly gets out of bed to go to the office, so Rosalie and I drag Stella out of our house to go to the mall.

"Check out this dress." Rosalie shrieks and all the heads in the store turn our way.

As if there weren't already enough gawkers.

Rosalie might not be that big of a name yet, but she's a big deal in her hometown. She's had at least a dozen fans ask for a picture or an autograph, and everyone else is staring and gossiping. Of course, I'm always hiding in some corner with my ball cap and sunglasses on, avoiding cameras like the plague. I don't know how she does it. It's kind of scary, everybody being in your business like that and recording every step you take. At least until Hulk's little brother, or as Rosalie calls him, her security, glares at them and they scatter.

"Oh, this one is for tomorrow." She gives a gold glittery cocktail dress to the assistant who's been trailing along behind us, taking every item Rosalie chooses to the dressing room. Which is nearly the whole damn store. I don't know why she bothers at this point, they should just close the store and let Rosalie use it as a dressing room.

"Damien called to invite me just before you guys came. Do you know what the theme will be?" Stella looks at the ungodly price tag on a blouse and quickly returns it. Neither of us can afford these clothes, but Stella can make similar ones if we like something. That's how I've got a closet full of designer-looking clothes without the labels and I've got no shame about it.

"Invite you to what?"

She looks at me like *I'm* confusing *her*. "To the party, duh."

"What party?"

Rosalie hands another couple of dresses to the assistant. "Didn't he tell you? He's throwing a coming back party tomorrow at the house. If the bastard lied to me I won't return his card for a month!"

"I thought he wasn't in party mode anymore?" I'm confused even more. "That's what he said yesterday, didn't he?"

"Classic Damien. Don't mind him when he says stuff like that. He always goes back to the rock-star life. It's second nature."

I'm not bothered by that. I used to be a regular at parties in my previous life too. Not the way he is, but I never missed a good one. "He didn't tell me, but we didn't speak a lot before he went out." My skin is still hot in that place where he woke me up with his tongue.

Rosalie squeals. "Aww, look at her blushing!"

"Somebody's in looovee." Stella singsongs.

"Come on." I chuckle with them. "I'm not in love."

"Oh, please. Your eyes turn into hearts every time we mention his name." Rosalie draws a heart with her fingers in the air but another piece of clothing quickly catches her attention. "Ivy, you have to try this! It's so perfect for you." She shoves a black dress into my hands and pushes me to the nearest dressing room.

Well, it wouldn't hurt or cost me anything to try it at least. I remove my clothes and stop at the reflection in the mirror. I have two massive hickeys on my left boob and one on the right, complemented by a path of red, almost purple lovebites all the way down to my belly button. I hadn't noticed them because I was busy staring at Damien when we were getting dressed. I love that he's marking me and now I want to do it to him too.

I put the dress on and the feel of the expensive satin on my skin takes me back to the days I had a closet full of these kind of clothes. I would never trade what I found in Rosehill for my old life.

Stella peeks through the curtains "Dio Mio, you'll blow his mind!"

You can never go wrong with a little black dress. This one is short, tight-fitting, with big gold hoops at the top of the spaghetti straps. It shows my cleavage and one of the hickeys is peeking out. The back is open and this might sound a bit narcissistic, but I look like a freaking sex bomb. I even have the best shoes to pair it with.

I look at the price tag and my fantasies fade out. "I could sell a kidney and I'm still not sure if I could afford it."

"Nonsense, girl, do you see this?" Rosalie waves Damien's black card in the air. "This is called payback. You deserve it for all the time you've put up with his annoying ass. Besides, if he finds out I didn't make you buy it, he'll never forgive me."

"No, I can't take it."

"Ivy, just take the dress. Trust me. I know Damien, he'll send someone to buy it for you if you don't," Stella says.

Rosalie fishes her phone out and before I can turn around, she snaps a picture of me. "There. Now I have a picture to show him if you don't take it."

I sigh. "I don't want to take advantage of whatever this relationship is." I take it off and put it on the hanger. She grabs it and hands it to the assistant.

"Well, I don't have a problem with that. It's family money after all. I'm taking it." I open my mouth to protest, but she raises her hand and stops me. "I don't want to hear it. You can thank me when you see the hearts in his eyes as soon as he sees you."

Damn that stubborn siblings' resemblance.

I don't try anything on in the next three stores because I don't want Rosalie to like anything else and make me feel any more obligated. But she tucks a ton of clothes in Stella's hands and despite her protests, buys her everything.

"Ivy, help me explain to her that I'm a designer and my wardrobe is full. I don't need any more clothes."

I give her a smug smile and raise my hands. *It's not cool to be in my place now, is it?* She rams her middle finger into my face, earning a disapproving look from the elderly lady at the checkout counter.

"How did you two manage to find each other, both so stubborn? The man's giving you an endless bank account, and you don't want to take advantage of it at least a little bit. There's no such thing as too many clothes. I don't get you." Rosalie shakes her head and raises her hands in defeat.

My belly rumbles and Stella nods. "I'm starving too. Let's go eat. There's a very nice restaurant on the top floor."

"Okay, but after Agent Provocateur, please. I promise it'll

be the last store." Rosalie makes a sad puppy dog face and pulls us both through the store's doors.

Unlike in the other stores, Hulk's brother doesn't follow us into this one and stays out front with all the shopping bags.

As much as I want to control myself, when it comes to lingerie, I always fail. I end up in the dressing room with over twenty hangers.

I'm trying on the last set when Stella and Rosalie peek through the door. "Gosh! You *must* let me buy this! Damien will go nuts. And those, the black ones. They'll go with the party dress. Pretty, pretty, please, he'll take my card for real this time," she's bouncing on her toes like that's really a possibility.

"Rosalie! Is that you?" A female voice with a Valley girl accent comes from the hallway. Stella and Rosalie freeze, look at each other and turn around. "I knew my eyes weren't lying. I can't believe it. How long has it been?"

"Since you almost stabbed my brother." Rosalie answers with a sugarcoated voice.

What the hell?

I put on a robe and go out. Rosalie and Stella stand with their arms crossed, eyes throwing daggers at the half-naked woman before them. She's in a hot pink bra, thong, and garters, strutting our way with more confidence than a supermodel on a catwalk. She's as tall as one, blonde hair, and sharp cheekbones. She also has the skinny body to fit the stereotype. But there's something in those bright eyes of hers...

"Hello to you too, Olivia," Stella hisses. I've never heard her use this tone before.

"Stella. I see you're still hanging on Blacks' mercy." Olivia looks down at her acrylic nails, dismissively.

Stella starts to take a step toward her but Rosalie grabs

her hand. "Not worth it," she whispers to Stella and turns to the other woman. "I see they let you out of the loony bin." Rosalie raises an eyebrow. Something flashes in the girl's eyes. "How was your stay?"

"It was a resort for emotionally confused people." Olivia hisses at her but immediately changes her tone. An evil bitch smile lights up her face. "It was super relaxing, if you must know. You should try it sometime. God knows you need it with that family of yours."

"Call it whatever you want. It doesn't change the fact you're bat-shit crazy," Stella bites out.

"I'm not crazy!" Olivia snaps, making her look every bit the crazy person. She regains her composure fast though and continues. "Damien doesn't know how to respect and love women. Don't worry, I'm not interested in him anymore." Her gaze is fixed on me when she says it.

"My brother needs a real woman to love and don't worry, he found her."

Olivia's face falls. She sizes me up and her lips curve back into a sinister smile. "I highly doubt that." She returns her eyes to Rosalie. "Anyway, it was nice seeing you. Toodles," she chirps as if this conversation never happened and disappears into one of the dressing rooms.

"I wouldn't call it that," Stella mutters, all three of us entering our rooms without saying anything more.

After we order at the Moroccan restaurant, heavy silence weighs on the table.

I decide to be the first to break it. "Seriously? Nobody? Who the hell was that and why did she try to stab Damien?"

"That's Olivia. She was slightly obsessed with him." Stella shrugs and Rosalie's eyebrows shoot up.

"Slightly? She's nuts. I mean, an absolute crazy, certified lunatic. Our parents are business partners and family friends.

We grew up together, but she wasn't like that as a kid. She's been in love with him for as long as I can remember, constantly chasing after him, but we all thought it was just a childhood crush. Until my brother decided to play dumb and sleep with her. Seriously, who sleeps with their stalker? Anyway, as you might guess, he didn't want to be exclusive. She misunderstood the situation with that crazy brain of hers, and when Damien passed on to the next girl, Olivia broke down and showed her true self." Rosalie stuffs some delicious-smelling bread into her mouth.

Stella picks up where Rosalie left off. "I was with him at the party when it happened. She'd been pursuing him for months, and he refused to speak to her. Then she finally made it to one of his friends' parties, cornered him, and after failing to climb him, literally, she started screaming he tried to rape her. She pulled out a pocket knife and tried to stab him, *in self-defense*. I was the only one who saw what really happened because I was looking for him and stumbled upon the scene, but the people only heard her screams and immediately ran to save her. One of them recorded the whole thing. Damien twisted her arm to get the knife out of her hands, but in the video it looked like he was attacking her."

My jaw drops so low the appetizer almost falls out of my mouth. I knew I felt something was off with her, but I didn't expect to hear *that*.

Rosalie swallows some wine and continues. "Her father knew about her "crush" and knew the whole thing was staged but didn't care about her condition. Instead, he sent her away, to *a resort for the emotionally disturbed* or, to put it another way, a paradise for the mentally ill who have enough money to drink green teas at five-star resorts and get high on legal drugs. I haven't seen her since. I didn't know she came back home. It was more convenient for him to keep her away, where she wouldn't cause trouble because he was always obsessed with taking over our company. When the idiot who shot the video uploaded it to YouTube, it broke out all over the other media outlets as well. The board wanted to remove Damien because he was the face of the company, and my entire family along with him, but thank goodness my mother managed to save the situation. Since then, Damien's been banned from any public displays that could harm his image or the company's. Not that this stops him from partying or sleeping around. He just does it more discreetly." She rolls her eyes and pops an olive into her mouth.

I don't know what to say, so I pick up my glass, staring through the ocean-view windows of the restaurant.

"Oh Gosh. Sometimes I talk without thinking, Ivy. I'm sorry." She fiddles with the corners of her napkin, looking down at her plate.

I shrug it off. "It's not like I don't know he's a player." As much as I hate to admit it, I have to keep my emotions in check if I don't want to get hurt. And this scenario is getting more real by the second. "The question is how long it'll take him before he gets tired of playing with me."

"Don't say that. He's different with you. Yes, he's no angel and sure the sins of his past are many, but who's sinless? We didn't grow up in a loving house and don't know what a real home is, so we're constantly chasing a high to escape our past. Traveling to other countries, alcohol, parties and sex. I found music and it saved me somewhat. But Damien never found his escape. He's always searching for something more. I was surprised when I got home and saw him so calm and grounded. He doesn't even want to leave the house because you're there. I think he finally found his thing and it's you. Give him more credit."

The server arrives with our dishes and more wine, so she goes silent.

"And you found out all of this in the however many days you've been here? Four? Five?" Stella shoots her a skeptical look.

"That's not important, Stells. I found out the first day I arrived. He couldn't stop talking about her and with such adoration, I've never heard him speak about anyone like that, even you. And you know you're his favorite."

Stella almost spits her food, snorting out a laugh.

"And you know *that* look. The one when you look at your beloved and your heart swells. You don't know you're looking at him that way, he doesn't either because he sees you through the same rose-colored glasses but everyone around you does. That's the way Damien looks at you. At first, I couldn't believe my eyes. But I always knew destiny had a woman that would put him in his place. And you, dear, look at him the same way." Rosalie cuts the meat on her plate and takes a bite. For a few minutes, we all fall silent and eat. I do more digging into my plate than eating.

Is she right? I haven't noticed Damien looking at me differently. Yes, he has certainly become more thoughtful around me, but that's because I took care of him. From gratitude.

And what about me? I don't want to delve deeper into my feelings, because then I'll have to face them and it scares the shit out of me. I've already let my lust for him become a liking. That's more than I can afford right now.

But deep inside I know it's not that simple, and I'm already too far down the rabbit hole.

We leave the mall shortly before it closes and we drop off Stella. Rosalie and I return to Damien's and she goes straight to bed, so I take a shower and lie down, watching some TV.

Damien isn't home, and I shoot him a message to ask when he'll be back, but he doesn't answer. The TV show draws me in and I close my eyes.

I wake up in the middle of the night and he still isn't here. I look at my phone, the clock showing 3:37 a.m. and there's no missed calls nor messages.

Where is he and why the hell isn't he answering? What if something bad happened? Or he's with a girl?

A bad feeling is brewing in my stomach. What if Rosalie was wrong? She might've confused his passion for love.

I curl up in a ball in the king-size empty bed, taking the silk sheets with me. Every bad thought goes through my mind until I tire my brain out and fall asleep again.

Chapter Twenty-Four

IVY

In the morning when I open my eyes, I feel a hot body tightly wrapped around me. I stir and Damien squeezes me tighter.

"What are you doing?" I try to turn around to face him.

He drops his hand and barely mutters, "Sleep."

The stench of alcohol catches up with me, and I jump to my feet. He scarcely opens one eye, then the other and sits up. "What are you doing?" He echoes my question and pulls me back. *Damn those muscles of his.* "Come back to me, please."

His plea mixed with his raspy sleepy voice does things to me I don't want to happen. Like the fool I am, I comply and lie next to him. He traps me with both hands and both legs wrapped around mine, tighter than before. There's definitely no moving.

"Where were you?"

Too late, he's already asleep again.

I lie there with my eyes closed for a few more minutes as I contemplate waking him and making a big scene, but I remember Rosalie's words. *Give him more credit.* Perhaps I'm overthinking. I'll let him sleep and then I'll ask for an explanation. He has to give me one if he wants me sleeping in his bed when he doesn't even bother coming home.

A few hours later, we're both awakened by a loud noise coming from downstairs.

Damien's erection is rubbing on my butt, and while I'm dying with desire, I can't let him distract me with his voodoo bedroom magic and make me dick-struck.

I jump off the bed, dress as quickly as possible, and run downstairs to see what happened. I stumble upon a dozen people running around, taking things in and out of the house. My best guess is this is the preparation for the party I'm not invited to.

A short guy in a work uniform comes my way. "Mrs. Black, we're sorry if we woke you. I dropped..."

"Miss Thanos. Not Mrs. Black," I correct him, but he's not looking my way anymore.

I feel a presence behind my back and turn to see Damien.

"It's okay, Garry. Keep working."

Garry nods and goes to the pool to help the others.

"What is this?" I decide to play dumb since he didn't invite me and he didn't come home. It's only fair.

"I'm having a party."

Nothing more.

Not an invitation or an explanation for last night.

"I see. Well, in that case, I'll grab my stuff, so it won't be in your way."

He scratches his head, smoothing his messy bedroom hair. "Okay?"

I run upstairs, tears welling in my eyes, and rush into the bedroom.

Damien doesn't follow me.

I pull out my bag and push every single item inside. I didn't even realize how many things I had in his house.

Proud that I didn't cry, I head downstairs. In the yard, Damien is talking to one of the maintenance men, and his eyes widen when he sees me walking toward the exit.

"Ivy, what are you doing?" he says softly behind my back.

I'm aware we have an audience, and I don't want to make a public scene.

"I'm taking my stuff," I reply quietly.

He catches up with me. "Where are you taking it?"

"Home."

He stops short and grabs my arm before I take the next step. "Why?"

"So it won't be in the way. I told you that a moment ago. Why are you making me repeat myself?"

"I thought you meant the shit from the common rooms. No one will enter our bedroom."

A warmth spreads through my chest when I hear "*our*" from his lips. It dissolves some of my anger, but I cling to the rest. "I'm going home. I'm not invited to your party, and I won't leave my *shit* here without me."

I try to tear myself away from his hand, but he squeezes me even harder.

"What are you talking about? I don't understand." He seems genuinely confused, and I'm wondering if I've read the party thing wrong. But even so, that doesn't explain his disappearance last night.

"You didn't invite me to your party. You didn't even tell me about it. I found out from your sister. The same way you didn't tell me where you were last night when you left me alone all night, worried and upset because I didn't know where you were or if you were even alive!" I say a little too loud and a few curious heads turn to us. I give them a cold stare and they quickly return to work.

"Can we move somewhere with no audience?" He nods with his head toward the rehearsal studio because it's the only place without people right now. As we enter, he nails me to the wall with an angry look. "What are you talking about, Ivy? You're always here. Why would I invite you to come, when I don't want to let you go?"

He melts a little more of my heart, but I quickly recover. He still hasn't answered the most important part of the question. "Where were you last night?"

He frowns and rubs his thumb and forefinger over his eyebrows. "It doesn't matter where I've been. I don't have to explain myself."

I can't believe his asshole attitude. "And I *have* to wait at your house, right?"

"Can't you just take my word and move on?"

"Move on? *Move. On*," I yell like a crazy person. Maybe I really am crazy if I'm still standing here listening to his bullshit. I throw my duffel bag on the floor and push at his chest. "Didn't you consider what I'd think when you refused to answer me and disappeared without warning? You expect me sleep calmly without knowing if you're with another woman or dead in a fucking ditch? Which planet do you live on? Don't you know me at least a little bit?"

He's standing like a statue, his eyes never leaving mine, different emotions passing through them. The anger is replaced by confusion and then realization. His arms shoot up, circling my waist before I can pull myself back. "Ivy, I'll never go to another woman when I know you're in my bed."

One hand rises and brushes a strand of hair from my face. "It's actually the first time someone's worried about me. I didn't even consider you wouldn't sleep because of this. I've never had to explain to anyone where I was or whether I'd come home, and no one ever asked me to, not even Melanie. I guess no one's been worried about me as much as you. I'm sorry I made you feel that way."

At that moment, I see what Rosalie is talking about.

Damien's looking at me with *that* look. I soften in his arms and rest my head on his chest, hearing his heartbeat calming down. "Don't do that again. Promise me you won't."

"I promise." He kisses my forehead and hugs me tightly.

"Will you tell me where you were?"

"I was at the office."

I pull out of his touch and fold my arms. "You're lying again? What, you got drunk at the office?"

He slams into one of the chairs in front of the stage and rubs his temple. "Damn stubborn woman. Nothing escapes you, does it?" I grin and shrug. He sighs and raises his hands. "I was at the office late when I got a call from one of the detectives who thinks he found some new information about the person who ran into me. According to him, the hit wasn't accidental, and the one who did it wanted to hurt me. He thinks it has something to do with some emails I received. Over the years I've received more than a few threats and I haven't really paid attention to them. But this one was more specific. There was too accurate information about me. So I called Robert and we tried to find some clues, unsuccessfully, and eventually, we got drunk in my office at Masquerade. So yes, basically I was at the office, getting drunk." He shrugs and leans back.

I sit in the chair next to him and lean my head on his

shoulder. If that theory is right, I might be able to help him. I'll never forgive myself if something happens to him when I could've done something. "I can track it." A sliver of the truth about me breaks the silence and Damien pulls back. "What do you mean?"

I've told him I'm a programmer and I'm building websites for side money. He doesn't know I'm one of the best hackers in the country, and I'm fixing the gaps in the computer language I've created so I can sell it when I get my life back. "I can try hacking the IP address the email came from."

His brows shoot up and he pushes at my shoulder playfully. "You didn't tell me you're a hacker, Miss Thanos. You keep surprising me. What else are you hiding?"

"I'm not a hacker, but I can try. It's not so different from building websites," I lie, hoping he doesn't know shit about programming. "I used to do it for friends when they wanted to get into their boyfriend's messages." I chuckle. Partly because it's true, partly because of the look on his face when he realizes there's nothing he can hide from me.

"Aren't you a bad girl? And you've kept it a secret. Tell me honestly, did you hack me already?" He laughs.

"I never felt the need to do it. I trust you. But if we get there, that means I've lost my trust in you and in that case, there'd be no point at continuing at all."

He stops laughing and his eyes soften. He pulls me onto his lap and buries his face in my neck. "I'll never let you lose it." Goose bumps rise on my skin with every word. His promise is much more than I asked for, but it makes me realize something. For the second time in my life, the first being Stella, I gave my trust to someone so quickly, easily, and without reservation. This thing between us, whatever it is, happened so naturally, we can't help it.

"So, will you let me try?" I bat my eyelashes.

"Baby, when you look at me like that, there's nothing I can deny you." He bites my lower lip, and I swear I hear the crackling of fireworks and sparklers whizzing.

Literally.

White and gold sparks light up the entire studio, and a few workers rush in the door. Damien and I jump out of the chair when we see the lit fireworks scattering across the floor and ceiling and hurling in every direction. He grabs my arm and leads me out before I realize my duffel is still on the floor with my computer inside. I rush straight toward the sparks and thank goodness they go out just before I reach it.

"Mrs. Black, what are you doing? You could injure yourself!" one of the workers shouts, but Damien is already by my side and takes the duffel from my hands.

"Miss Thanos!" I call out, annoyed that everyone here is confusing my name.

Damien laughs as we exit. "Don't you like my name?"

"On the contrary, but I like it on you, not me." I chuckle, but his laughing dies.

"Let's go, I have a few things to do before the party. I'll tell the housekeeper to make room in the closet for your clothes."

He catches me off guard as we're bypassing the people in the yard. I feel like they've doubled during the time we were in the studio. What the hell are they doing? We're not welcoming the queen.

"Um...I don't think that's necessary. I can keep them in my bag...or on the chairs like I used to." I shrug.

"Nonsense. I want you to feel at home and be as comfortable as possible." He puts his hand on the small of my back and gestures for me to enter first.

When he says things like that I can't protect my heart. I

know I should, but it's so darn hard when I'm a naturally sensitive and emphatic person. Honestly, I don't know if it's good or bad that I already feel at home, and it has nothing to do with the house. Damien is the one who makes me feel like I finally found my place in the world. And it's in his hands.

Chapter Twenty-Five

DAMIEN

I return to the house as fast as I can in hopes of having some more time with Ivy before the party starts, but it's too late. The parking lot is filled with cars, and there are people all over the yard. *Damn it*. Didn't they get the memo it's fashionable to be late?

"Looking great, sister." I hug Rose when I enter the house, and she gives me one of those fake-as-shit triple kisses on the cheek.

"I should thank you, brother. Your Amex did quite the job. And wait until you see what it did for Ivy. I'll expect your thanks in the form of something new. A car, couture, diamonds. Your choice and don't wait too long." She winks and all her pompous friends at the table burst out with that fake high-pitch laugh I should be accustomed to but always ticks me off.

Rosalie knows I'd give her the world if she asks, but she never does. If someone hears her talking shit like that, they'd only think she's a spoiled brat, but the reality is she only ever takes money to mess with me. Mother told her she won't fund her adventures in Hollywood so Rosalie is mostly living off the money she's earned herself since she doesn't get access to her trust fund for another two years, when she turns twenty-five. She doesn't let me pay for her living in LA nor does she want me to use my connections in the music world. She's trying hard to make it on her own, and of course, living with my mother and the lavish life she had before gave her some skills that she still keeps in her bag of tricks, but she mainly uses them as a defense mechanism against people in our circles. Nobody will bother with you if they think you're a privileged ass like them. It's a trick we both learned at a very young age.

"Speaking of which, where is Ivy?"

"I have no idea. I haven't seen her."

I run upstairs, and when I see Ivy's clothes in the closet, I let out the breath I didn't know I was holding.

This girl will be the death of me. I can feel it in my bones.

I can't believe the mere thought of her leaving tugs at my heartstrings. I've never wanted a relationship before. It's all so new to me, and I'm trying to go with my gut because I really don't know what to do.

What kind of sorcery has she performed on me that I can't picture a future without her?

A knock at the door drags me out of my thoughts. "Yes?"

Rose peeks from the door. "People are gathering and asking about you. Now would be the time to come down."

Sighing, I dress in the clothes laid out on the bed. I can't believe I don't even want to be at this party. I've never passed on a party before for the simple reason, it's my favorite activity. The music, the half-naked women, the booze. What's not to like?

But right now, I just want to hole up with Ivy in the bedroom and never leave. Unfortunately, I don't have this option because I am the host and as much as I don't care, it's a big part of my business and my image. That's how you get to know people, how you make contacts and that's how you stay on top.

My mom might run the business from her office, but thanks to my presence at these parties, and the media, our brand has become popular, attracting the richest people from all industries. Our hotels all over the world are booked out months in advance.

Now I have to do the same with my club, as I want to succeed in that industry as well. I can't let my personal relationships affect my goals.

I plaster my fake smile on my face in the mirror and I go downstairs. My eyes scan the space, but there's still no sign of Ivy. Then I look at the guests, consider who I should talk to and how drunk I should let them get first, and start circling.

An hour and a half later, I hide in the shadows at the side of my garage and look around. Still, no sign of her, although the party tripled in size already. I'm still on my second whiskey, and it's getting harder to deal with some of the guests. I have to wrap up the business part sooner and get the fun part started.

I light a cigar and take exactly three steps before I stop dead in my tracks.

Fuck. Me. Hard.

On the other side of the pool, the sexiest woman I've ever seen is confidently striding,

her black dress accentuating every curve, low-cut neckline revealing her lavish breasts. She walks like the fucking queen she is on some black fuck-me heels at the end of her long tan legs. Her long brown hair is curled and up in a high ponytail. She twists, probably looking for me, revealing her exposed back to me, something I never knew could be so seductive.

When she turns around her eyes connect with mine and she smiles timidly. I try to ignore my growing erection and head for her.

"Damien, buddy, I've been looking for fucking ever for you." One of my biggest clients appears in front of me, blocking my path. "Come sit with us. We have a lot of catching up to do." He pats me on the back and points to his table.

Shit. I can't refuse him.

When he moves, Ivy's no longer in the same place and I don't see her anywhere around.

The next hour I spend trying to get to her, but every time someone gets in my way, pulling me away from where I want to be. I've never hated a party but I'm close to that right now. I just want to get this over with as fast as I can so I can be with her.

IVY

"Well, you look like someone took a dump in your banana bread." Stella, and her culinary references, show up with two glasses in her hands and she places a Mimosa in front of me.

These small cocktail glasses make a mockery of alcohol. It's impossible to even get tipsy with them. I tip it back as soon as Stella hands it to me, and she eyes me suspiciously.

"I've been here for two hours and Damien hasn't even said hello. He's with his rich buddies, everywhere, all the time. I don't get it. Is he ashamed of me?"

"No, dear, he's just Damien. I used to joke with him that I'd tie a bell around his neck. You get used to it in time. The person you know is a different version of him, one that none of us has ever seen. But the real Damien is a very sociable persona. He has to network and keep up business relationships and if you want to be with him, you have to get used to the fact he won't be around you all the time."

If you didn't know she was Italian, you'd see it in the excessive hand-gesturing. It's a miracle and a gift the way she didn't spill a drop of her drink with all the waving.

It's not the *being around me* I'm worried about. It's him being around all these gorgeous women.

The female percentage is the larger part of the party and every model, actress, or socialite that is not hanging from someone's arm is following Damien with their eyes or literally following him. I saw at least ten girls trying to get close to him, and I arrived two hours late.

I have to give it to the party-planning guys from earlier, though. The whole yard is lit up with little white lights, including the palms. There are tall and low tables scattered everywhere. Inflatable toys float in the pool carrying women, men, or both taking pictures. The catering is top-notch, and there's an open bar at the other end beside the pool table.

When we arrived everyone was dressed for a party but acting like we were at a business meeting. Since then the alcohol consumption is quickly rising and the inhibitions are falling.

Speaking of which, some of the actresses I'm pretty sure I've watched in a teen drama TV show are just getting out of their clothes when a couple of guys grab them and toss them into the pool, screaming. Everyone turns in their direction. The DJ shouts something into the microphone and turns the music up, making people loosen up a bit more.

As I turn back to the table, I lock eyes with Damien yet again. He gives me a half-smile and I force one back. A blonde approaches him, puts a hand on his shoulder and whispers something in his ear. Damien smiles in response and the green monster in me makes me groan and yell in Stella's face. "Seriously?"

She jumps, startled, and puts the phone she was chatting on, on the table. I tilt my head in Damien's direction and the blonde who's clinging to his arm like she's drowning and he's the last life jacket in the ocean.

My ocean.

"This nightmare has been on repeat all night. I can live with him not paying attention to me, but I'm not putting up with him giving it to other women." I point at myself and pronounce every word clearly and distinctively. "I licked it. It's mine."

Stella bursts out laughing while I'm stealing sad little glimpses at the best-looking man at this party. He's dressed in a gray blazer accentuating his biceps and the muscles of his back, and designer dark blue jeans. The V-neck of his white shirt shows some of the tattoos on his chest. And don't get me started on his hair... his signature messy, freshly-fucked hairstyle.

I have two words for Damien Black.

Walking. Sex.

All mine fits the bill too.

"First of all," Stella says with tears in her eyes from all the laughing at my expense. "Ewww. He's like a brother to me." She makes a squeamish grimace and takes a sip from her Mimosa. "Second, did you talk about being exclusive?"

I raise an eyebrow. "Isn't that assumed when you're having all the sex, and you're falling asleep next to each other every night?"

"I would assume so, yes, but most men don't think like us. Don't kill me for saying it, but Damien has never had a serious relationship in his life. I'm not sure if he got the memo, or even if he agrees with it. Maybe you two should talk it through."

The look of pity on her face makes me feel even more pathetic than I felt before.

Great, now I'm the jealous woman that misunderstood.

Someone calls out "*body shots*" from the table Damien is sitting at, and we both turn just in time to see a man diving into the pool where a blonde woman wearing a scrap of pink fabric that could hardly be described as a swimsuit is lying on an inflatable pineapple and other women around her are setting shot glasses on her body.

The man licks the salt off her perfect abs and tips the shot back. Then he catches the lime out of her lips with his and everyone erupts in laughing, hollering, and undressing so they can get into the pool too.

The man throws the lime to the side and calls out. "Damien, come on, bro."

My hands start shaking and a wave of heat floods my body.

Damien shakes his head in refusal, but the man shouts once again. "Don't be such a pussy. You've been gone for eternity. You missed all the great parties."

My stomach sinks when I see Damien laughing in response and unfastening his diamond timepiece. Then he takes off his blazer, runs to the pool, and dives in.

My legs buckle and I feel a hundred pounds heavier. I didn't want to believe he never intended for us to be monogamous. And though he licks the salt from his own hand, not the girl's body, seeing him drink the shot from her belly feels like a gut punch. She winks at him and puts the lime in his mouth, her fingers lingering at his lips.

The DJ shouts "*Black is back*" and everyone starts cheering.

Me? I almost fall out of my chair.

Everything in me wants to curl up in a corner and cry because I was stupid to believe I'd be enough for him.

One thing is certain and I'll make sure Damien understands it clearly: I. Don't. Share.

Let's see how he'd like sharing me.

"What's with the wicked smile on your face? Should I be worried?" Stella asks me when I turn my head to her just as Damien's turns to me.

"Everything's under control. I'll just have to teach him a lesson." I smile at the man at the opposite table who's been throwing glances my way since we got here.

"What are you doing?" Stella looks behind her where the man has already disappeared somewhere.

"Nothing Damien isn't." I gather my pride, which is more than the pain, and straighten my spine. I smooth my dress and pull Stella aside to dance.

"Am I a bad friend if I'm glad someone is finally going to put him in his place?" Stella whispers as we sway to the beat of the music.

"My friend no. His...maybe." I snicker.

"Well, he might be like a brother to me, but sisters come before misters always." She shrugs, turns her back to me, and shimmies her booty against mine. I pull her away from the table that Damien is sitting at with his wet white T-shirt clinging to his abs, showing his tattoos for every girl here to enjoy, and a few minutes later, the stranger appears before me with two glasses in his hands.

"I didn't know what you were drinking, so I got you what I'm drinking." He hands me a glass with some type of brownish liquid. "Brandy," he explains when I consider whether or not to take it and smile.

I'm glad it's not whiskey. Damien's favorite drink.

After body shots, of course.

I roll my eyes at my pettiness, but the man takes my free hand, places a light kiss on it and introduces himself as Peter.

"So, Ivy, would you like to dance?" His smile is charming in a boyish way. Tall, broad shoulders, dark hair, and brown eyes make his appearance pleasing to the eye.

I realize I haven't noticed any man other than Damien in a long time.

Stop thinking of him, Ivy. He isn't thinking of you, my inner voice pipes in.

"I'd love to."

He pulls me to the dance floor, his hands going to my waist, and chills ripple all over me. Not the good ones. His very touch only serves to remind me of one thing. He's not Damien. I don't want to dance with anybody else but making him feel the same way I did is the only way to see if he cares.

The DJ changes the slow song to a sexier one, and I decide it's time I show some of my moves. I'm a professional, after all, and might I say, one with a smoking body as well since I've been training nonstop.

With every shake and twist, my confidence grows. Peter surprises me by showing some badass dancing skills I didn't expect. I get a little closer to him, feigning interest for what he's saying. He might've misunderstood because he pulls me into his arms, going for a kiss. I pull away before he manages to bend down and instinctively turn to see Damien, who's stomping toward us with rage in his eyes.

I scat out of there as fast as these heels can take me, running toward the house, and I climb the stairs, not paying any attention to Stella and Rosalie who are calling me. The only thing resonating in my ears are the steps behind me.

I reach the bedroom door as a familiar hand grips my wrist.

Chapter Twenty-Six

IVY

"What do you think you're doing, Ivy?" Damien roars, his eyes flashing with anger. I gather all my strength and pull my arm away from his. As soon as I enter the bedroom, two hands pin me to the wall. "Are you tired of me, Ivy? Is that why you're throwing yourself at the first fool?" He growls louder, and I question exactly how clever my idea was after all. Then, I remember the way that girl winked at him when her fingers touched his lips and my blood boils.

"You tell me, Damien. I thought we had something more than casual sex. But it looks like I'm the last to know, just after that girl whose fingers you licked," I scream at his face and push at him with all my force, but damn that man is as solid as a rock; he doesn't even budge.

"You know that's not true."

"Do I? Because it sure as hell looked like it when you didn't even acknowledge me all night, you were too busy being felt up by every other woman here." I push at him again, but he catches my hands and holds them at his ridiculously hot pecs.

"There's only one woman I want to touch me and that's you." His yelling makes me tremble. This is the first time I've heard him raise his voice. His heart is racing underneath my palm as his eyes burn holes in me. I turn my head to the side because his proximity makes me stupid. He runs a finger over my jaw and slides it down my neck. His gaze drops to my cleavage, one finger pulling the dress aside.

A wolfish smile appears on his face, and he traces the purple hickey on my breast. I didn't wear a bra and my nipples, those traitors, immediately harden at his touch. Raising his head, he whispers in my ear. "I never want anyone to touch you ever again. You're mine, understand? Only mine."

I growl as his teeth bite into the sensitive flesh under my ear, and his hands grab my thighs and lift me off the ground. He fits himself between my legs, wrapping them around his waist. The wet material of his jeans brushes against my panties, and I bite my lip. Being around this man is like an untended fire. All we need is a gentle breeze to ignite everything around us.

My fingers tangle in his soft hair, pulling his head back so he can look me in the eyes. I can't help but squeeze his jaw and bite that plump bottom lip of his until he roars out in pain. "I'm yours, but only if you're mine, Damien. I won't share, so it's your choice. It's either me or everyone else."

A low, sexy chuckle falls from his lips and one corner turns up, showing that left dimple I love so much. "I don't need anyone else, baby. It's just you and me."

We devour one another like hungry vultures. Everything is a mix of pain and pleasure. We're kissing as if the other is the last drop of water in the desert, and biting like rabid animals. His lips slide down my neck and suck. My nails dig into his back.

Releasing me, he takes off my dress and backs away. His hungry gaze is ravaging my body and the expensive lingerie I'm wearing just for him. "These are so sexy." He grabs the lace between his fingers. "I'll buy you new ones," he says and tears it, the sound of the material shredding exciting me all the more. I take off his wet T-shirt and bite on his chest. I want to mark him, as he did to me. Gritting my teeth, I put in all the effort until he growls out of pain. Then I suck on his neck as one of his hands plays with my nipple and the other slips down my body.

Damien glides a finger over my clit, and all it takes is a few swirls and I'm coming on his fingers. All the sensations flooding through me shake me to my core as I muffle my moan by biting into his bicep. He pushes a finger inside me, and the last wave of my release turns me to jelly in his hands.

Grabbing me by the waist, he turns me to the desk, bends me over, and slaps my butt. "This ass is all mine. Am I clear, Ivy?" His voice is imperious. The next slap comes to my pussy and my hips twist backward seeking more of his touch. "Let me clear it up for you." He groans and plunges into me to the deepest point.

Instinctively, I lift but his hand pushes me back down, smashing my boobs into the desk. The mix of the cool wood and the sweet pain of his cock stretching me is almost enough to make me come again.

Moving slowly inside me, gradually increasing the rhythm, he grabs both my hands and twists them back. I've never seen him so dominant. I'm completely at his mercy, and I like it more than I ever expected. The slapping sound of skin on skin, my moans, and his labored breathing are the best song I've ever heard.

Damien's banging me like it's the last time, and my next orgasm comes quickly. My walls choke him, my muscles clenching around his hardness. He drops my wrists and slides a finger down to my clit. That finishes me off and I scream his name, trembling over the wood desk.

As I turn my head to look at him, he towers over me, sliding his finger between my lips and I suck. My taste surprises me, salty but somehow sweet.

Damien continues thrusting in me without slowing down, and I can feel the edge of my third orgasm. "Come on, baby, give it to me. Come for me." His words shoot me even higher, and I lick his finger again. He returns it to my clit, and soon we're both trembling on the edge. I dig my nails into his arms, and he clutches my ass cheeks. Our bodies merge into one, and my orgasm overwhelms me when I feel his hot cum spilling into me. We both cry out in unison "*Mine.*"

For a few seconds, we're breathless and shaking, without moving from this position. He leans over me and leaves a trail of kisses down my spine. The contrast between the rough and primitive man who just fucked me and the gentle man who kisses me as if I'm his most precious possession makes me crazy all over again.

He stands up and pulls out of me, our combined release dripping down my inner thighs, and I'm just now realizing we had sex without a condom. I turn to ask him something but Damien is standing behind me, biting his lip, making me immediately forget what it was.

He hands me a napkin to clean myself, walks over, and kisses me on the forehead. "I'm glad we cleared that up." He smiles smugly and hugs me. "You're still on the pill, right?" I nod and wrap my arms around him. "Good, because I never want to wear a condom with you ever again. I didn't even know how good it would feel to come inside you, and I never want to know another feeling."

I pull away and head for the bathroom, but another slap

lands on my butt as I reach the door. "Where do you think you're going without me?"

"I'll take a shower and join you down there. People are probably wondering where you are."

"I don't care. By now, they're so drunk they forgot my name. All I'm going to do tonight is keep you in this room."

He follows me into the marble bathroom and slips into the glass shower cabin after me.

"Don't you have to send your guests away?" I take the sponge, the scent of the lavender body wash and sex surrounding us.

"They've been to enough parties here. They can handle themselves."

"Do you host parties often?" I run the sponge over his pecs, his abs.

"Yes, that's part of my job. That's how I made all my contacts and expanded my business." He takes the sponge from my hands and rubs it on my breasts, my arms, and back. "Does that bother you?"

"No, I don't mind. I like good parties. But I don't like when every woman looks at you like you're their dinner."

He smiles sweetly and I feel weak in the knees. "Don't be fooled, every man looks at you the same way. Next time, you'll be on my arm, so everyone knows we belong to each other."

I don't know where he learned to speak so smoothly. I can't help but give him what he wants. I reach up and kiss him, and he wraps his arms around my waist. We don't bathe, because in a minute, he's inside me again, fucking me against the wall.

Then on the bed.

On the floor.

All over the desk.

And back to the bed.

When the sun is rising, and the music outside stops, we finally fall asleep, exhausted, clinging to one another.

Chapter Twenty-Seven

IVY

I wake up alone in a complete mess. There are pillows and clothes all over the floor, and my torn panties are hanging from the chandelier. I get up and carefully step over the scattered pencils and paper, which used to be on the desk but now there's just an ass print on top.

My ass.

I smile at the memory, and don't bother to dress in anything other than Damien's shirt because if I did he'd just take it off of me faster than I put it on. Then I follow the divine smell of coffee to the kitchen. God knows I need a couple of cups; I feel like a desiccated vampire. But as soon as I enter, I freeze in place.

Talk 'bout vampires... Damien's mother is propped up on the countertop.

I shudder when I meet her cold green eyes, but she doesn't tremble at all, nor does she look surprised to see me. Her gaze travels over my half-naked body, my cheeks getting hotter with every silent second. Melanie sips from her cup and leaves it on the counter with more grace in her pinkie than I have in my whole body.

"I see you found the way to my son's home after all." This even, monotonous tone makes me want to curl up in a corner. I can't move and not a single thought pops into my head. I open my mouth to say Lord knows what, but she raises her hand and stops me. "Save it, I've seen many women like you. Don't think you'll stick around. Damien will never fall for your tricks."

It provokes something in me, and I open my mouth before I think. "Is that why I've been here for a month now?" This woman has no right to judge me when she didn't even come to see her son all this time.

She raises her perfectly shaped eyebrows. "Impressive. I don't know how you did it, but in the end, nature will play its role. You and I both know, you're just Damien's latest hookup, and once he's bored with you, you'll quickly return to wherever you came from."

I step closer to her. "Damien and I are together. As a couple."

For a moment, her cold façade falls, and just when I think I broke the Ice Queen, she whips her head back and dissolves into ominous laughter. Seriously, Cruella De Vil would kill 101 more puppies for that laugh. I stand, confused, pulling on the long sleeves of the shirt, wondering which one of us will be the first to have a mental breakdown.

Where the hell is Damien?

"Oh, dear." My heart skips a beat when I hear her sweet tone. This can't be good. "I feel sorry for you. I was young and naïve once too. Don't let that fool you. Men are men and they'll never change. You think you'll be enough for him? It's in his DNA. He may be smitten now, but once the first stage passes, he'll replace you before you blink. Damien is his father's son and nothing can change that. Adultery is in his blood. If it's love you're seeking, run before he breaks your heart. Money you won't find. I'll personally take care of that."

"Damien is nothing like his father," I raise my voice, feeling the need to protect him, even if it's from his mother.

She purses her lips, pity in her eyes. "You poor thing. You still believe in fairy tales. Take this advice from me and grow up. Save yourself the scandals and humiliation."

"Mother, is that you I'm hearing?" Rosalie's voice comes from the hallway. Melanie rolls her eyes and sips from the coffee when Rosalie shows at the door. "Are you trying to scare her off? It won't work. Ivy's tougher than the others."

Melanie's lips curve. "We'll see about that. I'm not giving it more than a month until Damien moves on to the next one."

I don't like the way they talk about me as if I'm not in the room. I open my mouth, but Rosalie beats me. "Wanna bet? My brother is head over heels in love."

Melanie chokes on her coffee, and I can feel all the blood draining from my face.

Damien's not in love with me. We only agreed last night that this is a relationship. It takes more time for someone to fall in love.

Right?

"Men aren't capable of such deep feelings. I've taught you better than that, Rosalie."

"When you treat them with care and love, you'd be surprised what men are capable of, mother."

With a mother like this, it's a miracle and a big achievement that Rosalie grew up to be a nice person.

"Give these documents to your brother. He was already out when I came. Nice seeing you." Melanie shoves a folder in Rosalie's hands. By no means, can you tell she's talking to her daughter and not to some random person on the staff.

"Don't forget to thank the girl for making sure your son didn't die while you were on vacation."

"Don't be ridiculous. Damien has staff that looks after him."

"No, actually everyone was taking time off then. I would've come if someone had told me. Thank goodness Ivy was selfless enough to take care of him without getting anything in return. You don't know that feeling, do you, mother? Being noble, having compassion?" she hisses through her teeth.

Why do I feel like this is about something different than me?

Melanie looks down at my shirt and her lips curve. "I'm sure she got something in return."

Oh, Earth, why do you never open up and swallow me when I need you to?

Her gaze returns to my eyes. "Thank you. But remember my words, Ivy. Sooner or later you'll realize I was right. Don't be stupid and do it early." She turns on her heels and leaves the house.

"Are you okay?" Rosalie looks at me.

"Yes, you?"

She shrugs and pours coffee into two mugs. "I'm used to it. That's like a regular Wednesday afternoon in the Blacks' house. Why do you think I stay with my brother every time I'm in town? You learn your limit."

"What's your father like?"

I can feel her revulsion the second I ask her. "He's a drunk, a junkie, a scumbag. Call it whatever you like. He always has been. When I was little, Damien told me he hid it at least, but then he lost all control. He barely got home and when he did, he brought different lovers every time and had crazy parties until morning."

I can't imagine the Ice Queen allowing something like that. "How does your mother put up with this?"

"He's the reason she hates all men alive or dead. She can't divorce him because her prenup says she'll get nothing and since Hyland was declared unfit because of his vices Damien took control of all the family's bank accounts. Not that my brother won't provide her everything she needs but she won't have access to the company, and this woman loves the business more than she loves us. When Damien replaced Hyland as CEO, she got some confidence, and I don't know how she did it, but she kicked him out of our mansion. Since then he's pretty much closed himself inside one of our other properties and we see him once a year. He's worse every time." Sadness sweeps through her eyes.

I can't imagine what it's like watching your parent self-destruct every day. Mine were at least decent people.

Oh, what am I thinking? They made the list of most-wanted criminals.

"I feel sorry for Melanie." I stop my mouth with a hand when I hear myself say the words out loud, but Rosalie laughs. No wonder Melanie told me all these things. And the way Damien lived his life... I understand why she thinks he'll follow in his father's steps. But I believe in him. Besides, he's no longer the party boy he was a few years ago. I see it in the way he talks about life, about his work. He's grown up.

"I'm beat. I'm going back to bed. You?"

"Where's Damien?" I finally remember to ask. I'm still shocked by this day's progress.

"I have no idea, probably working."

"Then I'll go to the studio. I have excess energy to burn."

This wake-up surprise gave me a headache.

DAMIEN

I walk into the rehearsal studio at my home to find Ivy hanging from the pole head down, legs up in the air in a pair of stripper shoes, and ass protruding from her pink shorty-shorts.

Perfection in its purest form.

She spins, sees me, and loses her balance. I jump forward and manage to catch her just before she falls.

"Thank you." She breathes the words out. Then she slaps me on the shoulder. "Don't startle me like that!" She laughs and jumps out of my hands.

It's impossible not to smile when I see her happy. And I came in so angry when Rose told me what happened...

"I'll always be here to catch you, baby." I wink at her and she smiles brighter. I take a chair and sit close to her. "Ivy, I want to apologize for my mother's behavior. I talked to her and she won't cause any problems in the future."

She takes a few steps toward me, puts her palm on my chest, pushes me back and whispers, "I don't want to talk about that. The past is in the past. Instead"—she slides a hand down my thigh and purrs in my ear—"let me show you how grateful I am for you letting me dance at the club."

Fuck.

The smartest thing I ever did was install this pole in here so she could rehearse at my home and away from fucking John. *And* the front row show is a huge bonus.

Ivy presses a button and the slow, seductive voice of Beyoncé starts singing the song "Dance for You."

Shit.

She kneels before me, her back to the pole, and that's all it takes for me to get hard for her. My girl slides her body across the floor, ass up, face down. She turns and opens her legs in the air in front of me. I barely keep myself from jumping up and fucking her right there on the spot, but I want to see the rest of the show she's putting on for me. She takes her pink top off, throws it at me, and spins around the pole. She slides her back on the metal support, lowering herself and spreading her knees. I clench the fabric in my hands when she slides a finger over the waistband of her shorts.

"Yes, baby, that's right." My voice is low and hoarse, but she's close enough to hear me.

She smiles mischievously, biting her index finger, and with one pull of the elastic, the shorts slide down her legs. She shimmies out of them, lies down on the floor, lifts her juicy ass, and rolls over. Her heels hit the floor with a thwap and my cock twitches.

I've had girls do a striptease for me a few times, and I've been to the best strip clubs in the world, but nothing compares to the feeling of watching *my* girl dance for me. When I see her moving that sexy body across the floor, it's like I'm seeing a woman for the first time.

She slides her hands all over my body, like a siren luring a poor sailor to certain death. I'm ready to die a thousand times, burned by the fire in her eyes.

The scent of vanilla wafts in the air and heightens my senses as her hair brushes my face. She turns her back to me and presses her hands on my knees, wiggling her ass in front of my crotch, but not touching it, making me crazy. I squeeze her hips, but she slaps my hands away and turns to face me. She rides me slowly, unbuttoning my shirt. She grabs my wrists, bending her spine back, and guides my hands across her chest, the white lace of her bra, and the soft skin of her tummy. I like watching her take the reins, knowing that she's doing this just for me. Purring in my ear, she rubs her damp thong over my hard-as-stone cock. I bite her neck and she squeals, standing she places her foot in my lap and grinds her sharp heel in my thigh. The pleasure-pain has an animalistic groan escaping from deep in my throat.

She pulls away before I can grab her ankle and swivels around the pole with one hand while unhooking her bra with the other.

My breath stops as I stare intensely and wait to see her divine tits.

Ivy turns to me and kneels on the ground. I jump out of the chair, but she quickly grabs my legs and pushes me back to sit. Her fingers slide up my thighs to unfasten my zipper and release my cock from hell. Her gentle hands caress me and I can't help but thrust into her hand. Ivy leans forward, looks into my eyes, and takes me deep into her mouth.

"Fuck, yes." I want it to last forever, but it's so good that everything in me is struggling to hold on. She slides her tongue from the base to the tip and laps up the droplet gathered on the crown. Slowly, she lowers her lips and wraps them around my cock until she's almost choking on it. I stroke her head. "Slowly, my good girl. You can take more." I grab a handful of her hair and feel her swallow when my cock hits the back of her throat. "You're going to make me come if you don't stop, Ivy," I growl and she starts moving her soft lips faster.

She works on me like she does everything else, relentlessly. She twists her tongue, strokes me, and sucks my last remaining sanity. I bend my head back and breathe deeply, trying to get control of myself. Her nipples are already hard, and I'm sure she's wet. When she groans, the vibrations almost make me come. I grab her hands and lift her. "Baby, I want to fuck you before you finish me."

She wipes the corners of her mouth with her thumb and I shudder. I swear this girl doesn't even know what she's doing to me. She's poisonous just like her name. Spreading her venom all over my veins, entangling my blood cells, and morphing my DNA to her mold. Until she's tainted every unit of mine, leaving her trace behind for me to follow.

And fuck if I don't like it.

"Show me those gymnastic skills on the floor baby."

My good girl lies down on the vinyl dance floor and opens her legs in the splits. I squat in front of her and run my finger over her pussy. I was right; she's dripping. I slide a finger inside her. She moans and lifts her pelvis for more. "Damien, I need you inside me." Her walls clench around me. I replace my finger with my cock and I bury myself inside her to the hilt. She calls out my name and her fingers find her clit. Her back arches and her eyes close, her muscles contracting around me and her body trembling in my arms. She opens her mouth in a little O, and I see every wave of ecstasy on her face.

When her eyes open she looks at me with adoration in a way I haven't seen before. I roll onto my back and pull her on top of me; she's straddling my waist and her breasts are swaying with her movements. Her hips move slowly over mine and she leans over until our lips meet. Initially, the kiss is light, but with every second, it deepens. There's something different about it; it's not frantic with raw desire, the way we usually devour each other. This kiss is slow and intense as if we're short of oxygen and we find it in the other's lips. Our bodies move like waves crashing onto the shore in a soothing cadence. Every part of Ivy is made in a perfect pattern to match every piece of me. Our heartbeats are synced and our movements are fluid as we gaze into each other's eyes.

Slow torture and complete satisfaction—that's what we are.

I watch her as she rides me, my hands squeezing the globes of her glorious ass as she rises before descending painfully slow. As her release gets closer and closer she moves her hips faster and farther, until she suddenly sinks to the deepest point, digging her fingertips into my chest and screaming with pleasure.

I'll never get tired of watching her come. I don't think I've ever seen a more beautiful sight.

I roll her over to lie on her back, her ankles wrapping around me, and I move slowly, rhythmically into her. I hug her, kiss her, everything around us is blurry.

I can feel the tingling in my spine before I fill her with my cum. A low growl rumbles in my chest and Ivy swallows it with a kiss. I pull her naked body to me and wrap her in my arms and for the next few minutes, neither of us can peel our hands or lips off the other.

I'm not sure because I've never done it before, but I think we just made love.

Chapter Twenty-Eight

IVY

I grab hold of the aerial silks, lift my leg, slip it through the hole and...twist like a ribbon on a Christmas present. Again.

I sigh and untie myself from the silk fabrics. I'll never be able to do the back rotation. We finished the rehearsal at the club half an hour ago, and all the girls are already gone. I'm the only one left to rehearse this stupid move because I couldn't get it right. It's not that difficult...it's just not my day.

It all started this morning when I stepped into Six's poop that he so generously left in front of the bedroom door. It got worse when Damien's driver dropped me off at Masquerade, late again, and some idiot drove past me so fast he splashed me with muddy water from head to toe.

What can I say...just my luck.

I clench the silks firmly and push my foot through again. One, two, three...lift the other and...

"If I'd known the view would be so good, I would've come sooner." A male voice startles me and I yelp, rolling over and hanging from the silks with one leg and hand tied.

Shit...I was so close.

Lifting up to untie myself, I hear footsteps on the stage.

"Do you need help with that?" His voice grows closer, and when I finally get unwound, I jump to the ground and turn around. Behind me is a large man with salt and pepper hair and clean-shaven face. His navy blue suit and leather briefcase scream expensive. I'm sure I haven't met him before, but his light blue eyes are very familiar and oddly unpleasant.

No one should have access to the club because it's daytime and it's closed. Rob went out to grab something to eat, and Damien should be arriving soon. I'm all alone.

"Who are you and how did you get in?" Before he answers, I head to the stairs on the side of the stage.

"What kind of welcome is that, Ivy? Shouldn't you treat your customers better?" His footsteps echo behind me and I hurry. But after two more steps, I realize what he just said.

He's a customer. I'm without a mask. And he knows my name.

What the hell?

I change the course and head straight to the bar where the knives are located. A hand grabs my shoulder and I bounce back. I turn around and the stranger looks at me with a curious, amused expression.

"Please..." I push his hand from my shoulder. "Don't touch me."

His eyes rake over my body and shivers run though me. I wrap my arms around my middle and slowly take a step closer to the bar, trying not to turn my back on him.

"Ivy Thanos, right?"

I finally reach the bar and calm down slightly when he doesn't follow me. The man stands in front of the bar and sets his briefcase on a chair.

"You know my name, but I don't know yours. Care to share?"

"Sweetheart, here's the deal..." he says with a sly smile on his wrinkled face and my breath hitches. *Where's my phone? Where's my phone? Oh no*! I left it in the dressing room. "You're going to pour me one of those nice scotches you have, and I won't tell your boss about the ugly attitude you greeted me with."

"The club isn't open. I don't know what you're doing here, but you should go." I gather some courage, clutching a knife under the counter, where he can't see it.

He laughs and I swear even his laughter is eerie. "A shot or make it two. I'm having a good day." He points to one of the bottles next to me. "You're brave, I'll give you that. You're also beautiful. I can see why Damien's into you. Greek did you say you were?"

I'm starting to feel more and more uncomfortable. This man knows too much to be a random customer. "I didn't." I put the glass in front of him and he takes a sip.

"Then tell me, when did you start working here? I didn't see you last time I came. I would've remembered that body." This is getting weirder.

"Recently," I answer hesitantly. *Where the hell is everyone?* At least Damien should've been here by now.

"What an interesting girl you are, *Ivy Thanos*." He says my name in a strange tone, and chill bumps erupt along my spine. He still isn't telling me where he knows me from or who he is.

"Do you know what made an impression on me? You young people, you love your social networks. You're always taking pictures for more likes. Even my daughter has thousands of followers." He pauses and takes another drink, anticipation killing me. "But you, Ivy..." I freeze on the spot. It can't be what I think. "I can't find you on any social networks. No Instagram, Twitter, or Facebook. It's as if you don't exist. Why is that?"

I swallow the lump in my throat and force myself to stay calm. Predators smell fear. "I don't like social networks. I think they detach the person from the real world." I give him my rehearsed response, but I'm sure he can hear my voice quiver.

"Interesting. I thought it was because of some clause in your contract here. You know, the secret club and masked staff and all. When did you sign the contract?"

I have to change the subject. "You haven't told me your name. I can't allow you to be here if I don't know..."

"Richard." I hear Damien's voice and we both turn to the door. He's walking fast toward us, and I can read the anger in his movements, despite his stoic expression. "What are you doing here?" His tone is all businesslike and unbothered. He slides behind the bar next to me and puts his hand on my waist. Instantly, my whole body relaxes, and the knife falls from my stiff hand into the sink with a clatter. Damien looks down at it, grabs my hand, and strokes it under the counter.

Richard's gaze never shifts from my face for a second. "I came by to check on my favorite partner. The beautiful Ivy here kept me company. Let me tell you, Damien, if all the dancers in your little club are this hot I might have to start coming more often."

I feel the tension in Damien's body behind me. Whoever Richard is, neither of us likes him, but you couldn't tell by the way Damien handles himself. "Let's move this conversation to my office."

Richard follows him.

I stay behind the bar, still shaking and very confused. What the hell just happened?

I avoid public appearances with Damien like the plague. The only place we show our affection is his home. Everywhere else, even in the club, I shy away from any physical contact with him, no matter how hard it is. I'm sure the girls suspect there's something between us, but I don't need to feed the gossip. I try to stay as inconspicuous as possible. I'm already exposing myself enough by dancing here, even with a mask.

How does this man know we're together? Should I be worried? Maybe he's just curious...

As much as I try to convince myself, everything inside me screams there's something more behind it. My heart is about to burst out of my chest. My breathing is labored and I grip the counter to get my bearings.

Oh my god. Not another panic attack. I can't bear it.

Inhale, exhale...inhale, exhale.

No one can find me. I deleted all traces of my existence. No one can find me. I repeat my mantra until my breathing begins to calm.

I take my stuff from the stage and head for the dressing room to change and wait for Damien. After a while I hear him come out of his office to accompany Richard out of Masquerade.

When Damien comes back wrinkles crease his forehead. "Are you okay?"

"Yeah, why wouldn't I be?" I shrug it off.

"Ivy, when I came in, you were pale, clutching a knife under the bar as if you were about to stab him."

Shit. I thought I was more nonchalant than that. "Yeah...well, he wouldn't tell me his name and he was asking all these weird questions. I was alone and worried he was some psychopath."

"What weird questions?"

"Where I'm from, when I started working here..."

Damien interrupts me sharply. "What did you tell him?"

"I didn't tell him I'm from Greece, but he seemed to know already."

"No, no. What did you tell him about the job?"

Oh, shit. *Here we go.* "Nothing. I only told him I started here recently."

"Okay. That's good. Recently can be a month, it can be a week. No wonder he threw all these hints at me. The bastard was digging for dirt."

"He asked weird questions about the contract too. I'm confused, why would he... Oh, God!" I slap my hand over my mouth when I realize who Richard is.

"Yes, exactly." Damien pauses, thinking. "Baby, I'm sorry, but you'll have to stop dancing. At least for a while until I figure out how to fix things."

It feels like someone just punched my heart from the inside.

I love my job, my coworkers. I got too comfortable. I knew this day was coming, but I was hoping I'd figure out how to exonerate myself before then. And here it is. And it happened so fast...it hasn't even been two full months since I started working here.

"Please don't look at me like that." He pulls me into a hug. "You know I'd do anything to make you happy, but this puts the future of the club at risk. Hell, even the company."

A tear rolls down my cheek and I raise a hand to wipe it away. This isn't about my happiness; it's about Damien's well-being. I wouldn't ruin his future for anything in the world.

I rise up on my tiptoes and kiss him. "Damien, I'll be fine. Don't worry. Now, the most important thing is for you to get out of the mess, I got you in. I'll get a job, but you need to be focused on your business. I'll be here to support you no matter what..." The words *I love you* get stuck in my throat, and a shockwave passes through me. Where did this come from? My emotions are all over the place right now, I'm not thinking clearly.

He squeezes me harder and rests his head on mine. "That means a lot to me, baby. Really. But you don't have to work. I'll take care of you."

I pull away from him and stare at him as if he's crazy. He definitely is, if he's offering something like that. Doesn't he know me even a little? "I'll go crazy if I don't work. What would I do all day?"

A big frown appears on his face. "There's no way you're going back to any of those shit-hole bars."

I don't like it when people tell me what to do with my life, but he's right. I won't do that to myself again. I guess I'll have to live on the little savings I have while I figure shit out.

"Definitely. I'll..."

"Actually, you'll keep working for me, but as a choreographer. There's no such position in the club, anyway, so no one will know I'm paying you under the table. You've been doing the job for free so far. Rose was right that I have to pay you double for that."

My eyes widen. He can't be serious. "Damien, I already told you, I'm not a choreographer. That's a job for someone more experienced than I am."

"Are you shitting me? You're the best we've ever had here. Hell, you're the best dancer I've ever seen. You came up with all of Rose's choreography as well as the last two shows at the club, all in the last three weeks while you were also taking care of me. You might not see the potential in yourself, but I do and I won't let you waste it."

"But..." I start to explain a choreographer is much more than that, but he raises a finger to my mouth to shush me.

"Consider yourself hired. I won't give up, so save your breath."

There's those words again... *I love you.* They're trying to get out of my chest, but they get stuck in my throat. My emotions are a mess. I'm confusing gratitude with love. It's not the right time for something so big. I can't afford it.

I bury my head in his chest. "Thank you. I'm the luckiest woman in the world to have you."

He kisses me on the head and raises my chin so I can look him in the eyes. "Baby, I'm the lucky one. With you by my side, I can conquer the world and when I do, I'll leave it at your feet."

I wrap my arms around his neck and kiss him before I say something I'm not ready for.

Chapter Twenty-Nine

IVY

"Come on, Six, leave the birds alone!" The stubborn Doberman once again gets distracted and starts chasing them. The sun is already setting, which tells me we've been walking on the beach for far too long. Well, it's not like I have anything else to do. *Cue dramatic sigh...*

The idleness will kill me. Three rehearsals a week at the club is not enough. I'm grateful for the opportunity to be a choreographer, but it's just not enough work to keep me busy. I've been working at least ten hours a day, every day, longer than I can remember. At least I have the rehearsal studio at Damien's so I can kill a few hours there.

I've been searching for traces of my parents and the stolen money. So far I'm failing spectacularly. It's as if they've disappeared from the face of the earth.

Even after all of this, I'm still left with too much time, which always leads to overthinking. Not good.

Rosalie is gone, Stella is up to her ears in work, and Damien is in his office putting in more hours that I am. Not that I mind, it's just that I miss him so much. I got used to spending all my time with him.

"Six, wait for me," I yell at my new best friend when he rushes toward the house. Well, at least I've got him. The dog shadows me everywhere I go, and I love him as if he's mine.

I almost jump out of my clothes when I see Damien sitting on the counter in the kitchen. The butterflies take flight in my stomach. God, you would think by now I should be used to seeing him every day, but no. Every time is like seeing him for the first time. "Hey, baby, what's up? Is there a problem?"

The vein on his forehead will pop any second as he types furiously on his phone. "One of our investors is trying to renege on our deal."

I've never seen him so tense. "Can I help with something?" I rub his shoulders, but he swats my hands away and stands up.

"No, I have everything under control. I have to go back to the office. I'm so swamped that I forgot about my mother's ball. Here"—he pulls out his credit card—"take it and buy a dress. I'll be in a black tux, so get whatever color you want."

"I'm sorry, what?"

"You didn't hear or you don't get it?" he barks at me while tapping his foot impatiently.

"I obviously don't get it, because I don't recall being invited to a ball."

"Again with this invitation thing. Ivy, don't you realize that you're with me now, which automatically means you're invited everywhere I am?" The arrogant way he says it makes me want to pinch myself. This isn't my Damien. This is the stranger I ran into at the hotel.

"You could've at least asked me if I wanted to go. I don't think your mother will be pleased by my presence."

"I told you already, I forgot. Melanie would never forgive me if I missed it. She throws this ball every year for Halloween, and it's more business than anything else. Thank goodness Vicky reminded me."

If my eyes rolled any harder they'd be in the back of my head. Vicky is his new assistant. A blonde bombshell with blue eyes that I'm going to poke out if they doesn't stop undressing my man. Seriously...she doesn't even bother trying to hide it when she comes to the house and I'm right there in the same room.

"Get yourself something elegant. It's a masked ball, so get a mask too. Don't wait for me tonight. I'll be in the office late." He pushes the black card at me and dodges my kiss as he collects his things.

Oh, hell no. Why do I feel like I've watched this episode of Desperate Housewives?

Damien and I are going to get a few things straight. I'm not the girlfriend who'll happily put up with his attitude as long as he throws money at her. I thought we'd made it past that phase.

I open my mouth and raise a finger to interrupt and explain to him how inconsiderate that is when the harsh reality hits me like a brick to the head. "I can't come with you." He finally raises his gaze, confused. "I just... I can't."

"Ivy, what's the problem?" He comes toward me, but I pull back, leaving his arms hanging in the air.

Shit, I knew this moment would come. I just hoped like a fool it wouldn't happen until I came up with a reasonable explanation.

"There'll be photographers, the media. I don't want to be in the spotlight, and if I come with you, there's no way to avoid it."

"Everyone will be wearing a mask. Besides, I'm not

going to let anything happen to you. What scares you so much? I know you're running from something. What is it?"

Frankly, I'm surprised it took him so long to ask. During all our time together, he never once brought it up. I know he's curious and I love him even more for respecting my personal space, but this day was inevitable. "I don't want to talk about it. Can't you just go without me?"

"No, Ivy!" he explodes, pacing the room. "I want you to be on my arm when I go inside. It's important to me. Why can't you come? I want a real answer. I've been patient because I was waiting for you to decide to share with me. How can you still not trust me after everything we've been through together?"

"I trust you, Damien. It's..." The lump in my throat stops me from telling him. I trust him, but I'm not sure he will trust me if he learns my story.

I'm a fugitive because the police accused my parents of stealing billions of dollars, and they're looking for me too, and somehow I accidentally ended up in a billionaire's club, then at his home and now in his bed.

Yes, I thought so, too. No man in his right mind would ever believe I'm not here to con him.

"It's what? I trust you completely, and you don't give two shits about me. Is that what you're trying to tell me?" He hits the wall, his fist creating a dent.

I step back until my butt hits the counter. I know he wouldn't hurt me and I'd rather deal with his anger than lose him for good. I'll find a way to show him I'm not guilty and then I'll tell him everything. "I trust you, okay? I do. I'm just not ready to tell you. Please don't push me." I'm trying to hold it together and not let him see me cry.

"And when the fuck might that be? Because it seems like the only thing I do is help you while you make up excuses."

His phone rings but he rejects the call. "I have to go. But, Ivy, I'm done waiting. I want an answer when I get home. If not..." His phone starts ringing again, interrupting his ultimatum, which I'm pretty sure I didn't want to hear in the first place. "We'll talk later." He says bye with a promise in his eyes, accepts the call, and walks out the door.

I just stand there, glued to the counter for the next few minutes, tears streaming down my face.

What just happened? Did we break up?

Damien gave me an ultimatum, but I just can't do it. If I stay here and tell him everything, what are the chances it'll take more than two seconds for him to call the police?

Love or freedom? This is the hardest choice I've ever had to make.

I'd give anything to be with Damien, but how will I do that if I'm locked in a cell? My only option is to distance myself from him and keep looking for a way to acquit myself. And then beg him to forgive me and take me back. I can't imagine even a day without him, let alone a lifetime.

The whole time I'm packing my stuff, my tears are flowing. I have to believe this is temporary. Maybe we rushed the whole thing. I mean, I'm practically living with him. His behavior today, his anger and his ultimatum, that's not how I see our future together. He probably needs some alone time too.

This is temporary. I keep repeating this to myself all the way home. But it hurts so fucking bad. Why can't I be with him? Why is life so unfair? I'm his, and yet I can never be.

"Hey, stranger! I didn't expect you," Stella calls out when I enter. She's sewing something at her workspace in the living room, but as soon as she notices the duffel in my hand, she frowns and the sewing machine stops. "What did the motherfucker do?"

I almost bare my teeth, feeling the need to protect him, but then I remember the real reason everything happened. Me. "He didn't do anything. He just wants things I can't give him."

She looks at me questioningly and I sigh. Better to tell her now than to spend all night under cross-examination. "He wanted me to tell him my story...but I can't. You understand, right? It's just not the right time. He gave me an ultimatum so I left."

"I understand," she says in a somber voice. I knew she'd get it. After all, we're both hiding something.

"He's wrong to pressure you, but are you sure you can't tell him? I mean... Damien's one of the most supportive people I know. Not to mention he'll protect you with his life."

"I can't, Stells. I don't want to lose him," I say wearily. I just want to go to bed. I get off the couch and head for my tiny box of a room.

"What happened before things escalated to an ultimatum?" Stella follows me.

"He wanted me to go with him to his mom's ball and I refused." I undress and throw myself onto the bed.

"Oh..." I suppose, she finally got it. She's the one who warned me to stay away from him from the beginning for this very reason.

"Goodnight, Stells."

She leaves and soon I hear the sound of the sewing machine again. But even this can't stop me from passing out after I cry all my tears out.

DAMIEN

The house is quiet when I come home.

"I can bring the documents to you, Mr. Black." Vicky purrs my name through the phone. The last thing I want to do at midnight is more work.

I set my briefcase on the bench near the front door and remove my shoes. "Don't worry. I can go through it tomorrow." My neck hurts from clutching the phone between my shoulder and my ear. I put her on speaker while I walk toward the great room, unbuttoning my shirt.

I can't wait to get out of this suit I've worn for the last sixteen hours. All this sitting around the house for a month in nothing more than my boxers, or sweats on the rare occasions, have me rethinking my clothing choices. Maybe I should become a stay-at-home boss. You know, one of those filthy rich bastards that play golf all day and have their work delivered to their mansions, ready for signing.

"Hello? Are you still there?" Vicky's voice breaks through my musings as I drop my shirt to the floor and start with the pants.

"Yes. I'm done with work for today. See you tomorrow at eight."

"Okay. Have a good night, Mr. Black." She does the same purring sound before ending the call. Maybe she's getting a kick out of it because she's been using that tone every time she says my last name. I'm too tired to read anything into it.

I'm in the mood to have a drink and fall into bed. Maybe even a dip in the Jacuzzi before that.

The conversation I had with Ivy flashes through my head when I reach the kitchen. Fucking hell. I was really mad and took it out on her like an asshole. Maybe if I bring her a drink and some chocolate she'll let me apologize the best way I know how. With my cock, so deep inside her pussy the neighbors will hear her screaming my name from the hot tub.

With a glass full of whiskey in each hand along with a chocolate bar I head upstairs to our bedroom.

"Baby?" I call out. Maybe it was a bad idea to warn her of my presence in case she's ready to aim and throw a book or something even heavier at my head.

I step through the door carefully, slanting my gaze all over the bedroom to make sure it's safe to enter. But the only thing I find is Six curled up on the empty bed.

"What's mommy up to, boy?" I leave the glasses on the desk and scratch him behind the ear. He yelps and sniffs in the direction of the closet.

A-ha!

"Can't hide from me, baby. I'm coming for your sweet ass."

I open the doors of the closet expecting the worst. But what I see is close to bringing me to my knees. My vision goes blurry and I blink rapidly hoping I was mistaken. When I open my eyes again my heart drops to my stomach and I realize…she's gone.

She's fucking gone.

The floor feels like it's moving beneath my feet as I walk over to inspect the shelf where all her stuff used to be, but all I find is the empty space mocking me.

No, this has to be a misunderstanding. She wouldn't just leave me, right?

The piercing pain in my chest has me digging deeper, opening every single drawer, frantically sliding the hangers looking for one of her dresses, hoping this is just a prank and all her things are hidden. A lesson she wants me to learn. I expect her to pop out of the corner any second now and laugh at my pathetic ass for falling for it.

But the seconds pass. And the minutes pass. And I've

thrown every item I own to the floor. And still, there's not a single one of her possessions among them.

My eyes are red when I reach the desk and down the whiskey one after the other.

She left me.

It fucking hurts more than the wreck. More than the hope that dies a little more every time I see my deadbeat father drunk on another Christmas Eve.

It's different this time. It's not just my heart that hurts. It's like someone punched the air out of my lungs and left me to suffocate. I know only one thing, I have to get her back or there won't be anything left of me to hurt.

Chapter Thirty

IVY

The next day I'm equally relieved and disappointed that Damien didn't call. He didn't even show up for the rehearsal at the club. I guess he's busy with work.

When I get home, Stella is standing in the living room with a huge smile on her face, looking at me as if she just won the lottery. "Guess what?" she screams and bounces enthusiastically.

"If you've won the lottery, as my best friend, you're obligated to take me with you wherever you decide to go."

She stops and shakes her head. "Come on, let's go to your room." She grabs my hand and pulls me that way.

"What is this?" Suspiciously, I look from her to the glittering sand-colored dress on my bed.

"A dress!" She squeaks and jumps, clapping her hands.

"I can see that, but why are you so excited about it, and why is it on my bed?"

She smacks her palm against her forehead. "It's not my dress, silly. Damien left it for you."

"Why would Damien leave me a dress?" I ask, confused. I thought he was avoiding me.

"You really are daft. To wear to the ball, of course. And as an apology."

"I don't want his apologies, and you know I can't go to the ball with him."

Her smile turns mischievous and she disappears for a bit, only to return with a glittering green dress in her hand. "That's why he brought one for me too. We'll go to the ball together. That way you won't attract attention. You will meet him secretly inside," she says dreamily. I'm speechless, my stunned gaze bouncing between the shiny dress on my bed to Stella who's hugging hers as if it's her most precious. "I wasn't planning to attend because I'm so swamped with work, but, Ivy, it's just so romantic. Like that fairy tale, *Beauty and the Beast*. No, more like *Romeo and Juliet*." She's humming a waltz melody, spinning and swirling the skirt of her long dress, all the way to the living room.

As I follow her, I pronounce each word slowly because she clearly isn't getting it. "I. Can't. Go."

"Of course you can. No one will pay you any attention. There'll be hundreds of guests, and we'll just blend in with the crowd. And these beautiful dresses..." She presses the green dress to her chest and rubs it against her cheek. "We can't return them." She looks at me with her big, sad blue eyes and pouts. I head for my room to avoid this conversation but she's on my heels in a heartbeat. "You can't refuse. He's your prince. You can't miss the chance to get back with the love of your life. Not all of us get second chances." Her gaze falls to the floor.

"I don't know about the love of my life thing." As the words leave my mouth, they feel like a lie I don't want to look at too closely. "Trouble in paradise? Are you sick of

Max already?" Her eyes watering instantly make me regret my comeback.

"No, things with Max are okay, although I don't think he's the one." She wipes a single tear from her cheek and softly whispers, "My prince died a long time ago."

I hug her. "Oh, honey, I didn't know. I didn't mean to upset you. Do you want to talk about it?"

"I believe you only get one soul mate in your lifetime and for me, it was him. It doesn't matter now. I couldn't have done anything to save him. But"—she pleads, wiping her eyes and standing up—"promise me you won't let something as stupid as a misunderstanding keep you from your happily ever after. Life isn't as long as we think it is."

Stella is right in theory. I don't even want to think about what my life would be like without Damien in it. He's been close to death at least once already. "Honey, I want to promise you, but he didn't even call me all day. And then what? He leaves some fancy dress here and that's supposed to make everything all better?"

Stella looks at me like I've insulted her and squeezes the dress closer to her chest. "This is not some dress. This is Elie Saab's Haute Couture!"

"I don't care if it's covered in diamonds and gold. He can't throw money at people and expect everything to be forgotten."

"It's not like that, I swear. Trust me, he's sorry for the way he treated you. Besides, I gave him a lecture. He left you a letter with the dress. Just read it and then decide."

Stella leaves my room and I turn to the dress. To say it's magnificent is an understatement. It's floor-length with a slit on the side that goes all the way to the hip. The wide straps fall off the shoulders, tastefully. The sun from the window reflects the thousands of tiny glittery particles sewed on the sand-colored fabric, and I'm sure this is what it would look like if the stars came down to the seashore. It looks like something a Greek Goddess would wear. I run my hand over it, barely keeping myself from squeezing it the way Stella did because it's the most exquisite fabric I've ever touched.

Beside the dress, there's a masquerade mask of the same color with stones and golden flecks details, and a black feather on the side. Exquisite.

Beneath it lays an envelope with a gold seal.

Well I'll be damned, this really is like a fairy tale.

Ivy,

I'm sorry for my behavior yesterday. I was upset about something that happened at work, and I was wrong to take it out on you. I don't want to pressure you, I'm sorry for giving you an ultimatum and I won't do it again, but I hope that someday you'll tell me all the secrets you're keeping from me.

When you're ready.

Until then, I don't want to spend another night without you. Please forgive me and come to the ball.

P.S. I promise you'll get your apology, just the way you like it.

D.B.

"I'm texting him that we're going." Stella barges into my room, already dressed in her one-shoulder, shiny, olive-green dress.

"Don't. Let it be a surprise."

Our taxi stops in front of Melanie's Victorian-style mansion, with a trail of limousines twisting behind us. The valet opens my door and gives me a hand out of the car.

Wow.

Forget mansion, this thing is like a freaking castle. It's made of stone, and it even has two towers.

We're greeted by a staff member who welcomes us and directs us to the ballroom.

The ballroom is exactly what I imagine every fairy tale depicts. Geometric and floral designs combined to make the flooring's gold and blue marble design a work of art, tall beige arches with gold elements and resplendent chandeliers hanging overhead. In the middle, there's a stage where a string quartet performs classical renditions of modern songs.

"Wow." The only word in my vocabulary apparently.

Stella shrugs. "The ballroom in my home was much more impressive, but Aunt Melanie's is nice too."

I turn to ask her where the hell she lived, but I lose my train of thought when I see Damien across the hall. His strong body beneath a tailored tux, a black mask covering half his face. He's greeting everyone who walks through the door. I look around and notice there are two doors, and unfortunately we came through the other one. A camera flashes in front of him and I quickly turn to Stella, who's busy grabbing two flutes of champagne from a passing waiter's tray. She hands me one and takes me by the hand. "Let's hide in the back until things calm down."

Three hours later, Stella is drunk on the dance floor, and I'm still hiding out at one of the back tables, watching Damien like a stalker. I don't know if he's seen me because he hasn't approached me, or even met my eyes. It cuts me even deeper having to watch all these beautiful people waltzing on the dance floor and laughing and having fun. I wish I could enjoy this with Damien. I want to know what kind of a dancer he is. I want to be in his arms. I want him to kiss me while he dips me on the dance floor. All night, I've been trying to figure out a way to get to him without attracting attention, but it's impossible. Most of the press remains outside interviewing and taking photos of the attendees as they arrive, but there are two photographers inside that have been capturing his and his mother's every move.

This is like a repeat of the party he threw at his house but on a much grander scale. There are at least four hundred people here, and he seems intent on greeting every single one of them. I don't know how he does it; I don't think he's even made it halfway through all of them.

He's being photographed with yet another guest and for the first time tonight, our eyes collide. Or so I think. He quickly moves on to the next couple who've come to say hello and looks this way again. This time I'm sure he sees me and he smiles. Turning around, he seems to be heading to the back door. Is this his way of telling me to follow him and meet him in secret? I put my glass on the table and keep to the outer edges of the ballroom to escape unnoticed. Before I make it to the door, I notice a strangely familiar blonde exiting through it in front of me.

Shit. Nobody can see us together.

I pause for a second to consider whether I should follow. I don't know what's behind that door. What if he didn't see me and just went out to get some air?

Damien's mother is approaching with her photographer, and her gaze stops on me. Her fake smile falls for a second when she recognizes me, and I decide to disappear before I become the unwelcome subject of another scene.

Behind the door, there's a barely lit corridor with a hell of a lot of rooms. What do rich people need all these rooms for? How do I know which one Damien is in?

"Hello." I hear his voice and hurry to the room, excitement tickling in my stomach. *He really is waiting for me.*

Just as I reach the door, I hear a female voice from inside. "Hi."

I'm startled, thinking I'm hearing wrong and I stumble, pushing the door just a little, enough for my heart to hit the wooden floor.

Under the dim light of the lamp, I see Damien leaning against a desk and the blonde woman, whom I now recognize as Vicky, *the assistant*, wraps her arms around his neck, her tongue down his throat.

My hand falls from the door and it closes quietly. I step back, shocked, and stumble over the dress, my arms reaching out to the wall for support when suddenly everything starts spinning. I run down the corridor to find Stella, I need her to tell me what I saw was just a hallucination. A joke or a trick. It couldn't have been Damien. It must've been someone who looks like him.

Yes, maybe Damien's still in the ballroom. I have to find him.

At the door to the ballroom, however, is Melanie and her eyes tell me everything I don't want to be true. "Don't say I didn't warn you."

I stop in front of her and blink a few times. A tear rolls down my cheek and then a few more follow.

Melanie narrows her eyes and speaks in a softer tone. "Don't worry, it gets easier after the first one."

I pass her and walk out the door. The sounds of the music and laughter are amplified in my head, making me feel like it'll burst any second. Tears blur my vision and everything before me is distorted. I look around for Stella, but I can't see her anywhere. My chest is tightening and my breathing is labored. It's like I'm running out of oxygen.

I have to get out of here.

I rush to the nearest exit and almost crash into a couple getting into their limo. *Shit*, there's not one taxi in sight. "Excuse me, can you give me a lift into town? It's urgent," I beg them and they look at each other, communicating silently. Pity is written on the woman's face when she sees the tears flowing down my cheeks and she nods.

Chapter Thirty-One

DAMIEN

"What are you doing?" I push Vicky away, but maybe a bit too hard because she staggers back, and I reach out to catch her before she falls.

"See? You want me too, Damien. There's no point in denying it just because we work together." She comes at me again but this time I'm faster and I manage to avoid her.

"Are you insane? You know I'm with Ivy." I stalk to the door, furious, but she blocks my way.

"She's not good enough for a man like you. She'll never understand what you need." Vicky slides her fingers on my shoulders, and I push her away even harder this time.

"You're crazy. I. Have. A. Girlfriend." My growl scares her, and she steps aside with wide eyes. "I'll expect your resignation to be on my desk by Monday morning."

I leave her in the room, take two steps into the corridor and see a feminine figure in the dark. Fuck, I hope it's not Ivy. Who knows what she'll think when she sees Vicky following me.

"Mother?" My eyes widen when I recognize the woman

looking at me with the coldest look even by her standards. Her eyes drift behind me, where I hear Vicky's heels clicking as she passes around us, her head hung low. "It's not what it looks like." I raise my hands like that would help me defend myself.

"I've heard that one before." She spits the words in my face.

"You don't understand. She came after me."

"Your father would be proud of you," she hisses with the venom of a thousand snakes. "It's not me you should be explaining yourself to."

It feels like I've been struck by lightning. My luck can't be that fucking bad. "Where's Ivy?"

A sinister smile spreads on my mother's face, and she answers with a sugarcoated voice. "If she's smart, she'll be as far away from you as possible."

Chapter Thirty-Two

IVY

Lightning splits the dark sky, and the drizzling rain turns into a heavy downpour. There's not a single person on the sidewalk, and the few passing cars spray water all over me. Not that it makes any difference; I'm soaked, anyway, after the limo dropped me off in the outskirts of the city.

Another flash of lightning followed by angry thunder announces the approaching storm. Not that I care. I stopped feeling anything a mile back.

I feel not the cold, the raindrops, nor my heart. It's as if it was never there.

I've been told when someone hurts you, you suffer. They lied too.

I don't even feel the pebbles on the asphalt under my bare feet.

As I enter my house, I drop my shoes to the floor and head for the living room, but the reflection in the mirror stops me. I step back and my spine presses against the wall.

The girl staring back can't be me; it's a stranger.

Her carefully crafted curls are now a matted nest, running mascara and eyeliner make her look like a raccoon. The once beautiful designer dress is now a wet, ripped and muddy mess.

That's what you get for believing in fairy tales. The carriage turns into a pumpkin, you turn into a mess, and the prince turns out to be a filthy liar.

Welcome to the grown-up world of fiction.

I slide down the wall until my ass hits the floor.

Somewhere deep inside, I want to rip my clothes off and tear into my skin until I find the heart I can no longer feel beating in my chest.

But I don't.

I just sit in a puddle of rainwater and blink with dry eyes, watching the woman in the mirror.

"Don't say I didn't warn you." Melanie's words echo in my head. She was right from the beginning. About everything. And she did warn me. I'm sure if I had even one feeling left in my body, I'd be humiliated for the way I treated her. I thought she was a bad person when she was just trying to protect me.

Damien was lying to me the whole time. About us, about his feelings. You don't do that to the person you like. Hell, maybe even love.

I know I love him. I was ready to tell him tonight.

A lone tear rolls down slowly, coating my cheek in smudged mascara.

What a fool I am.

It hasn't been twenty-four hours since I left and he's already replaced me. He didn't even wait to see if I'd come. Fuck, he could've been lying to me the whole time. Sometimes you think you know someone only to find out you never knew them at all.

I'm surprised I still have any tears left after two more run down. I thought my eyes had dried up by the time I stopped feeling anything.

"Ivy?!" I hear Stella's voice, and I feel a body fall to the floor beside me. "Are you okay? I called you a million times. What happened?"

Without moving my gaze, I drop my phone so she can see it has no battery left.

"Who did you leave with? Why do you look like that? What happened?"

I shrug, my eyes on the girl looking at me from the mirror. This girl's a stranger. Her eyes are blank, her shoulders are slack, and her face has no emotion.

"Ivy talk to me. What the hell happened? Why did you leave? Damien and I came to the house..."

I shudder and the words come out of my mouth in a whisper. "He's not here, is he?"

Stella looks at me puzzled. "No, he's not. We came to the house earlier, but you weren't here so we parted ways to search for you. Where were you?"

I only now notice her hair and dress are wet. "Did he leave you in the rain too?"

"What do you mean too? Did Damien leave you in the rain?"

"No, a limo."

She starts rubbing her hands up and down my arms to warm me, but I can't feel a thing.

Not cold, not warm.

Nothing.

"Ivy, you're shaking. I'll call Damien, and you'll come with me to the bath."

I pull the phone out of her hands. "No, don't call him."

"There's a terrible storm outside. He's worried out of his

mind. We've been searching for you for two hours. Why shouldn't I call him?"

Two hours? Is that how much time has passed while I was walking home? "Please, just don't call him. I don't want him to know where I am."

"Ivy, you're starting to freak me out. If he did something to you, you need to tell me right now."

"No, no. He didn't do anything to me."

"Come with me." She helps me up and drags me to the bathroom. She literally tears the dress from my body. It makes me appreciate Stella all-the-more. Being *Saab Couture* or whatever...

I step into the tub, lie there and just stare out into the dark flashing sky through the small window. Rain beats on the glass and the wind is blowing, both working to break it.

I feel something warm and wet and I turn to Stella, who's spraying me with the handheld showerhead with one hand and talking on the phone with the other.

"Yes, she's here. Damien, tell me what happened. She's not herself."

At the mention of his name, I jump and my eyes widen. I don't want to see him. Not now or ever. I can't look him in the face.

Stella steals a glance at me and continues. "No, I don't want to wait until you come! Tell me now or I won't let you in."

Every nerve in my body lights up. I start waving my hands, whisper-yelling *"No"*, but she has her back to me. Finally, I find my voice and scream as loud as I can. "*No*! I don't want Damien here." It makes Stella jump and drop the handheld sprayer in my lap. Tears stream down my cheeks and I frantically wipe them. I can't start feeling now. I shouldn't.

"She doesn't want you to come. Please don't. Give her some time to come to her senses." My best friend hangs up the phone and strokes my hair. "Relax, I'll keep him away until you're ready, but one of you has to tell me what the hell happened."

"He... I saw him with another woman," I whisper and something in my chest tightens.

So my heart is here after all.

Her face turns red and she stands up from the edge of the tub. "That idiot! I warned him. I cannot believe I thought he could change," she screams while pacing the bathroom. Hysterical laughter comes out of my chest, and my body shakes with the vibration. Stella stops short and looks at me as if I'm crazy. "Dio, he really broke you. Ivy, do we need to go to the hospital? I can make an appointment with a psychologist."

That just makes me laugh harder. I couldn't go to the hospital if I was dying. Before I would be discharged, the police would arrest me.

"What's funny?" She stares at me like I've grown a second head.

"You're angry and I don't feel anything." I shrug and my laughter dies a little.

"What do you mean you don't feel anything? Don't you like him?"

I swear I hear the ice around my heart crack. Maybe I am going crazy. "I love him. I just... I feel nothing, absolutely nothing, my body is numb."

Stella pushes me forward and climbs in behind me in our little bathtub. She wraps her arms around me and I lean back and rest my head on her shoulder.

I don't know how long this numbness will last, but I have to guard it with everything in me. The alternative is my complete ruin.

Chapter Thirty-Three

DAMIEN

I spend all night in the rain in front of Ivy's door like a fucking dog, only going home to change my soaked tux, and now, once again, I'm sitting on the fucking swing, cursing my fucking luck. The yellow grass in the yard is flat from my constant pacing.

The doorknob turns and I bounce off the swing like it scalded me.

Please be Ivy.

"Here, take this. You need it."

I take the glass from Stella's hands before she even completes her sentence, and I gulp the liquor down. "Is she awake yet?" The desperation in my voice is pathetic. Stella starts to say something but stops, and I can see the pity in her eyes. "Please, let me come in. I have to see her, try to explain."

"I told you the last twenty times, Damien. She doesn't want to see you."

"What happened is a fucking misunderstanding. You know I'd never hurt her."

"No, actually, I don't know." She sighs. "I wanted to

believe you could change, but in the back of my mind I think I expected it."

Why the hell doesn't anyone believe me? Am I that bad? I never lied to women about what I wanted from them. "I've changed, Stella. Can't you see how much I've changed? It's all because of her."

She pats me on the shoulder with a frown. "It'll be dark soon. I think it's best if you go. Give her some time to realize what's happening."

Hell no.

"She doesn't need time. The more time that passes, the faster she'll forget about me."

"I don't think there's much chance of that," she says under her breath. "But you still have to leave. Ivy needs to breathe freely, and she won't be able to do that if you spend another night pacing the yard." She takes my glass and walks back into the house.

I start stomping around the small yard, the anger I've been trying to hold back getting the best of me. I need to direct it somewhere before I end up breaking their door, kidnapping Ivy, and locking her in my house so she can never run away from me again.

Just when I stop in front of the door and seriously consider how much she'd hate me if I did that, my phone rings. I pull it out of my pocket to turn it off, but I see it's Rob. Maybe if I listen to Stella and step away for a bit, Ivy will come outside and when I get back in the late evening, I'll be able to catch her in the yard.

"Hey, man." Rob sounds oddly sluggish. I look at my watch and it's only seven thirty p.m. It's unusual for him to be drunk this early, and it's his day off. He should be out somewhere with his fiancée.

"Is everything all right?"

"That answer depends on the number of drinks I've had. So far I'd say it's okayish," he slurs. "What about you? Are you good?" If I wasn't so stupid, I would've been good right now.

"Did something happen? Why are you drunk?"

"Isn't the answer to these questions always a woman?" There's a horn blaring in the background, followed by Rob swearing.

"Tell me you're not driving, fucktard."

"Then I'll have to lie, and you're my best friend and my boss. I think that would break one of your rules." The horn keeps blaring and he laughs.

"Where are you? Pull over before you kill yourself and someone else, you dumb bastard."

Robert tells me a familiar street name, and when I finally get there, I find him half-asleep in the driver's seat. "What happened?" I take him by the shirt and pull him out of the car so he can straighten up a bit.

"She killed it. The motherfucking bitch killed it." I can't understand a word coming out of his drunken mouth.

"Tracy?" I don't think his witless pretentious fiancée could kill a fly. He must be really drunk.

"I didn't even know I wanted it until she told me. And then she killed it because she's a selfish bitch."

I'm beginning to understand how Stella felt last night when she found Ivy. My heart feels like it'll burst from the memory of hearing her cry when she heard my name. At that moment, I realized she has the power to break me into a million pieces.

Robert staggers toward the road, and I barely stop him before he falls in front of a moving car. "Don't stop me. I want to get rid of this agony."

"What is the fucking matter with you?" I use all my strength to pull him back and shove him against the car because the bastard's heavier than me. He leans back and tears start falling from his eyes. *Fuck.* "Talk, Robert. What the fuck happened?"

"Our baby. She killed our baby, man. Because it would ruin her body. She didn't even tell me she was pregnant until I found the test and questioned her. I begged her to keep it, and she went and had an abortion without even telling me." He slides down the car until his ass hits the ground. He pulls out a blunt and lights it, the smell of pot spreading around us.

"Shit, man. I didn't expect that." I sit on the ground next to him and he passes the blunt to me.

"I knew she's self-absorbed, but I thought there was a heart behind her fake tits somewhere."

I hand it back to him and we keep passing it for a few silent minutes as the cars pass in front of us.

When the weed hits me, my body relaxes and my thoughts begin flowing more clearly.

Maybe I'm smothering Ivy, and I should give her some space and time. But God, do I miss her.

Rob breaks the silence. "Judging by your appearance, you're in no better shape than me." He knows a little about my situation because he saw me leaving my mother's house last night, enough that he can probably guess the rest.

"Ivy doesn't want to talk to me. Stella wouldn't even let me in the house."

"Man, how did we get here?" The false humor in his voice is sadder than anything.

A few more silent minutes pass until Rob's phone rings. His conversation is short, ending with "Yes, we're coming."

"Where are we going?" I lift myself from the ground and hold out a hand for him.

"Milo's having a party at his house."

"I don't feel like fucking partying, Rob."

"What other options do you have? Sit in front of her door and beg her to let you in? You can act like a fucking stray dog later. At least drive me there, if you don't want me to drive myself."

Out of the two of us, I'm the more sober one. At least I'm not drunk. There's no way I'll leave him to his own execution. And he's right. One hour won't change Ivy's mind. I have to be reasonable. I'll give her another one without me, and if she doesn't want to talk to me then, I'll rush in and kidnap her.

We walk into Milo's house and the party is already at full force, despite the early hour. One look at this scene tells me everything I've subconsciously known for a while. I'm getting too old for this shit. Everyone here is in college or in their twenties. Drunk or high. Unlike before, it doesn't tempt me in the least. All I want to do right now is be on the couch with Ivy in my arms and Six on my legs.

"Damien?" A woman's shrill voice jerks me out of my thoughts and I turn. At first, I don't recognize her because of the dark hair, but a few seconds later, it comes to me.

"Olivia?" I say, uncertain, but when she laughs and comes closer, it's confirmed.

"Come on, it hasn't been that long." She flutters her long false eyelashes in my face. I still can't get used to her with this brown hair; I've never seen her with anything other than platinum blonde. "What're you doing here? I thought you stopped partying." You can't tell from her friendly tone that she's the reason I stopped going. Or rather, why I started hiding from the media.

"I just dropped off Robert. I'm leaving."

She grabs me by the arm and pouts her lips. "Hey, not so

fast. Stay and have a drink with me. You know, for old times' sake..."

"I have to be somewhere, Ollie." I want to kick myself for calling her the nickname I used as a child when I see the enthusiasm in her eyes. The last thing I need is the crazy-in-love version of Olivia.

"Come on, just one drink. We've got so much catching up to do. I don't want things between us to be awkward, Damien."

"You tried to stab me after twenty years of friendship Olivia. Does it get more awkward than that?"

She tears up and her gaze falls to the ground. "But I... I..." She sniffles and a tear rolls down her cheek.

Dammit, I hate seeing women cry.

"Please, just give me a chance to apologize. I wasn't well then. I swear, I'm better now. I'm so sorry for what I did to you." She starts whimpering. She wraps her arms around my neck and stands on her toes to whine in my ear because the music is too loud. "Please, let me explain what I've been through. And then decide if you can forgive me."

On one hand, my gut tells me to run as far away as possible from the nutjob, but on the other, I feel guilty because if I hadn't slept with her, she probably wouldn't have ended up in a mental hospital. Everyone deserves forgiveness, right? I should know that...

I sigh and agree. Either way, I have thirty-five more minutes from this torturing hour until I can go back to Ivy.

Olivia disappears for a few minutes and comes back, handing me one of the two cups in her hands. She apologizes again and starts telling me stories about the "resort" she went to and all the celebrities she met there, and the atmosphere quickly lightens.

Maybe that's exactly what I need. If I can forgive Olivia

after she almost ruined my life, then maybe Ivy will forgive me after Vicky tried to ruin ours, right? I keep telling myself this while Olivia keeps talking about herself. I don't know how long it's been since we started talking, because my thoughts are thinning out.

After a while, my limbs start feeling heavy. What the hell? This can't be the pot. I grab the edge of the bar to hold on to when I feel myself starting to slip. The people around me blur and the last thing I remember is Olivia pulling my arm around her shoulders.

Chapter Thirty-Four

DAMIEN

An obnoxiously loud noise violates my ears. I lift my head up to scan for the source just when it stops and a few seconds later it starts again. I feel like my head is stuck between a sumo wrestler and a sharp rock. The room is dark, but a small ray of light breaks through the curtains. What day is it and what's happening? I feel as if my head is stuffed with cotton.

I find the source on the other side of the bed and answer the phone without bothering to look at the caller's ID.

"Where the hell are you, you fucking moron?" Melanie's furious voice snaps me back into reality. What the... I've never heard my mother curse, not even once in my whole life, and even weirder is that she's not hiding her anger behind that eternal ice queen mask.

"I..." I look around and realize I don't know where I am. Nothing is familiar to me. "What's going on, mother?"

"How dare you ask me what's going on?" she screams, and a foreboding anxiety spreads through me. Melanie never screams. Ever.

She clears her throat, gathering her composure, and

continues with a sharp bite. "If you want to keep your job, you better be at the office in twenty!" Then she just hangs up.

I can only form one sentence in my head: *What the fucking hell?*

I get up and open the curtains, wincing as the light burns my eyes. Slowly, because I don't have any strength in my legs, I start searching the room for my shirt. The weird thing is it's not only my head that hurts; it's my whole body. Like every muscle is stiff. My jeans are still on me, which is weird too, because I never sleep with clothes, and I find my shirt crumpled and tossed on the floor where I don't remember putting it. But actually, I don't even remember coming here. And where the hell is *here*?

I look around the big room and notice it's feminine. Dark pink wallpaper, a bunch of dresses on a white chair, tons of cosmetic products.

Oh, no.

I bolt out of the room, trying to find some explanation as to where I am. The last memory I have is the call from Rob, but this isn't his condo. Following the smell of coffee I head down a dark hallway with some odd small paintings until eventually I reach the kitchen and freeze.

"Ivy?" My voice is weak and my throat is dry. The woman standing with her back to me is wearing only white lingerie and has hair the exact same color as Ivy's. But this woman has a skinnier, bonier body than hers. As she turns to me, the memories start hitting me like a ton of bricks.

"Are you up already, baby?" Olivia's candied tone goes perfectly with her angel expression.

Hot shivers of hellish anger start crawling on my body as I realize why I feel like the walking dead. The bitch drugged me. "Olivia, what did you do?" My livid glare causes her spine to bend, but her psychotic puppet face doesn't change.

"Baby, I don't know what you're talking about." A jury would fall for her innocent, sweet voice, but I know better. This is not my first rodeo, and if I have to judge by my own experience, the freak poured me a happy dose of some cheap opiate.

Adrenaline is racing through my body, and I can barely control myself. If she wasn't a woman, she'd be dead by now. But since I can't physically harm her, I resort to a menacing glare and a threatening stance, and with every step I take toward her, Olivia shrinks back. "You drugged me, you psycho. I don't remember anything from last night. What did you give me?" I squeeze her shoulders, barely stopping myself from shaking her.

"Nothing, I just wanted you to relax. You wouldn't stop talking about that Ivy girl." The venom with which she says her name makes me squeeze her harder.

A wave of guilt floods me as I look around and realize I was supposed to be at my girlfriend's door last night, but it's not evening anymore. I look at the clock on the wall and I'm shocked to see that it's already noon.

Remembering my mother's words, a cold sweat breaks out on my forehead. What the hell did she mean by keep my job? No one can take it from me.

As I release Olivia, I notice her hair is even cut in the same style as Ivy's hair and has the same highlighted strand on the left side. What the hell? "Nothing has happened between us and nothing will ever happen, Olivia. I forbid you to approach Ivy, myself, or any of my family. The next time you do it, I'll issue a restraining order." There's no room for doubt in my tone, and Olivia finally slips off her mask.

She raises an eyebrow, and her demented smile spreads. "Keep on repeating that if it'll make you feel better."

I don't listen to her as I head for the door. I know nothing happened between us, I can vaguely remember passing out as soon as I hit the bed.

In the elevator of what I now recognize as one of Olivia's father's buildings, I find my keys and hope I came here in my car. Last night is still a blur with a few glimpses coming now and then.

I'm at the headquarters in less than ten minutes. I don't bother greeting anyone as I head straight for my office on the top floor. I find my mother in my chair behind my desk, and her eyes widen when she sees me. She jumps to her feet and smacks her palms on the desk.

I'm not the type of man who is intimidated by his mother, nor do I allow her to interfere in my life, but the anger radiating from her in waves makes me anxious. Nothing so bad could've happened, could it?

Unfortunately, my gut is telling me I'm not going to like what she has to tell me.

She grabs the large pile of newspapers and magazines next to her and starts throwing them across the desk one by one. "*The Heir to The Blacks' Empire Wasted Again. Bimbos, alcohol, and drugs—that's how a billion dollar empire is run. Damien and Olivia: A Renewed Romance. Black Rose Shares Falling Due to Drug Scandal.*" My mother continues reading headlines and captions, and I manage to take a glimpse of the photos of me on the pages of every newspaper from the tabloids to the broadsheets and a couple of magazines. I can only assume what's swirling in the social media and the news sites right now. *Dammit!*

There's no longer any doubt as to why the fucking bitch drugged me. She didn't want forgiveness; she wanted revenge.

"Mother." I raise my hands and approach her cautiously

as one would do with a mountain lion. "I have an explanation."

"I don't care about your explanations! I'm sick of them. I hoped that you wouldn't follow in your father's footsteps, but you keep on disappointing me day after day. Save your explanations for the board." She saunters toward me, every word and every step harsher than the last. "If they're even willing to listen. Look at yourself." She wrinkles her nose in disgust. "You smell like a keg." She passes me, her heels echoing down the hall to the conference room.

I look at myself in the mirror and step back. *Shit, there's no chance they'll believe me.* My blue button-down shirt is torn, my jeans are stained, and my face looks exactly like I feel. Crushed.

I walk into the boardroom right behind her and sit down. Richard, as always, is sitting across from me. He's grinning. The fucker knows what his daughter did. Hell, they might've even worked together.

As expected, no one believes my explanation when it's my turn to speak.

"How dare you insult my daughter and try to blame her for your behavior! Old habits die hard, we knew it would be only a matter of time before you were back to your shenanigans. I think I speak for everyone here when I say you're unfit for the position of CEO. The negative publicity is damaging our brand equity and the investors are losing confidence in our ability to maintain the high standards they expect from us. I vote to remove you from the company." Richard's fist lands on the table, earning him a disapproving stare from the rest of the board. Everyone knows he hates me and he's been trying to get rid of me for a long time.

One thing's for sure. I won't just roll over and let them

rob me of my family's legacy that we've built with blood, sweat, and tears. Richard can suck it.

"Who's with me?" He raises his hand and looks at the other members. One by one they start raising their hands and my pulse speeds up. They can't throw me out just like that, because of a minor mistake. Okay, it's not minor, but there are ways to fix it.

My mother clears her throat and stands up.

In general, she shouldn't be attending these meetings, but everyone is aware of my father's situation, and everyone respects her too much to throw her out. She's also with me, and I have the larger share of the company. Not that this would help if the board decides to remove me from the management. Then my mother will have to leave too. We'll keep receiving a check from the company, but it'll be in Richard's hands.

I don't care that no one believes me. I'll fight for what's mine until my last breath.

"Richard. Respected members," she begins with her convincingly sweet tone, which has won her thousands of deals. "I believe there's a way to resolve this situation without such drastic measures. Damien and I have a wealth of experience and contacts between us, we've built up close relationships with our clients and you'd risk losing them as well. I agree that this situation is serious, but it was unintentional and probably exaggerated by the media. I believe with my proposal, everyone will be satisfied, and with the help of the PR team we can turn this around in our favor."

A slight smile lifts the corners of my lips. My mother can be a royal pain in the ass, but she's a genius. If there's anyone who can convince them, it's her. I knew she'd stand up for me.

She looks at everyone at the table. "The media portrays

Damien as the eternal bachelor, frivolous and juvenile." She turns to Richard. "Richie, you're concerned for your daughter because of the pictures of her with Damien. But we all know what happened a few years ago, the truth was suppressed while my son suffered the consequences. No one forced Olivia to be in Damien's company last night and don't forget I can easily turn the media's attention to her mental issues faster than you could throw us and our things out of the building. But that would only lead to more losses for the company and more black marks on your resume. How about we make a mutually beneficial deal and end the feud between our families once and for all?"

Yes!

"You want to protect your daughter's honor, and I want the company to stay in the family." Her eyes stop on me. A devilish smile replaces her serious face and my body tenses. "Damien will marry Olivia."

"I agree," Richard says at the same time I shout, "No way."

I jump from my chair and smack my fists against the wooden table. She can't be serious. "Tell me you're joking?!" I growl in her face but her smug smile says it all.

I grit my teeth. I won't allow this to happen, and I won't leave my company in their hands! But first, I need to calm down and come up with something before they have security throw me out.

"Melanie, a word." I point at the door, and we both leave the room where Richard and the members are already agreeing to her crazy idea. "What the hell are you thinking? How could you do this to me?" I growl as soon as we enter my office, but she doesn't even blink.

"This, my son, is called karma." For the first time since forever she slips off her mask and talks with her real voice that I haven't heard since I was a child. "I didn't raise you to be a liar and that's what you get."

"What the hell, I didn't do anything! I swear I didn't cheat on Ivy. And I thought you of all people would believe me when I tell you that psycho set me up again by drugging me. Why does nobody believe me? It's all a big fucking misunderstanding. I fucking love Ivy." The words come out unexpectedly but the moment I say them, I know they're true. I've loved her since the first time she fell asleep in my arms. I just didn't want to admit it to myself. But none of that matters because I know my mother will never believe a man.

"How can I believe you when you continue to let me down again and again? That's exactly why I raised you not to fall in love. Because the men in the Black family are incapable of keeping their dicks in their pants. I knew it was inevitable that you would hurt her." She shakes her head, and for the second time in my life, I want to grab a woman and shake some sense into her.

"You don't even like Ivy?!"

"It doesn't matter if I like her. No woman deserves to hurt like I did. You might not understand now, but someday you'll thank me."

"Mother, you don't know what you're saying. Nothing can make me give her up. I'll marry, but only if it's Ivy."

"Do you think I want this freak Olivia for my daughter-in-law? This is the only way. It's time to grow up and show you're a man who can take care of his family. Otherwise, I'll make sure you don't see a penny of your inheritance."

My cold tone lets her know there's not an ounce of doubt in my words. "I don't care about your money if it means losing Ivy."

"You've lost her already," she calls after me, but I'm already storming out the door. There's no point in her wasting her breath. I know I can fix things between Ivy and me. She'll believe me. She has to believe me. There is no other option. I wouldn't touch another woman, and I'm sure nothing happened between Olivia and me. I'll spend all of eternity proving to Ivy there's no one else for me.

I know she loves me too. She'll marry me, and even if it's to save the company, I know she's the one for me. I can't imagine life without her. I'd rather die.

I get in the car and step on the gas. I know where I'm going.

First stop, the store where I saw the ring a few days ago. Even then, I knew that one day it'd be on her finger. Damn, I wanted to give it to her that same day, but I didn't want to scare her off.

Well, fate decided it for me.

Chapter Thirty-Five

IVY

I take my duffel bag and head to the afternoon rehearsal at Masquerade. I'm sure Damien won't make a scene in front of his staff, and that gives me some relief. I'll just sneak out early so he won't catch me alone.

If he comes for me at all.

I expected to spend the night hiding in my bedroom, but he left and didn't come back. I don't know if I'm happy or sad about that. Frankly, I don't know anything anymore. I still feel lifeless. Although the pain in my chest and my head has been growing since I woke up, I'm still holding on tightly to the numbness. I'll keep it as long as I can.

At least I have the choreographer job, for now. I hope Damien doesn't decide to punish me for his mistakes and take this away from me. I don't know how I'll survive otherwise.

The second I enter the studio at Masquerade, five pairs of eyes pierce me like knives. *Crap.* There's no way they found out about the scandal, right?

Judging by the pity in their eyes, they did.

Oh, come on, who could've told them?

"Oh, honey, you look terrible. I'm so sorry. Come here." Tasha reaches out to me.

Apparently, the three layers of makeup didn't help. I hug her quickly and pull away. I don't need pity. If I give in to it, it means giving in to my feelings, and that is scary. Lord knows I've hidden so many feelings in the pits of my soul, they'd tear me to ribbons if I let them out.

"I'm fine. Let's get started." I start changing my shoes in the corner.

"Are you sure you don't want to talk about it? We're here for you, you know. Girlfriends support each other."

"Yes, Ivy. If I didn't need this job so much, I would've thrown in my bodysuit in a second. How dare he pull you from the show and then humiliate you in that way!" Christy almost makes me laugh when she literally throws her black bodysuit on the ground and kicks it like a grumpy kid.

My chest warms when all the girls agree with her. I knew I'd found friends here, but I didn't know they'd be so loyal. "Thank you, but I'll be fine." I send an air kiss to them and a little more of the ice around my heart melts.

Shit.

I close my lids for a moment to push my feelings back into the abyss, but when I open them, my eyes land on Damien's photograph in a magazine on a chair.

"What's that?" I grab it and read the headline. *Damien and Olivia: The New Power Couple or Just Another Drunken Night?*

What the hell?

Damien's eyes are glassy and bloodshot, and his arm is draped over Olivia's shoulders, she's hugging him around the waist and grinning at the cameras. Below, in a smaller font, is written: *The billionaire heir celebrates with alcohol, drugs, and a socialite girlfriend.*

I take a couple of steps back and sit in the chair that has another newspaper with a similar headline.

So that's why Damien didn't come back. My heart cracks a little more, and I ram my nails into my palms, trying to stop it.

Wow. He's quick to replace me. I cannot believe a part of me was trying to justify his behavior at the ball wanting to believe he's innocent.

"Honey, you're pale. You want me to bring you some water or something sweet?" One of the girls asks, but I can't see which one.

"No, I have to dance." My answer comes out before I can figure out what's happening. I jump out of the chair and suddenly I feel lightheaded and my vision is getting blurry. Next thing I know I'm falling to the floor.

"Oh my god! Ivy, are you okay?" Several hands grip my body and help me get up.

"Yes, low blood pressure, that's all. We have to dance. Come on." I stand in front of the mirror. The other girls look at each other and stand in position.

I can't think about this bullshit. The only thing that can save me from falling apart now is music.

Tasha presses the button for the music and we warm up.

"Ivy!" A painfully familiar voice calls out from the hallway and I freeze in place.

No, this can't be happening. I'm hearing things. Damien wouldn't...

"Ivy!" Damien flies through the door and heads straight for me. He wraps his arms around my body and lifts me into the air. Still paralyzed, I only manage to make some inarticulate sound between shrieking and a dying cat. Another bit of my ice starts melting and I yell at him. "Let me go!" I punch him in the chest and he steps back.

My body is arguing with that decision because it wants to be in his warm embrace. I barely manage to keep from throwing myself into his strong arms again, which is why I decide to ignore him and turn to the mirror. "Girls, let's move to shoulders." I start my stretching exercise but none of the girls follow me. Everyone looks at me as if I'm crazy.

Hell, maybe I did finally go crazy.

Damien grabs my arm and pulls me toward him. "Ivy, don't ignore me. You can punish me any way you want, but please don't make me live without you." He kisses my hand and squeezes it in his palm.

"You don't seem to have a problem living without me. It even looks like it was a lot of fun." I pull my hand away, pick up the magazine from the chair, and open it in front of his face. "I believed you, Damien. I believed you had changed, and you were lying to me the whole time." I'm shouting like a crazy woman. I dig my nails into my palms again and again in an attempt to return to the numbness I've been feeling, but it's too late. As much as I try to drown my feelings, they swim back to the surface. "Take your apologies and shove them up your ass!" I hurl the magazine at his face but Damien dodges it and strides toward me. I raise my hands in front of his chest. "Don't you dare touch me. I don't want anything to do with you," I shout. Around us the five girls just stand there with their eyes bugging, so I lower my voice. "This isn't the place, and the time will never come."

"I don't give a damn if the whole world hears. Ivy, you have to believe me. I didn't do any of those things. Olivia and Richard set this whole thing up. The bitch drugged me and she probably called the press herself. I swear, I barely remember anything from last night. I didn't even want to be at that party, but I went for Rob. I would never touch another woman."

His last sentence crosses the line. If he wants a show, I'll give him a fucking spectacle. I can't hold back my feelings anymore.

My disbelieving laugh must confuse him because he reaches out to me. I swat his hands away and yell in his face. "And Vicky? Is she a big coincidence too? All week, late nights at the office. You didn't even have the decency to wait and see if I showed up at the ball. Why did you send me that dress? And the fucking letter? Vicky probably wrote it while you were fucking her behind my back."

"I swear on everything holy, I never touched her. She came on to me and I pushed her away. I don't care about anyone but you." His eyes well with tears. He looks so sincere that everything in me wants to believe him. "I promise I'll never hurt you again. I love you." He reaches out and wipes the tear that trickles down my cheek.

He grabs my hand and suddenly drops to one knee. My eyes widen, and a group gasp comes from the women behind him.

What is happening?

"Ivy, I've never loved another woman. You're the only one I want to fall asleep with and wake up to. I know I hurt you, but please believe me, I'd never touch another woman. You're it for me. I can feel it with every cell of my body."

Damien pulls a small blue box from his pocket and my legs start shaking. I could faint right about now.

"Before I do this, I have to be honest with you. The board is trying to control my life. By marrying you I'll either win my company back or lose it for good. But in either case, I'm winning because I'll get to call you my wife. I've wanted you to be mine since the moment I first saw you, and even though this proposal seems rushed, I have not a single doubt that we are meant for each other. Hell, I wanted to propose when I heard the maintenance man call you Mrs. Black, but I was afraid.

"I can't survive a day more without you, and I don't want to do it. Ivy Thanos, will you marry me?"

My tears start flowing faster when I hear my false name on his lips. He doesn't even know who I am. I'm the one who's been lying to him all this time.

A mix of feelings overwhelm me, and as much as I want to shout *yes, I feel the same way*, I can't do it. I can't marry Damien while I'm still a fugitive, and he still doesn't know the truth.

I wipe my tears with my free hand and grit my teeth. Now, more than ever, I have to be strong. "I can't do it, Damien." It tears me up from the inside out to watch his eyes lose hope. All his feelings are written on his face.

I believe him when he says that he didn't betray me, but this thing between us is impossible. I was a fool to believe otherwise.

He rises from the floor and grabs my face in his hands. "You can Ivy. I know you want it too. I know you love me. I can see it in your eyes. What's stopping you?"

"I just...can't," I whisper. His touch is like hot coals burning my skin. His hands stroke my cheeks, jaw, lips and leave burning traces of love and pain.

"Okay. I assumed I'd hear that answer and I promised I wouldn't push you. Fuck my inheritance. Let them take the fucking company. I'll build a new one. They can take everything if I still have you."

His words shock me and I pull back. "What do you mean take everything?"

I can't let Damien lose everything for me. For a future that's not even certain. I might end up in jail for all I know, and everything he did would be in vain. Even if I exonerate myself by some miracle, who's going to do business with a man whose wife was a wanted criminal for stealing money?

I don't care if he has a dime to his name, but he likes his lifestyle. He loves his job, his house, and his family. If he loses them because of me, I know one day he'll look back and hate me.

That's if he doesn't hate me after he finds out my secret.

I'd rather break my own heart, trample it, and throw it in the dumpster before I see the hatred in his eyes, which is inevitable if I let him give up everything for a liar.

"I already have everything." He wipes my last tear and bends down to kiss me. I pull away from him before his lips reach mine and ram my nails into my palms so deep there's a danger of them bleeding. I grit my teeth, swallow the lump in my throat, and put my emotionless mask in the mirror behind him.

I look him straight in those teary emerald eyes and lie with the coldest tone that leaves no room for doubt. "Damien, I didn't mean for things to get this far. It was fun, but it was just a game. I'm sorry to have misled you, but the truth is, you were convenient because you gave me a job and the sex was great. I don't want to be with someone like you forever. Please don't call me anymore and forget you ever met me. I'll do the same."

Then I do what I do best.

I run away.

Chapter Thirty-Six

IVY

A month later

I hear barking through the open window, and my heart squeezes at how much it reminds me of Six. *That damn cute dog.*

I shudder and pull my blanket over my head.

Everything reminds me of *him*. Every stupid movie we watched. Every one of his T-shirts I took with me when I left. The scent of his cologne, his soap, and his house.

Every breath.

I'm not sorry I did what I did that day. It was the most selfless thing I've ever done and I'm proud of it. The only thing I regret is I didn't prepare myself for the pain that followed.

The first few days were unbearable. I couldn't stop crying, I couldn't eat, I didn't get out of bed.

Every single feeling I ever hid hit me like a tidal wave and flooded me like a tsunami.

A tsunami that almost drowned me.

That numbness I felt at the beginning... Turns out it was

just a stepping stone from which I fell into a bottomless pit of pain.

I lost myself; I lost the man I love. I have no one and no reason to live. The only thing that keeps me relatively sane is that Stella doesn't let me out of her sight for more than a few hours at a time.

Damien kept looking for me for the first few weeks after I dumped him in front of everyone at Masquerade. He called nonstop; stayed at my front door day and night, tried to peek at me through the windows, did everything possible. It only made me close myself off even more, spending all my time in my little box called a bedroom and crying until I fall asleep or sleep until I wake up to cry.

The latter describes my daily routine throughout the last month.

I haven't set foot in Masquerade. I can't bear seeing him and I don't think I'd be strong enough to refuse him again. The show I gave was a one-time only deal, and I wouldn't survive a repeat.

I haven't even looked for a job yet because I'm still not functioning properly. I don't think I've left the house more than four times in those four weeks. I live off my parents' stolen money that I brought with me in my duffel bag when I ran away. I was keeping it as emergency money in case I had to flee the country again, but at this point, I don't care even if the Bulgarian police come knocking on my door.

My life will never be the same, and I don't think I'll ever be truly happy again. My only hope is someday I'll be able to look in the mirror and see something other than a walking dead person staring back. But for now, I'm riding this wave.

I hear the dog bark again and sigh. *You're imagining it, Ivy. It can't be Six.* There's scratching and banging on the door, then barking again.

I get out of bed reluctantly to see which neighbor's dog got lost and insists on entering my home. I love dogs so much, but our neighbors are annoying, and I have no desire to listen to their monologue about the lawnmower or the new petunias when I return their dog to them.

I open the door and before I can react, he jumps on me and licks my whole face. "Six, what are you doing here?"

Of course, I don't get an answer because it's a dog. A dog that's too far from home.

I look around the yard, cautiously, fearing Damien has switched to a new strategy to get my attention, but no one's there.

The big black-and-brown dog, the height of a baby horse, sits on my step with a wide smile and his tongue out, slobbering.

"Come in, boy." I open the door wider for him, and he enters like he's being chased, pushing everything out of his way and sniffing every corner he hasn't sniffed since I last brought him here.

It's obvious he got lost because he's missing his collar and he's really dirty.

I call Stella a few times but she's not picking up, so I think about my options. No taxi would agree to drive him unaccompanied to Damien's house, and there's no way I'm going there.

I grumble and glare at him. "Is that your plan, Six? How did you even get here?"

A long silence follows, and then he yelps and lies on the carpet.

I can't leave him here. If I were in Damien's shoes I'd be worried sick. I don't know how long he's been out there, and it's not fair of me to hide him until Stella returns, because no one knows how long that'll take. It's time for me to grow up.

"Ivy?" My heart shrinks when I hear Damien's voice on the telephone. The hope in his voice when he says my name tears me apart.

"Yes," comes out of the lump in my throat and I cough. "Yes, it's me. I wanted to let you know that Six is at my house. I don't know how he got here. You can send your driver to pick him up." I'm proud I'm able to say it with such confidence.

"Will you let me see you?" I can barely hear him with the music and noise in the background.

"I said everything I had to say. I don't want to see you." I hope he didn't hear my voice breaking on that last sentence.

"Then you can keep the fucking dog too. You already took everything else from me." I pull away from the phone to see if I've dialed the right number. Damien loves that dog. "He likes you more, anyway." Damien's slurring his words.

I look at the clock and see it's lunchtime. Then I look at the calendar because in my permanent Zombie-like state I have no clue what day it is. It's not even the weekend. This isn't normal.

"Damien, are you okay?" I may not be with him, but I still love him from the depths of my soul, and I want the best for him. Even if that isn't me.

He laughs in a higher pitch and calls out sarcastically, "Wonderful. How can I not be? I'm celebrating an engagement, after all."

The next thing I hear is complete silence. He hung up.

The same feeling, like someone is stabbing me in the ribs, which never left me since the Halloween Ball is getting worse now.

Engagement.

I lie on the carpet and snuggle against Six.

Engagement.

The word repeats in my head, over and over again, and I can feel the tears trying to push their way out. I swallow them and get up to pour myself a glass of wine as Stella enters. *Great.* She couldn't pick up the phone or show up five minutes early, so I had to go through this.

She looks at me, puzzled. I guess because she didn't think I'd be out of bed, and screams when the dog touches her with his wet nose. "Dio Mio! Six, what are you doing here?" she asks, then turns to me with an accusing stare. "Ivy, tell me you didn't steal him."

I choke on the sip of wine and spit it out in the sink. "Are you insane? Why would I steal a dog? And how do you think I'd be able to get into that fortress Damien calls a house?" I try not to show how much it hurts me to even think of his home. The place that felt like my home.

"I don't know. Then why is Six here?" she says in a baby voice as she strokes his head.

I pour her a glass of wine, and the three of us cuddle on the carpet while I tell her the whole story. One of the reasons I love her is because she's always ready to day drink with me.

"Will you return Six to Damien? I know he doesn't mean what he said and he'll miss him. And while you're there, would you check on him for me? He was very drunk, and although he said he's celebrating an engagement, he didn't sound good."

A stream of wine sputters out of Stella's mouth onto the green carpet and she turns wide-eyed to look at me. "Engagement? You mean he got engaged to that nutjob?"

Straight with the salt in the wounds.

"I don't know who he got engaged to. He hung up on me."

"I knew he wasn't good because he refused to take calls from me, Rosalie, Melanie...everyone." Stella narrows her eyes at me because I do the exact same thing. I refuse to let anyone in. The girls at the club and Rob called me several times, but what good is it to keep in touch, knowing eventually I'll have to let them go too. The only person I can't avoid is Stella because I live with her, but I wouldn't replace her for anything in this world. And I know she wouldn't judge me if she knew the truth. "He even forbade the security guards to let us in. But I didn't think he'd accept his mother's offer."

We both go silent, pondering until Stella gets up and taps Six on the butt. "Come on, buddy, let's get you home."

I help her load him into a taxi, and a few more tears slip down my cheeks because I know this is probably the last time I'm seeing the big mutt. I go inside and curl up in my bed, my sobs growing stronger, no longer entirely because of the dog. It's because deep down in my heart, I still hoped that one day I'd be able to clear my name, and Damien would accept me back. A selfish hope, but still…hope.

But soon he'll be married and I refuse to be a homewrecker. Which leaves no hope at all for me.

The ringing of a phone I haven't heard in more than half a year takes me out of my self-pity, and I jump out of bed to pry it out of the abyss of my duffel bag.

"Hello?" I pick up the satellite phone my aunt gave me and my nonna's soft voice breaks my heart into another hundred pieces.

"Ivonne, my child." The tears start again when I hear my real name and the Bulgarian language for the first time in almost a year. Since the last time I talked to her.

"Nonna." I finally break and start crying out loud.

"Oh, my dear. What's wrong?"

"Nothing, nothing. I'm just glad to hear your voice."

Unfortunately, I know she won't believe me, because neither my tone nor my tears are of happiness, they're sadness. Sadness for her, sadness for Damien. Sadness for my life, the false one and the real. I don't even know which is which anymore.

"Girl, you know you can never lie to me. It's a boy, isn't it?" Nonna always sees right through me. I don't know how she does it, like she has a key to my soul.

"Yes, but it doesn't matter because he's marrying another woman."

"I'm so sorry, my dear." Her gentle voice is like a sedative, making me stop crying and wobbling in place. "Life has a way of sorting the puzzle, kid. Have faith in it and everything will fall into place."

"Not in my life. The parts of my puzzle are long lost."

"That's just the way you see it, honey. You'll be surprised at what fate can bring." Nonna starts coughing deeply on the phone, and I immediately jump to my feet as if I could do something from five thousand miles away.

"Nonna, what's with this cough? Are you okay?"

"I just have a cold." She keeps on coughing, but it doesn't sound like *just* a cold. My body tenses and I'm already pulling the laptop from my bag before she can say the next word.

"I miss you a lot. I'll find a way to see you soon," I tell her as I open and start the computer.

"Don't worry about me, child. Your aunt says hello. I have to go. She's calling me downstairs. I love you."

"Kiss her for me. I love you too, Nonna. Take care."

This time the silence on the phone hurts even more.

I don't get to talk to my Nonna and aunt often, because we don't want to raise suspicions. But oh, how I want to pick up the phone and fall into another world while talking with her for hours like we did as I grew up.

I clench my teeth and wonder how I haven't broken any

yet. I sense something different about me. Something that comes to life and swims to the surface. Some hope, mixed with love and determination. I may be too late for Damien, but I won't be too late for Nonna. I'll never forgive myself if something happens to her before I can see her again.

I open the program on my computer, enter the code, and start checking every corner of the internet for traces of my parents.

I close the laptop with a growl.

A week and a half of witch-hunting. And nothing. Again.

I leave my room just as Stella enters the front door with some huge bags in her hands.

"Oh, great, I won't have to drag you out of your room. Guess what?" She drops the bags on the ground and pads to me. I shrug and she rolls her eyes. "You're no fun at all when you're so focused. What are you doing in your room so much that you don't ever leave it?"

"You're changing the subject. Am I supposed to guess?"

"Guess who's going to New York for a week," she singsongs. "Raquel wants to meet a few representatives of some big stores out there, and she thinks there's potential they'd take on my clothes." She jumps and for the first time since... I don't remember when, I smile genuinely.

"I'm so happy for you, Stells." I hug her. "Don't forget to get a magnet for the fridge."

"You can take care of that because you're coming with me!" she screams.

I freeze in place and look at her, puzzled. "Stella, I don't have a job. I can barely afford to stay alive let alone travel to New York." I give her the most logical explanation, instead of *I used to live there until I had to hide from the authorities.*

"That's why I convinced Raquel you're a very important part of the process and you should be with me. Everything is paid," she screams again and starts dancing her victory dance. "What's wrong? Why aren't you dancing with me?"

"Because I can't come to New York." I don't know how to explain it to her. I've run out of lies, and frankly, I'm tired of them.

"Forget it, you're going. I won't leave you here all week. Who knows if you'll even feed yourself? No way. If you're not going then I'm not going."

I sigh heavily and start padding to my room, but I hear the footsteps of the blonde tornado behind me. "Ivy Thanos, don't think you can run away from me. I'll get you to New York if I have to drag you by your hair."

I turn around with another sigh to explain to her Lord knows what, when she jumps on my bed, right on my laptop.

"Ouch," she yelps and moves away from it. "Dio, Ivy, I'm so sorry. I'll buy you a new one."

I swear my heart stops for a second.

She grabs the laptop with her shaking hands and hands it to me. I open it and press the on button. The computer turns on, but the screen remains black.

Oh, no, no, no. What am I going to do now? How will I look for clues?

I press the keys frantically, but it's hopeless, and it'll need a change of the screen. Which means a lot of money and at least a week. *Shit.*

"Ivy, I'm so sorry. We'll get a new one or fix it." Stella's voice trembles, but I just don't have the strength to deal with anything more. That was the last straw. I didn't sleep more than two hours last night. I need to recharge and come up with a new plan.

"It's okay, Stells. Would you mind leaving me alone? I need to get a little rest." I yawn and she leaves the room with a guilty expression. I feel really bad for shitting on her happiness but I'm drained.

In less than a minute, I'm already dreaming of my favorite country house and Nonna's banitsa.

The next day, while digging in the duffel bag for the money I brought with me when I escaped Bulgaria, I find my old laptop at the bottom. I'd completely forgotten my parents had put it in there before fleeing.

At least they were helpful with one thing.

All of my programs are on an external hard-drive, which means I can keep digging for clues the week and a half that my other laptop will be out of commission.

Nostalgia creeps in when I open it. I was like seventeen or so the last time I used this laptop. There's still a picture of me and my only Bulgarian friend on it from one of the times we stole Nonna's moonshine. I chuckle at the memory of how fun it was, and then how nasty it got.

Everything on my screen is perfectly arranged, like I do with all my computers. Except for a folder in the top-right corner with the name *IVONNE*. That's weird. It's possible I forgot it, but it's unlikely.

I open it to see which folder I should put it in before I get started, but there's only one file inside. A photo of my parents in the New York apartment.

What the hell?

My parents never allow anyone to take photos of them.

Even for homecoming, Nonna barely convinced them to take a picture with me. And when they do allow it, they never show affection for one another. I always wondered how they could be married for so many years and still behave like strangers. In this photo they're hugging.

There's something weird about it, but I can't put my finger on it. I look at it from corner to corner and everything looks normal. Except...the painting.

I don't remember that painting being in the apartment; after all, I chose all the art. Upon closer inspection, if the little knowledge I have doesn't lie to me, it looks like a Monet. I'm positive we don't have one of those. Almost all the art in the apartment is abstract. I'd remember if there was impressionism. It doesn't even match the décor.

Something's wrong.

I open the properties and almost fall off the chair. The date the file was created was one day after I escaped from Bulgaria. *Impossible.* I haven't opened my laptop. I couldn't have done it.

Unless someone put it here.

I consider all the possibilities as I pace the house, and the only conclusion I come to is no one but my parents would have a reason to put it on my computer. This laptop is not as secure as my others, simply because even if someone gets to it, there's nothing to see but my baby pictures. That means they could've hacked into it and put the photo there.

But why? What does it mean? They must've planned it because they're the ones who left this particular computer with the money in the bag. I thought my mother threw in the first laptop she grabbed so I could keep up with my programming, in case I forgot mine in my hurry to escape. But there must be some other reason. This is no accident.

Besides, in the photo my father is wearing his new pants,

which my mother gave him a few days before everything went to hell. That means they were in the apartment after they disappeared.

Why would they risk getting caught to take a picture with a painting? I have to go there and find out what they're trying to tell me.

Shit, what if I see someone I know? I may have changed my hair color, but my old friends will recognize me if they see me.

I have to tell Stella I'll go with her to New York, convince her to choose a hotel as far as possible from my old apartment and dance studio and shop for a little disguise.

Chapter Thirty-Seven

IVY

Three days later, Stella and I are already in New York.

I had to tell her I lived here for a few years and didn't want to run into any old friends to explain why I didn't want to go out much and when I did I wore sunglasses and a scarf around my head with only my nose showing.

Thank goodness I was able to convince her not to ask any more questions, promising I'd tell her everything soon. I don't know whether to thank her for being so trusting or to scold her.

But given that she still hasn't told me a thing about her family, and I don't know anything about her life before moving to the Blacks, I guess she understands why I don't want to talk.

I promised to take her to Times Square, in return she agreed not to make me leave the hotel for the rest of the week. I can't believe she's never been to New York, considering she's been unofficially adopted by one of the wealthiest families in the US. Black Rose is one of the largest hotels here.

Stella left for her appointment half an hour ago, which gives me about three hours to get to the apartment and return so she won't know I left. The lie I told her and Damien was that my family lived in Utah after we moved from Greece. They think I only lived in New York for two years while I was dancing. I can't tell her I've lived most of my life in an apartment in downtown Manhattan. That would raise too many questions about my parents' financial status. Which wasn't too bad, considering they had millions in the bank. That's why I'll never understand why they embezzled all that money. We were far from poor; what more did they want?

I hop into the first cab I see and the driver raises an eyebrow when he sees me but he doesn't say a thing. I guess it's because I'm wearing the most avant-garde snobbish clothes I could find, and sunglasses in December when the weather is as dark as it can be. I press my lips together and give him the address.

When I step onto the sidewalk, I look around, taking in my surroundings. The traffic, the people on the streets, and the tourists looking up at the large buildings in awe, used to be so familiar to me.

They say you slip off the masks you wear for society, friends, and family when you're alone. That's as big a lie as what we sell to others. We wear camouflage even when we're alone. The mask of false self-esteem in the mirror, and the disguise of what we try to be but we're not, garnished with small parts left over of every other mask we show to the world. Over time, all of them merge with our perception of who we are and we create a new mask, just for us. Then we lose the real parts of ourselves that we've neglected for the benefit of all our other personalities.

The only time you can see glimpses of the real person is when you catch their first unadulterated second of emotion.

That's why I used to love living and walking around midtown Manhattan and just looking at all the different faces, to catch that first pure emotion when they see something that's either enchanting or repulsive to them.

Right now I'm standing at the corner on Twenty-First and Seventh Avenue next to my favorite Japanese restaurant, trying to feel some nostalgia, but I don't. I don't feel anything looking at the beautiful building that used to be my home for so many years.

I walk inside as if I'm on a catwalk and flash a beaming grin at the guard. I'm trying to distract and fool him into letting me in without having to give my name. Hence, the snobby clothes and swaying hips. Thank goodness, it works and he opens the door with a smile.

I feel like the elevator is taking forever and I'm shaking with trepidation. Nobody can know I was here and some of the neighbors know me well enough to recognize me. I finally reach my floor, but I almost bump into the old lady from the next apartment on the way out.

"Young lady, watch where you're going!" The old eternally angry owl, who always used to call the police because of the loud music, nudges me with her cane and I give her a stiff smile. She stares at me, and my pulse accelerates. "Don't I know you from somewhere?"

"It's my first time here, ma'am," I answer in a slightly higher pitch.

"Hmm... Where are you going?"

I freeze and my heart stops for a second.

"Visiting Margo, of course," I reply arrogantly with the only name I know on this floor, that of my neighbor with the three children. They hate each other.

The old lady narrows her wrinkled eyes and walks into the elevator. "Be careful next time," she mutters.

When the doors close, I take a deep breath and exhale in relief. My heart is hammering like crazy. I unlock the apartment door and enter quickly. Without wasting any time, I run to the living room, where the photo was taken. My breath stops when I see the painting on the wall.

Damn.

I was doubting my memory, but now that I'm standing in front of it, I'm sure this Monet wasn't here before. I look around the apartment and everything seems to be in the same place, covered in layers of dust. I take the painting off the wall and examine it closely, but there's nothing. Still, my gut tells me there must be something. I take a closer look and then I see it. The canvas is slightly sunken below the frame, and there's something black stuffed into it. I push it with my fingernail and a micro SD card falls on the table.

Yes! I knew it! This could be the proof I've been searching for. It saddens me to think this little thing might be the key to my freedom and I wasted all year in fear when it was right in front of me all this time. I have to get home as quickly as possible.

I return the painting to its place on the wall, readjust my disguise, and leave the apartment without looking back. Without a single doubt, I know my place was never here.

It took me the whole week in New York and half a week after we returned to Rosehill to make any progress with the micro SD card. It has one of the best firewalls I ever built, with my mother's help of course, when I was seventeen. Her idea of bonding was spending every free second after school and dance classes in her office where she made up games to entertain me but were really to challenge me to make or break a good firewall.

I decrypted the binary code that showed up as the wall lifted, but for the last half an hour I've been trying to figure out what the numbers on it mean. I think it's virtual bank account data, but there are some symbols that are hidden and protected with another firewall. I need to break through this one as well.

Chances are my parents either made a new account to send me some money or they're giving me access to the original bank account with all of the money. Either way, I'm not touching their dirty money with a ten-foot pole. They might not know the real me very well, but they know the type of person I've always been. I won't cover for them. I'd send it directly to Europol and beg them for a probationary sentence. So why give me access to it?

I hope there might be some heart left in their ice-cold chests. Maybe they're ready to give me a chance at living a free life, now that they're safely hidden and have spent a few million.

The problem is, until I track down the account, I can't just waltz into the police station and wave the paper with the numbers and tell them to figure it out. If they had good enough specialists to trace the account, they would've already found me and my parents.

I'm running my program to start working on breaking the next firewall, just when Stella enters the house with a huge box in her hands.

"What you got, Stells?" I get up from the couch in the living room and go hide my laptop in my bedroom so I can help her with the rest of the boxes. "These weigh a ton. Are you moving a third roommate in?"

She beams with excitement and claps her hands. "It's Christmas Eve."

"So?" I don't really care; I've never loved the holidays, anyway. The only thing I liked about them is that I always got to see Nonna. Given there's no snow in Florida, unlike in Bulgaria or New York, where I've spent every Christmas so far, the atmosphere doesn't predispose me to celebrate.

"Don't give me that frown!" Stella snaps at me. "Last year, we didn't celebrate, decorate, or even cook. I'm changing all that. I bought all the toys and groceries I could afford." She places her hands on her hips and looks at the four boxes and the three paper bags proudly.

"You didn't have to do that. You know I don't have a job and I can't pay you back. I promise when I have enough money..."

She raises a hand and stops me. "When I was alone, needed a home and a friend, you took care of me. I can't repay you for that with all the Christmases. Accept it as my early present for being the best friend in the world." She hugs me and my eyes tear up. I could never part with Stella. "I know this is a temporary place for both of us, but it's starting to feel like home. I'm ready to make some changes to the house if you agree."

I nod. Stella is right; this tiny old house has enchanted us with its charm, and little by little it has become our home. Or maybe it's because of who we're sharing it with. It makes me so sad not knowing if this will be my last Christmas here. Regardless, I know that whatever happens next, I'll find my way back to Stella again eventually.

We spend the rest of the day assembling and decorating the huge artificial tree. I almost fall off the ladder as we put the outdoor lights around the house. Stella even picked up a Santa

Claus who greets the people passing by the rusted gate. Then, as I'm putting some decorations on the front of the house, I literally fall off the ladder when I hear him greet the old lady with the ten cats who's always in our business, with "*Ho-ho-ho you fucking ho.*" She shrieks and hits him with her bag, and he responds with the voice of the man from *Home Alone "Merry Christmas, you filthy animal."* Stella and I roll on the ground with tears of laughter, unable to catch our breath for at least five minutes, thinking of her indignant face. Best. Santa Claus. Ever.

"That should teach her not to gossip about us," Stella says with a laugh.

"You're brilliant." I pant as I wipe my tears.

"I also got presents for the neighbors' kids who pull their pranks on our sidewalk." She opens a box and pulls out a Santa Claus giving the middle finger. "If they choose to ignore our requests, it's time to show them we're fed up."

We burst out laughing again. Then we play some Christmas music and prepare all the food Stella bought. I give up this day for fun and force myself not to think about the bad stuff.

We decide to eat outside because Florida's weather is warm and pleasant. We put a blanket on the grass, and have a picnic with potatoes, lasagna, cookies, and all the other dishes, and spend the evening laughing and talking about everything and nothing.

Chapter Thirty-Eight

IVY

I'm losing my mind.

The first two days after Christmas, I broke the first two walls, but as much as I try with the next, it's always a dead end. Something's not right. I tried every possible program and language and still nothing. What am I missing?

I run the program again and get up to stretch a little, glaring at the calendar as if I can make it move forward twenty-four hours.

Today is New Year's Eve. And my birthday. Whatever you call it, I hate this day.

I never liked the concept of the whole new year, new me thing. In reality, this "new you" lasts about a month until your new fitness card expires, you get bored with your diet, or go back to your ex. People know that very well, and yet they repeat the same thing every year, lying to themselves. I would've liked my birthday if it didn't fall on that day. I only have one day a year. Why the hell does it have to be on a holiday?

Birthdays should make you feel special, right? Well, alas,

anyone born on this date can tell you there's nothing special about it. After a while, I even stopped doing anything for it. People always turned my celebration around that annoying day. I just kept my birthday to myself, showed up at New Year's Eve parties and got wasted or stayed at home and curled up with my favorite book. The irony is the second has always seemed more like a celebration to me.

And that's exactly what I intended to do this year until Stella found out about it and insisted I couldn't be alone on my birthday.

And here we are again having the same argument, and the scales seem to be tilting in her favor. "Please, please, please. Don't leave me alone with Tasha and her boyfriend. I don't want to be the third wheel. It'll be just the four of us at his villa outside the city. I promise you it won't be boring. Please be my date for the night." She puts her hands in prayer position before her pursed lips and makes a sad puppy dog face.

Damn her.

"Why can't Max go?" I'm desperately trying to save myself, though I know they've taken a step back from their relationship.

"I don't want to be with Max. He was good fun and long-awaited sex but that's it. Neither of us feels the thrills. Please, please. I promise I'll bake your favorite cake."

"That's just not fair. You know I have a weakness for your cooking." I point at her accusingly, but knowing that I'm losing the argument, I flop onto the couch and sigh heavily. "I shouldn't have gotten drunk on Christmas and told you when my birthday was."

"I would've found out, anyway. I waited all year for this information, and I would've asked either you or Damien eventually." She rubs her hands triumphantly, but as soon as she realizes what she said, she loses her smile. "Sorry."

I sigh and give her a sappy smile. Ever since Stella brought Six back, we've both avoided mentioning Damien. Every now and then, Stella brings home a magazine or a newspaper that has an article about the upcoming wedding of two of the richest heirs in the country. I avoid the internet like the plague, afraid if I Google him, I'll go down the rabbit hole so I limit myself to stealing a glance or two at the articles, and Stella pretends she doesn't know. Photos of them together are rare; usually, the pages are full of pictures of Olivia. I swear this woman is nuts. I'm positive that at one point, her hair was an exact copy of mine before she dyed it blonde again.

Or maybe I'm just the bitter ex creeping on them.

In either case, it hurts like hell to see her beside Damien. I keep trying to convince myself I have to move on and so I force myself to look at the magazines, torturing myself and trying to hate him but the opposite effect is what really happens. With every day that passes I miss Damien and hate myself more for running away from the best thing that's ever happened to me.

"Hey, have you heard from him? How's he doing?" Maybe I'm a masochist to ask this question, but worry has been eating me up ever since I talked to him on the phone. Despite everything that's happened between us, I want the best for him.

Stella drops onto the couch next to me. "No. I call him every day, but he doesn't pick up. I've only managed to talk to him twice, and he was dead drunk both times. When I brought Six back to him he was out of it, too. He doesn't answer Melanie's calls either, and he stopped going to work. I'm really worried about him. I think he's going back to his old ways."

We both go silent for a while, probably thinking the same

thing. It's my fault. But it was the right decision. I can't let him lose everything he loves for an uncertain future with me. If I could go back, I'd do it again. My life is already ruined. I love him too much to let him sink and drown with me.

I change the subject and get up to pack a bag. "What should I wear?" Stella said we'd sleep there and I have twenty minutes until they come to pick us up.

"Whatever you feel comfortable in, but make it sparkly!" she calls after me.

I swear this is her universal answer. *Add a little glitter and everything gets better*.

"Yeah, like that's an option," I mutter. Last I checked, they don't make *sparkly* baggy T-shirts or hoodies.

Twenty-five minutes later, the four of us are traveling to Noel's—Tasha's boyfriend's—villa.

It turns out Stella and Tasha used to study together in high school when Stella moved here and they still keep in touch. Stella invited Tasha to our house just before we went to New York and seeing her made me muster up the courage to call the other girls and Robert and apologize. Maybe if things hadn't worked out that way, we would've been a girl posse, gathering to drink wine and bitch about our men like in the movies.

We reach the Myakka River State Park, where Noel's villa is. It looks more like a log cabin with a big place for a bonfire in front of the beautiful Myakka Lake reflecting the sun as it sets for the last time this year.

"Come on, Ivy! Stop staring. You'll have time to look at it later," Stella calls out too enthusiastically, and I roll my eyes. *People and their New Year's Eve fever*. I walk to her and we enter the house.

"*Surprise!*" many voices shout, and faces spring up from all corners of the room. Christy and the three other girls from the club jump from behind a brown couch, and two men I don't know come out from behind the leather armchairs. I'm just standing at the door with my jaw on the floor, and I can't believe it.

Dozens of white and gold balloons are scattered throughout the house, with a banner that says *Happy Birthday, Bitch. You're getting old!* hanging in the middle of the room and everyone's wearing gold party hats.

"Wh-what is this?" I stutter, my eyes tearing up.

"A surprise party for your birthday. You don't think I care *that* much about New Year's Eve to spend all day begging you, do you?" Stella winks at me and hugs me.

One of the boys opens a bottle of champagne and the cork flies up and hits the ceiling. We all laugh when it overflows and he sprays himself with bubbles, and the girls start coming one by one to wish me a happy birthday. I hug and thank everyone. "I can't believe it. You did this for me?" With the realization, the tears come. No one has thrown a party for me since I was ten years old, and even before that, it was only my nonna who organized my birthdays. Everyone had too many responsibilities to bother with me.

"Of course. You deserve a great party and we're giving it to you." She hugs me for the hundredth time.

"You don't know how much this means to me."

Tom, one of the girls' boyfriends, hands me a glass of champagne. "Bottoms up!" I shout, the music plays, and we all raise our glasses.

The next few hours we spend around the fire outside, enjoying the beautiful view and laughing at childhood stories. Even *I* relax and tell a few that won't raise suspicion. We roast marshmallows on a stick, drink lots of booze, and have a lot of fun.

I can say with certainty this is my best birthday ever and

no matter how stupid it is, I feel special because these people, my friends, could be anywhere in the world celebrating the new year, but they chose to be here and celebrate with me.

"Ten minutes to midnight," one of the guys calls out, and the other two get up to help him with the fireworks.

The girls had split into groups, talking about different topics. I'm sitting on a stump, wrapped in a blanket, staring at the reddish-orange flames of the fire. I'm feeling grateful and take this time to count my blessings and thank the Lord for all he has given me.

They say on this day you should think about everything that has happened to you in the past year and decide what you'll take with you into the new one and what you'll leave behind.

This is the only thing I like about New Year's Eve—this balance. I do it every year, but instead of making promises, I think about the good and the bad.

Throughout the year, I couldn't find it in myself to forgive my parents for what they'd done, and it weighed on me. But today's different. I'm finally ready to give them my forgiveness in order to find inner peace.

Today I am thankful that if it wasn't for their actions, I wouldn't have found these great people I'm surrounded with. Whom I can call my friends and who fill my soul with love. I wouldn't have found Stella, who became one of the most important people in my life, my ride or die.

And most of all, I am thankful for experiencing what true love is, albeit for a brief moment. I'll always be grateful for Damien.

"One minute," Tom calls out, interrupting my thoughts, and I look out at the peaceful water of the lake, merging with the horizon.

From all I can take with me, I choose the love and the pain.

Thanks to Damien, I experienced what truly devastating pain is, and I wouldn't trade it. It made me stronger.

Thanks to this man, I learned what it's like to put someone else's needs before my own, even if it means destroying a part of myself.

What saddens me the most is I know I have to leave Damien in the old year. He's already at another place in his life, and I have to let him go.

But God, how it hurts.

"Three, two, one," they all shout in one voice, and beautiful fireworks illuminate the sky from all over the lake. "Happy New Year!"

"Make a wish," Stella calls out.

I close my eyes and whisper out loud what I feel deep in my heart. "I wish for Damien." But the moment I say the words, I know how wrong and selfish they are.

Instead, I wish I never leave him behind. I will take a piece of that man for life. If not, I shall leave my heart with him. It`s his for life, regardless.

DAMIEN

I open my eyes and it's dark in the room. Is it day or night? Doesn't matter.

Days and nights, dates and times, it's all a blur.

I get up and turn on the light. It's all a big mess.

My room, my head, my heart.

I don't have to wonder what day it is for long because the hundred people in my yard start counting down. I've woken up just in time for the fireworks. I stand at my bedroom window and watch as everyone turns to kiss their partner at the stroke of midnight.

Fucking delusional people. Don't they know love is the biggest-selling lie?!

They make me close my eyes and imagine the impossible. That Ivy is somewhere among the crowd, waiting for me to find her and kiss her, and hold her forever.

Alas, when I open my eyes, she isn't here, again. And it's not these people's fault.

Every fucking day, it's the same thing, like a broken record. I don't even know how I made it to New Year's Eve. How long has it been now? A month and a half or two, drunk off my ass. Each day merges with the previous. I wake up and she's not there, my arms are empty. Every day it's like my heart breaks again and again. And then every day, I drink whatever I see first to numb the pain. Until I pass out, just so I can see her in my dreams. That's all I have left of her.

Again, I'm thinking too much and my heart hurts like it's being pierced by a thousand knives over and over again. Shouldn't I have died of this constant pain by now? They say time heals everything. Then how is it possible it's getting worse every day?

Frankly, I don't even care anymore. I don't care about the people coming and going out of my house. I don't care that the nonstop partying is destroying my house. I don't care about anything.

I look at my phone out of habit. Twenty missed calls from Melanie.

I don't care.

I don't want to hear about the fucking company; I'm giving it to her. It means more to her than her son's happiness, anyway. She can wed me to anyone she wants. She can take all my money if she wants.

Guess what?

I don't fucking care, if the only thing I've cared about in my whole damn life doesn't want to have anything to do with me.

They can play this whole charade on my behalf as long as they don't expect anything from me. I'll have my fun as soon as I see their faces when I show up at the wedding drunk like the clown they're trying to make of me. It'll be a miracle if I recognize the bride.

But after all, it won't matter who she is, because she's not my girl.

Shit got too deep. It's time for a drink.

I go downstairs without bothering to dress in anything other than my Calvins. Why would I spend another painful moment of my life when I can use it to get drunk faster and fall asleep again.

Several people holler at me, but I don't even glance at them. What does it matter? Every day they're different, anyway.

I reach the kitchen and open the fridge. It's empty again. Another fucking thing that reminds me she's gone.

I didn't want to fire my cook, so I moved him to Black Rose. Who needs food, anyway?

I take out the whiskey bottle, pick up an ice bucket, and walk back to my bedroom, trying to avoid any conversations along the way. A girl with a too-short dress is trying to follow me upstairs, but I stop her on the first step.

"Do you know who I am?" she raises an eyebrow.

"I don't care. I know who you're not." I don't bother to look at her face; I just continue up the stairs. The faster I start, the faster I can see *her* again.

I fill my empty glass and take the first sweet sip. Whiskey dulls the thoughts in my head. I give myself more time to enjoy the second one. From between the bitter heat, a soft sweetness creeps in, awakening a fire at the end of my throat and a blossoming warmth in my chest. The irony almost makes me laugh. I thought everything left there was iced.

My phone rings for the first time tonight, and I get up to turn it off. Stella's picture on the screen tells me who's calling, and I don't know if it's because I'm still drunk or not drunk enough, but I feel bad for ignoring her all the time. Before I think, I slide my finger to answer.

"Damien?" Her voice sounds genuinely surprised and confused.

"Stella." I retort. I can almost see her astonished face through the phone. There's a long second of silence, so I tease her. "You called me, so if you don't want to talk, I'm hanging up."

"No, no. I just...didn't expect you to pick up. B-but it doesn't m-matter," She stutters.

"Stella, are you drunk?" I can't believe Stella's drunk before me.

"Teeny-tiny bit." She hiccups. *Yeah, right.* "How are you, Damien? I called to wish you a happy new year and..."

I cut her off before she gives me the same lecture as everyone else. "I don't want any of this new year, new me bullshit. I can assure you I'm the same fucker I was half an hour ago. Is there anything else I can help you with?" I hate to be rude to her, but my family needs to understand I'm my own man, and I'll handle my grief as I wish. It's not their decision.

"Actually, yes, I wanted to ask you for something..."

"Stella, I can barely hear you over that music in the background." I interrupt her again. "Is that the birthday song?" I'm sorry for the poor bastard. It must suck for your birthday to be on such a big holiday.

"That's exactly why I'm calling you. Just a second, let me go outside." She shouts into the phone, and the music in the background fades. "It's Ivy's birthday."

I freeze when I hear her name.

"We threw her a surprise party with all her friends, but she still looks lost. I thought maybe if you sent her a text or call to wish her a happy birthday, it would cheer her up. You know, take the first step toward friendship at least."

I don't know whether to strangle Stella for thinking my love for this girl is less than what it is, or for thinking that we can be just friends. Surely she knows better than that. On the other hand, I want to thank her for telling me about Ivy's birthday. When I asked Ivy about it while we were together, she just told me she hated it and didn't want to talk about it. Now I understand why. Stella gave me at least a chance, and I won't waste it. I don't know if I could ever be her friend, but I certainly won't miss an opportunity to see her. Even if it's only for a minute.

"Where are you? I'll come to you." I grab my towel and go straight to the bathroom to take a shower.

"I don't think that's a good idea, Damie."

"Stells, what did you think would happen when you called? That I, being the good ex-boyfriend that I am, would send her a happy-fucking-birthday text? You know that's not my style. I want to see her in person and give her a gift, the right way." I'm already halfway in the shower.

"Is that water? Oh, Damie, I shouldn't have said anything. Please don't ruin this day for her. I finally managed to get her out of the house and it was so good to see her smile for real."

The fact she doesn't want to leave her home makes me think there might be something else going on with her. She convinced me she didn't want to be with me, but if she's suffering too, this situation isn't as black and white as I thought. I would never be able to break her heart and stomp on it like she did with mine, but Ivy's a stronger and more stubborn person than I am.

"I promise I won't make a scene, Stells. I'm not that selfish. This is her day. I just...just want to see her, and I promise I'll leave in peace." It'll only take me one look and I'll know if she really doesn't feel anything for me or if she's hiding something. In either case, I won't ruin her day. If it's the second, I'll start digging until I find out what she's afraid of and root it out so I can claim her. Whatever the hell happened, we can work through it, I know I'm the only fucking one that made her truly happy.

"Don't make me regret this, Damie. I'm only doing this because I accidentally overheard her New Year's wish. Behave yourself." I sigh and roll my eyes. It's nice to know your friends trust you. "Wait a minute, where will you get her a gift at this hour? I thought you didn't know about her birthday."

"I didn't until you told me. Don't worry, I have the perfect gift."

Someone calls her name and Stella quickly tells me the address before hanging up. Then I hurry with my shower, put on some clean clothes, and grab the little box hidden in the top of the closet. I bought it to give to Ivy the day of the ball, but when all hell rained down on my head I never got the chance. I hope it brings me better luck this time.

Chapter Thirty-Nine

IVY

I go out of the cabin, where we were dancing on the sofas and tabletops, to get some fresh air and cool off a bit. I'm not even drunk yet, and I'm having more fun than any other year. But on the other hand, I feel an absence I've never experienced before. My feelings are fighting. I'm grateful there's so much space and I can dance to shut down my brain.

I haven't danced since...too long and I miss it. That is one of the hardest things about my breakup with Damien. The lack of space is a factor, but the biggest reason I don't want to admit to myself is that I lost my muse. I'm like a bird whose wings were clipped. So what good is being a bird if you can't fly?

I round the house and check my satellite phone for missed calls. None, just as I expected. I know I shouldn't talk with Nonna and aunt so often but it still hurts that I can't hear them on *my* day.

Just as I turn to go back, I hear the roar of an engine and bright lights blind me. I rub my eyes and when I open them, my breath stops short like someone just kicked me in the gut.

It's not possible. My mind's playing tricks on me.

Or maybe this is my stop and it's time to board the crazy train.

My heart that I left behind just got out of his Aston Martin and is walking toward me without taking his gaze off mine. Those eyes...the rarest, most precious Trapiche emeralds piercing me and sneaking into the abyss of my soul. I don't know whether to scream and run away or throw myself into his arms. I stay locked in place, incapable of looking away.

His hair looks darker, almost black in this light, and his stubble gives him a sharper look, all of it contrasting with his light blue shirt.

My eyes are drying up and I realize I've stopped blinking.

Damn. What is he doing here?

Damien stops an arm's length in front of me and gives me that panty-dropping smile I love so much. "Happy Birthday, Ivy." His voice is both soft and masculine, just like in my dreams. A dangerous combination.

As much as I want to speak, the lump in my throat won't let me. I drink him in. That perfect face... I don't know if I'm imagining it or it's the light, but his eyes look swollen and his cheekbones sharper. He smiles wider and takes another step closer to me. Some strange sound comes out of my chest.

Did I just squeal? Oh my god, what's wrong with me?

"I hope I'm not intruding. I just wanted to wish you a happy birthday in person and give you a present." His hand touches my palm, and I immediately pull back from the burning feeling. How can he be so hot when it's fifty degrees outside? He looks down to the hand I'm clasping and then back to my face with a raised eyebrow and a smug smile.

Damn him and damn these feelings he's stirring in me.

"Thank..." I start, but my voice is so soft I can barely hear it. I clear my throat and try again. "Thank you."

"Well, aren't you going to take your gift?"

My eyes dart to his hand. I didn't even notice him holding a white box about the size of his palm.

Oh, no, no. My knees weaken. The last time he held a box in his hand it was catastrophic.

I carefully pick it up with two fingers, as if it might contain something poisonous. "What is it?" I don't want to open it unprepared.

Before he answers, I hear Noel and Tasha's voices behind me, and without thinking, I grab Damien's hand and pull him toward the back door of the cabin. I still feel awkward about my scandalous behavior in front of all these girls who are in the cabin right now. I don't need any witnesses to whatever is about to happen. Nor do I want them to see Damien and ask me questions when I don't have any answers for them.

I look around the hallway, trying to find something closer, but it seems the only way to sneak in without them seeing us is to go to the second floor. I open the door to the first room I see and push Damien inside. Closing it behind me, I realize what a big mistake I just made when I feel the heat of his body radiating only inches from me, in the smallest room that ever existed.

Dammit, Ivy. You should've run when you had the chance.

"Well? Are you going to open it?" Damien's the first to break the heavy silence, looking down at the box.

"It's not a ring, is it?" My eyes widen when I realize I said that out loud.

Damien chuckles bitterly. "No, I'm done giving those. This is a symbol."

"Of what?" I'm confused. What could he possibly want to symbolize? The breaking of our hearts?

"Go on, open it."

I lift the lid off the pearl-white box, and I gasp when I see the exquisite silver bracelet. I hesitantly lift it out of the box and see three charms hanging from it.

Before I can ask, Damien explains. "The dog's for Six because I know how much you love him and you always take him everywhere with you." He puts his hand on the side of his mouth and whispers, "Don't tell him it looks like a pinscher. That's all they had." I giggle like a twelve-year-old and he winks at me. "The mask's for Masquerade. If it wasn't for the club I would've never found the best thing that's ever happened to me."

I look up from the silver mask to meet Damien's eyes. They're incinerating me. He grabs the last charm and lifts it between us. "I bought this bracelet to give it to you on the day of the ball. I chose the infinity symbol to represent how long we'd be together."

My heart aches at the pain in his eyes. A reflection of mine. "Damien..."

He puts a finger to my lips and my body tingles at his touch. "Ivy, don't. It's in the past. Now, this charm symbolizes that infinity's the period I'll love you for."

Before I take my next breath, my lips are on his. The kiss is hot and filled with a coarse, primitive need. He devours me like I'm the air he breathes. I drop the box to the ground and hug his body as if I can't get close enough to him. His tongue tangles with mine, and my legs turn to jelly.

Every kiss with this man feels like the first time, but this one's different. It's full of loss and love, pain and passion, desperation and regret. We eagerly leave our prints on each other's souls.

A sudden realization penetrates my love-drunk brain and I push him away from me. "We can't, Damien. We can't do this." He looks at me bewildered, and that pain returns to his eyes. "It's not right. You're engaged. You're marrying Olivia, and you shouldn't cheat on her." The words coming out of my mouth feel like a punch to the gut.

Damien seems confused for a moment but then a throaty chuckle escapes. "Are you fucking kidding me? Do you really think I'd lay a finger on that nutjob? I've forbidden her to touch me or even come near me unless we're making a public appearance. The whole fucking wedding is a sham for the media."

This time I'm the one who raises an eyebrow, then the other in disbelief.

Damien's smile falls and he grabs my face in his hands. His eyes are filled with so much intensity and sincerity that I'd believe him if he said he was Santa Claus. "The only reason I agreed to this circus is because that business is my mother's life. But, even though I love her, I'd throw it all away, every business and every penny, if it meant I could have you. Otherwise, I don't care if they sell me. The truth is, I haven't been with another woman since I was with you that first night at the hotel. I don't want to touch anyone else. I love you, and I don't think that'll ever change."

I don't want to think about what his words mean. I don't want to think who I am and where I come from. I just want Damien and the way he makes me forget everything.

I can't be strong anymore. Tonight I want to let myself fall apart in his arms, and tomorrow...tomorrow I'll collect the pieces.

DAMIEN

Ivy's chocolate eyes are full of love. Love I knew she still felt for me when I first saw her as I was getting out of the car.

My girl still loves me.

My heart can't bear it. I wasted so much time believing the lies she sold me for Lord knows what reason. Never again.

Her love gives me power I didn't know a man could possess. With it, I'll protect her from everything in the world, and I'll never let her go again.

I bend down and lick that spot on her neck that makes her squirm. My good girl doesn't disappoint me, she digs her nails into my arms. Our lips meet and our connection is stronger than before, it's as if we've unleashed a nuclear bomb. Our tongues start twisting together we're nipping and biting each other until we bleed.

Ivy pushes me back until my calves hit the bed, I fall back and pull her onto the mattress with me. Our hands work feverishly as if we're in a race to see who can strip the other first. Our naked bodies rub against each other like flints, creating a spark that's likely to catch fire and burn everything inside us.

I glide a finger over her pussy and she moans. "You're so wet baby. You're going to drip all over me and I'm going to lick up every drop of you like honey."

Ivy groans and digs her teeth into my neck as I push a finger inside her. She scratches my back with one hand as she grabs my dick with the other.

Having her in my arms after so long, knowing that she's finally mine to touch is almost too much. Too intense. It's messing with my head. I like to watch her take control, but it's time I show her who she belongs to.

I wrap my arms around her waist and flip her over on her back. My lips quickly find her pussy and I circle her clit, my tongue going for the victory. I'd worship her all night, as slowly and carefully as she deserves, but right now, all I want is to feel her fall apart in my hands.

I want to feel she's mine again.

She's already pulling on my hair and riding my face. Her moans, strong and incessant, are music to my ears. "Damien," she whispers and her entire body shakes with her release.

Before she can even get through the last wave of her orgasm, I push my throbbing cock into her warm center and slowly sink home with the words, "You're mine, Ivy. I'll never let you go again."

She shivers beneath me and a quiet, barely above a whisper *"Don't say it"* falls out of her swollen lips. I start thrusting in and out of her slowly, teasingly. She's scratching my back and biting my chest.

"You're driving me crazy. Please," she pleads, and though I'm fighting for control, I clench my teeth and keep a steady pace.

"Say it," I command, and she tries to give me a puzzled look, but we both know what I want to hear.

"Please. Please." She tries to persuade me, but that only motivates me. She's still holding back, and I want the next time she comes to be with the full awareness she's mine.

My hand slips between us and I start making lazy circles on her clit. "You know you want it. Come on, baby."

She moans and squeezes my butt cheeks, trying to keep me inside her longer, but I pull out and press on her clit even more. "Say it. Just say it and I'll give you anything you want."

Groaning, she pulls my body against hers and purrs in my ear, "I love you."

My body's overwhelmed by all the feelings those three words evoke in me. I thrust into her again and again and she cries out with pleasure. Our bodies merge as one, and we fuck like animals. It isn't long before I feel her orgasm building again. Her body is twisting under mine, and she has to tear her lips away from mine when her moans become too much.

"I fucking love you, baby. Give me everything."

She freezes, her walls closing around my cock, and she falls apart into my arms, biting my neck, trying to silence her cries. Hot shivers run down my spine and I feel my balls tighten in preparation for my release. One, two, three more pumps and I bury my face in her neck to muffle my roar.

There's something so primitive about the feeling of ownership when my cum fills the girl I love. I feel the pleasure twice as much when I know I have enough confidence in her to take the risk. Hell, I love her so much I'd even give her a child.

"Happy New Year, baby," I wrap my arms around her, pull her to me tightly, and whisper in her ear, "It's only you and me. Now and forever."

Chapter Forty

DAMIEN

For the first time in forever, I wake up with a smile on my face and no hangover. And I don't want to wake up any other way for the rest of my life.

Last night after we bathed together and had a much needed come-to-Jesus talk, we collapsed from exhaustion, wrapped around each other in the tiny room.

Ivy trembles in my arms, and I get up to throw a thicker blanket over her because this thin sheet doesn't do much in the cold early hours. I put on my pants and head for the bathroom when my forgotten phone vibrates in my pocket. Ten missed calls from Rob. That's odd; he never calls me this much unless it's an emergency.

"This better be important."

"I'm pretty sure this qualifies as important." He seems worried. "First thing, I screwed up. Big time."

"Don't care. You're ruining a very good morning. Tell me some other time."

"Second, and you might want to get your head out of your ass for this one. Do you remember my Russian friend I mentioned some time ago? Well, I gave him Ivy's profile when she started working for us, and you'll never guess what he found."

I knew he'd ruin my morning. Frankly, right about now I don't fucking want to know. "I don't care if she's skinning puppies and making them into coats."

"Bro, you'll be interested in this. Get out of your drunken comatose and come over to my place. My friend's one of the best hackers and it took him four months to find this little bit of information. Your girl...sorry...Ivy is more protected than the CIA."

I don't like the way he corrects himself.

"Ivy is my girl. Clear?" I growl at him. "By the way, she'll be dancing tonight."

"Ivy's dancing tonight? Did you two make up?"

I hear a girl's voice call his name in the background and color me crazy but it sounds like Olivia's.

"That voice sounds familiar."

And that's the reason I didn't want to pick up. Reality. It follows me everywhere, even in my head. But as much as I want to avoid it, sooner or later it'll catch up with me.

"Umm, that's kind of the other thing we need to talk about."

"Fucking shit." I can't help but snicker. "If the thing you screwed was Olivia, Lord help us both."

"Just get here as quickly as possible."

"Fine, but there better not be any lunatic blonde surprises waiting for me."

He hangs up as soon as the female voice starts calling again.

When I walk out of the bathroom the cold air in the hallway hits me like a slap. *Damn*. I shouldn't have answered. I could've been still sleeping, wound around Ivy's warm body. But Rob's right; I want to know. About the Ivy thing. I couldn't give two shits who Olivia's sleeping with. And I'll have to talk to him about investigating my girlfriend without my permission. If I'd wanted it done, I'd do it myself, but I chose to respect her boundaries.

And see where that led you, my inner voice scolds me.

I need to know the reason Ivy broke up with me. I can't let her run away a second time. Whatever it is, I don't care. At this point, if she tells me she killed a man, I'd dig a hole and carry the body so it wouldn't weigh on her.

I go back to the room, kiss her, and quietly promise myself this won't be the last time. I won't let anything else get between us.

From now on, Ivy and I are until death do us part.

IVY

When I wake up, I instinctively turn to the other side, but Damien's not there.

Oh no, did I dream it?

I jump to my feet to check every corner for traces of him, clothes, shoes, anything that shows he's still here. But he's not. It's only when I turn to pick my clothes up from the floor that I see the white box. I take a deep breath and grin as wide as my face allows.

I wasn't dreaming; it all happened.

Putting on the bracelet, I head downstairs to find everyone. No one looked for me last night, which means Stella figured out where I was. And she's the first one I lay my eyes on. She's sipping coffee with Tasha on the couch.

"Good morning."

"Look who finally woke up," Tasha chirps. "Did you have

a happy ending to your birthday?" She winks at me and Stella chokes, trying to suppress her laughter.

I don't answer, but my burning cheeks and the smile I can't wipe off my face say plenty.

"Look how happy she is." Stella claps her hands.

"Where's everyone?"

"Girls left in Christy's car, and the boys drove Tom to the hospital because the moron ate some wild mushrooms and puked his guts out this morning." Tasha crinkles her nose.

"Are they coming back?" I sit next to them.

"Nope, it's just us. We're ready to hit the road as soon as you say."

"Why didn't you wake me up? You shouldn't have to wait for me."

"After we saw Damien sneaking out this morning, half-naked, a shirt in his hand, we guessed you needed a little more sleep." Stella gives me her cunning smile and I throw a pillow at her, feeling a little embarrassed. "What's that bijou on your wrist?" She pulls my hand. "Is that Six?" She snorts out a laugh while examining the charm that looks like a mini version of a Doberman.

"Don't make fun of him." I pull my hand back. "If he hears you, he'll leave you a pinscher-sized poop at the door."

She can't hold it anymore and her shoulders shake with her ringing laughter.

"But seriously girls, the best party ever. Thank you so much." I lean my head on Stella's shoulder after she calms down.

"You can thank me by driving. I have a headache from hell." Tasha throws the car keys at me as we all get off the couch.

Stella stares at me like I've grown a second head. "You

telling me I've been living with you for a year and a half, and I didn't know you have a license?!"

"You haven't asked." I shrug and exit through the door. "And I don't have enough money to buy a car, so there's that."

"Come on, Bambi!" Tasha calls her, chuckling and tapping on the front doorframe with her long nails, as she's waiting to lock it. Stella frowns at the nickname the dancers gave her and quickly grabs her bags and exits, flipping us off. I smile at her slyly with a look that says *It's not so cool when it's on you, is it?* and Stella narrows her eyes at me saying *Blow me*.

She rolls her eyes, "Ugh, what an imposter. It's like I don't even know you anymore," she says dramatically, emphasizing her Italian accent and throwing in the universal Italian hand gesture with pinched fingers just for the show, making us chortle harder.

We climb into Tasha's SUV and I start the engine. It's been a long time since I last drove and I miss that too. Driving always helps me clear my mind. And of course, the first and only thing that pops into my head is Damien as I drive out of the Myakka River State Park.

I want to scold myself for what I did last night, but I can't say I regret it. As much as I'm fooling myself that I could live without him, I just can't. Without him it's not life, but it's not death either. It's worse. I never want to go back to that black pit of pain. I don't know how we'll make this thing work but I'm more motivated than ever to figure it out. I hope the clue I found in New York will help me. But before I do anything, I need to tell Damien the truth. Today. We can't move on if I'm lying to him. I think he'll understand I didn't want any of it to happen. After last night, I'm convinced he loves me enough to support me.

And then there's the problem with his company... I don't want him to lose his job because of me, no matter what he says. We'll have to figure it out together. I hope it's not too late.

I look at the passenger seat where Tasha has drifted off already. In the rear view mirror Stella is fiercely chatting with someone on the phone and doesn't pay any attention to the empty side road we just took. With my new mindset, I turn on the radio and start singing quietly along with it.

As we approach Masquerade, Tasha wakes up from her nap. "What are we doing here?" she says drowsily.

"I'm dropping myself off." I explain. Last night Damien and I talked and decided it will be best if I come back to work. He told me he couldn't replace me and they're still one dancer short so I could start immediately with the New Year's Day routine we started practicing just days before I dropped my heart on Masquerade's floor and stormed out. "I've been gone for too long and I need to rehearse the hell out of this routine. You know how complicated it is."

"First of all, girl, you're coming back?!" Tasha shrieks. "I'm so happy. It wasn't the same without you." She gives me a half-hug and backs away. "And second, you're crazy, you know that?" She shakes her head. "It's freaking New Year's Day. Go get some sleep. We'll do it in the evening rehearsal."

I don't have anything better to do and staying at home overthinking everything that happened and is about to happen with Damien won't do me any good. I might as well burn off some of the excess energy I've felt since I woke up.

"I love you too." I hug her and turn around to face Stella. "Eat, drink some water and go to sleep." She couldn't have slept more than two hours. "You look like hell and I want you front row tonight."

"Yes, mom." She blows me a kiss and I get out of the car.

I have a spare key for Masquerade that Damien gave me when he got tired of calling Rob whenever I wanted to rehearse. And I admit, I tend to be a perfectionist when it comes to dancing and I regularly overwork myself. I know it's not healthy but when you want to be the best at something and when you love what you do, all the hours you spend on it feel like seconds.

My dance workout clothes are still in my locker when I open it. I change and head for the stage in the empty club. I leave Damien a text that I'm here in case he gets a message that someone entered the building from the security alarm system.

As I enter the empty hall I feel goose bumps erupting on my arms and the hairs on the back of my neck stand on end. The lights are on, which isn't that unusual as Rob tends to forget to switch them off sometimes.

"Hello?" I call out and look around. I have the odd feeling that I'm being watched but I can't see anyone.

I head for the stage and begin warming up. I notice the aerial silks we'll be using for tonight's performance are still hanging from the rafters. I'll start there. When I'm stretched enough I start with some easy twists and turns close to the ground until I'm finally ready to tackle the real work.

This show is more dangerous than any we've done before, most of the performance we're so high above the ground. It's performed by two dancers on silks and two dancers on hoops. It's complicated with a lot of new tricks and I'm proud to say I came up with most of the choreography. Of course, it wouldn't be what it is without the input of my girls. God, I've missed them so much.

I start climbing the silks so I can work on the ending which is supposed to resemble an angel falling from grace. I prepare myself for an angel flip which is basically hanging downward while I wrap the fabric around my body and flip around floating like an angel in the air with my hands reaching for the skies. But when I start flipping I hear the fabric hiss on one end and look up to see it's torn. I quickly unhook myself and jump to the ground before an accident happens.

I have no idea how this fabric could tear because it's supposed to be of gymnastic quality. My hands are getting sweaty and my heart speeds up as a memory floats to the surface.

I was ten when Nonna took me to the circus. It was cool and all, but what enchanted me most were the acrobats doing aerial stunts. It was then I decided I wanted to be just like them. But during the final performance one of the women, a beautiful blonde, hooked her legs in the wrong position and fell from her hoop. The gasp of the audience and the cracking sound when her body hit the rail haunt me to this day but I try hard to press the memory down. Nonna led me out in a hurry but I managed to swivel around and see the girl's body curled in an awkward position on the floor. Later that night she came to me in my dreams and told me to be fearless, so I've never let that memory stop me.

But as I stand silent staring at the torn fabric, I contemplate starting over on the other silks set. As much as I want to move, my legs are cemented. The odd feeling I had earlier never left and I scan the empty hall again. Something doesn't feel right but after a few more minutes of uncomfortable silence and breathing exercises I manage to calm myself and decide to shake it off. I missed more than a month's worth of rehearsals. I have to get it right at least once before tonight's rehearsal.

Ignoring my trembling hands, I start over. I do some easy moves on the other silks until my fear makes room for my excitement and I start the final trick again. As I wrap the silks around myself, I'm interrupted by the ringing of my phone, and it's Damien's ringtone.

Yes, I have a ringtone just for him. Don't judge me.

I chuckle to myself like a teenager. Butterflies take flight in my stomach and I use my voice command and yell from the top of the silks "Answer."

"Hey." I manage to keep myself from giggling like a fourteen-year-old, amid the bubbling feelings in me.

"Hey." His voice echoes in the hall through the speaker and it doesn't sound very happy. "Ivy, we need to talk about what happened yesterday and about...other things."

"Yes, I..." A noise coming from backstage startles me and I turn my head so fast I almost lose my balance.

"Don't back away, Ivy. This time I won't let you escape."

I try to focus on his words and answer him. "I won't. I have to tell you something..."

"I already know. But I can't hear you very well and we should do this in person." His words immediately stop my brain spinning, and I bring my gaze to the stage underneath me where my phone is sitting on my towel.

Shit. What does he know?

I have to get down.

I yell at him to wait a second but he says he doesn't understand a word. I'm pretty trussed and getting down would be faster with the final trick in the show—the crucifix drop, which looks exactly as it sounds—instead of unhooking myself.

He continues talking while I do the angel flip and wrap the silks behind my back for the drop. "What I told you earlier is true. I'll protect you from everyth—"

His words are muffled by a loud bang behind me and I let out a startled yelp. I quickly roll down when suddenly, just as

I end tied in the crucifix position a few feet above the stage, I hear the hissing sound of fabric tearing and I fly downward. My head hits the floor and my body falls like a sack of potatoes.

"Ivy?" Damien's voice comes from the speaker of the phone.

I blink a few times, but the pain in my head is too intense and my vision is clouded. I try to focus on the PAR light on the bottom of the stage until it's hidden by a figure. Am I hallucinating? The only thing I can distinguish is something light. Hair?

"St—" I try to scream for Stella, but my voice betrays me and the next moment, everything goes dark.

Chapter Forty-One

DAMIEN

I've always hated hospitals.

It doesn't matter that the wing we're in has my last name on it, and the private room has a laminated floor instead of the industrial gray, or the walls are soft beige instead of sterile white. The smell of the hospital makes me sick.

I don't care if the best doctors come in every twenty minutes to check on Ivy. My heart has been squeezed tight as if I'm on the verge of a heart attack since the moment I heard the thud of her body falling to the ground.

When I saw my girl unconscious, blood dried on her pretty little head… I didn't know that kind of pain was possible. The fear I might lose the love of my life when I just got her back fills me with so much rage I could kill whoever manufactured those fucking silks with my bare hands.

If it was the manufacturer's fault.

Stella told me both sets of silks had fallen to the stage when she and Tasha got to Masquerade but they didn't have time to investigate because they had to meet me at the hospital with an unconscious Ivy. She only woke up for a minute while in the car with them and said something about the fabric being torn and a guardian angel.

A cold hand wraps around my clenched fist and I stop pacing the room, every cell in me wanting to punch the person daring to interrupt me. But when I meet Stella's swollen eyes, my fingers relax.

"Take it easy, Damie. Ivy will be fine. You heard the doctors. She just needs rest." I don't know how the hell she thinks it's possible to calm down. I won't be able to relax until she wakes up, and I hear that she's okay from her own lips and not from some doctors. Everyone says the same thing; but she hasn't woken up yet. What if that blow to the head caused more damage on the inside than the outside? When I don't answer, Stella goes on. "I'm sorry. I'm so sorry. I shouldn't have let her rehearse alone. I'm so stupid." She whimpers and buries her head in my crumpled shirt.

"None of this is your fault. We're lucky Tasha decided to stay at your house for lunch." I was at my house when it happened and I called Stella. She and Tasha managed to get to Ivy faster than I could have. I shudder at the thought that Ivy could've laid unconscious on the stage for hours until she woke up on her own if I wasn't on the phone with her. Or worse, someone from the staff could've found her and called for an ambulance.

"I'll go get us some coffee." She exits the room, no doubt needing to walk the anxiety out.

Thank goodness this hospital values our partnership, given half of it was built by Black Rose Group, and agreed to keep Ivy off the records. I can't risk exposing her real identity and fake ID. I won't let anyone take her from me again, no matter who her parents are.

God, when I think of how angry I was at her. I don't care if she helped them or not. I'm angry she didn't trust me enough to tell me. I would've protected her and hid her from the world. I understand it's an enormous secret, and you can't just share it with someone you've only known for two months, but I thought we were different.

In the end, life-threatening accidents once again put things in perspective. I can't be angry when she's lying helpless in a hospital bed. I have to support her like she did with me when I was in the same position a few months ago. Thank goodness the thin exercise mat protected her and, apart from a few stitches on her head and some bruising, there are no serious fractures on her body.

Still, this doesn't calm me much.

The monitor starts beeping out of the normal range and I see her pulse accelerating. Her hand trembles and I reach out and cover it with mine.

"Ivy?" I kiss her forehead. Her body moves under my lips, and my pulse jumps along with hers. "Ivy, can you hear me?"

She squeezes my hand weakly and opens her eyes slightly. "Damien?"

"Yes, yes. It's me." I kiss her hands and her trembling body is soothed by my touch.

"What happened? Where am I?" She tries to rise from the bed, but I grab her by the shoulders and gently press her back onto the bed.

"Don't stress yourself. The doctor said you could have a concussion. You fell from the silks and you're in the hospital now."

Her eyes widen. "No, I can't be in the hospital. They'll find me. I have to leave." Her scared face only confirms the information I received earlier.

"No one will touch you. I took care of it."

She attempts to rise. "You don't understand. I don't want to leave. I don't want to be taken away from you."

"The only way you'll leave me is over my dead body. I know who you are, and I don't care what you've done. I won't let anyone get to you, Ivonne." Her real name sounds so unfamiliar on my lips, but when I say it, the little color that came back to her face drains away and she turns white as a sheet.

"I...I..." Her lips tremble, hands shaking and eyes tearing up.

I crawl up on the bed with her and pull her into my arms. "Shh...don't talk baby. I don't care what your name is. The important thing is you're alive. I'm never ever letting you go again. Do you understand me? Never." Her quiet sobs tear me up inside, but she needs to let everything out. I hold her through the pain and she falls asleep after the nurse puts something in her IV.

IVY

I wake up to the constant hum of something in the distance and sit up in bed. Jesus, everything hurts like I got ran over by a bus. When I feel around to find that Damien isn't with me, my pulse speeds up. I search the room with my blurred vision and finally manage to focus on his body, leaning over a table. "Damien." He turns and it takes me a few seconds to realize the black thing in his hand is my purse and the sound is coming from it.

"Shh...go to sleep. I'll take care of it," he tells me, but when I lie back, the sound starts again and I realize where it's coming from.

"Phone. Please." I don't know why the sentence in my

head comes out as single words. Everything is messed up, though I feel much better now than I did when I woke up before.

Damien searches the bag and the shock on his face is almost audible when he pulls out the thick black satellite phone. Maybe I should feel guilty or worried that he had discovered my secret before I had a chance to tell him, but everything except the joy of seeing him is numbed. The painkillers are doing their job and yet every part of me still hurts like a bitch.

He comes up to me and hands me the phone, which stops, and before I can dial the number, rings again.

"Hello?" I answer and hear something muffled like crying from the other side. "Aunt, can you hear me?" I ask Aunt Maria, and one of Damien's eyebrows rises when he hears the Bulgarian language coming from my lips.

"Ivonne, where are you?" She whimpers.

"What's happening? Why are you crying?" I don't answer her question in case there's someone around her who can hear me. Shit, if anyone has found out she's hiding me, it's only a matter of time before they find me.

"Mother. She doesn't have much time left."

My heart tightens and a lump forms in my throat. Little by little panic seizes me, and I try to focus on one spot on the wall. "What do you mean? Is Nonna alright?" I try to ask in a calm way, but my trembling voice betrays me.

"The doctor said it was just a cold, but it got worse, and now he's saying she won't have twenty-four hours to live."

Remember when I said painkillers numb my feelings? Right now, I can feel their effect vanishing and all the bad feelings are overwhelming me until I no longer have air to breathe.

Damien sits in the chair next to me and stares at me

intently. His hand slides over and squeezes mine, but I pull my fingers away from his and grasp the phone with two hands as if it's suddenly weighing twenty pounds more. "I don't understand, twenty-four hours? Where is she?"

"We've been in every hospital I could get her to, but the doctors can't find out what the problem is. They can't hold her anymore and discharged her. Ivonne, I'm so scared. It's very bad and I don't think she'll hold on for those twenty-four hours. She wants to hear you."

The sound of the beeping monitor when my pulse quickens resonates in my head, and it's like someone is hammering a nail in it. My breathing is ragged, and every time I force myself to inhale, it's like someone is kicking me in the stomach. The pain is much stronger than the bruising from the fall. I look at Damien, who looks at me, then the monitor and back with concern.

"Ivonne," I hear nonna's raspy voice and tears start flowing from my eyes without warning. "Ivonne, is that you, my child?"

"Nonna, tell me you're going to be fine. That you won't give up. Hold on tight. I'll come to you and everything will be fine. I promise." Before I realize what I'm promising her, I already know I'll find a way to see her before... I struggle to hold in my sobs, trying to hide them from her. I can't even think about it. It can't end like this. I'll never forgive myself if something happens to her while I'm on the other side of the planet.

"Don't, you'll get caught. Promise me you'll be happy, sweetie. I want the best for you. Don't let your parents' mistake stop you from living your life."

I jump to my feet and try to rip out the wires tangled around me. Damien pushes me back to a sitting position and pulls my hand so I don't hurt myself. I growl and shove at him with all my might. He obviously wasn't expecting it, because he steps back and blinks rapidly. Instead of fighting me, he squats beside me and squeezes my hand in his.

"I promise you, Nonna. Now, promise me you'll be fine. Tell me you'll hold on until I get there." My voice breaks as my sobbing gets louder.

Damien sits next to me, hugs me, and asks me in a quiet voice, "What can I do?"

I hear coughing through the telephone, and I can barely hear my nonna's weak words. "I love you, Ivonne." Then the cough intensifies and I hear her choking. My heart stops for a second while I process the information.

Nonna's dying. The most important person in my life is dying. *And I'm not with her.*

I bend forward and my crying becomes uncontrollable. Sobbing my heart out, I'm shaking and wailing out my fear and pain, unable to hold back my despair. Everything hurts. It hurts as if every bit of me is trying to rip my skin open, tear my heart and head out until my every cell falls apart.

"You have to come home immediately, Ivonne. I can't handle this alone. I checked the flights from Rosehill and there's one in two hours. Please tell me you'll make it," Aunt cries on the phone and I promise to get there as soon as I can.

As I end the call, I turn to Damien, who's typing on his phone and looking at me expectantly.

"My nonna's dying." The words said aloud send me into another wave of wailing and he gets a determined look on his face.

"I'm calling our pilot. The jet should be ready within a few hours. Bulgaria, right?"

I stare at him, shocked, when he squats down and starts putting my shoes on my feet. "You'll help me get there? On your plane?"

He raises an eyebrow and I remember he knows who I am, and yet he's still willing to hide me. Of course, he'd want to help me. I mumble a quiet *thank you*. He takes his phone and starts talking to someone.

From here on, I hear nothing else because I can't stop crying. Damien talks to the doctors, and after two hours he and I board the plane along with one of the nurses he insisted on taking with us for my safety. She sits in the front, giving us plenty of privacy to speak freely, and we sit in the back.

I manage to calm my sobs, or maybe I finally run out of tears, but my pain is increasing every minute. I don't know how I'll survive if Nonna dies. I feel like I'm just going to lie down and die with her. The only thing still holding me together is the man opposite me. Damien is unshakable through all of this and manages to take care of everything while keeping me reasonably sane. Without him, I'd be a wreck right now. Instead, I try to take in some of his calm determination and reassure myself, hoping that once we get to her, we'll do our best to save her. I don't care if the police catch me. Damien's here and he won't let anything happen to Nonna.

"Layla?" I ask, surprised when my only Bulgarian friend picks up on the first ring.

"Who is this?"

"Ivonne Molerov. Layla, listen I don't have much time. I'm coming to Bulgaria. I'll be arriving on a private jet, and I need your father to do me a favor."

"Girl, I'm so glad to hear from you. My father's not here right now, but I'll take care of it for you. When are you arriving? I'll be there waiting for you."

I tell her the time that the pilot told us and rest back in my seat, closing my eyes and praying.

"Who was that?" I open my eyes when Damien asks,

sitting in the beige seat across from me, resting his foot over his knee.

"A friend. Her father owns the airport. She'll help me get past security."

His half-smile turns into a frown. "Is that how you escaped?" His question weighs heavily between us. It's written on his face how much my lies hurt him. They're hurting me too, and I think the time for full disclosure has come.

"Yes, I escaped in one of their jets. My aunt made me some fake documents and put Ivy Thanos into the system, enough that I would pass the first check if anyone looked into me. She works for the government and she warns me of any problems."

His posture relaxes at my confession, but his gaze doesn't change. "And have there been?"

"So far, no. I managed to bury all traces of Ivonne Molerov as if she never existed."

"The hacker who found you told me that already. You must be good." A slight smile returns to his face. "Who is Ivonne Molerov?"

At first, his question catches me off guard. I was expecting him to yell, to be angry with me, or to judge me for not telling him. But instead, he's trying to get to know me. A warm feeling settles inside me and I relax a little more. "Ivonne's dead. She was a girl who tried to please everyone. Her parents didn't respect her. Her friends used her. She lived a false, miserable, and meaningless life hidden behind a mask." I can't stop the words pouring out of my lips. The truth that I've thought about a thousand times but never dared to say out loud because then I'd have to admit I was a criminal. Not a thief but a con artist. I tricked myself into believing I had to take care of everyone else, but I was avoiding taking care of my own feelings. Cheating in life because I didn't want to learn how to embrace them and start the journey to finding myself. Because maybe then I'd turn out to be someone my parents or the world didn't like. "The truth is, the day I slipped on Ivy's mask, I became my true self. My parents caged me in, but at the same time, they set me free to fly. I no longer owed them every hour of my time, controlled by guilt to keep me working nonstop. Nor was I obligated to tolerate my fellow dance school students who used me because I had more money than they did. I was free to be who I wanted to be, but I didn't know who that was."

"And did you find out who Ivy Thanos is?" His eyes are soft, his hand resting on the little table between us.

"I found out without even realizing it. Ivy's the girl you know better than anyone. She has a true friend in Stella. She loves performing on stage with her friends and fellow dancers that are ready to help her with anything, even though she doesn't have a dime to her name. She's a brave girl, ready to pursue her dream of being a choreographer." I reach out to meet his hand halfway on the table and look into his beautiful eyes. "Ivy's the luckiest girl in the world. Luck carried her to a man she never even dreamed of. He taught her how to trust, how to endure the most painful things in life with her head held high and most of all...how to love unconditionally with her whole heart. This girl would've never found herself without you, Damien, because you were the missing piece that made everything fit together."

Damien stretches out his long arms and pulls me onto his lap. His lips brush mine and our kiss quickly turns into something more. A burning desire for the other person.

He smiles against my lips. "I love you too, baby."

Chapter Forty-Two

IVY

"You're lucky I love you. You haven't called me in a year and a half. I've been worried sick about you, miss. And how could you not tell me about the delicious piece you brought with you? Does he have any brothers?" I chuckle at Layla's chatter and Damien's confused face when he senses we might be talking about him in Bulgarian.

"You know I love you too, right?" I send her a kiss through the rearview mirror from the back seat of her SUV. At least her babbling keeps me from overthinking. My hands are shaking and sweating more with every mile closer we get to Nonna's village.

"Yeah, but seriously." She gives me her don't-shit-me face in the mirror, "Brothers? Cousins? Hot friends?"

Damien looks at us suspiciously.

"No, no brothers. I haven't met all the relatives but he has some hot friends."

Layla squeals, drops the wheel for a second, and claps her hands. Damien squeezes me with the arm he has wrapped around my shoulders, his forehead creasing. It was hard enough to convince him at the airport to let Layla drive so we could sit in the backseat, where the windows are tinted. The nurse is in the front seat because Damien refused to leave her behind in case my head hurts again.

Like I can feel anything with the adrenaline surging through me.

He's just too worried about me. Since I woke up in the hospital, he doesn't want to let me out of his sight, and he's constantly touching me.

"Watch the road, Lay, and speak English so Damien can understand you." To be honest, I'm not the best at Bulgarian since I've spent my whole life in the US.

"Damien, ohhh..." She fans herself and her black hair flutters. "That name is so sexy. How did you manage to escape and end up with the whole package? Maybe I should commit a crime or two..."

Damien pulls me in and whispers in my ear. "Is that what you were talking about the whole time?"

Layla keeps babbling. "Iv, babe, I have to tell you, if that man has skills in the bedroom to match his looks and his wallet, you better put a ring on that finger before some model bitch steals him away."

Once more my petite friend makes me laugh with her big mouth until my mirth dies when I remember Damien actually has a ring, though he isn't wearing it, and it's not from me but from that lunatic. What's wrong with me? Why do I keep forgetting that?

"Don't worry, Layla, I'm not going anywhere. I'm the one who should be careful because this girl keeps running away from me." His nose caresses my cheek, his breath hot on my jaw as his lips kiss a path to my neck, making me stupid. Damn, how does this man manage to erase my every single thought?

Layla's voice quickly brings me back to reality. "Aww...you two are so cute. Like two fluffy bunnies who want to fuck. Oh Gosh, he doesn't fuck like a rabbit, does he, Iv?"

Damien's eyes widen and it's very hard to hold back my laughter. He's not used to Layla's crudeness. From the passenger seat, the nurse clears her throat, and the three of us shut up for the rest of the way.

The closer we get to the outskirts of the capital, the higher the lump in my throat is rising and the more labored my breathing becomes. I have to believe Nonna's still alive. I know she wouldn't give up before she sees me. Damien senses my anxiety as we pass the welcome sign for the village and he rubs my shoulders to soothe me. His touch grounds me somewhat, and I close my eyes, trying to turn off all negative thoughts and concentrate on my breathing.

Inhale, exhale. Nonna will be fine.

Inhale, exhale. She'll be fine.

"Iv, do you want us to go inside with you?" Layla's voice pulls me out of my trance, and all the effort I put into regulating my breathing goes to hell when I open my eyes and see Nonna's small white house. I swear I can hear my heartbeat thrumming in my ears.

Grabbing the door handle that feels like lead, I open the door and jump out of the car right into twenty inches of snow. A warm feeling spreads through me, that comforting feeling you can get only when you come home, despite the freezing weather. Winters in Bulgaria are tough, and January is usually the coldest.

Damien slides over the seat and gets out after me.

"Please, don't. I want some time alone with her," I tell him, tears trying to break free.

He gives me his second phone because mine is somewhere on the stage at Masquerade and hugs me tightly. "I'll be here. If you need me just call."

"Thank you, but there's no need to wait in the car. It could be a while. Go to Layla's villa."

"No, I want to be close to you." He squeezes my hand and although I know this is hard for him too, I don't want to feel pressured by them waiting.

"Please, baby. Nothing will happen to me, the only people in this village are Nonna's age. Besides the villa's only ten minutes from here."

I know he wants to say no, but his compassion doesn't let him. He hugs me one more time and they drive away to Layla's villa, which qualifies more as a winery, because of all the grapes her father grows. He's an Abu Dhabi sheikh who fell in love with a Bulgarian woman and left his home to chase her all the way to this little Balkan country. He's a true Bulgarian villager now though, since he spends all his time growing fruit and making wine and rakia to drink with his friends, when he's not closing million-dollar deals.

Locked in place, I stand in the snow in my summer sneakers and thin clothes that are almost soaked now, and look after their car until they're out of sight. I slowly turn to face my favorite house and make the first hard step. With every one that follows, it feels like my heart is fighting to escape the cage of my chest.

I open the creaking metal door and a single tear slips over my lower lid. The snow-covered backyard holds so many memories of me and my grandparents playing hide and seek before Grandpa got sick and came to live with us in the US while he was getting treatment. Every summer after that, we came for a month to Bulgaria, and I spent all my time running around the small village. The concave in the white Renaissance façade and the crack beneath it are the mark of mine and Layla's friendship. We were crazy kids and no one could stop us from causing trouble. This small house feels like home more than the luxurious Manhattan apartment me and my parents lived in.

Another tear burns a trail down my icy cheek. I wipe it off with the cardigan I borrowed from Layla and take the next step up the stairs. The wood groans under my weight, and the sound is so familiar it hurts. I climb to the top and stop before knocking on the door. Aunt's car wasn't in the front, but she might've come in a taxi. Maybe I should just go in, in case she's not here and Nonna can't get up.

I don't even know why I worry so much; after all, it's my home too. I grab the handle, when all of a sudden, a past conversation with my aunt flashes through my head in retrospection and stops on a sentence I hadn't paid attention to at the time.

"I checked the flights from Rosehill..."

How did she know where I was? I never told her or Nonna. Not that I don't trust them, they proved their loyalty when they got me out of Bulgaria and kept my secret, but the less they know the better. I didn't want to put them at risk. Did I slip up in one of our conversations?

A niggling feeling in my gut worries me and I try to remember all of our conversations. No, it's not possible I told them. How the hell did she find out?

I raise my fist to knock on the door, but something stops me. Should I call Damien to come back? No, no need to worry him further. Everything will be fine. Maybe I don't remember well, and I told her.

Before I can knock, I hear aunt's voice from inside. "Come in."

The hair on the back of my neck rises, but I take a deep

breath and tell myself I'm just imagining things. She must have seen Layla's car and heard the creaking of the stairs.

With each step on the wooden floor of the hallway, the feeling in my stomach tightens. I reach the door of the living room and open it cautiously. I don't know what I was expecting to see, but it was certainly not Aunt resting her hands on the wooden table, her face a grimace of pain, tears streaming from her eyes, and smeared mascara on her cheeks. I relax my shoulders. How could I have ever thought Aunt would cause me any harm when all she's done for a year and a half is help me and protect me?

"Ivonne, you're here!" She sits up straight on the wood chair, sniffles and taps on the chair beside her. "Come here, kiddo. I haven't seen you in so long." I sit on the chair and hug her, and she whimpers on my shoulder.

"Aunt, it's going to be okay. Where's Nonna?"

"She's resting, leave her for a bit, she's tired. Tell me, how's life going for you? How are you handling New York?"

A warning sign pops into my head when I hear her mention New York. I'm sure she said Rosehill when we spoke on the phone. Why is she changing the city now?

"I'm fine. I made friends and I was able to adjust. But you know how winter in the Big Apple is...cold and ruthless." I decide to toss New York in again; maybe she just got it wrong.

"Yes, the only time I visited your mother there was in the winter, and I'll never go back to that hideous, noisy city ever again."

Everything in me screams something's wrong. "How are you, Auntie? Is there any news on my parents?"

"No trace of them. They've disappeared into thin air. As for me, I'm fine." She seems to change her sad mood to casual in a matter of seconds.

"What about Nonna Ivanka? When did she get worse? And what do the doctors say?"

"Her cold turned into pneumonia and everything moved so fast from there. In one night it was so advanced that no one could help her. All the hospitals refused to take her in because they said they couldn't do anything and she's dying." Her expression changes back to sadness again as she talks about her.

"God, how do you suddenly go from a cold to dying?" My tears are on the verge of breaking free, but I keep telling myself I won't cry in front of her and swallow them back. "Layla's father knows a lot of doctors. Maybe one of them can do something. I won't give up. I'll take her to the States with me if I have to..."

Aunt puts her hand on mine and stops me. "Listen, kid, look after yourself. Your grandmother's old, and her days on this earth are numbered, anyway." Her words are so cold, for a moment I'm shocked into silence. How could she say that about her own mother? As indifferent as my mother was to me growing up, if she was dying I'd do anything I could for her, and my Nonna who's the sweetest and kindest person I know, even more so.

"Where did you say she is? I want to see her and judge for myself." My tone mimics hers perfectly.

She huffs and rolls her eyes, and pushes me down on the chair by the knees. "Let the woman rest. You'll have plenty of time to see her."

There's that feeling again. Something is wrong. And the expressiveness on Maria's face, something she could never hide, betrays her.

I slip out from under her arms and walk to Nonna's bedroom. "I don't care. She'll be glad to see me."

A hand grips my shoulder and squeezes, painfully. Chills

crawl up my spine. I turn around and meet the most sinister look I've ever seen.

"What are you doing? Why are you stopping me from seeing Nonna?" I push her off me.

A huge calloused hand covers my mouth and my eyes widen. *What the…?* There's someone behind me. A male. I can feel his muscles.

My nails dig into his arm which is cutting off my oxygen, but Maria pulls my hands away from his arm and twists them behind me. I try to scream, but with his hand over my mouth muffled mumbling is all that comes out. His other hand is holding my wrists and he squeezes them as if he's trying to break my bones.

"Take her to the old bat." Maria's voice and steps are getting distant.

The man's hand falls from my mouth but before I can scream, it's back with a wet rag that has a pungent smell. I try not to breathe it in, but I can only hold my breath for a short time. Eventually, I take a breath, my knees give out.

Oh no. This is just like the movies.

I do my best to get out of his grip, wiggling and writhing around, but he's too strong.

I can't.

A few more breaths and my vision blurs. I hear a cry, but it seems so far away and the next moment I slump to the ground, everything around me darkening.

Chapter Forty-Three

IVY

Slowly my eyes open, but my head hurts more than when I woke up in the hospital. My instinct is to rub my eyes, but when I try to raise my hands, I can't. *What the hell?* Something is cutting into my wrists, it feels like the rough fibers of a rope. Where am I?

A bright light is blinding and I struggle to make anything out when I look around. The black spot on the concrete floor helps me identify where I am, the basement at Nonna's house. This stain has been here for as long as I can remember, we've tried everything to get it out but nothing can clean it.

It takes a few seconds for my eyes to get used to the light, and just when I start to make out a large figure, a hand pulls the lamp away.

"I told you she'd wake up faster with the light." The man's voice is raspy and familiar. Too familiar. I lift my gaze to his face and my eyes widen.

"Vladimir." My ex's name falls out of my mouth and a sly smile appears on his face.

"Surprise, princess."

That boyfriend that hit me, who was also an ex-partner in

my parents' firm until my mother caught him stealing and fired him, stands in front of me. Casual as fuck with his black slicked-back hair, Guns N' Roses T-shirt and hands tucked into the pockets of his jeans, sizing me up as if I'm a Beluga caviar hors d'oeuvre and he's starving.

He reaches out and his rough palm slides down my jaw and stops at my dry, cracked lips. "I didn't want to sedate you, but she insisted. I could've brought you here without the rag..." His gentle gaze morphs with annoyance and he turns back, where now I see my aunt sitting in a chair. He looks back at me with a tenderness that belies the ropes he tied me with. "You know I can carry you without you being passed out, right, baby?" The pet name immediately brings my thoughts to Damien. Where's the phone, I have to call him?!

"Although you've gained a few pounds..." Vladimir's pointless rattling continues, while I'm trying to reach my back pocket without attracting too much attention.

"Is this what you're looking for?" Aunt Maria drops Damien's second phone on the ground, and the sole of her thick boot smashes into the screen. "Oops."

I hear a muffled whimper from somewhere behind Vladimir and he turns, revealing a sight that steals my breath.

"Nonna?" My voice is weak and desperate when I see her on the other side of the basement tied to a chair, hands and feet with a rag stuck in her mouth.

"That's right, Ivonne, your nonna is suffering because of you. Because of your stupidity, you couldn't just sit on your butt and leave me alone, could you?" Maria spits out.

"What are you talking about? I didn't do anything to you!" I shout at her, and suddenly a hand comes out of nowhere and slaps me so hard my ears are ringing.

"Don't lie to her like you lied to me." When I hear his words, I realize the slap came from Vladimir.

"I never lied to you or her! I don't know what you're talking about!"

The sound of another slap echoes off the walls of the basement and my mouth fills with the metallic taste of blood. "I warned you, baby."

"Don't call her baby," Maria barks out and comes closer. I grit my teeth, but instead of another slap, she turns to Vladimir, an adoring expression on her face, and she kisses him.

What the actual fuck?

I spit a mouthful of saliva and blood on the ground and Aunt turns back to me. I don't recognize the woman standing before me, with the rapid changes of her expressions a person would say she's more of an actress than a hacker. "Give me your programming language niece, and I promise I'll let one of you live."

"I don't understand you." I decide to stick to the cold tone, instead of the angry one, if I want to remain conscious at least for a bit, before this idiot beats the life out of me.

"Did I stutter, what aren't you understanding? I. Want. Your. Programming. Language," she barks in my face. "Oh, and the bank account you risked your life for when you went to New York. If you were just a tad bit smarter you would've left everything to me, but no, you had to take after my brainless sister."

Little by little the pieces of the puzzle are starting to fit, and I can see what's happening here, although I still don't understand why. I know my aunt and mom aren't close. Okay, they hate each other, but she's always been good to me. "Why are you doing this? My language won't help you with anything. It's not even finished yet."

"Stupid child. That is exactly the problem. Your stupid language is keeping me from accessing the money because of its unresolved errors. I want you to fix them and hand it over to me. Simple as that."

"What money? The language is not even launched yet." The moment I say it, everything clicks into place. This is why I can't break the last level of the firewall. It's encoded in my language. It's the only one I haven't checked. There's no other explanation.

"I can see by your expression that you've figured it out, you're not as dumb if you're given the right push."

"Why do you need my parents' stolen money when you have your own? You can't be that greedy."

She smacks her forehead and rolls her eyes with an exasperated sigh. "You haven't put two and two together yet. You disappoint me, Ivonne. I had high hopes for you. I stole the money. I don't know how you ever thought your stupid mother and your brainless father would be able to do something so big. Honestly, I was disappointed the day I told you that unbelievable story and you believed it, without any doubts. I taught you better than that, how could you be so naïve?"

"What does he have to do with all of this?" I nod to Vladimir, who's standing in the corner, tugging on the door of an old cabinet.

"He does what he's told for the right amount of money and he's not bad in the sack either. I'll need someone to rub suntan lotion on my back when I'm basking in the sun on a tropical island."

I feel like I'm going to vomit and don't know if it's because my life's in danger, the fact my aunt is sleeping with the man who was in my bed three years ago, or because my nonna's face is turning blue. Who knows how long she's been here. She could freeze to death.

"If I agree to help you, you have to free Nonna." I try to

ignore Nonna's shaking head, trying to tell me no. *Shit*, she tried to warn me when she told me not to come.

Maria smiles devilishly and her eyes light up. "Of course." Her candied voice doesn't persuade me one bit, but what other choice do I have. "But first, let me show you what happens if you try to escape when I untie your hands."

Vladimir fishes something from his pocket that gleams under the light and heads for Nonna. With the push of a button the blade of the pocket knife rests on her throat.

Aunt turns to face Nonna. "You could've saved yourself that punch in the gut if you hadn't tried to warn her."

My heart skips a beat when I realize that was the reason Nonna was coughing up a lung on the phone. What kind of person gut-punches their own elderly mother?! A psychopath.

Aunt turns to me with a wicked grin. "This old hag almost ruined everything with her big mouth, but I knew once I told you she was dying you'd come running. If she'd been better at obeying orders she might've been in a nursing home now, rather than tied up. Cut her."

The blade slices through the skin of her neck and a few drops of blood slide across the steel, at the same time I scream "No!"

Vladimir stops and Maria looks at me with an eyebrow raised.

"I get it. I get it. I won't try anything."

She smiles and makes a sign to her partner. "Bring her the laptop."

DAMIEN

"Her phone's still turned off. I'm not waiting any more,

Layla, I'll find her myself if you don't want to help." It's been three hours since we dropped Ivy off.

She sighs and puts down her cup of coffee. "Relax, macho man. You look like you're ready to tear someone up. The battery must be dead."

"I gave it to her with the battery at one hundred percent. That's not possible. Something's wrong, I can feel it. I'm going." I head to the door, but Layla beats me to it.

"Okay, if you insist we'll go. I'm not leaving you alone. I don't want Barbie to be pissed at me for breaking Ken. A city boy like you wouldn't last five minutes in the winter conditions of a Bulgarian village." This is strange coming from a girl whose "*village house*" looks like a mansion that Bloomingdale's threw up in. I try to ignore the nicknames she gave me and Ivy and her constant jokes. At any other time, I'd laugh with her but right now everything in my body is strung tight. I have this weird feeling in my gut and I don't like it.

It takes all of my mental strength not to force Layla to let me drive so we can get there faster. I could've already been there if Ivy hadn't made me leave our rental car at the airport so we could ride with her friend. Never making that mistake again.

"Tell me, now, what's the deal with you marrying another woman?" Her question surprises me but I guess she googled me.

"A job. That's it."

She looks at me like I just told her I might or might not kill innocent kittens for fun, and I have to grab the wheel. "Watch the road."

"What does a job mean? You want to break my girl's heart? What are you going to do, make her your mistress?" She growls at me with a tone that says I'll be pushing up daisies if I hurt her girl, and that kind of warms my heart. I'm glad she has friends that have her back, but I'd end myself first if I hurt her again.

I sigh and tell her the truth. "I haven't worked out how I'll handle things yet, but there's no way I'd do that to her."

She smiles. "That's right because my girl isn't cut out to be someone's second choice. If you don't appreciate her, someone else will."

I clench my teeth at the thought of someone else touching her, but right now I need to concentrate on the more important issue. "Have you seen her grandma? Do you know what the deal is with her? Maybe we should've taken the nurse with us."

"I have no idea. I haven't seen her in months."

A few minutes later, we're in front of the house, where an old lady with a babushka, wearing a brown knit cardigan, long peignoir and black slippers, is standing in front of the fence, shouting. I don't know Bulgarian and don't understand what she's saying, but it seems like a name. I think it's Ivanka.

Layla goes to her, hugs her, and they talk for a bit while I stand on the sidewalk, contemplating a break-in, anxious to see Ivy and reassure myself that she's safe so I can relax. A few minutes later the lady goes into the house next door and Layla returns wearing an expression I don't like.

"Very strange. The neighbor–Grandma Mina–said Ivy's grandmother hasn't been ill at all. They had coffee two days ago and she was just fine. Then Maria came by with a man and Nonna Ivanka stopped going out at all. She went to see her but no one answered the door, so she thought they were gone, but she saw the man enter and leave the house a while ago."

The feeling in my gut is getting stronger. I knew it. "Layla, do you have a gun?"

She looks at me as if I asked for something absurd and laughs. "You clearly have never been to Bulgaria. We don't have permission for guns here. The only thing you can find around here are gas or air rifles. I'll ask Grandma Mina."

"Let's look around first."

We slip through the small gap in the door, trying not to make any noise. We don't see anything strange in the backyard, through the windows of the house, or in the shed. As we're getting ready to go back to the front we hear a noise coming from the basement. We stealthily approach the outside window, which is the size of my hand. I see a woman's shoe; it's tapping impatiently next to someone sitting in a chair with the same type of skirt as the old lady next door. I can't take a closer look without them seeing me, but something's not right. If the grandmother is sick, why would she sit in the basement where it's cold? Why would she even be sitting in a basement in the first place?

"I want you to go to the neighbor and stay there. Don't go in the house, no matter what, but watch the backyard. If you see anything unusual call the police. This is a last resort. I can't risk Ivy if I'm confusing the situation," I whisper to her.

She salutes me. "Don't worry captain. I've got your back."

"Go, Layla!"

With quiet footsteps, she disappears out of the yard just as the basement door opens. I hide around the corner and watch a big man with Rob's physique, but shorter than me, enter the house.

It's time to find out what's going on.

Chapter Forty-Four

IVY

I try to work as slow as I can to buy us some time, but I'm worried about my nonna being too cold. I still have hope I can figure out a way to escape. They tied my legs when they untied my hands, but Vladimir left out a moment ago, so if I can come up with a good plan, I think I can take out my aunt.

I scan the room and see the pocket knife he left on the shelf. I try to measure the distance between me and it's pretty far so not much chance I could make it.

I focus on some movement near the door and sigh in frustration that Vladimir's returning so fast. But the eyes staring at me through the small gap aren't his. Damien is peeking inside, just inches from Aunt, who, thank God, is too busy typing on her phone to notice.

I want to scream at him *What are you doing here*? Now they'll kill him too, because of me.

"Why did you stop?" Maria's voice startles me, and she turns to me with crossed arms, giving Damien her back. I have to signal him somehow to leave and call the police.

"I'm trying to remember the code I used for this setting. Something with white and blue...and sirens...hmm..."

Aunt puffs, frustrated, and rolls her eyes at my "genius" hint aimed at Damien. "I can't believe I couldn't break your firewall if your codes are so dumb." She stops in front of me and leans over my face, blocking my side view to the door. Her fingers caress my cheek, and for a moment, her eyes change into that caring look I know. "I knew I taught you well." She sighs and just like that they change again, only this time there's something sad in them. Pain. "You could've been my child and then all this would have never happened. If only your father..." Her voice breaks, and she stops to blink away the moisture gathering.

I have to distract her to give Damien some time.

"My father what? What were you going to say?" I ask and start typing some nonsense and bang on the keyboard as loud as I can.

"Did your mother ever tell you that before you were born, your father and I were going to get married?"

I freeze. "Married?" Remembering the more important thing than a crazy woman's tales, I start clicking the keyboard again, trying to distract her.

"It's a funny story, really. Maybe if I tell you, you'll understand me better and start cooperating voluntarily." She starts fidgeting and taps her foot nervously, which makes me think the story is anything but fun.

"I have nothing else to listen to right now, so go ahead." Hopefully, this will keep her distracted. In my peripheral I see Damien is no longer at the door. I sigh, relieved he was able to understand my message so I try to relax. We may still have a chance of getting out of here alive.

"Your father was my boyfriend in high school. You know

how first love is. You don't see anyone else and you're extremely stupid. Anyway, we made love on our prom night and a few months later I found out I was pregnant."

My fingers stop on the keyboard and I turn to her, shocked.

"Yes, that look." She points at me. "That's what I looked like when I told him, and he made me have an abortion. At first, I didn't want to, but he told me now wasn't the time for babies. He had to pursue a career and promised once he was financially stable, we'd have a big family. I was so happy I'd have a family. I dreamed of being a mother from the time I was a child." Her lips curve up at the corners.

I can't believe what she's saying. Aunt doesn't have a family and as long as I've known her, she never wanted one. She always told me her life wasn't cut out for children.

"Can you guess what happened?" Her face twists into the meanest grimace mixed with pain, and when I don't reply, she continues, spitting out the words like venom. "One year later, I was at home cleaning, washing, and cooking like a good housewife, while your father and my sister made this basement into their office so they could pursue their dream of a career they planned to share. I was so happy my little sister was working with him, I liked the idea of keeping my family close. But I didn't know what else they were sharing. Six months later her rounded belly became obvious and she told your father she was pregnant before the eyes and ears of half the village, he fell to his knees and cried tears of happiness."

If I wasn't tied to this chair I'm sure I would've fallen out of it. *Oh my god.* All these years my aunt hated my mother and didn't talk to her, but she was very good to me, and I always wondered what caused the feud between the two of them. I did. I'm the feud.

"Both of them were selfish career-driven workaholics, I couldn't understand why they were so happy to have something that would interfere with their dream."

"Auntie, I'm so—"

She stops me with a hand in front of my face, wipes the only tear daring to flow, and puts on her stone face. "Don't feel sorry for me. I got enough pity when the two of them ran off to America with our savings, and I was left here to bear my shame. I didn't have a dime, but I couldn't stay in this village anymore, so I packed up and moved to the capital. Actually, I have to thank them. Because of my determination to defeat them, I became one of the best hackers. But the time for my revenge never came...until now. Honestly, you're the only one I ever liked in the whole family, even though you're the apple of discord. Children shouldn't be blamed for their parents being insensitive bastards. I didn't want to be here...but sacrifices had to be made. I won't let anything get in the way of my revenge."

We both pause for a few seconds, frozen in place, until the sound of a cracking beam has us turning our heads in sync. Before she realizes what's happening, a metal crowbar hits her on the head, and she falls to the ground like a sack of potatoes. I blink a few times in stunned silence until I realize the blow came from Damien and hope rushes through my veins.

"On the shelf." I point to the knife, and he dashes toward it. Tears are trying to get the best of me, a mixture of happiness and the sorrow over aunt's tragic tale, but I blink them back. "Hurry up. Vladimir will be back soon."

Damien works at my feet, using the knife to cut the rope binding me to the chair, but he only frees one leg before Vladimir enters the room, slamming the door behind him with a bang. His eyes widen when he sees Maria on the floor, unconscious, and Damien crouched next to me.

Damien quickly stands up and lunges at Vladimir with the knife, but he grabs his arm and twists it. Damien jabs at his chin with his free hand, and Vladimir steps back a few steps, releasing Damien's other arm and hitting the door. Damien charges at him, throwing punch after punch, but Vladimir somehow manages to duck under his arm, spin around, and grab him from behind.

Oh, no, no, no. If he gets Damien, then we're all dead. I have to do something.

I look around the room as the two men wrestle on the floor and see the knife on the floor near my chair. But it's still too far for me to reach it. If I tip myself and the chair sideways, I can get to it, but I might fall on Maria, and there's a good chance of waking her up, which I don't want to risk.

"You son of a bitch. I'm going to send you to hell along with that bitch, after I fuck her one more time, while you watch," Vladimir growls and my gaze returns to the two men on the floor. Vladimir's on top of Damien and he's pounding his face. *Shit*.

"You'll never touch her again, you motherfucker," Damien roars at him, spitting blood in his face.

I scream, trying to distract Vladimir, and it works because he stands up and walks away from Damien and stalks toward me. But he's no genius, and he has too much self-confidence, he barely has his back turned and a second later Damien's already on his feet and standing between me and Vladimir. He's punching him in the face, blow after blow, then to the stomach and ribs with some fancy boxing moves as the blood from both of the men's mouths flies through the air and paints the concrete floor.

The door slams open and the three of us freeze when we

hear the lever-action of a shotgun behind Vladimir. The tip rests against his head and he slowly raises both hands.

"Move and I'll shoot you on the spot," Layla's voice sounds in the basement, and her small body appears behind Vladimir's large form.

Damien grabs him by the throat and he reddens, choking, blood spilling from his lip and his eyes beginning to swell. At the same time, Aunt Maria rises from the floor, the four of us failing to notice she's regained consciousness.

Vladimir uses the element of surprise and as soon as Layla and Damien turn to look at her he snaps out of Damien's grip. He turns to grab Layla and she screams. The next thing we hear is a gunshot and Vladimir's screeching. He falls to the ground at Layla's feet, her eyes wide open and her finger still on the trigger of the gas rifle.

"You crazy bitch! You shot me in the knee!" Vladimir yells and rolls over, holding his leg in his hands.

"You'll pay for this," cries Maria, who took advantage of our shock to reach the other side of the room unnoticed. She fishes something out of her purse and stretches her trembling hand out in front of her, pointing a small gun at Layla.

I don't know much about guns, but years of living in New York where you need a weapon to protect yourself, I know it's neither gas nor an air gun; it's a real gun. The kind with bullets that leave holes in people.

My brain kicks in and I tip my chair over and fall sideways feigning shock, which puts me an inch closer to the knife on the ground.

Maria doesn't look away for a second from where Layla stands with her mouth hanging open, the rifle in her hand. Vladimir sits hugging his leg, still sobbing on the floor at her feet. Damien—with a bloodied face and an even bloodier once-white shirt—stands in front of Layla, trying to protect her from my crazy aunt.

I cannot believe that this man, who could've left long ago and by now boarded a plane far away from my crazy life, is putting his life in danger to protect me and my friend. He loves me so much he'd give his life for me. And I'd do the same for him without blinking an eye.

My aunt grips the gun in both hands and moves toward Damien. I take that instant to reach out and grab the knife from the floor without her seeing me and curl up, trying to saw through the thick rope. As Maria flips the safety and moves her finger over the trigger I'm cutting through the last strand of rope until finally, my second leg is free.

Then everything happens at once.

I grab the chair, creep up behind Maria, and hit her with it. She flies forward, stumbles, and the deafening sound of a shot and a scream pierces the air. In the next moment, several men in dark blue uniforms burst into the basement.

"Police! Everyone on the ground, hands where we can see them," the officer that seems to be in charge shouts, and Layla and I lie down on the ground with our arms spread out, while Damien stays in place and raises his hands.

"*Nooo!*" my aunt screams and charges toward Vladimir, who lies on the ground. Only now do I notice a puddle of blood is forming beneath his body. *Fuck, she shot him.* She keeps yelling "*No! No! No!*" holding his head on her lap, but he appears to be unconscious. The hole in his black T-shirt, above the ribs on the left side, is barely noticeable with all the dark blood covering it.

"Ma'am, please stand up slowly, with your hands up." Maria stands, still sobbing. "You're under arrest." The officer handcuffs her while reciting her rights.

"Ms. Molerov, we have a warrant for your arrest. You

have the right to remain silent. Anything you say..." one of the other cops continues the same speech after I stand up, and he fastens the handcuffs, that I managed to avoid for so long, onto my wrists.

"You can't take Ms. Molerov. She's innocent," Damien snaps at the cop.

"Sir, step away from the suspect, keep your hands up if you don't want to be arrested as well," the policeman warns him with his bad English.

Damien's eyes flash with anger and he growls in his face, "Go ahead, arrest me. You'll lose your job before we make it to the police station."

There he is, my arrogant fool. I love him so much.

"Damien, calm down. Nothing will happen to me. They'll question me, find out who's responsible, and then they'll release me. I need you to stay outside the cell. Can you take care of Nonna for me?"

Anger is still sparkling in his eyes, but his face relaxes as we both look at the petite old woman, crouching and crying in the corner. The cops freed her from the ropes at the same time they arrested me.

"I'll take her to the best doctors, baby, as soon as I call my lawyer. Don't say a word until your lawyer shows up." He gives me a quick kiss on the lips, interrupted by the officer's grunting beside me.

Damien turns to him with a murderous look that would scare a serial killer. "If a hair on my girlfriend's head is harmed, I'll level you to the ground. Understood?"

The policeman's grip on my biceps trembles, and he shifts in place. "Sir, one more threat and I'm arresting you. Step back peacefully." I can hardly hold back a laugh when he tries to sound authoritative, but his squeaky voice betrays him.

Damien comes closer and kisses me again, this time more passionately, causing all the adrenaline in my blood to move south. "I promise you, we'll be sleeping together in a warm bed tonight, baby. I won't let anyone take you from me for too long."

Chapter Forty-Five

IVY

Damien kept his word, and a few hours after I gave my statement, the chief of police and the head prosecutor appear in the interrogation room, along with him, as if they're best friends. I have no idea what this man did, but apparently he's got a lot more power and money than I thought if his connections extend to the other end of the world in a small Balkan country. His explanation was "I don't want you to worry about anything."

Frankly, sometimes I want to strangle him and kiss him at the same time. "How do you do these things? You probably know God or something."

"Not exactly." He laughs and hugs me. "You just have to know the right people for every situation. And I'm either a friend or in business with them." He winks at me and we get into the black armored jeep, which he rented for no reason. It's not like someone wants to kill me. At least not anymore, now it's my aunt that is being charged with stealing the money and shooting a man. She confessed everything when the police found some papers in her car proving she's guilty. Once Vladimir wakes up in the hospital and recovers from the bullet that barely missed his heart he'll also be charged and imprisoned for being complicit in the theft and the kidnapping of my nonna and me.

Everything happened so fast I didn't even realize what was going on until a few hours ago when Layla's father showed up, furious the police had detained his daughter for defending herself. A few minutes later, the four of us were leaving the station, and he drove us to their home in the capital city Sofia, where a Bulgarian doctor and the nurse we brought were examining Nonna. They checked me out too and gave me some more painkillers because once my adrenaline rush wore off while I was sitting alone in the interrogation room, the pain from the fall and everything that happened after hit me like a truck.

"Wait a minute. I thought your business was clean. Are you telling me you're dealing in something illegal on the down-low?" I joke and push him with my shoulder.

Damien wraps his arms around me, looks at me with a sexy smirk, and whispers in my ear, "Baby, there's a lot you don't know about me. But I'll answer you when we're not among so many witnesses."

My panties nearly go up in flames. I don't know why danger and bad boys are always such a turn on. And it seems my man can be both, hidden under beautiful, neat packaging.

Damien kisses me on the ear and continues. "As soon as you are no longer able to testify against me." He rubs my ring finger to emphasize his words.

I try not to think about what that means. Right now, I just want to stay in this bubble, protected from everything in the world and safe in his arms, for as long as possible. In twenty minutes we'll be at the airport, heading back to the other world, where our problems are not even close to over.

And so it begins, again. The flashing of his phone for the

hundredth time, and though he ignored it most of the time, now he lets me go and slides to the other end of the seat to take the call.

Nonna, who's sitting next to the nurse in the front row of the SUV turns to me, her face still flushed with all the tears she's cried. No matter what, aunt is her daughter, and I know she's hurt by her betrayal. "My girl, you've found a good man. Keep him," she whispers in Bulgarian and squeezes my hand. "He was relentless in convincing me to fly back with you. Didn't take no for an answer. Any man who goes through all of this and is ready to do it again for you is invaluable. You won't find it a second time. Believe me, I know, because your grandfather was just like him."

Her eyes fill with tears again and I come closer to hug her as much as I can around the seat. "I know, Nonna, I know."

Damien ends his call and I cuddle into him and nestle under his big shoulders. The sun is already rising on the horizon when the car stops before the jet, but none of us are sleepy even though we've been at the police station most of the day and then all night at Layla's.

Damien rests his head on mine, but I can feel the tension in his body that wasn't there before. "What's going on?" I whisper in his ear.

"Nothing to worry about. Things are under control."

"Damien," I push back and look into his emerald green eyes that are flashing with a hint of anxiety. "You put all my problems on your shoulders and carry them as if they don't weigh an ounce. I can do the same for you. I want to. Whatever happens, I want you to promise me we'll handle it together."

His eyes soften, he kisses my head, and whispers, "I promise. But don't think you have to fix my problems. I'm strong enough to take care of myself and you. All I want from you is to be happy."

I didn't think it was possible to love him more, but with each passing minute, my adoration is growing stronger. "I love you," I whisper.

He answers me with a kiss, but the driver opens the door and interrupts us. We go out to the tarmac where the jet is waiting with the door open and the flight attendant waiting to greet us. Damien helps Nonna up the stairs and helps her get buckled in. The nurse gives her a sedative and reclines her chair to rest during the flight home. When Damien and I are at the back of the plane huddled together, I turn to him and ask again. "Tell me what's wrong?"

He takes in a deep breath. "Rob found out what happened at the club. It was an attempted murder."

I flinch in his arms and he grips me tighter.

Okay, I'm retracting my words. Apparently, there is someone who wants to kill me.

I get off the plane and step forward, looking at my feet so I don't stumble, when I hear a female voice. "You fucking bitch! You just don't want to die, do you?" A familiar feminine voice shrieks. "Robert, what is she doing here? You told me Damien was waiting for me!"

I'm shocked for a few seconds until I realize it's not a dream. Olivia really is in one of Damien's cars and she's struggling with the window Rob is closing as if her life depends on it. I turn to him, sure the question *What the hell?!* is written across my face.

Before I can voice it, Damien speaks. "Nicky, will you take the ladies to the other car?" It's an order, not a question, but Nicky, the flight attendant, doesn't hesitate. She nods and takes Nonna Ivanka's hand.

"Hell no! I'm not leaving you with that freak. I want to know what's happening, Damien."

He sighs and runs his hand over his face. "Robert took Olivia home last night after she got smashed at Masquerade. While he was there, he saw a room full of photographs of you, hate notes, threats toward you and other creepy stalker stuff. He suspects her of some other things as well and brought her here so I could question her before she realizes something's up and runs away. You weren't supposed to see her..."

"What things?"

"I'll sit in the back to hold her down in case she tries to reach out to harm you, and you'll sit in the front seat next to Robert. You may be of use when I question her, especially after seeing the way she exploded when she saw you. Just...don't believe anything I say in the car. Remember it's all a show." His face is indistinguishable, like that of a skilled poker player, and his tone is cold as if he's suddenly speaking to a stranger. I guess it's part of the show. When will this charade end? I'm tired of tiptoeing around landmines. I just want to be with Damien. I can put on one more mask...but God, I hope this is the last one.

The two of us get into the car, and as soon as Damien closes the door, Olivia throws herself at him like a starving lioness. I clench my fists and my teeth, ready to tear her apart if she keeps touching my man like that, but Rob holds my arm and winks. Damien releases her but she's sitting beside him and he's got an arm around her waist.

"I knew you'd come back to me!" Olivia chirps, looking at him with hearts in her crazy eyes.

He answers with a syrupy voice. "Of course. But if we're

going to be together, we need to be honest with each other. I want to know a few things, and if you lie to me, I can't be with you, Ollie."

"I'll tell you anything you want to know, honey bear, but—" She stops abruptly. Her eyes slant over to me as if she didn't see me before. By the way she's looking at me, I'm sure she wants to stab me with a thousand knives. "What is *she* doing here? Why were you with her on the plane?"

He pulls her closer to him and his gaze passes through me and Rob. "She's here so you can apologize to her for what you did, bear."

Olivia opens her mouth to say something, but Damien strokes her cheek, and she melts into his hand. *Talk about moody.*

"If you tell her what you did and apologize, I'll be with you. Ivy doesn't mean anything to me and as soon as she gets out of this car, I'll forget her." He talks to her like she's a fragile baby, and by the way she looks and behaves, I have no doubt her mental condition has deteriorated. At our previous meeting, she looked like a Barbie doll—absolutely flawless. Now that I'm looking at her in the dark car, her makeup is smeared under her eyes, and her face looks like she's been awake for a decade. Her wide blue eyes sparkling in the dark and tattered blouse make her look like every psychopath I've seen in the movies. A Joker-like smile spreads across her face and a shiver runs through my body. What did she do and why is she so happy about it?

"I'm sorry," she spits out. Damien looks at me, his eyes telling me something. Perhaps now is the time to play my part.

"What are you apologizing for?" I ask, mimicking Damien's attentive tone.

"For trying to kill you," she murmurs, crossing her arms like an angry child. "Twice."

Both of Damien's eyebrows rise in question, but he masks his face faster than I do. "What do you mean twice, bear?"

She nestles into him, rubbing against him like a cat. *One crazy, crazy cat.*

I'm still shocked when she speaks with the sweet tone of a serial killer. "I wouldn't have had to slice those veils or whatever you call them and mess with the hoops if you had just stayed away from my man. Is it that hard to stay away from him and his club?" She snorts out a laugh. "I was this close," she pinches her fingers, "to getting rid of you when that bitch Stella and her friend had to come to your rescue. Why are you always so needy?" She grunts, exasperated.

Shit, I knew I saw blonde hair, but I thought it was Stella. She couldn't get to me that fast. When I look at Olivia again, I see all the signs of a psychopath on her crooked face, in the irises of her blue eyes, in her predatory smile. She's crazier than I thought she was.

She rubs on Damien again, doing a good job of putting on her innocent mask. "You know I slept with Robert just to get back at you, honey bear. Well, and to steal his key to Masquerade. But it didn't mean anything. I swear."

I stare at Rob, mouth open wide and shock running through me in waves. He raises his hands and purses his lips.

"I was so drunk on New Year's Eve I don't even remember how I got home. She had on a wig and a shit-ton of makeup. I swear I didn't even realize it was her until I woke up in the morning."

"That's cuz I gave you my favorite pink pills, duh. The doctors at my clinic, um, resort, told me they're the best ones." Olivia rolls her eyes. "Whatever. You don't care, right honey bear?"

"You said twice, bear. When was the second time?" Damien's mask is starting to slip.

Olivia sits up straight in the seat next to him and suddenly starts bouncing and screaming, pointing at me. "It's her fault. Hers. If she stayed away from the club, I wouldn't have had to do it." She gets close to me, her teeth snapping like a rabid animal. "You're the reason he was in the hospital. I hit him because of you. It should've been you."

Rob, Damien, and I just sit there with our jaw on the floor of the Mercedes and we all yell at the same time, "*What?*"

Olivia pulls away from Damien and grabs for the door the moment Rob presses the child lock. "Let me out. Let me out," she screams, pulling the handle with all her might but to no avail. Damien grabs her by the wrists, not a trace of his sweet face remaining, and shakes her until she stops screaming and looks at him with such innocent eyes she could fool a judge. "You have to understand, bear. I did it for us. I ran out of that clinic to be with you, but she decided to show up and interfere with everything. She should've been on the motorcycle too. I had a plan. I'd let her die, and I'd save your life. You would've been so grateful, we would've been together forever. You understand me, right, bear?" Crocodile tears are flowing from her eyes.

A few seconds of silence pass in the car, each of us frozen and staring at the psychopath shaking and wailing in the back seat.

"Do we have it?" Damien asks, still looking at Olivia.

"I'm sending it to Richard," Rob replies, showing him a phone I didn't notice.

"What the hell?" Olivia snaps. "What do you have and why are you sending it to my father?"

"Olivia you need help," Damien answers coldly, and the lunatic in his hands pulls on the handle harder.

"No, no. I love you. I did it for you. I'm not going back to that place."

"Olivia, please, calm down," Rob tells her and she turns to us.

"You! You bitch! It's all your fault." She reaches out and scratches my hand with her long acrylic nails but Damien wraps himself around her like a strait jacket.

"Ivy, please go to the other car. I have to take care of this."

I'm not about to dispute him. I don't want to be close to that freak a second longer. I jump out of the car, just when she manages to pull one hand out of his hold and swings at me.

"*I'm not crazy!*" she screams, her eyes wide, breathing labored and nails trying to claw the leather seats of Damien's Mercedes.

Yeah, she definitely doesn't seem crazy.

Chapter Forty-Six

IVY

Two months later

I'm sitting on the bathroom floor in Masquerade, staring at the little stick in my hand, showing a pink plus sign, and I can't believe my eyes.

I knew something was off when I started getting sick at rehearsals soon after I persuaded Damien to let me dance in the club again by showing him some sexy acrobatic tricks in the bedroom. *Dammit, just when I finally got what I wanted, doing what I love most full-time.*

"I told you your boobs look huge." Stella laughs on the phone I'm clutching in my other hand. The moment I peed on that stick, I was already dialing her. My emotions are all over the place today, and I need my best friend.

"But the time is so inconvenient. My career is just getting started. Damien is up to his ears in work, and he barely has time for me. What if he decides he doesn't have time to be a dad?"

Insecurity is killing me. Damien promised he wouldn't give the recording of Olivia confessing to two murder attempts to the police if Richard agreed to leave the company and get her to a secure mental health hospital, this time with real security guards and high walls. Then it turned out he had to work overtime trying to put out all the fires Richard started with his constant sabotage. The first month, Damien was barely home. Now he at least has time to sleep at night, but his workday is maxed out with work for Black Rose Group and preparations for the opening of the new Masquerade club in New York.

"You're still in shock. Don't rush things and try to work out everything right away. Think about it, relax, and then tell him. Do you want me to come to you?"

"No, don't. I have to go home anyway. I'm sending Nonna and Layla to Bulgaria tonight."

"Okay, if you need me, call me anytime and I'll come over, or you can come home." I miss Stella so much since I moved in with Damien. Correction, since *he* packed my stuff and *he* moved me in with him, without asking, just telling me we were living together. I kind of wanted to kill him, but that other part of me that kinda likes his bossy side and didn't want to spend another day without him overruled. "I can distract you with silly stories from my childhood. At least you'll know what kind of a mother not to be." She laughs bitterly.

The lump in my throat tightens at the mention of her past. When I finally told her my whole story over a bottle of wine, she opened another one and told me hers. To say I did not expect that is an understatement. To think of all the times I thought my story was more dangerous than hers... I would've never guessed what her life was like.

"Stells, thank you. For everything."

"Just wait until I throw you a baby shower, then you can

thank me." She chirps and yelps, "Eep, I'm gonna be an aunt."

As usual, her enthusiasm is contagious and I smile. "Wait to see if there's going to be a baby for sure before you start sewing baby clothes."

My hand unconsciously goes to my tummy, which is still flat and shows no evidence of what's growing inside, but I feel it in my heart. My period is always on time but it skipped this month. My breasts are swollen, and almost every smell lately makes me sick. I'm sure the doctor's appointment will tell me the same thing the five tests did.

I go out to the car where the driver is waiting every day. Damien refuses to listen to my pleas to let me walk or at least drive. It's sweet that he worries about me, but at some point, he'll have to accept the fact I want to be independent. I'll just have to negotiate it like everything else, in the bedroom.

A few weeks after my aunt and Vladimir were sentenced, Nonna decided she wanted to go back to the village. I tried to talk her out of it, but in the end she won because I want her to be where she feels happy. Of course, I didn't give up until she promised me she'd fly to us for every holiday, and we plan to visit her more often in Bulgaria. Damien suggested we demolish the old house with too many bad memories and build her a new one, and to my surprise, Nonna agreed instantly.

Layla called two weeks ago and told me she's coming to Rosehill for a week to find herself a Damien. She was more than happy to extend her visit another week, so Nonna's house could be finished and they could go home together. She didn't like any of Damien's cousins but she told me she had a moment with some guy at Masquerade last night. I didn't ask who and she didn't tell. But I'm looking forward to finding out his name as soon as I figure out my current situation.

I enter the house and Six welcomes me with face-licking as usual.

"I'm almost ready. I just have to stuff all of this in the suitcase," Layla calls out, running toward the guest room with a bunch of clothes in her hands. Clothes she insisted we shop for every day for the two weeks she's been here. I can't say I was too reluctant because now that I finally have access to my money, I desperately needed some new clothes.

I laugh and squeeze Six in a big hug.

"Stop torturing the dog," Nonna calls out from the kitchen when Six yowls, and I let him go. He runs straight to her and sits at her feet. She's his new favorite human because she's constantly cooking him all kinds of unhealthy treats. I'm pretty sure he worships her like a goddess.

"How are you today?" I sit at the island, where she's propped up with a cup in her hand. I've gotten so used to her being around these last two months, it's really going to be hard for me to let her go today.

"Wonderful, kiddo. Do you want a cup of tea?" she asks with kind eyes and twirls a few strands of her dark red hair. For as long as I can remember, Nonna refused to be white-haired. She says it makes her look old when she's young. You'd never peg her for seventy-five.

"Yes, thank you." She puts the cup of tea in front of me, and I inhale the divine aroma of linden and honey.

"I want to talk to you about something before we leave." She sits down next to me.

"I have something to tell you, too." I lean my head on her shoulder.

"I'm very glad you're happy, baby. Damien's a wonderful man. I prayed every day for you to find someone like him, but he exceeded my expectations." She pinches me on the cheek like she did when I was a kid, and her hand slides over my shoulder, down, and stops at my stomach. "You've looked different recently. You're glowing. You're even prettier, like you're blossoming..."

Before she continues, the words roll out of my mouth. "I think I'm pregnant."

She smiles warmly and hugs me. "I know, my girl."

I haven't said the P word out loud until now. I felt like if I say it, everything will change, but I couldn't keep it from her. And now that the realization hits me, I whimper in her arms. "I'm scared, Nonna."

She pulls back to look me in the eyes. "There's nothing to be afraid of. This will be the best experience of your life."

"Please, stay with me. I don't know how I'll handle everything alone."

"You're not alone, dear. You have Damien. You two have to build the foundation of your family."

"But..." I sniff.

"No buts. There's no place for elders in the relationships of the young." She caresses my cheek and pulls away to lean on the counter. "I'm staying in the beautiful house Damien built for me. Your place is here, and my home is in Bulgaria. Besides, you don't want Grandma Mina to die of boredom without me, do you? We've still got a good twenty to thirty years of active life left." She winks at me.

"Well, who's ready for a ride on the private jet of that gorgeous man of yours?" Layla shouts somewhere in the house and we both laugh.

I accompany them to the airport and send them away with lots and lots of crying and promises, then head home. I lie on the couch, wrapped around Six with a warm blanket, pretending to look at some TV show when the only thing I can think about is how to tell Damien about the baby and what his reaction will be. Maybe he'll be late like most days, and I can wait and tell him tomorrow after the doctor appointment.

"Ivy?" His voice in the hallway startles me. My fake name sounds so real on his lips. When we returned from Bulgaria, I decided I'd keep it. It's close enough to mine and there's nothing of life as Ivonne I want to keep. Aside of Nonna and Layla.

"Here," I shout back and wave my hand from the couch.

"Hey. How's my favorite girl and my favorite boy?" He kneels on the floor and kisses me and Six.

"I'm just...thinking." I don't want to lie to him anymore and this feels like a lie.

"About what?" He takes off his suit jacket.

I look at this beautiful man before me, in his dark-blue shirt, black slacks, and messy brown hair and catch myself wondering if our child will have eyes like his.

"About family."

He smiles, takes off his socks, then his clothes and slips under the blanket beside me. The moment his hot skin touches mine, a fire ignites in me. I run my hands over his muscular arms, the tattoo on his chest, and over his abs. I don't know what I did to deserve this god, but I know my need for him will never die. Every time he touches me it's like the first time.

"You're home early today."

He smiles with that million-dollar smile and rubs his nose on mine like a bunny. "I wanted to see you sooner. I should've come with you to send off Nonna, but I got held up." His fingers slide across my lips, neck, stopping at my chest. He whispers in my ear. "Besides, I couldn't stop thinking about this body all day."

His finger slides under my bra and he twirls it around my nipple. Even with this tiny little touch, I know I'm wet as a waterfall. My needy clit trembles in response, but my tension isn't only from the pleasure. My stomach is in knots... I have to tell him.

"Damien, we need to talk about something." I moan as he kisses my neck.

"What's up, baby?" His warm breath sends shivers through me.

"I... I think..." I stutter.

He pulls his head away and lies on one side with me. "You..." he prompts me.

"I think I'm pregnant," I shoot out so quickly that *I* barely understand what I'm saying.

He pulls away, and looks from my face to my belly and back. A smug smile spreads over his face and mischief sparkles in his eyes. "I know. I'm pretty sure your nonna knows too."

"What? How did everyone except me know?"

"Well for instance, I know you missed taking your pills around New Year's when everything happened. And didn't you think it was weird that I started bringing home the smelliest cheeses after I heard you throw up a week ago? I wanted to be sure."

"So you've known the whole time? Why didn't you say something?"

"I was giving you space to process it and tell me yourself when you were ready. Isn't that the arrangement we had?" He smirks at me. I want to bite those lips off his face. Or shove his head between my legs. Damn, hormonal isn't a good look on me.

"And you're not mad?"

"Why would I be mad? You're giving me everything I've always wanted. A family."

"What is that devious smile about? You're hiding something. What did you do?" I narrow my eyes at him. This is not the face of an innocent man, and definitely not the reaction I was expecting.

He pulls back an inch farther, looking like he's ready to bolt. "I might or might not have chosen to fuck you in the positions you're most likely to get pregnant in."

My eyes widen and I push the blanket away. "*You did that on purpose?*"

He stands from the couch and dares to shrug, that smugness never leaving his face. "I warned you. I won't let you run away again."

"I thought we were just having fun, you idiot!" I shriek at him, jumping to my feet. I start chasing him around the house with a pillow in my hands, planning to suffocate him. "I'm going to kill you!" I'm pretty sure if the judge is female, I can convince her the murder was justified.

I bump into him when he stops abruptly at the kitchen counter and his hands wrap around my waist before I fall backward. "Oh, come on. Don't play coy with me. You knew you skipped the pills and you let me come inside you. Multiple times. Don't tell me you haven't thought about it.."

I blame it on hormones but I melt in his hands like hot wax and lean my head against his chest. "I might have thought about it a couple of times...but, Damien, my choreography career's just starting. I have another video for Rosalie coming soon, and I have to pick the dancers for New York and I have..."

He stops me with a finger to my lips. "Baby, I'll give you whatever you want. I'll give you a studio or come with you to every job you get. Or you'll keep dancing in the club if that's what you want. I'll support you in every decision you make, and I promise you, you'll be able to combine work with family, and I'll be there every step of the way to help you.

We're equals. I'll never put you in second place." His hand goes to my belly, and he lifts my shirt to kiss it. It feels like he lifts all the weight off me.

I cuddle into him, holding him tightly. "I'm scared. I'm scared we'll repeat our parents' mistakes."

My parents haven't even contacted me yet. I don't know if they know what happened, but I certainly won't look for them. They deserve to stay in oblivion for what they did to my aunt. I can't even imagine what I would've done if Damien told me he wanted me to have an abortion. I probably would've stabbed him on the spot instead of waiting for revenge.

He removes a few strands of hair from my face and kisses my forehead. "Baby, you're going to be the best mother. You're the smartest, most beautiful and loving woman I know."

"I hope so. At least I know for sure you'll the best dad ever. I can't even imagine how much you're going to spoil our baby." My heart speeds up. "Oh God, a baby. I'm so scared Damien…"

His lips swallow my words, and I forget them the moment his tongue invades my mouth and takes me in a new way as if we're back in that first moment in the elevator. He pulls away with a slight smile on his face. "It's good that we both have shitty parents. At least there's no way to confuse what not to do."

I kiss him on the chest. "The rest we'll just have to figure out together."

He winks at me with a playful look, and his hand slides from my belly down under my panties, lighting a fire in me. A little moan falls out of my lips and I bite his lower lip. His tongue dives in, chasing mine in an endless spiral of passion.

We're like gasoline on fire. It's dangerous, explosive… It

could burn the ground beneath us and destroy everything around us. But the fiery dance of the flames is too enchanting.

Too beautiful.

Too hot.

And somehow soothing.

We're different in our masks, yet the same in our souls.

Two pieces of life's puzzle. Broken, incomplete on our own. But combined, we possess a power stronger than anything else.

A power that could destroy a whole galaxy...or create a new universe.

Epilogue

IVY

Six months later

"Come on, Ivy, it's starting in five," Rob calls out from the door of the dressing room, where I'm fixing my makeup.

I get off the chair and walk to him in my five-inch heels, which I think I'll be wearing for the last time because my feet are getting more swollen with each day. My pink mini tulle dress with a huge tutu skirt bounces with every step, successfully hiding my grown belly.

Rob gives me his hand and the two of us head to the stage of the new Masquerade club in New York, where a single spotlight shines and awaits Damien for the official grand opening. The club is crowded with people and I can barely see anything in the darkness. "Stella should've been here an hour ago. Have you seen her?" I ask and Rob shakes his head.

That girl wants to kill me. She doesn't know New York, and yet she still wanted to fly alone in coach today, instead of coming with us a few days ago. Who knows where she got lost. I'm thinking about calling her when suddenly the music stops, and Damien comes on stage in all his sexy splendor—bedroom messy hair, dressed in a black suit made to perfectly fit his divine body, which has only improved since he started doing sports again. With that sexy smug smile, every girl here falls under his spell, including me. It was hard for me to resist him before, but now that my hormones are going crazy, I can barely keep myself from climbing him like a tree. It doesn't matter that we had amazing sex just this morning, I plan on dragging him to the nearest dressing room as soon as he leaves the stage.

Behind him are the new dancers that I personally selected and trained, dressed in gold and silver stage outfits that Stella sewed, and masks.

"Welcome, everyone. I'm Damien Black, your host for the night." The crowd bursts into applause and whistles and I smile widely. With the baby coming, Damien's at home much more, and I'd forgotten how popular he is at these parties. "Tonight's very special for me because I'll fulfill not one, but two of my dreams. My amazing dancers and staff will make sure to give you an unforgettable experience, but before I leave you to enjoy yourselves, I want to thank everyone who helped..." I zone out for a minute to shoot Stella a message. "...and finally, I want to thank Ivy." I raise my gaze to the stage, where two green eyes are looking at me. "Baby, can you join me please?" Damien winks at me.

I'm going to kill him.

Tonight is supposed to be all about him. I've had my fair share of the spotlight in every magazine and social media I can think of, as soon as we came out as a couple, and then when they dug up my past. Now that my pregnancy is showing, I even have paparazzi following me around like I'm a freaking celebrity or something.

Rob gives me a hand and I climb the stairs. Damien hugs

me and kisses me, eliciting a few cheerful whistles from the crowd.

"Ivy, without you I wouldn't be the man I am today. All the highs and all the lows showed me there's no woman more perfect for me. Only one girl can fight you for my love and that will be our daughter." He puts his hand on my tummy, and my heart melts into a puddle at our feet. I whisper the words "*I love you*" and he smiles. Several *awws* follow in unison from the crowd.

He hands the microphone to one of the dancers and before I realize what's happening, he drops to one knee before me and opens a small black box with a big shiny ring. It's an emerald pear cut Chopard ring I saw a few days ago and told him how much it reminds me of his eyes. It's like they're made of the same gemstone and it's a damn precious one.

I can't believe it. We haven't even talked about this. My hand shoots up to hide my open mouth, and tears well up in my eyes. I'm trying to blink them back when he takes my hand and continues. "The first time I saw you was on a stage like this in Rosehill. Even then, I knew there was something special about you. The last time I proposed to you, we weren't ready to take our masks off. But today we're here, knowing if one jumps into the fire, the other will follow. You make me a better person every day, and I promise to make you happy until one of us kills the other."

In his eyes, I can see all the love in the world.

"Ivy Thanos, or Ivonne Molerov, it doesn't really matter to me, since the only name I want to call you is mine. Will you put me out of my misery and be my wife?"

Grave silence spreads and I swear I can hear his breath stop.

"Yes," I whisper, my eyes watering.

I hear clapping and cheers in the background, but the

moment he stands up and lifts me in his arms, everything and everyone around us disappears, and again, it's just the two of us.

Just two bodies, two people, no masks and no restraints.
Just us.

THE END

Acknowledgments

There are not enough words to express my gratitude toward all the people who helped me achieve this dream but I'll try to put it in a few without crying my eyes out. (*Edited: Mission unsuccessful.*)

Life is nothing without friends so I'd like to take a second to acknowledge mine.

To **Komal Chandwani**, the only person to read my god-awful first draft and still fall in love with Ivy and Damien. You are a godsend! You have been my rock through everything, never ever skipping a beat even though you're going through the wringer yourself. Thank you for always answering my daily anxiety questions and for believing in me even when I didn't. I can't repay you in this lifetime but I'll start by buying us all the lasagna and wine once we get to Italy.

P.S. You have first dibs on Damien.

To **Kylie Ebner** and **Jessie Stafford**. You girls… Never in a million years have I thought I'd find such amazing friends on another continent through the wonderful book community. But miracles do happen and it appears I have found my unicorn beta readers. Thank you for everything you did for this book.

To **Milena**, **Pamela**, **Rally** and **Radoslav**, and to my cousin **Angel**, thank you for listening to my endless rattles, for picking me up when I fall, and for always having my back. **Rally**, thank you for the late night evenings on my terrace plotting fight scenes.

To my family. **Dedi Miti**—my one and only grandfather, thank you for stepping up when I needed a father and for always supporting me. **Dedi Blagoi**—my late great grandfather, thank you for keeping an eye on me from above and for teaching me to be positive. **Baba Peni**—there will never be anyone like you, granny. No one has ever cared for me as much as you do even if you show it in your own special way. **Baba Slavka**—my great grandmother, your kindness is unattainable. Thank you for supporting this book since day one. **Baba Lidia**—for teaching me to be as independent and adventurous as you are. **Baba Stella**—for always being there to help me and baba Slavka. **Baba Zagorka**—I never got to tell you about this book before you left us, but I know you'd be the proudest, nanny. Thank you for being the most supportive. **Mommy Anny**—for giving up your life to give me mine. I love you even if I don't show it all the time. **Aunty Vanina and Uncle Ilian**—thank you for letting me skip work to chase after my dream. I could never be grateful enough for you.

To my angel and my brightest star, **my father Plamen**. When everyone else fails to support me, you never do. Knowing you, you're probably bragging about me to all your friends in heaven and you brought my dogs as well. Thank you for giving me the greatest gift of them all—my love for the arts. You truly saved my soul.

To my amazing editors – **Lia Fairchild,** and **Jen Coleman**. This book would be nothing without your input. I am so grateful to be working with all of you.

To all the **bloggers** and **bookstagrammers**, I couldn't do this without you. Thank you for believing in me.

I am surely forgetting someone so to everyone else who helped me or supported me in any way, thank you!

Xoxo, Leah

About the Author

Get all the details about future releases here:
Website: www.leahkplamm.com
Subscribe to her newsletter.
Join her private Facebook group.
Follow her on social media:
Instagram (@leahkplamm)
Facebook (@authorleahkplamm)
Pinterest (@authorleahkplamm)
Goodreads (Leah K. Plamm)
YouTube (Leah K. Plamm)

Thank you!

To you:

Thank you for trusting me! As an avid reader myself, I know how many books there are to choose from, and you chose to spend your time and money on mine. I don't take it for granted!
If you would have a minute or two, would you be so kind to leave <u>an honest</u> **review** on Amazon or Goodreads.
Reviews can help indie authors tremendously!

All my love,
Leah

I hope you enjoyed Ivy and Damien's story. Stella and Lucifer's book is next and it's promising to be a whirlwind, [stay tuned](#) for ***Good Girls Go To Hell***!

Milton Keynes UK
Ingram Content Group UK Ltd.
UKHW041318260124
436751UK00002B/443